WELCOME TO ZODIAC ACADEMY

Note to all students: Vampire bites, loss of limbs or getting lost in The Wailing Wood will not count as a valid excuse for being late to class.

ZODIAC
ACADEMY
THE AWAKENING

CAROLINE
PECKHAM

SUSANNE
VALENTI

Place
Terra House
Hall
Mars Laboratory
King's Hollow
The Howling Meadow
The Wailing Wood
The Orb
Earth Observatory
Venus Library
Aer House
Fire Arena

DARCY

CHAPTER ONE

I was halfway through the window when the police sirens sounded.

Pause. Breathe. Wriggle hips.

The window was a tiny thing with a metal latch digging into my belly. But I was under fed and had the determination of a pitbull. *You've met your match Mr Window.*

Sirens again.

My heart thumped a warning tune in my ears. I lifted my head, the bathroom below me familiar and haunting. I didn't have to do this. Breaking and entering. Although technically I wasn't breaking anything.

My sister was *way* better at this kind of thing. But maybe that was why I was here instead of her. I wanted to prove I could do it. So I was damn-well going to.

Sirens. Closer this time. And whoosh, I was mentally carried away to a jail cell. Then weeping dramatically on a stand in court. *"Guilty!"* the jury chimed then *bam*, a metal door slamming in my face while I turned to my cellmate Patrice who had a gut the size of a beach ball and a menacing gleam in her eye.

At least she's well-fed.

Maybe prison was the answer to my prayers. Tory would kill me though. Although, to be fair, she was one mistake away from ending up behind bars herself. We'd be a force to be reckoned with in jail, queens of the condemned. Like Thelma and Louise if they hadn't driven themselves off a cliff.

Mental note: ask Tor if jail is a decent Plan B.

For now, prison wasn't on my to-do list. My senses were alive with adrenaline and okay just a little bit of fear.

Can I do this?

Yes I can dammit.

I took a bracing breath. The chances were those cops weren't coming for me. I just had to be fast as a precaution.

I braced my hands against the ice-cold tiles and pushed, my hips getting jammed and my butt waving like a flag as I hung out the back of the house. The midnight blue tips of my ebony hair were waving around like a sheet in a storm.

Push – wriggle – *yes!*

I clambered onto the toilet without grace and jumped down, my beat-up Converses as quiet as air as they hit the tiles. I took a moment to internally celebrate what I'd just achieved, rocking my ass to a silent tune.

I did it!

I yanked the door open, darting further into the house which I knew was empty and yet...

A knot frayed and tugged apart in my chest. A floorboard creaked beneath my feet as I moved and the sound was a thunder crack in my ears.

Pete's at work. No one's here.

His name in my head sent a violent chill through me. Up until three months ago this house had been mine and Tory's home. If you could call it that. Pete had never thought of us as his kin. We'd been stuck here for our final year in foster care. And the day before we'd turned eighteen he'd shoved us out on our asses, since he was no longer entitled to the state fund for 'looking after us'. But the only thing he ever looked after was a bottle of Jack and his precious fifty eight inch TV.

I slipped into the room which had been mine and Tory's. Stripped bare already. He wouldn't be getting any more foster kids now that Darla had left him. Nearly two months before our birthday she'd walked out and I couldn't blame her. He'd conveniently forgotten to mention that to our social worker and we'd been too close to freedom to kick up a fuss.

There hadn't been much to remove from the room except the bunk bed that had been too damn small and too damn degrading for a couple of grown-ass girls. *Oh no, did I forget to thank you for that set-up Pete? I'll be sure to do it on my way out.*

I threw caution to the wind and jogged loudly across the room. I pressed my palms flush to the wall, moving, searching. I grinned as I found the right spot and my heart bounced with hope. I gripped the edges of the brick and pulled, the masonry coming loose until I revealed the little cubby hole Tory and I had used to stash stuff.

Reaching inside, I bit down on my lip in concentration as I tried to feel out what I was looking for.

Cash. A whole wad. We'd been thrown out of Pete's house so hard and fast we hadn't had time to grab it. And it wasn't the type of thing we could have asked Pete to hand back to us. He'd have spent it on one night at the local casino. But we'd been saving for years. While I'd been hustling for money from students at school, buying and selling their unwanted crap for them and taking a profit, Tory had been doing something much more illegal. She never really went into it because she didn't want to implicate me but I could hazard a guess at what it was. She always came home at ungodly hours of the night smelling of gasoline and adrenaline.

I couldn't find it in me to care about the source of our funds. This money was our future. In this precious brick hole was nearly two thousand dollars. Enough for six months rent on our apartment. And a shitheap it might have been, but it was certainly better than a cold sidewalk.

Knuckles rapped against the front door – hard.

My gut plummeted. Pete didn't have friends. He was a loner. A loser.

Cops imminent.

My fingers brushed the pile of cash and I snatched it in my fist, bundling what I hoped was the whole contents between my fingers.

A crash sounded as the cops battered the front door down. *No no no no.*

Heart in throat, I ran like there was a fire up my ass.

A door burst open down the hall.

"Freeze!" a male voice shouted. I threw a glance over my shoulder and all I saw was the barrel of a gun.

"Holy shit – don't shoot!" I crashed into a wall in my panic, my shoulder bruising on impact.

"I said freeze!" the cop yelled.

Desperate, I lurched toward the bathroom, slamming the door shut and shoving the bolt into place.

No shots fired yet. That's gotta be a good thing. Cops don't shoot unarmed teenage girls, do they?

I shoved the cash into the back pocket of my pants, scooped up Pete's toothbrush and dunked it in the toilet bowl. A thump sounded on the other side of the door but I was already halfway through the window and Pete's toothbrush was back in its holder. Totally worth the five seconds it had cost me.

I squeezed out and hit the ground running, fleeing toward the back fence where I knew for a fact the neighbour's Rottweiler had dug a sizeable hole. More shouts followed me. But the wind was tugging at my hair and my lungs were expanding with freedom. It was pure ecstasy, tumbling through me like a drug.

I pictured Tory's face when I told her what I'd done to Pete's toothbrush and couldn't wait to hear her laugh over it. I'd doubted whether I could pull this off. I was usually the one who tripped over her own feet on a regular basis- but not today *dammit*.

"Hey – stop!" a female cop this time.

My dream died and my heart turned to ice. I dropped into a flowerbed and hauled myself through the hole under the fence. My jeans snagged on the underside of the sharp wood. It scratched my skin and I yelped as the sound of footsteps closed in.

"I need this money – it's not even his!" I shouted, my heart wailing just as loudly in my chest.

Hands caught my ankles and my heart nearly combusted. I unhooked my belt and in that minute, I felt it. All of it. The cash cascaded down to the mud, brushing across my torn skin and falling to the ground.

I hadn't tucked it in my pocket. I'd stuck it in my damn belt.

"No!" I kicked out at the cop, but she didn't let go, her nails digging in.

"Sarge!" she yelled for back up and I could see my life fading before my eyes. Screw jail – it was a terrible Plan B!

A forbidding male voice filled the air which cut into me like a knife. *"Let go of her."*

The cop released me and I thanked my lucky stars as I scrambled onto my knees. I turned back but a pair of large male hands were already wrapping all of our lovely green cash up in a ball.

That's our life you're taking!

I booted the fence hard, yelling my rage before turning and running as fast and as hard as I could in the opposite direction.

Whoever that guy was, he'd both saved my ass and ruined my life.

Thanks asshole.

11

I trudged up the four floors to our apartment, caked in mud and furious as hell with myself. My hands were jammed in my pockets and I was soaked through from the downpour I'd just experienced for ten blocks. Chicago was having mood-swings. If it wasn't the wind, it was the rain. It was September dammit, they were still sunbathing in Springfield!

I shivered as the cold trickled into my bones and made every single part of me numb apart from the pain of losing that cash and the shame that I'd failed us so deeply.

I twisted my key in the lock, marching into the tiny studio with flaky green paint on the walls and exposed brickwork which didn't look hipster, it looked like a half-finished job.

Tory was stretched out on the couch, thumbing her cellphone which had a jagged crack up the centre of the screen. At least she'd secured herself a smartphone, I was stuck with a Nokia from the 90s which did nothing but make calls – as if *that* was what a phone was for.

I shed my leather jacket with a dramatic huff and she glanced up, arching a brow. Her face transformed as she pulled herself out of technology brain and sprang to her feet.

"Where have you been?" she asked, confusion gleaming from her olive green eyes which were the exact same shade as mine. Like everything about us. Bronzed skin, our lips full and wide. We were a mirror version of each other except for my hair's dark blue tips. Maybe that was why we drove each other crazy sometimes.

I threw my jacket on the floor without answering, tempted to stamp on it but Tory sucked in a breath, pointing at me. I looked down, finding my hem stained red with blood from the fence catastrophe.

"It's fine." I tore the shirt off, dumping it in the garbage bag we'd strung up in the two foot kitchenette which didn't even include a toaster. I swallowed my pride and prepared to tell Tory just how much I'd failed us. "I decided to get our money back from Pete's but the cops showed up. I ran...then I dropped the cash." I was so angry with myself that I bashed my fist down on the counter. *Clumsy idiot.*

"That was two grand," Tory gasped.

"I know." I shut my eyes, my embarrassment devouring me from the inside out. I had to keep my head. I had to figure this out. Because we were so effing screwed if we didn't. We'd only managed a few month's rent here because we'd sold the single item of value we'd had when we left Pete's. A Gucci handbag I'd spotted in a thrift store labelled as a knock-off. Pete hadn't known that it was the real deal or he would have gotten his greasy palms all over it the second he could.

"Did they see you?" Tory demanded.

"Yes," I sighed. "Pete must have gotten cameras installed...or maybe the neighbour. Who knows? It all amounts to the same thing. I messed up and we're screwed."

"They don't know where we live," Tory said thoughtfully.

"It's the money though, Tor." I flung myself on the threadbare couch we'd found down an alley – yeah things were that shit – and groaned. "How are we going to pay the rent?"

Tory perched on the edge of the couch, punching my shoulder in the way she always did to say she loved me. Tory wasn't much for the feelings type, but that didn't mean they weren't there. And though I sometimes wished for a few more warm hugs, she always showed me she cared in her own way. "It's cool, Darcy. I'm doing a job tonight. We'll figure it out after that."

"You are?" I glanced up at her with a hopeful look, my eyes anime wide.

"Yep." She grinned, but I could tell she was still disappointed about the cash.

Dammit, if only I'd pocketed it. Why do I always mess everything up?

The rain was slowing to a drizzle as the evening rolled in and my stomach growled for a meal it wasn't going to get.

"Sorry," I sighed as Tory stared out of the window to the street. "But one good thing came out of it."

She glanced over her shoulder at me, giving me a curious look. "What?"

"I wiped Pete's toothbrush around the toilet bowl. The rim and all."

Her mouth opened then she burst out laughing. My anger finally fizzled away as my own laughter joined hers and our hollow little apartment was filled with something good for once.

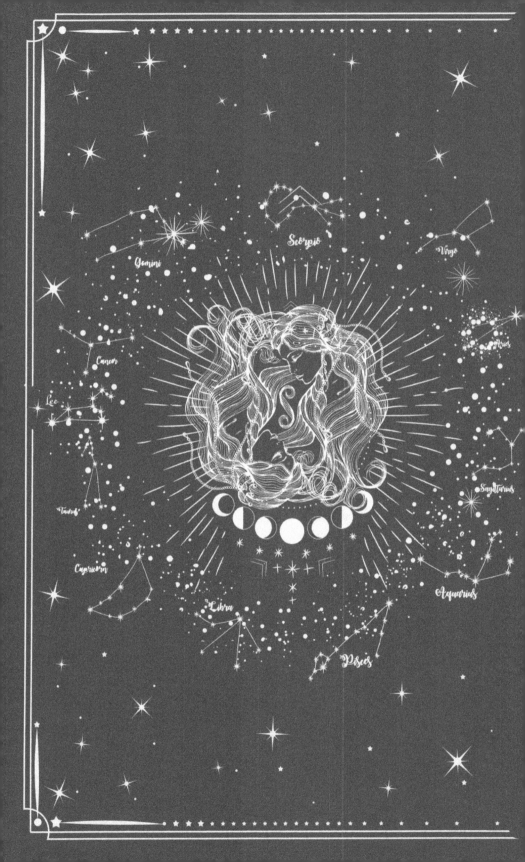

TORY

CHAPTER TWO

"**S**park," I cursed, glancing over my shoulder to make sure I was still alone out here. The night was dark, shadows thick and silence deep in my particular spot of the multi-storey car park but I could never be too careful. The beautiful silver bike beside me was hiding me for the most part but if anyone spotted me, the game would be up. *"Spark, c'mon!"*

I brushed the wires together again and still nothing happened. Was there an extra security feature on this model that I didn't know about? I'd done my research but limited editions were prone to random upgrades.

I half considered cutting my losses and getting the hell out there.

A high-pitched laugh sounded somewhere between the cars, my heart rate spiking in response.

Can't see me back here. Not yet. They're nowhere near close enough yet.

I wrangled my frayed nerves into line, releasing a slow breath through my nose as I forced my heartbeat to slow down. One last shot before I gave up.

I ground my teeth together, picturing the little spark of energy that I needed so desperately. If I wanted it enough it would happen. One final try...

I brushed the wires together and the stunning creature beside me purred as life was breathed into its engine.

Oh yes.

I stood quickly, pulling the black helmet down onto my head and sliding the visor into place so that my face was completely hidden. I made sure any final strands of my long, black hair were tucked up out of sight and kicked my leg over the bike.

"Let's go for a ride," I breathed, anticipation stroking my spine like a feather-light caress.

My fingers tightened around the throttle and I gave it a little tug, letting the engine growl beneath me. I bit my lip, a smile splitting my face. I wasn't clear yet, I had to get this beauty across town to Joey's if I wanted this to pay off. But I couldn't help but spend a moment bathing in my victory as I admired the sleek, silver beast I was about to ride off on.

"Hey!"

My head snapped up as a security guard stepped out of the stairwell to my left. He obviously knew the owner of this beauty and the fact that that wasn't me. "You there, what do you think you're-"

I kicked the bike into gear and released the throttle before he could finish that thought. I shot forward, leaning low as I guided the super bike down the steep, spiralling ramp as quickly as humanly possible. If anyone was coming the other way then I was dead. Splat. Gone. Bye bye Tory. But not today.

The ground levelled out and I shot towards the exit. The barriers were down but that didn't matter; the pedestrian access was wide open and I had a huge six inch leeway to guide the bike through. With no time to slow down it felt a little hairier than it should have and I inhaled sharply as I shot through the narrow opening, my left knee brushing the wall.

My heart was pounding, adrenaline shivering along my limbs but I was out. Now I just had to keep going until I made it to Joey's and hope the cops didn't catch me first. Not that they stood much chance while I was on this bad boy. With a top speed of one-hundred and eighty-six miles per hour and the freedom to take back alleys and sidewalks, I was pretty much home dry already.

I zigzagged between the traffic, sliding through a set of lights as they switched from amber to red and swung a left.

The flash of red and blue lights came from my right a moment before I heard the sirens and I threw another left hand turn into the mix before shooting down an alley between two apartment blocks and skidding out onto the street on the far side.

With the cops officially lost, I let the throttle loose on the long stretch of road before me, weaving other vehicles and narrowly avoiding a collision as I ran a red light.

My heart was pounding even harder now but not with fear. This was it. Half the reason I took these risks. Riding these machines made me feel alive unlike anything else. I wished I could take my helmet off and let the wind race through my hair at top speed with nothing but an open road ahead of me. Unfortunately my disguise would be ruined if I attempted such a thing. The baggy jeans and oversized brown leather jacket were not, in fact, an indication of my terrible taste in fashion but were actually cleverly selected to make anyone who saw me believe I was a man. With my long hair and feminine curves hidden plus the fact that people just preferred to think of men as criminals, my cover was pretty airtight. So long as I didn't get caught.

The city lights sped by and I added an extra circle to my route just to make absolutely sure that no one had followed me. And if I was being totally honest, I wasn't going to complain about giving this beauty another five minutes of my time either.

My bones thrummed with the power of the engine beneath me and for a moment I let myself feel the ache to just keep the bike for myself. Of course the idea was absurd. Where would a girl who could scarcely afford a cellphone have gotten a limited edition super bike from? No, I was destined to ride the bus as usual and my night time exploits would have to remain hidden.

Once I was doubly confident that no one was tailing me, I turned the bike down a sloping alleyway and rolled it to a halt beside the black shutters which marked the service entrance to Joey's.

I revved the engine once before cutting it and stepping off of the machine I so wished to keep.

The seconds dragged as I waited for Joey to let me in and the tension in my gut coiled tighter as I glanced over my shoulder towards the road at the far end of the alley. If he didn't hurry up I was going to reacquaint him with my left hook.

With a deep rattle which made me jump half out of my skin, the shutter was lifted. I didn't wait for it to open all the way, pushing the bike inside and ducking beneath it quickly.

The shutter fell to the ground and I kicked the stand down before pulling my helmet off and turning my gaze to Joey.

He was a tall man, his dark hair slicked back with gel and his leather jacket stamped with the insignia of his bike gang, not that I had any interest in that. He was in his late thirties; not old enough to have stopped him from trying his luck with me in the past but too old for me to be interested. I was eighteen. He'd been my age when I was born. Gross.

Joey let out a long whistle as his gaze traveled over the bike. I didn't waste my breath pointing out all of its features; he was one of the few people I knew whose knowledge on these machines rivalled my own.

"Pretty good, huh?" I asked with a smirk. This was by far the most expensive bike I'd ever stolen for him.

"Depends on your definition," he replied, his gaze raking over the machine hungrily.

"C'mon, I know what it's worth, don't try and screw me over," I said irritably.

"Yeah, it's worth a lot alright. It's also a limited edition."

"I'm aware," I replied dryly.

"As in *very* limited; they only made eighty-five of these beauties. How do you expect me to shift that? It may as well have a big flashing sign on it saying 'stolen'." Joey tore his eyes from the bike, raising an eyebrow at me as my heart sank.

I'd been caught up in the challenge of it. The moment I'd seen the bike I knew I just *had* to ride it. What I didn't think about was this situation.

"Shit," I cursed. "What does that mean for me?"

Joey tilted his head, eyeing the super bike again. "Four-hundred."

"Fuck off, Joey. That bike cost over forty grand new and it's only a few months old." My palms grew slick as I kept my face in a mask of outrage and worry began to gnaw at me. We needed the money from this job. I'd been hoping for three grand at the very least and that bike was supposed to secure it for me.

"Take it or leave it," he said with a shrug, moving towards the shutters as if he was going to open them again.

"*Please,*" I bit out, the word nearly burning my tongue. "I need the money from this."

"Why are you so desperate for cash all of a sudden?" he asked, eyeing me with something that almost looked like concern.

Because I need every penny I can get to get me and my sister the hell out of this backwards corner of nowhere and start our goddamn lives.

"None of your business," I replied steadily.

Joey tutted. "Eight-hundred. Not a penny more."

"Done," I growled. It wasn't as much as I'd wanted but it was better than nothing.

Joey moved away to locate the cash, heading up a wooden staircase to the building above us.

I pulled the old leather jacket off of me before I followed; it smelled of tobacco and peppermint. The guy I'd stolen it from obviously believed he could cover the one smell with the other. He was wrong.

I kicked the baggy jeans off next. Beneath them I was wearing a pair of skin tight yoga pants and my black boots came up to my knee. The red tank top I'd coupled with it was just dressy enough to pass for something I'd wear clubbing, especially as I tugged it lower to make my cleavage more prominent.

I yanked the clips from my hair last, letting my black locks tumble to my waist as I ran my hands through it. No one would recognise me now. The man who had stolen that bike was long gone and I was just one of many girls out enjoying a drink tonight.

I followed Joey up the stairs, pausing outside his office as I waited for my money. He handed me a thick envelope and I didn't bother to count the contents; he was always good to his word where finances were concerned.

I gave him a nod before heading further along the corridor and through the back entrance to the bar which acted as a front for his less than legal exploits downstairs.

The stench of strong liquor and unwashed man assaulted me as I passed through the crowd of bikers.

The bartender spotted me and poured a shot of tequila into a glass before sliding it my way. I slipped between the bodies and accepted the drink as I leaned an elbow on the bar. I had no intention to stay long but I couldn't turn down free booze.

I knocked the drink back, my throat burning from the sting of the liquor as I slammed the glass down again.

I turned to leave and found my way blocked by a wall of muscular chest wrapped up in a crisp white shirt.

"Can I have a word with you?" he asked as I glanced up at him.

He was tall, his brown hair pushed back in the kind of careless I've-spent-ages-making-this-look-accidental way that guys with too much time and money on their hands often went for. I guessed he was five or six years older than me, probably mid-twenties. Kinda hot in a straight-laced way which wasn't really my bag.

"Are you lost?" I asked with a smirk. This was a biker bar. Facial hair, leather jackets and jeans were pretty much the uniform here and Mr expensive shirt and grey slacks stood out like a sore thumb. He did have a beard but it was carefully styled to look a certain way. The beards in here were more along the lines of crumb-hoarding face wigs than designer stubble. He was drawing attention and the last thing I needed right now was any extra attention.

"No. I've found exactly what I'm looking for," he replied, his deep tone almost lost to the heavy metal playing in the background.

"Good for you. I'll see you around." I started to walk away from him but he caught my arm.

"What the hell do you think you're-"

"*Take a seat with me,*" he said, his tone firm.

I dropped into a chair by the bar and he sat down beside me, releasing my arm.

Joey had made an appearance behind the counter and he raised an eyebrow at my choice of companion. I hadn't actually meant to sit down and I frowned as I tried to figure out why I had.

"You drinking tonight then, Tory?" Joey asked with a smirk as he filled another shot of tequila for me with half a smile. He knew I wouldn't waste my money on alcohol but he was also pretty generous with freebies when I wanted them. No doubt it was a ploy to keep me sweet so I didn't find anyone else to deliver my liberated merchandise to.

"I think I'll give it a miss after the events of last weekend," I reminded him. Me and a free bar weren't always the best combination and dancing on a table before falling from it wasn't exactly my proudest moment. I still had a purple bruise the size of Utah on my ass.

"Well one of these days I might-"

"*Leave.*" The guy beside me said irritably and Joey headed to the far end of the bar without so much as a word of protest.

I raised an eyebrow at his rudeness but he didn't seem to care. I guessed douchebag ran through his veins too deeply for him to acknowledge it.

"I think that's my cue too," I said, hopping from my seat and slipping back between the crowd of leather-clad bodies.

Fancy-shirt snatched my arm again and said something which was drowned out in the crowd of voices and background music.

"Back the fuck off," I snapped, twisting my arm out of his grip as I slid into the throng of bodies. A few of Joey's gang overheard me and stepped in to halt Mr Expensive's advance as he tried to follow me.

I took my chance at escape and headed for the exit. *Must be the full moon bringing out the pushy weirdos again.*

I ignored any further attention which was cast my way as I crossed the crowded bar. I didn't want to drink tonight. I just wanted to get back and show Darcy the cash I'd managed to earn.

Eight-hundred dollars. I sighed as I fingered the envelope which was at least half as fat as I'd have liked. Next time I'd have to set my sights on something a little less flashy.

Although, as I thought back to the ride I'd taken to get here, my lips lifted a little. So maybe the payout hadn't been quite what I would have wanted. But *man* that was a good ride.

The usual line-up of douchebags decorated the wall outside the bar, posing with their Harley Davidsons and bad facial hair. A couple of the younger guys eyed me with interest and I decided to skip the bus journey tonight.

"Any of you fellas fancy showing me what those machines can do?" I asked with a smile which was way sweeter than my personality.

My face was well enough known around here to allow me a measure of trust with the gang members though I'd made it clear I had zero interest in signing up.

"What'll you give me for it?" asked a guy with a handlebar moustache.

Nothing you're hoping for asshat.

"Which way are you headed?" a less gross male asked next. He didn't even have any facial hair which *may* have been because he was incapable of growing any yet but that was okay. Young and hopeful topped old and lechy any day of the week. He was actually kinda nice looking and he had a bike so that was two ticks for him.

"Just outside Riverdale on the south side," I replied hopefully. It was a fifteen minute ride at best but a good hour on the urine stained rust-box that served as a bus around here.

"Hop on then," Babyface said with a grin as he pulled his bike out of the lineup, throwing his leg over it as I drew closer.

I gave the bike an appreciative once over. "Nice upgrades, dude," I said with a smile. Either he was spending way too much money on putting this baby in the shop or he knew his way around a bike and a toolbox.

"Thanks, I did it all myself," he replied with a smirk. My kinda guy.

I slid onto the bike behind him, wrapping my arms around his waist as he started her up.

Flashy-shirt stepped out of the bar just as the engine roared to life beneath us, his dark gaze set on me. He looked more than a little pissed as he took a step towards us, calling something I couldn't hear over the growl of the engine.

Take a hint, dude.

I tightened my grip on my companion and a smile pulled at my lips as we shot away.

The wind braided my hair with icy fingers as we left the bar behind at a fast pace. Babyface knew what he was doing with the bike, easing past the speed limit and weaving the traffic in a way that set my heart racing with joy and my skin tingling with exhilaration.

In no time at all, we arrived at the outskirts of my less than great neighbourhood and he pulled over to let me off. I was still four blocks from home but there was no need to show the nice stranger where I lived.

"Thanks for the ride," I said with a grin as I started to back away.

"You gonna give me your number this time, Tory?" he asked and I tilted my head, surprised that he knew my name. He seemed to realise it too and gave me more of an explanation. "I gave you a ride a few months ago and you said you'd give me your number next time."

I couldn't remember that. I eyed the bike. Nope, I'd definitely never ridden it before, though my memory of faces wasn't so good.

"I used to have a Triumph," he said, noticing my confusion.

"Oh, you've upgraded," I said as the memory clicked together.

"I have. So what do you say? Will you let me buy you dinner some time?"

Hard to say no to free dinner. And he *did* know his way around a bike. And he was fairly easy on the eye.

"Can't say no to that, can I?" I asked, reaching for his cellphone so that I could key in my number. "I didn't catch your name."

"Matt," he supplied with a smile.

He hit dial as I handed his cellphone back and I smirked as I lifted the vibrating device from my pocket to show him that his call had come through. "Don't you trust me?"

"Just checking," he replied, giving me an appreciative glance. "I'll call you."

I watched as he rode away down the street with a faint smile pulling at my lips before I turned and started heading for home. I picked up a fast pace; the evenings were getting cooler now that we'd hit September and I was beginning to wish I'd brought a jacket out with me.

I jogged the last block, heading into our apartment with a sigh of relief as I pulled open the door at the foot of the stairwell.

"We didn't finish our chat," a deep voice came from behind me and I flinched in surprise as I turned back to the street. There, standing beneath the flickering streetlight was none other than Mr Expensive himself.

Terror coursed down my spine and sent my heart into overdrive.

I didn't waste time on chit-chat with the stalker as I turned and bolted for the stairs, my heart thundering in my chest.

I could hear his footsteps behind me and my mind filled with images of my broken body abandoned in a dumpster, food for the rats and a one-liner in the newspaper tomorrow.

Holy fucking shit on a cornflake.

"Stop!" He called and for some unknown, utterly terrifying reason, I *did.*

My lips parted in fear as he gained on me and I managed to shake off the desire to stay still as I bolted again. I made it to the fourth floor, sprinting towards our door at the end of the corridor with the upside down seven hanging from it.

I heard him cursing a moment before his solid weight collided with me. I was *fast* and had a good headstart, so how the hell had he caught up to me? He shoved me back against the door to our apartment and released a huff of irritation.

I opened my mouth to scream and his hand slapped down over my mouth.

The corridor was abandoned, even nosey Mrs Ergu from next door hadn't stuck her beak out to moan about noise or cooking smells or goddamn trash collections and for the first time ever I wished to see her narrow-eyed glare.

"I'm Professor Orion. I'm not going to hurt you and *you're not going to scream. You want to let me in."* He released his grip on me and stepped back as I stared up at him, fear still strangling me but the desire to scream for help gone.

I opened my mouth to tell him I absolutely *didn't* want to let a random stranger into our apartment at midnight on a Sunday but my hands seemed to

27

have other ideas. I shoved my key in the lock and turned it before I could stop myself.

"Come in," I said sweetly. *What the hell?* I wasn't sweet, especially with strangers. Especially, *especially* with stalker strangers.

Fancy-shirt stepped right into my personal space, offering me a flat smile as he followed me inside and pushed the door closed behind him. My heart was pounding, my palms slick and I was filled with the feeling that I'd just let a fox into my chicken coop.

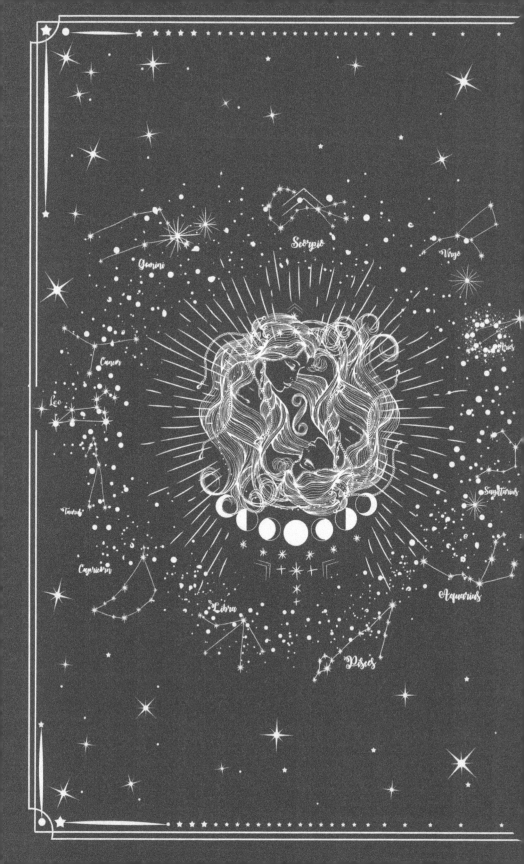

DARCY

CHAPTER THREE

I was snuggled up on the couch in my favourite pyjamas when the front door opened. I turned away from the episode of Breaking Bad where I'd maybe (not maybe) been taking mental notes on ways to solve our current predicament. Hope bloomed inside me as Tory walked in, but my smile fell away as I spotted two disturbing things: her bitter scowl, and a complete stranger marching into our apartment behind her.

I clung to the edge of the couch as the man side-stepped Tory, taking in our small apartment with a single, sweeping look. Heat invaded every cell in my body as his eyes fell on me, coal-like and dark as sin. He looked like a quarterback squeezed into a nice shirt and grey pants. His sleeves were rolled up to reveal muscular forearms and that trend continued from his biceps to his battering-ram shoulders.

A short beard clung to his chin, but he had an air of youth about him which suggested he was only a few years older than Tory and I. That could only mean one thing...

"Hell no." I stood up, pointing at the couch which converted into the only bed in our apartment. "Go to his place, Tor, are you crazy? Are you really expecting me to clear out so you can defile our only bed?"

Tory shook her head, her lips pinching together tightly as she gave me a stare that said I'd gotten the wrong end of the stick. "Obviously not. This guy just...well he wanted to come in alright?"

"And that's acceptable why?" I asked in utter confusion.

I realised Mr Shoulders was staring at my pyjamas with an expression that said he was wholly amused.

"What are you staring at?" I demanded, but heat slammed into my cheeks beneath my defensive facade.

"I thought I was coming here to collect a couple of eighteen year olds. Must have gotten the wrong apartment, little bunny." He laughed at his own joke and I cocked my head, fury bubbling up inside me.

Bunny? I glanced down at the bright-eyed rabbits lining my PJs and planted my hands on my hips. My mouth dried up. Damn, why did I pick these today of all days? I quickly went on the defensive, wanting to divert as much attention away from my cutsie PJs as possible. "Who the hell are you? And why are you in my home insulting me?" I looked to Tory again and she gave me an apologetic shrug before turning to face him.

I moved to join her, slipping off of the couch and standing shoulder to shoulder with my sister. We were a wall, barring him from stepping a foot further into our apartment, but up close he seemed even bigger and I could have sworn those muscles were getting twitchy.

"You were getting me a drink," the stranger shot at Tory and she promptly walked into the kitchen and poured him a glass of water.

What on earth?

I stared at him, his gravelly tone suddenly sending a bolt of recognition through me. Crap. My mouth opened as the penny dropped. "You're a cop. You were there today."

He gave me an innocent look, a dimple puncturing his right cheek. "Where exactly?"

"Don't play dumb with me." I pointed at him as my heart rate ratcheted up. I could almost see the walls of the prison surrounding me and my cellmate Patrice cracking her inked knuckles.

Tory returned, thrusting the water into his hand with a strange look on her face. I wondered why she'd bothered. It wasn't like her to comply with the orders of strangers. Or anyone for that matter.

The guy took it with a word of thanks then tipped it into his mouth. Glug glug glug. I watched his throat the whole time, lined with stubble, moving up and down.

When he'd drained the glass, he sighed satisfactorily and placed it on the kitchen counter. I dug my nails into my palms as I watched him take his time to make the arrest. Was he enjoying this? Or was he really just that damn thirsty?

Maybe I should run for the door. But I'm not going anywhere without Tory. And besides, I can't see any handcuffs. Maybe he's off duty. But then why is he here?

"I've been chasing around after you two all day." He strode to the couch, throwing himself down in my spot and stacking his hands on his stomach.

"Just leave Tory out of this. I was the one who took the cash." I glanced at her and she gave me an accusatory look for incriminating myself with the admission.

"Except you didn't get the cash, you dropped it," she pointed out and I pursed my lips.

"You mean *this* cash?" The guy lifted his ass and tugged something out of his back pocket, waving it above his head. And there it was: the wad of our beautiful two thousand dollars now bound together by a rubber band.

My heart did backflips as I stared at the impossible sight before me. Tory strode forward and snatched it out of his hand, perching on the coffee table as she counted every last note. He hadn't even tried to stop her.

When she was satisfied it was all there, she looked up and pinned him with one of her coldest glares. He didn't so much as raise an eyebrow, gazing at her with an equally cool look.

"So what do you want?" she demanded. "People don't just hand cash over unless they want something for it, Mr Orion."

Oh so he has a name.

"Professor," he corrected and I frowned.

And a title apparently.

"How old are you?" No way was this guy a professor. Unless he was some hipster DJ who'd labelled himself as Professor Dizzy D or something equally lame. But he just didn't have the tool vibe that accompanied that kind of lifestyle choice. He was entirely at ease except for a vaguely tense air about him that said we were the ones who were imposing on *his* day.

"Old enough to be a professor." His eyes swung to me and seemed to suck everything in like a blackhole. My heart accelerated and I started to deeply fear having this stranger in our home.

I moved to stand before the couch, folding my arms as I waited for an explanation while trying to keep my cool. I wasn't sure I managed the indifferent glare Tory was pulling off. Especially not in these pyjamas.

"You're going to listen to me and remain calm and collected," he said in a powerful tone and I felt an instant desire to obey. I nodded easily, half aware that I didn't want to listen to this random guy, but doing it anyway. I dropped down beside Tory on the coffee table and we both gave him our full attention.

He beamed at us and there was that dimple again. Just the one. Denting his masterpiece of a face and somehow making him even damn hotter.

"Since your eighteenth birthday, you have both been giving off a signature that my kind can sense from a world away. Literally." He paused, letting those odd words sink in.

I opened my mouth to ask a question but he held up a hand to stop me, continuing in his gruff, baritone voice. "I will explain, just *keep calm*."

I nodded, a lightness replacing the sneaking unease in my chest.

"Go on," Tory encouraged, a frown lining her forehead.

He leaned back in his chair, rubbing a hand across the back of his neck. "I'm not a beat-around-the-bush kinda guy, so here it is: you're not human. You're Fae. Which means you have an unawakened power in you defined by the stars themselves. You belong in Solaria: a mirror world of earth where Fae rule. Are we keeping up?" A flash of dry amusement swept over his face and though I couldn't find it in me to be angry, I was certainly frustrated.

I wanted to scream at him that he was crazy and he needed to leave or I was going to call the cops. But I couldn't get past the floating calm taking hold of my body.

I shared a look with Tory, her nose crinkling as she gave me a *he's batshit crazy* expression.

"You're both Gemini," he stated. "Hot-headed, hence the Coercion I've used on you to keep this all running smoothly. Especially as we're already running late," he muttered, lifting his wrist to check his watch. Dials and silver cogs spun wildly on the strange thing; it was unlike any watch I'd ever seen.

"Gemini...as in the star sign?" Tory asked. I'd always secretly liked reading horoscopes but Tory didn't buy into stuff like that. I wouldn't have gone as far as to say my star sign had any real impact on my life though. It just sort of intrigued me.

"Precisely," Orion said. "Gemini is an air sign so once your powers are Awakened you'll-"

"Hang on," I spoke over him and his expression told me he didn't like that one bit. "Do you really expect us to believe we have powers? Like *magic*?"

"Honestly? I don't care what you believe. But I have a job to do and part of that job is explaining this to you. Frankly, I'd rather not waste my breath as you're going to find out soon enough anyway."

"What does that mean?" Tory asked with less fury than I'd have expected from her.

"It means I've been trying to speak with you all day, but apparently breaking and entering and stealing motorbikes was on your agendas so I've been running around after you like a dog. And I really don't like chasing people about so let's just say I'm not in the best of moods right now."

I pursed my lips. He was rebuking us like a school teacher. But he was just some strange psycho who'd strolled into our house and was apparently pissed at us for not making this easier on him.

His lips twitched with irritation as he checked his watch for a second time. "Right, we're going." He stood, tugging something out of his pocket and I stared up at him in utter confusion.

"Wait a minute." I stood too but it did little to compete with his towering height. "You said we're Fae? What does that even mean?"

"We're a different race. A better one." He shrugged and I scowled. "Careful Miss Vega expressions like that are punishable in my classroom."

"Vega?" My nose wrinkled. "That's not my name. Wait, please tell me you've got the wrong twins?"

He shook his head. "That is your true surname in Solaria. No one will call you anything else once you get there, mark my words."

"Er- excuse me?" Tory cut in. Her jaw was gritted as if she wished she could have shouted those words. "We're not going anywhere with some creep from the lobby. What drug are you on exactly? Judging by the fancy attire I'm gonna guess coke?"

The 'Professor' gave her a predator's smile that made my stomach knot. "Look, I have far better things to be doing with my time than standing here in a dingy apartment with a couple of girls who think I'm an addict with a screw loose. But I didn't get a choice in the matter. So just humour me, will you?"

"You haven't explained anything." I shook my head and could feel an inch of my former fear raising its head. "And why should we believe anything you say anyway?"

36

He snatched up his satchel, flipping it over and pouring the contents out on our coffee table. A waterfall of papers fell everywhere, pages and pages. Pictures of us as babies, newspaper articles about the day our parents had died in a house fire. How we'd been pulled out of the ashes, two perfectly unharmed babies. A complete miracle. Amongst it all was our file for foster care. Every detail we knew about our history could be found amongst these cascading sheets of paper. So why on earth did this guy have them?

Orion sifted through all of it, extracting a photograph of our parents arm in arm on their wedding day. My father's hand lay on our mother's large belly, their eyes gleaming with happiness. I'd never known them, and I never would. And having that picture held in my face right at that second undid every chain that seemed to hold my emotions in check.

I snatched it from his hand, hugging it to my chest as the tears threatened a dramatic outburst which I couldn't afford in front of this shiny prep guy.

"What are you doing with a photo of our parents?" Tory hissed.

"They're not your parents," he said coolly as if that didn't rock the foundations of everything we'd ever known about ourselves. "You're Changelings. Fae born. Elementals with natural magic flowing in your veins. Your real parents swapped you for the twins born to that couple." He pointed at the photo in my hand and my brows dragged together. His expression was so impassive – how could he be so heartless? To just say such devastating things with not even a hint of emotion.

"That's not true. You're insane. Why would they do that?" I demanded.

"My guess? You were in danger," he said with a shrug. "Or maybe you just annoyed them as much as you're annoying me right now and they decided to swap you for less irritating twins."

Tory looked like she was about to punch him and I wouldn't have stopped her in the slightest.

"Get out," she said in a measured tone.

"Fine, I tried." He took a small silk black bag from his pocket and untied the strings. "Shame to lose out on your inheritance though. Your real parents were the wealthiest family in Solaria."

"Right," I muttered, fighting an eye-roll. This was like one of those scam emails where an African Prince had randomly chosen to give us two million dollars. Except this time the email had walked in the front door looking like a sport's model – *the balls on this guy!*

"Wait...wealthy?" Tory asked, stepping closer, her anger seriously lessened.

"It can't be true Tor," I said under my breath.

She shrugged one shoulder. "Let's hear him out." She gave me a look that said *jackpot* but I wasn't convinced.

"Yes. *Hear me out,*" he insisted and suddenly I nodded, wanting him to go on. He tugged the photo from my grip, eyeing it for a moment with a vague frown. "Look, I'm not trying to shatter your little daydreams about this couple but they're just two random humans who got caught up in something much bigger. You don't know them from Adam. And neither do I for that matter. The fact that they're dead is a tragedy but they aren't your blood. And blood's all that matters in my opinion." He shrugged, glancing between us. "You two would do anything for each other, I hope? Because this shitty life can go away like *that.*" He snapped his fingers. "All you have to do is agree to enroll at Zodiac Academy. You'll get full board, have your own beds-" He gave the couch a pointed look, "-and your inheritance will cover the cost of your stay plus you'll receive a monthly stipend from it. Once you graduate, it's all yours. But only when you graduate. That's the law."

"So you want us to go to some school?" Tory asked.

"Yes. But not just any school. The best school." His eyes glittered with his belief in that. "So what do you say?"

"I say you're crazy," I said.

"Yeah... but I do want the money." Tory elbowed me in the ribs and I frowned.

"It's full board?" I looked to Orion.

"Every meal," he swore. "So?" He tapped his foot impatiently.

Neither of us answered.

"Just say yes and come with me," Orion growled.

"Yes," we both said in unison without a moment's hesitation.

Wait – what just happened?

Orion grinned from ear to ear. "Should've done that in the first place." He jerked his chin at me. *"Go get dressed,* if you show up like that at Zodiac you'll be eaten alive by the other students."

My legs moved of their own accord and I cursed myself inwardly for obeying yet another of his commands. When I returned from the bathroom in jeans and a black tank top, some of my fear had kicked back in.

"You mentioned magic…" I said, changing tact to see if I could break through Orion's hard walls.

"Yes," he said. "Water, air, fire, earth. You will both possess one Element, perhaps two. Your parents were very powerful, so I expect you will be immeasurably gifted." Something about his tone told me he wasn't happy about that.

He prised open his small silk bag, pinched something between his fingers and sprinkled it in his palm.

"What's that?" Tory whispered as I inched closer.

"The rarest substance in Solaria and the quickest way to travel: stardust." He lifted his head with a demonic smile. "Welcome to your Awakening."

He blew the stuff right into our faces and I gasped. Thick, black glitter cascaded over us and I prepared to splutter, lifting a hand to shield myself, but instead my body felt like it had turned to vapour. Our apartment faded away and all I could see was the sparkling black substance clouding around me. It seemed to spread out and out until I appeared to be floating within an entire galaxy of the stuff.

My body reformed and my feet hit firm ground. I staggered forward and my forehead bumped into a hard body. I blinked as my vision restored and found myself face to chest with Orion. My hand was pressed flush to his stomach and I realised it much too late as he took hold of my shoulders and jerked me around to face the opposite direction.

My heart bolted into top gear as I found myself in a sprawling meadow beneath a crystal clear night sky, the stars brighter than I'd ever seen them. Before us were over two hundred people all around our age, standing in a huge circle in an expansive meadow surrounded by trees.

Tory sucked in a breath and I moved nearer to her, goosebumps lining my skin as I promptly stepped away from Orion. I was tempted to reach out to my sister in a gesture of comfort, but my hand balled into a fist instead, knowing she probably wouldn't appreciate it.

I glanced back at Orion in alarm. "What's going on?" I asked, panicked.

"Did you just drug us?" Tory rounded on him.

"What is it with you and drugs?" he muttered. "*Remember to keep calm,*" he commanded a second later and that wishy washy feeling stole away my fear again.

A female voice rang through the air but I couldn't see who it belonged to beyond the circle of teenagers.

"Get in the ring." Orion pointed and we reluctantly moved forward to join the masses.

Two girls parted to allow us to stand between them, their eyes roaming over us curiously. They took our hands and Orion caught hold of mine and Tory's wrists, pushing our fingers together to link the circle. Then he stepped back into the night and disappeared into the darkness.

At the centre of the ring was a tall woman in flowing blue robes. She had her arms raised in the air as she gazed up at the heavens and everyone else in the ring was watching her attentively. I had no idea what was about to happen and I shared a quick look with Tory to confirm she felt as lost as I did.

The long meadow grass tickled my knees and a cool wind pushed at my back. The woman dropped her arms and the wind fell deathly still, the whole world seeming to hold its breath.

"Welcome to Zodiac Academy. I am Professor Zenith of the Astrology department and it's my greatest pleasure to Awaken your Elements this very night. Please lift your faces to the sky, students. It's time for the stars to rouse your inner power." Her tone was slow and dramatic and even though this whole thing sounded ludicrous I couldn't help but hang on her every word.

She pushed the hood back from her head and midnight locks tumbled down around her. She was middle-aged, her skin pale and glimmering and her lips painted in a dark red lipstick. Her eyes fell on Tory and I and she jerked her finger toward the sky in an order. I realised everyone in the circle had looked up and we promptly followed suit.

The navy quilt above was aglow with stars and the milky way weaved through the centre of it all like a shimmering band of pink and purple dust. My mouth parted at the beautiful sight. In Chicago, you were lucky if you saw one star at night, let alone this spectacle. It was as if every other light in the world had been extinguished to allow the sky to dominate. There was no sign of the moon but even without it the stars were bright enough to cast a hazy silver glow over the meadow.

"Virtus aquae invocabo!" called Zenith in what sounded like Latin.

Okay this is going from weird to mental asylum real fast.

Silence stretched out and I almost dropped my head to figure out what was going on when rain dotted my cheeks. Several others in the circle gasped and I looked to Tory, finding droplets peppering her cheeks too. But how was that possible? There wasn't a cloud in the sky.

A deep whirlpool of power seemed to open up inside me and my breathing stalled as I felt its strength coil around my veins.

This can't be happening.

But it is. And I can actually feel it.

"If you feel rain, please raise your right arm," Zenith called.

Tory and I lifted our arms and I spotted around fifty others in the circle doing the same.

"Good!" Zenith said excitedly. "You hold the Element of water inside you, just like myself."

Some of the others who'd raised their hands started muttering keenly and a few without their hands raised grumbled and sighed.

"Quiet," Zenith hushed them. "Eyes to the sky once more. You will be tested for all Elements, though you are unlikely to have more than one my dears."

I raised my eyes, my heart hammering as I thought over what she'd said. The Element of water? Did Tory and I really hold that gift? Even as I thought it, I was sure it was true. Like an innate part of me had awoken and it embodied water itself.

Holy crap we really do belong here.

"Rogo vim aeris!" Professor Zenith called out and a strong wind gusted through my hair. I looked to Tory, finding her hair moving in the same powerful breeze. Another fifty or so of the group seemed to be in the depths of the maelstrom but everyone else in the circle were clearly unaffected. My gut swirled and a fluttering feeling filled my stomach and sailed through my veins. It felt so natural, like my body had a whole other channel inside me alongside my veins and now it was flowing with the magic of two Elements.

"Raise your right arm if you feel the power of the wind!" Zenith commanded.

Tory and I raised our arms along with another random selection of the circle. A couple of which had raised their arms for water.

Eyes fell on us and a few words were exchanged which I didn't catch. Zenith faced us, her brows lifting with delight. "You are of air and water girls. Your powers will be great indeed just like your parents'."

I nodded but Tory gazed down at her hands, turning them over as if expecting to find something more tangible there.

"Is this really happening?" she asked me under her breath.

"I think so," I whispered. "Either that or that dodgy Professor slipped us something in his fairy dust."

Tory snorted a laugh and Zenith fixed us with a glare. "Quiet! Eyes to the sky. You may be done here, but everyone else is not."

We nodded, looking up again.

Air and water...could we really use magic related to those Elements? I could hardly wait to try it.

"Rogo vim terrae!" Zenith cried and I glanced down at the other students, wondering what would happen to those who had the next power. The edges of the grass tickled my knees and I searched the circle for signs of the next Element taking effect.

A deep well seemed to open inside me, filled with a pulsing kind of energy. It tingled and then coiled and rippled like an ever-changing being that lived within me.

Something brushed against my arm then curled around it. I glanced down, frowning as I found the grass growing up and spiralling around my wrist, as gentle as a caress. More of the fronds wrapped around my arms and I spotted the same happening to Tory.

She looked to me with her brows arched. "I thought it was rare to get two?"

I shrugged, confused as I spotted the other pupils in the circle who also had the grass hugging in around them. It took me a moment to realise everyone was staring at us, Zenith included.

"I- oh my..." she breathed, clapping a hand to her mouth. When she dropped it, she was smiling widely. "My dears, how wonderful. You have Earth as well. Three Elements is very rarely heard of. You will be amongst the most powerful students at Zodiac."

A lump formed in my throat as that news settled over me. I supposed that was a good thing, but it all felt too surreal to really hit home. The other students were muttering and I caught strange words like 'Celestial Heirs' and 'Vega Twins'.

"Eyes to the sky!" Zenith commanded once more and I looked up again with my heart pounding an uncomfortable tune. Why was everyone looking at us like that? Was it really that unheard of to have three Elements?

"Invoco virtutem ignis!" Zenith yelled.

Heat flared at my feet instantaneously and fire scored through the ground around me in a tight circle. The fire flickered out into embers, leaving a glowing red ring in the grass around my Converses. The exact same thing shone around Tory's boots too.

My heart stalled as I stared down at the sight in confusion.

Four Elements? But Zenith said...

"By the stars!" Zenith cried and my head snapped up.

Everyone was staring. Hard. And not in a good way. Nearly a quarter of the circle had the same rings around their feet too but no one seemed to care about them.

"You hold *every* Element," Zenith gasped, shaking her head as if she couldn't believe it were true.

"Is that...bad?" I asked.

"Seems like it," Tory whispered so only I could hear.

Zenith recomposed herself, clearing her throat while mutters broke out around us, loud and unavoidable.

"Of course not," Zenith finally answered me.

"Looks like my boyfriend has competition," one girl said, throwing a sharp glare in our direction. Her hair was a rich gold colour and perfectly straight, her face the kind of pretty you usually found in a make-up commercial.

The girl beside her narrowed her eyes. "Are you *really* dating one of the Heirs, Kylie?"

"Yeah we've been together since forever, he texts me like every other week." Kylie tossed her hair over her shoulder with an expression that said that was something to be proud of.

The chatter grew louder and Professor Zenith finally seemed to notice it. "Enough! Quiet! Your Awakening is over. If you have two – *or more*- powers you will choose between them and pick an Elemental house to join. Your head of year will now take you to The Orb where you'll join the rest of the students and make that decision."

I spotted Orion emerging from the shadows at her words, beckoning us to follow him. As the students moved in a tide toward him, his eyes locked on me. His gaze drank me in for an endless second, then he turned and looked away toward the dark line of trees at the edge of the meadow.

Tory moved to my side and I stepped close to her, biting my lip. "Why does everyone seem pissed at us?"

She shrugged one shoulder as if it didn't remotely affect her but her eyes told a different story. "Guess we're about to find out."

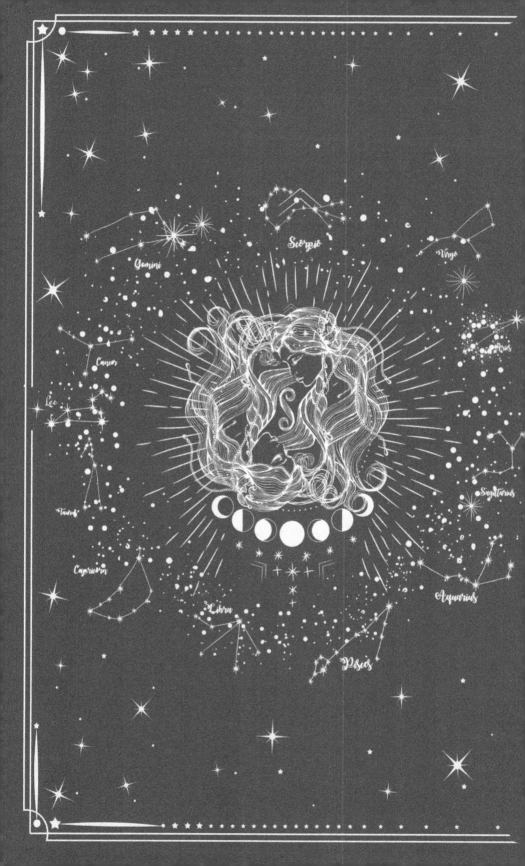

TORY

CHAPTER FOUR

The awakening had left me reeling, trapped within my own body as I tried to adjust to the sudden onslaught of power which had filled a void I'd never known I had. For the first time in my life, I was struck speechless. This power had crept up on me, whispered sweet nothings in my ear then slapped my face so hard it was left pink and stinging for the whole world to see.

My veins were alive with the force of what I was now. And I could no longer deny the truth of everything Orion had said to us since he'd turned up at our front door.

How could this have happened? How could it *be* happening? Everything I thought I knew about the world had just been flipped on its axis and I should have been left floundering in its wake and yet... I wasn't.

Yes, my newfound power had overwhelmed me but I couldn't deny just how *good* it felt as it writhed beneath my skin. It made me feel fearless, powerful, unstoppable. Every dream I'd ever had suddenly seemed irrelevant.

The world held so much more than it ever had. And it was ready for Darcy and I to take our places amongst it.

In my power-drunk daze, I hadn't noticed everyone filing away across the meadow but a sharp cough drew my attention to the fact. Orion raised an eyebrow at me, pointing me towards the line of freshmen who had already headed away. Only Darcy remained, taking a few hesitant steps before waiting for me while her eyes lit from within with the same writhing power I could feel harnessing itself to my soul.

I moved to her side at a quick jog, falling into step with her as we hurried after the group of our peers.

The path was winding beneath the dark sky and I was sure that under any other circumstances I would have tripped. But with the miracle of magic flowing through me, I managed to stay true to my course without upsetting so much as a lonely pebble.

The path led into a thick forest and we stepped beneath its branches where flaming torches sprang to life to guide the way on.

We caught up to some of the other students and they eyed us with interest. A short girl with a blonde pixie cut and freckles dotted across her nose offered us a friendly smile.

"I'm Sofia," she breathed, casting a glance behind us at the teachers before obviously deciding they didn't mind if we talked. "I've never met a Changeling before," she gushed, looking between my sister and I.

"Hi," Darcy replied with a smile.

"I'm Tory, that's Darcy," I supplied.

"I guess this whole place is super confusing to you?" she asked sympathetically. "I could be your walking, talking info source if you like?"

"Oh," I said in surprise. It wasn't really programmed in me to expect help from people I didn't know. Or those who I did know for that matter. Where we'd grown up, people didn't just do something for nothing, but as I looked at Sofia's earnest expression, I couldn't help but think her offer was just that. "That would be... great. Thanks," I said, trying out a warm smile while wondering if I was managing to pull it off. I probably looked like a hyena on crack but Sofia seemed satisfied with my attempt.

The path beneath my feet turned from dirt to gravel to shining gold. I tore my mind away from the caress of my energy and looked up at the building we were approaching instead.

It was a huge, golden dome, so big that I couldn't see anything else aside from it. Carved all over its surface were swirling decorations which looked almost like living flames, especially as the clouds shifted over the moon and shadows danced along the whorls in the metal. The gold markings which we were walking on shimmered too and I realised what the building was designed to mimic. It was a giant model of the sun, the ground beneath us decorated to look like beams of light reaching away from it.

"The Orb is where we'll take all our meals and gather for announcements like this one to declare the start of term," Sofia supplied as she noticed my widening eyes. "It's designed to look that way because the zodiac is directed by the sun. Without it, we would have nothing. Everything begins and ends with it."

"Poetic," I muttered, still not completely buying in to the whole horoscope idea, though I had to admit that the arrival of my magic was throwing my assumptions into confused overdrive.

"It's... amazing," Darcy said, her mouth falling open with awe.

We moved inside the double doors lined with symbols depicting each sign of the zodiac. We found ourselves standing before a whole crowd of students so big that I could hardly distinguish one face from the next. I only knew there were hundreds of them. And they were all looking our way.

At the centre of the room, beside a roaring fire pit which was surrounded by a ring of water, a curving red couch stood out amongst all the others. Its four occupants all looked deliciously bored, barely sparing a glance at the new additions to their ranks as the rest of the freshmen began to file into the huge room, taking whatever chairs were left available in the circular space. I wasn't sure I'd ever seen a group of guys who were quite as alluring as them. It was like I could feel a deep hum of power emanating from them and the hairs on the back of my neck raised accordingly.

They hadn't looked our way yet and I found myself glad to have the opportunity to study them without being noticed.

Each of them held a deep aura which set them apart from the rest of the people in the room. I would have thought they were siblings except that they looked so different that I knew it couldn't be the case. Something bonded them together though, something so clear that I could almost see it.

They were all tall and strongly built with muscles in a way that made my gaze roam over them a little inappropriately. They oozed power, wearing it as comfortably as the designer clothes they'd clad themselves in.

On the left was a guy with skin as dark as coffee, his black hair shaved into a mohawk which should have made him look like a total douchebag and yet somehow made me want to run my fingers over it instead.

He said something to the guy beside him who tossed his head back in laughter so loud that I wished I'd heard the joke too. The smile which accompanied that laugh drew my gaze for just long enough to rouse its owner's attention.

My heart raced a little like I was a kid caught taking candy as his dark blue eyes trailed over me. He pushed a hand through his curling golden hair, drawing my gaze to his broad shoulders for a moment before I looked away without studying the other two so closely.

My gaze trailed over the curved roof above our heads and I noticed a set of elaborate carvings cut into the gold ceiling which depicted constellations and planets. There were too many for me to even begin to count but my gaze roamed over them hungrily and I knew I'd be compelled to look up at them every time I entered this room.

Darcy moved closer to me as we began to follow the others and I raised an eyebrow at her as I tried to gauge her reaction to this. We hadn't exactly had time to discuss the life-altering, mind-crushing, new reality we'd found ourselves dumped in but the smile she was trying to hide let me know that she was just as energised about this place as me. I couldn't quite put my finger on what it was, but something about Zodiac Academy just felt *right*. It was like coming home after months abroad. Except for the fact that I'd never been abroad or ever really felt like I had a home in my entire life so that couldn't be right.

Home was where my ass landed. But I was glad to find that that was here for now.

I glanced down at my feet and paused as I realised that the ground which I'd thought was decorated with tiles was actually carved stone. It was as if someone had spent years etching spirals and images into a giant slab of rock; the length of time it would have taken to do such a thing blew my mind.

Before I could take another step, a hand clamped around my elbow and I turned to look at the owner of it with a frown. The woman was tall, with long black hair twisted into a bun on the back of her head and her skin pale and glimmering like starlight. Her gaze roamed over my sister and I hungrily as she drank in every detail on display and I found myself wishing I'd opted to change out of the low-cut red tank top. After seeing the rest of the students it was abundantly clear that this was supposed to be a dressy affair and my efforts at biker girl on a night out weren't really meeting the bar. Then again, I'd started this night with the sole intention of stealing a motorcycle, not joining a mystical species in a realm I never knew existed... Even thinking that made my brain wrestle against the reality of this situation once more.

"I'm Principal Nova, your guiding star here at Zodiac Academy," she said warmly. "I hear we have two things to celebrate with you both tonight."

"You do?" Darcy asked, glancing at me with a small shrug.

"Of course!" Nova gasped. "When Orion informed me that the girls he'd been tracking were indeed the lost Vega Twins I couldn't have been more delighted to welcome you back into the fold and return you to your people! But to then discover that the two of you hold *all four* Elements within your grasp... it's unheard of. Your return will be the talk of the entire Fae population, not just the school. Your every move will be watched and assessed as we all clamour to find out if you can truly reclaim the throne and-"

"Throne?" Darcy squeaked.

"Yes, didn't Professor Orion explain your heritage to you?" Principal Nova asked, looking around as if she hoped to spot the man in question.

I glanced over my shoulder and noticed him slipping away through the crowd as if he'd overheard her and didn't want to be caught.

"He just broke into our apartment and forced us to come here," I said.

"He told us our parents weren't who we thought they were," Darcy added. "And that we had to come here to claim our inheritance."

"That's... a very brief overview," Nova said, her lips pressing to a firm line that told me she wasn't pleased with Orion. "Your parents were the last King and Queen of Solaria, you return here as joint Heirs to the throne."

My lips parted but no words came out. I caught Darcy's eye, almost laughed then looked back at Nova and found I couldn't actually come up with a response at all.

"You mean we're like... princesses?" Darcy asked and the disbelief in her tone was punctuated by my scoff of laughter.

"Well, yes. Which is why you've caused quite a stir. Since the demise of your mother and father, the four Celestial families have held the power of the throne between them equally. They had intended to keep hold of that power with their own Heirs in the knowledge that the royal line had fallen. But with your return, everything could be about to change once more."

Nova seemed excited by that idea as her eyes whipped between Darcy and me but in my head all I could think was *hell no*. We didn't know the first thing about this place, let alone the family we'd supposedly been born into. How could she be standing there like Prince Charming with a glass slipper expecting us to shove our feet straight in?

"I really don't think-" I began but Nova cut me off.

"Of course, the throne won't just be handed to you. You will have to graduate from the Academy and prove your worth before that could ever happen. And you'll soon learn that Fae have to claim their own power if they want it. You have a lot of catching up to do if you want to reclaim the throne from the Celestial Heirs."

I stared at her in a weird non-blinking way for several seconds too long before my mind snagged on the one part of her announcement that my brain could process with ease.

"So if our parents were royal, does that mean they left us a load of crown jewels and a castle in their will?" I asked.

Darcy's eyes twinkled at the idea of that and a smile hooked the corner of my mouth.

Nova tittered a laugh. "Well of course your inheritance is quite sizeable - presuming you graduate and become eligible to claim it. And in the meantime you can acquaint yourselves with everything you will need to know to live up to your birthrights. And of course there will be interviews and exclusives, I've even heard talk of a documentary being made to detail your return and-"

"We don't want any attention like that," I said firmly, not knowing what the hell she was going on about and not really wanting to either. "We're here because that Orion dude said we had to come to claim our inheritance. That's it." I didn't mention the fact that since my magic had been Awakened I'd begun to think coming to this school could give me so much more than just money because it didn't matter. Whatever way I looked at it, I knew neither my sister or I would want the kind of attention she was suggesting.

The Principal's eyes widened in surprise but she covered it with the kind of fake-ass smile which wasn't really a smile at all but held something much more calculated in check.

"It must be a lot to take in," she conceded gently. "Of course you can spend a bit of time settling in before you have to make any choices about how you'll handle your claim or anything else besides that. Perhaps we'll hold the media off for a while so that you can get your bearings."

"Great," I bit out, not bothering to hide the fact that as far as I was concerned there wasn't any choice to be made. I tried to step away but Principal Nova had her claws in my sister and I and she didn't seem to be willing to let go any time soon.

A lump formed in the pit of my stomach as I realised she'd decided to make a spectacle of us on our very first day in front of the entire school and I couldn't quite shake her off before she turned to address the crowd of students who filled the huge room.

"Can I have everyone's attention?" Nova called and all eyes in The Orb swung to us as silence fell amongst the gathered students. I noticed several older men and women lining the edges of the room and spotted Orion amongst them which I guessed meant they were the faculty. Their eyes were on us too and I promptly looked away.

"I'd really rather not make a fuss," Darcy muttered but the Principal continued as if she hadn't spoken.

My gaze slid over the crowd and hooked on the group of guys sitting around the fire once more. They were looking at us curiously now and I tried not to let my gaze linger on them too long but it was difficult. Somehow, they commanded the room despite the fact that it was full to the brim with more people than I could count.

The guy on the right tilted his head to the side, his long, chestnut hair tipping over his fist as he leant his chin against his knuckles. There was something deeply animal in the way he eyed us and I found myself lifting my chin, refusing to cower beneath the challenge in his earthy brown eyes.

"This year's attendees have been joined by two particularly important girls," Principal Nova said, a wide smile pulling at her lips as I tried to ignore the fact that the entire student body of the Academy were looking at us now.

"I am delighted to announce that we have recovered the missing Vega Heirs and brought them back under the protection of our great nation. For seventeen years the Vega Twins were lost to us, believed to be dead. But to our great surprise, with the surfacing of their powers on their eighteenth birthday we were able to track them down in the mortal realm and return them to their rightful place amongst us."

No applause followed her words, though the long pause she gave suggested she was expecting one. Instead a pregnant silence had built in the room and I held my breath as I waited for someone to break it.

A high-pitched shriek of excitement broke the silence as a tall, broad shouldered girl with long, brown hair leapt to her feet. She started applauding so quickly that her hands were almost a blur and the wide smile on her face looked more than a little manic.

Her movement set off a little tidal wave of enthusiastic applauders who were dotted around the room, though there were still plenty of people sitting stock still and seeming less than impressed by my sister and me. I wasn't sure which response was worse.

Slow movement caught my eye and I glanced back at the couch dominated by the four heartbreakers as the final guy leaned forward to get a better look at us.

He rested his elbows on his knees, his dark eyes crawling over my flesh in a way that made heat rise along my spine. He was broader than the others, his muscles tight beneath a maroon t-shirt which clung to the curves of his powerful frame. His hair was jet black, and just long enough to shadow his eyes as it spilled over his forehead. Ink lined his biceps, disappearing beneath the short sleeves of his t-shirt, the designs intricate yet powerful in a way I couldn't quite name. His face was cut from my very own personal fantasy, as if someone had delved into my deepest desires and drawn them into strong angles and perfect temptation made just for me. My gaze caught on his muscular body, his mouth, the stubble gracing his jaw, his mouth again...

My heart raced a little faster as his eyes met mine for a moment and I felt like a lamb caught in the gaze of a lion. He was dangerous in all the right ways and I knew without doubt that the fire in his eyes would burn me up if I strayed too close.

The applause took way too long to run its course and our number one fan was the last to stop. She reclaimed her chair but didn't tear her adoring gaze from us for a second. We were left standing there as a thousand pairs of eyes ripped us apart, curiosity ready to tear every secret from us.

I pulled my gaze away from the hungry crowd and found my sister's green eyes instead.

The same nervous energy danced in her gaze as I felt writhing beneath my skin and I released a slow breath as I pulled my arm out of the Principal's grip. She wasn't so easily deterred and swiftly hooked her arm behind my back instead before pushing us forward so we started walking. Straight towards the group of guys whose faces were set in expressions that seemed anything but friendly.

"Gentlemen," Principal Nova purred as she gave me a little shove so that I was forced to stand before them like a sacrificial offering. "These are the Celestial Heirs," she explained to me and Darcy, naming them from left to right. "Max Rigel," (the dark skinned demi-god). "Caleb Altair," (the blonde haired beaux next door), "Darius Acrux," (my sin-filled fantasy). "And Seth Capella," (the long haired lothario). "This is Gwendalina and Roxanya Vega-"

"Those aren't our names," I interrupted, refusing to keep standing there like a lemon while the pack of muscle-filled daydreams assessed us like we were fresh meat. "I'm Tory and that's Darcy."

"I'm aware that your Changeling family gave you the names of their birth children," Nova said, like she was pacifying a small child, much to the delight of the blonde guy she'd named as Caleb. "But now that you're home you don't have to keep using-"

"I like my name," Darcy interjected.

"I'm sure as shit not going to start going by Roxanya," I agreed in a tone that closed the subject for further discussion.

Principal Nova eyed us like she was considering arguing further but I guessed the answer she saw in our eyes encouraged her to leave it. She sighed dramatically before continuing to address the distractingly good looking specimens before us. "Well whatever names you go by, you're still Vegas. The last in your line and rightful holders of the Solarian throne once you come of age. So long as you pass your assessments here and go on to graduate from Zodiac you will reclaim the throne from the Celestial Heirs." She indicated the four guys who sat before us and I frowned as I tried to comprehend exactly what she was suggesting. Before she gave me a moment to compute that little nugget of information, she continued to address the Heirs. "I do hope you hadn't gotten too comfortable with the idea of holding the throne together. I'm sure you'll want to be the first to offer the girls the hand of friendship as they embark upon this journey of education."

The four guys looked at us like offering the hand of friendship was the last thing on their minds. In fact, I got the distinct feeling that Dark and Dangerous might be trying to set us on fire with his eyes alone.

To my surprise, he was the one to speak first, a smile lighting his face which was no doubt meant to look friendly but seemed like a mask to me. I was a specialist in detecting bullshit and this guy looked like he was stuffing himself full of it especially for the Principal's benefit.

"Did you say they've been hiding in the mortal realm?" Darius asked curiously. "Without an ounce of training at all?" His voice was deep and rough in a way that made my skin tingle and I couldn't help but glance at his mouth as the corner of it lifted in amusement.

"Well I'm sure you boys will be more than willing to bring them up to speed." Nova patted me and Darcy like we were good children and moved away, leaving us standing before the wolves.

"Can you feel that power?" Caleb asked, leaning towards us as if he intended to sniff us like a dog.

Darcy stepped back and I frowned at him. The other three were looking at us curiously and I found myself wanting to be anywhere other than here.

"I guess we'll see you around," I said dismissively, turning my back on them as I tried to draw Darcy away.

Before we could get two steps, I came face to face with a broad chest as the four Heirs suddenly rose to stand around us.

"That was a little rude," Seth murmured, his voice almost like an animal growl as he looked down at me, his long hair spilling over his shoulders.

"Cut them some slack, Seth," Darius said as he stepped closer too and we found ourselves boxed in by a wall of testosterone-fuelled muscle. I didn't much like being forced into a corner like that. "They don't know how it works here yet. I'm guessing you didn't realise that turning your back on your superiors is considered an insult?" His tone was almost kind but his words sent a trickle of fuck you right along my spine and I straightened as I turned my gaze on him instead. He was even more intimidating now that he was upright, his broad chest in line with my face so I was forced to tilt my head to look up at him.

"Superiors?" I asked, arching an eyebrow at him. "I don't see anyone superior to me around here."

"Well maybe you should look a little closer, *Roxy*," he taunted, using that name to try and get a rise out of me. *Poking fun at my dead parents' choice in baby names. Classy.*

I made a show of trailing my gaze across the four of them before shrugging dismissively. "I can't see anyone better than us here. How about you, Darcy?"

"Nope," my sister replied dismissively.

Before he could reply, I turned my back on him again, pushing between Max and Caleb as we began to walk away.

"I think they could do with a lesson in how things work around here,"

Max growled as we gained some distance from them but I didn't bother to look back. I'd never made a habit of being popular in any of our other schools and I wasn't bothered about that now either.

Darcy raised an eyebrow at me as we walked away from them and my lips lifted. She'd never been quite so keen to rock the boat as me but I'd never been too concerned with making friends. Especially not the kind who demanded respect instead of making sure they earned it.

Before I could say anything else to her, a solid weight slammed into my side and I released a cry of surprise as I was propelled around and shoved up against the golden wall of the curving room.

My heart leapt with fear as I tried to break loose of my attacker's grip and Caleb smiled at me as he pressed his strong body against mine, pinning me in place.

"Wanna beg for forgiveness?" he purred and a shiver raced down my spine as my sister yelled at him to stop and tried to come to my aid. Max grabbed her before she got close and my gaze slid around the room, hunting out the teachers but none of them seemed to care about what the Heirs were doing to us.

My heart was pounding and I struggled feebly against Caleb's hold on my wrists before trying to slam my knee into his crotch. He avoided my attack easily, pressing his body to mine so that I couldn't repeat it.

"Last chance," he offered, his gaze sliding over me in a way that sent fear crawling through my limbs despite his devastatingly good looks.

"Fuck you," I growled, my fists clenching with the desire to punch his pretty face.

"I hoped you'd say that." His mouth dipped to my neck and for half a second I thought he was going to kiss me before the sting of his teeth pierced my flesh.

I cried out, bucking against him in disbelief as the most horrifying sucking sensation pulled at my blood and worse than that - my newfound power. I could feel him draining it, drawing it out of me and into himself.

Holy shit, what the hell is he?

Everyone in The Orb was staring at us now but no one took so much as a step forward to help.

My gaze fell on Sofia who looked like she wished she could intervene, Orion who seemed mildly bored, the Principal who appeared disappointed and finally the other three Heirs. Max held my sister back as easily as if she were a child, despite the fact that she was thrashing and cursing at him. Darius and Seth had moved to stand beside him as they watched the show with amused expressions. They watched their friend feed on me with a sickening sense of satisfaction rolling from them. Darius caught my eye and for a moment I felt like I was looking at a monster instead of a man.

He smiled at me with all the smug satisfaction of a mainstream asshole who thought he could win just by throwing his weight around.

My heart slammed against my ribs and my knees grew weak as Darcy shouted for someone to do something. Somewhere deep inside my chest a defiant little spark lit beneath the pyre of my panic and I clung onto it like a life raft. I wasn't going to let this touch that flame. And together we'd ride out the dark.

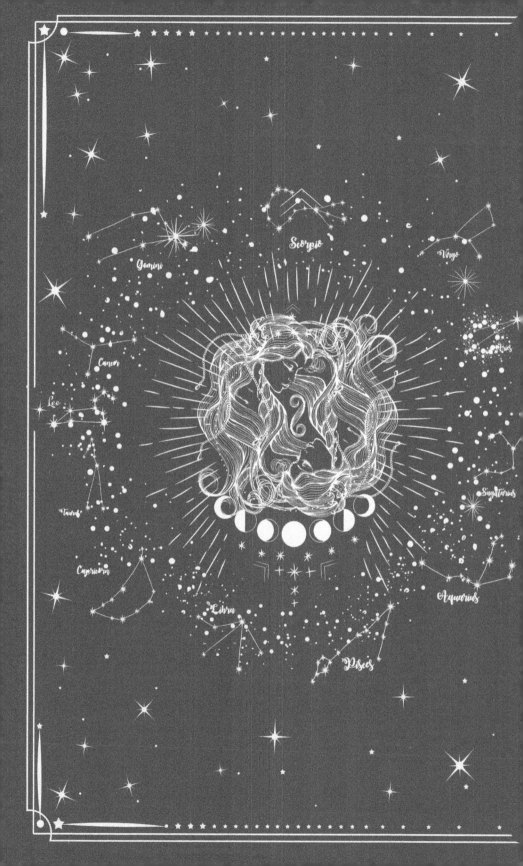

DARCY

CHAPTER FIVE

I elbowed the muscular Heir who held me back from my sister, looking to the room for anyone who might help.

"Let me go," I snarled.

The beast continued to chomp on Tory's neck like a complete freak and she struggled wildly to push him off. I managed to twist my wrist free of Max's hold and thrust my palm against his chest in anger. A flood of power crashed through the barriers of my skin and a storm of air sent him careering over the heads of the crowded lounge and slamming into the back wall.

My heart turned to a solid, unthawing lump of ice.

Caleb released Tory and everyone stared on in shock at what I'd done. I gazed at my hands, beginning to shake as the truth of our current situation finally sank in. I could do magic. Actual, real life magic. And I'd just used it to throw that two hundred pound guy across the room.

And pissed him off real good no doubt.

Oh crap.

"You're gonna regret that," Darius said coolly, flexing his muscles. The long-haired one, Seth with the etched-from-stone jawline, smiled around at the chaos.

Tory shoved Caleb back, clutching her neck as she staggered toward me. "What the hell is wrong with you, you psycho!?" she snapped at him and Caleb started laughing. Several girls close by giggled as if they were involved, glancing hopefully at Caleb for a crumb of recognition.

Did all Fae bite people? What kind of crazy species are they?

"Are you alright?" I asked Tory as she inspected her blood-stained fingers. She nodded stiffly, her pride clearly wounded more than she was.

I looked toward the teachers at the back of the room, hunting down Orion and discovering that he was the only one paying us any attention. A wild intrigue lit his eyes and fury bled through my veins like magma. *Is he for real right now? He's supposed to be a teacher!*

Max reemerged, rolling up his sleeves as he barrelled through the crowd like a stampeding rhino.

"Back off," Tory spat at him, moving to my side as fear crushed my heart.

"Or what?" Darius asked while his friend, Seth, continued to laugh like this was the most amusing thing he'd ever witnessed.

The group of our apparent supporters closed in, headed by the dark haired girl who was built like a viking warrior. "Or we'll fight for our queens," she announced and I shared a surprised look with Tory.

Max opened his palm as if he was about to cast some spell and fear daggered into my heart.

"Multiple Element freshmen it's time to choose your houses!" Principal Nova called, stepping away from a few members of the faculty who she'd been deep in conversation with. So deep that she hadn't noticed one of her students biting Tory? I didn't think so. But what kind of school let their students attack each other without so much as a verbal warning?

The other Heirs surrounded Max, pushing him back with shakes of their heads and a heavy sigh of relief left me.

I was thankful for the excuse to end our altercation with them and Nova clapped her hands to hurry us up. Tory and I strode over to join the small division of freshmen who were bundling together in front of the faculty.

The rest of the students fell back into their seats but the Heirs remained standing, folding their arms as they watched us go.

"House Captains," Nova beckoned them and I turned, my gut sinking and sinking until I was fairly sure it was wedged in my left sock. The four Celestial Heirs were the House Captains. *Of course they were.* "State the name of your house and why the freshmen should pledge to join you. And for a little suspense, we'll leave the newest Heirs till last," she said excitedly.

"Great," Tory said to me under her breath. "Which asshole are we picking?"

"Umm." I gazed at our abysmal options with a frown and they stared back with looks that said they were gonna eat us up. And one of them had already had a go with Tory. So he was definitely ruled out.

Max stepped forward first, brushing a hand over his mohawk with a smirk and his bicep hardened. He was a tower of pure masculinity and those eyes held nothing but a sea storm. He looked at Nova but somehow I sensed his words were for us. "Water focus, House Aqua. My house is for those who have what it takes to face the deadly sea of life in Zodiac without flinching."

"Thank you for that poetic description," Nova said, clearing her throat as she pointed to the bitey blonde guy, Caleb. My heart pounded harder at his angelic face which hid a demon beneath it.

"Earth focus, House Terra. And terror is exactly what you'll get if you don't fit in." He gazed firmly at Tory and my gut shrivelled into a tight ball.

"Not him," Tory hissed, her eyes spilling venom in his direction.

"Agreed." I nodded.

The long-haired guy stood forward next and my gaze scraped over his muscular frame. Everything about him was tempting and distinctly predatory. "Air focus, House Aer. Life with us is a breeze." His eyes swept our way and he smiled. It looked pretty genuine and my shoulders relaxed a little. Yep. He looked like the one. Especially as the last one, Darius, was built like a fortress and had eyes as sharp as knives.

"Fire focus, House Ignis. We aren't for the faint of heart. And frankly I don't see anyone in this line-up who's good enough to join us." He glared at us as if daring us to join his House and I could almost see him thinking up ways to make our lives insufferable if we did.

Nova moved along the line of twelve students beside us and one by one they picked from the two Elements they'd been gifted and joined their House Captains. The pretty girl who'd glared at us in the Awakening chose Seth, running forward and wrapping her arms around him.

"Baby!" she cried, tossing a straight golden lock over her shoulder.

Seth squeezed her against his athletic body and I wondered for half a second what an embrace from those arms might feel like. "So glad you got air, Kylie," he said but his eyes didn't say the same thing. "What's your other Element?"

She swatted his chest. "You know I got Earth, Sethy, I'm a Capricorn." She leaned up for a kiss and he rammed his tongue down her throat in an overt display that lasted nearly a whole minute. *Nice*.

The line finally dwindled away until only Tory and I remained.

"Air?" I confirmed with her in a quiet voice. She nodded, opening her mouth to announce it when Nova spoke.

"You will have to pick differently girls I'm afraid. Each House is very competitive and we encourage everyone to take part in the healthy rivalry. As you have so much power, it wouldn't be fair for one House to be at such an advantage."

Horror bloomed in my chest. Part with Tory? My twin? I mean...we were independent but we were also a constant in each other's lives. She was like my left arm. I could manage without it most of the time but if it was cut off I wouldn't be whole.

Tory looked to me with a dark frown. "Well that's just perfect."

"We'll be housed separately?" I confirmed with Nova.

"Ohh are you gonna cry?" Max called to me and I wanted to rip his face off for it as sniggers filled the room.

I swallowed hard, shaking my head as I tried to inwardly deal with my surging emotions.

"I choose fire," Tory announced loudly, brushing her fingers over my back for the briefest of moments. She leaned in to speak in my ear and I felt a goodbye passing between us. "Take air but don't take any shit."

She stalked away, standing beside Darius who gave her a calculating look which told me she was gonna be in trouble with him. My gut unravelled as she joined the most demonic-looking Heir in the entire line up. She never had taken the easy route in life. But I wished she'd done so just this once.

"Air," I said, trying to keep my spirits up as I walked cautiously toward Seth. He moved forward to meet me and suddenly wrapped me in his arms. The exact arms I'd just been having a two second day dream about. Damn, it felt like eating a too-hot cookie fresh out of the oven. It burned all the way down but tasted divine.

"Welcome to the tribe, babe." He smelt like musk and something almost animal. I tried to pull away as he held me in what was fast becoming an inappropriately close embrace for several more seconds. When he released me, his girlfriend drew closer with a bright smile on her face.

"Hey girl, just so you know, my bae is in charge. So long as you get that, we're totally cool."

I shrugged, not giving one damn about taking power from her *bae*.

She linked her arm through mine as Nova dismissed us all and the rest of the Air Element freshmen joined us.

This has gotta be better than being in Caleb's House.

"Let's show the newbies how Aer House works," Seth said, throwing me a wink as he led the way out of The Orb. Many more older students stood up, joining our ranks as we filed out of the building.

As I glanced over at Max's new recruits in Aqua, I was overly relieved that I wasn't in his House. He had them standing on their heads and was in the process of pouring water all over them. I shook my head in disbelief as the teachers continued to chat away as if that was entirely acceptable even when one of them started choking.

I spotted Tory in a tense-looking conversation with Darius, but I knew she could handle herself. My sister was as tough as nails. But I was going to miss her.

We headed east away from The Orb and Kylie parted from me, moving to join a girl with large eyes and raven hair.

We passed by big stone buildings which seemed to ring The Orb and a huge, crescent-shaped structure which resembled the moon. Seth had an excited prance in his stride as we followed the winding path toward a thick group of trees in the distance.

My heart hammered and I looked around me for a friendly face as the group jostled me along, but no one met my eye.

We headed into the thick forest and the amber glow of lanterns lit the path, the trees grouping close together on either side of the track and arching overhead. A chill brushed across my skin accompanied by a lick of adrenaline.

I half expected to wake up tomorrow and find that all of this was a dream. Despite the fear the Heirs had struck in me, this place called to me. It was beautiful and a deep vibration in my soul told me I belonged here. Like the stars themselves had been waiting for me to arrive at this very spot.

We emerged from the trees and found ourselves on a sprawling clifftop where the crash of waves sounded from below. A huge tower stretched up high above us, the dark grey bricks ancient and weathered. Vertical windows were built into the walls and at the very top was an enormous rotating wooden turbine which moved in a breeze I couldn't feel.

Seth turned back to face us, standing before the arching doorway made of black iron. Above it, carved into the stone, was a large symbol of a triangle with a horizontal line intersecting the top half of it. Seth raised a palm and the symbol glowed with an intense white light, the sight making my heart thrum excitedly. The iron door clunked heavily, sounding it unlocking.

"Freshmen, get your asses in front of me because I'm only gonna say this once," Seth announced.

Me and the fifty or so other newbies headed toward the front of the group. I moved to Kylie's side, stepping between her and a guy with a beanie hat on and an excited look on his face.

Seth devoured the attention, his gaze flitting across all of us as several of the older students grouped around him. Many rubbed shoulders with him or brushed their hands over his back and arms. It was totally weird but he let them continue as if it was a regular occurrence.

"You don't get into Aer unless you use your power on that symbol." He pointed to the triangle above the door. "As it's your first day, I've already opened it but as of tomorrow if you can't conjure air, you don't get a bed in my House."

I rubbed my fingers together, hoping I'd be able to use my power again but I wasn't entirely sure how I'd done it before. Power coiled inside me in anticipation but I couldn't will it into my hands.

The guy beside me bobbed on his heels with a keen energy; he glanced my way and gave me one of the friendliest smiles I'd received so far. My shoulders relaxed as I smiled back, glad to have the prospect of a friend in my new House.

"Now." Seth smiled and for a moment he looked like a hungry wolf who hadn't eaten for a few days. "Let's get on with it." His eyes whipped to me and he curled a finger to beckon me over.

My mouth dried up and it took a second for me to make my legs move as I stepped forward. He turned me to face the group of freshmen, slinging an arm around my shoulders. His fingers stroked my bare skin and I stiffened in surprise at his tactile behaviour. I tried to duck away, but he plucked the back of my shirt and tugged me against his hip again, his hand suddenly in my hair.

Was he petting me?

"Initiation!" Seth called and the swarm of older students behind the freshmen descended on them, shoving black linen bags over their heads.

Seth kept his attention on me and my heart crashed against my ribcage as he moved his nose to my hair and inhaled deeply. A shudder ran through me and I tried to push him back, but he was frighteningly strong. The hot, wet, pad of his tongue suddenly dragged up my right cheek and revulsion slammed into me.

"Ergh!" I brought a hand up to slap him, but he caught it with ease, his eyes glittering as if we were playing some game.

He laughed heartily. "Chill out, babe. This is how I say hello."

My heart slowed a fraction as I gazed at him. He cocked his head and gave me an innocent expression, making the remainder of my anger melt away. Maybe in Solaria this was normal. And I didn't want to be accused of culture shaming...

"Right," I said uneasily. "I'm just still trying to figure this all out."

He laughed as if I'd said something funny then turned back to the crowd, his arm still locked tightly around me.

My gut fluttered with nerves as I took in the hooded group of freshmen, but I noticed Kylie was standing to the side of them, her hand on her hip. Evidently the House Captain's girlfriend got a free pass.

"What's your Order, babe?" Seth nuzzled into my ear and my body seized up at the intimacy of his gestures.

"Err.. what?"

"You know...Siren, Vampire...Werewolf?" he asked with a note of curiosity.

Someone behind me started touching my hair and I was pretty sure they were braiding it.

What the crap is happening right now?

"I don't know what you're talking about," I said, trying to keep my thoughts in line as Seth moved his face to my neck and breathed in deeply again.

He chuckled, pulling away. "You really are from the mortal world. Don't worry babe, those powers will surface soon." He nodded to someone behind me and a linen bag was yanked over my head, blinding me in an instant. I steadied myself against Seth as my breath quickly heated the air surrounding my face.

Seth released me and I tried to hold my nerve as I was left alone all of a sudden. My pulse raced as I waited for something to happen.

"If you don't pass my initiation you don't stay in Aer, got it?" Seth barked and his voice was so forceful I couldn't fight a flinch.

A murmur of ascent went up from the freshmen.

"You will reply with 'yes Alpha'. Let's try again," Seth commanded. "Have you got that?"

"Yes Alpha!" the freshmen called but I couldn't bring myself to do it. It was just too degrading.

I was suddenly yanked against a hard body and I felt sure it was Seth. "Answer me, pledge."

Gah.

"Yes Alpha," I forced out through my teeth.

He released me and I stumbled forward as he stepped away.

"MOVE!" Seth bellowed like a drill sergeant and hands snared my arms, pulling me along at a fast pace. A cold breeze gusted over me and the thumping of hundreds of footfalls filled my ears.

The air became noticeably warmer and I guessed I was inside the tower as I was guided across a hard stone floor. The toe of my Converses hit a step and I staggered, but the hands holding me kept me upright.

We started climbing a winding staircase, round and round and round. I was dizzy and hot and fear was making a good effort at making me freak out. But this was just a game. Even mortal colleges did crap like this. I just had to get through tonight. Pass their stupid initiation. Then hopefully I'd get a warm bed and a moment alone to process this whole day. It must have been well past midnight already and exhaustion was starting to seep into my bones.

Someone jabbed me in the back and I grumbled as I was forced higher and higher.

Finally, we stepped onto flat ground. My leg muscles burned and I panted heavily. Whoever was holding me didn't seem to be out of breath at all. In fact, I couldn't hear many people around me who sounded as exhausted as I was.

I'm not that unfit am I?

"Forward," Seth commanded and I was guided across hard flooring, twisting left and right.

A cold wind hit me and a shiver ran through my body as I realised I must have been outside again.

"You're now at the top of Aer Tower," Seth announced and murmurs of fear escaped the other freshmen.

My heart doubled its pace as the icy wind increased, pressing against my back.

"Line them up on the edge," Seth growled.

The edge!?

My heart thundered as the two people holding my arms dragged me forward. I dug my heels in as some of the freshmen called out, "Wait!" and "I'm not ready!"

I was pushed forward then released and I felt myself teetering on a precipice, my toes hanging over the edge.

I lurched backwards in fear, but strong hands shoved me into place again.

"You are air born, pledges!" Seth shouted at us from behind. "The wind is your ally. If you can't harness it, you don't deserve to live here. Or at all for that matter."

Terror clutched my heart and I shook my head as I realised what was about to happen. The wind gusted at my back again and a murmur of fear escaped me.

Someone sniggered and I was fairly sure it was Kylie. I gritted my teeth, hating feeling so vulnerable in front of everyone. But at least the other freshmen were beside me. I tried to reach out for the closest one, but my hand just flailed and I quickly pulled it back to my side.

Movement sounded around me, the shuffle of feet and the odd giggle.

How was this funny? I didn't know how to use my powers! Did the rest of the freshmen have some training? Maybe I was the only one who didn't. And if that was true I had to let them know.

"Wait," I choked out. "I don't know what I'm doing."

"You'll figure it out, girl," Kylie called in encouragement.

I started to tremble, picturing the huge drop stretching out far below me.

"On the count of three you'll jump and if you don't stop yourself from hitting the ground, then you're gonna go splat. And if you don't jump, you'll be pushed," Seth explained in a bright tone.

"What the fuck?" I snapped, suddenly losing it.

"One!" Seth called, ignoring me.

I shook my head, panic dashing my heart to pieces. I didn't know what I was doing. How could I catch myself with a power I'd just found out I had a few hours ago!? I rubbed my fingers together, trying to draw that rippling sensation to them again but it wouldn't obey.

"Two!"

A quiet, resolute voice in my head told me I had to do this. I couldn't be the weak link in this crazy group of students. School was always about hierarchy and if I failed at the first hurdle, I'd never earn my place here.

"Three!"

I took a breath, shut my eyes and placed every ounce of faith I had in myself.

I jumped.

My feet hit the floor. Someone ripped my hood off and raucous laughter filled my ears. It took me a painfully long second to realise I'd just jumped from a one foot step at the heart of a crowded room. All of the other freshmen had been pulled aside to watch me do it. Alone.

Heat scorched my cheeks, my neck, everywhere. I wanted to vanish, hide away from their mocking eyes and never come out again.

The cold wind I'd felt was coming from the outstretched hands of several seniors and now that their cruel prank was done, the wind died and they buckled over in hysterics. The freshmen were laughing just as loudly, their linen hoods now gripped in their fists.

Seth stepped into view, grinning a wolf's grin.

"That's not funny," I blew out, trying to smile it off.

He caught my wrist, dragging me forward, his hands everywhere again. The sizzling look in his gaze made my smile drop away like a falling brick.

"What's really not funny is you and your sister showing up here to steal *our* throne. We've worked our asses off to earn that right. Our four families have ruled for nearly twenty years since the fall of King Vega and Solaria has been much better off for it. Our parents divide the power between themselves and as the sons of the Celestial Council, we will soon take that responsibility from them. So we don't intend to just sit back and let you take the throne from us and return Solaria to the shitheap it was when your father ruled," he snarled, his eyes two hollow pits of cruelty. There was no friendliness left, his touches weren't curious now, they were possessive and degrading.

His words sent my mind into a desperate spiral as I tried to understand them.

"I don't want your throne." I tried to wrench my wrist free from his grip but he wouldn't let go.

He turned me to the room. "Who says we really throw her off the tower this time?"

"What?" I gasped as the whole of House Aer roared their ascent. "Get off of me!" I threw my shoulder at Seth but he barely noticed, tugging me through a grey stone lounge filled with woollen rugs and cream armchairs. Seth hauled me toward a huge set of glass doors that led onto a balcony and fear spread through me like a forest fire.

The older students crowded in behind us as Seth forced me to the edge where a stone wall parted us from a sea of nothingness.

"Are you crazy?!" I yelled desperately as I tried to get his hands off of me.

The group who had been all over him before lifted their heads to the sky and started howling. The piercing noise sent my heart skittering.

I clawed at Seth's hands as he lifted me, planting me up on the wall.

I stood there, refusing to look over the ledge, gazing back at the lounge through the glass windows where everyone in Aer was fighting to look out.

Seth glared up at me, the king of this group of madmen. I didn't want to beg, but death seemed one shove away and I didn't know how far he would take this.

"Please, just let me down," I whispered, just to him, my voice betraying my fear as it quavered on the last word.

Seth tilted his head with a smirk and I spotted Kylie pushing through the crowd to reach him. I looked to her, wondering if she might tell him to back down but instead she linked her fingers with his and gazed at me with a vicious grin.

"Jump," she said, her eyes sparkling.

My throat constricted as I searched for a single friendly face amongst the masses. But I couldn't find one. I was alone in this. And the only person I had to rely on was myself. They'd played me like a fool.

I clenched my fists. "Let me down."

Seth released Kylie as he moved right up to the wall and gripped my ankles. Fear shot through me like a lightning bolt. My life was in his hands, he could uproot me at any second.

"Alright," Seth said after a long pause. "But you can only get down when you've cut off all of your hair."

On cue, Kylie produced a sharp pair of scissors from her pocket, her gaze venomous as she passed them to Seth.

"What?" I gasped.

"It's that or jump." Seth shrugged and laughter rang out from every direction.

I wanted to curl up into a ball, but I refused to let them see me break. Seth held out the scissors, his face cast in shadow.

I clenched my jaw, furious that I was backed into a corner like this. It was clear this had been his plan all along. He wanted me wholly ridiculed. He wanted the entire House to laugh at me, to humiliate me beyond repair. It wasn't just my hair he was trying to take, it was my dignity.

The wind pressed at my back and a trickle of energy met my fingertips. The air moved between my hands, dancing, floating, completely under my command.

My throat tightened and I threw a glance over my shoulder. My heart screamed at me not to do it, but this was the only way I wasn't going to be destroyed by Seth Capella on my first day at Zodiac Academy.

His brows pinched together as he realised what I was about to do.

I sucked in air and felt it moving through my body with a promise. And I simply had to have blind faith in that feeling. It was the only thing I had to hold onto as I threw myself over the edge.

Screams and gasps followed me as I cascaded through the air, my heart trying to break free of my chest. I tumbled and lost sight of everything, panic invading me and gripping onto every cell in my body.

I spread my hands desperately, knowing the seconds were ticking by.

That I was only feet away from smashing into the hard ground below.

The well inside me spilled over and I felt a shift. A rush of energy like a hurricane unleashed itself in my body. The moment it met my fingertips, the power exploded from my skin in a gigantic gust. At the last second, I begged it to stop my fall and I came to a swooping halt.

I hung suspended, ungraceful but completely alive as I gazed down at the ground a few feet below me.

I'd been so close to failing. So close to dying. And as cheers called to me from above, a smile forced my lips wide. The cushion of air collapsed and I crashed to the ground in a heap.

Adrenaline surged. My entire body trembled. But I was alive. And for now, I'd damn well earned my place in Aer. And it sounded like the rest of the House knew it too.

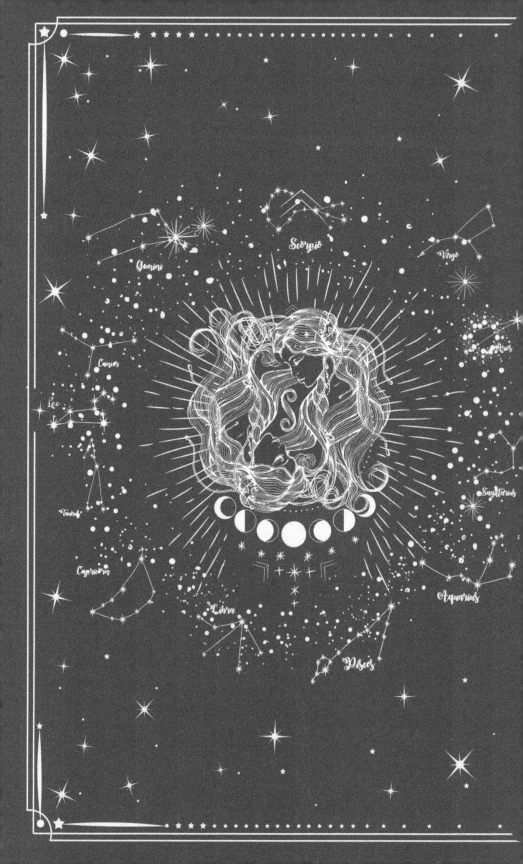

TORY

CHAPTER SIX

I followed the crowd of Fire Elementals away from the Orb and down a curving path which led around to the south of the building before dropping down a steep hill.

Pillars of stone sat either side of the path every few meters with flames burning in plinths on top of them. As the older students began to pass them, the flames took the forms of various creatures and my lips parted as I stared at horses, wolves, birds and men built out of nothing but flame. My mind wanted to cast it off as some kind of illusion but I knew it wasn't. The power roiling within me responded to the fire and each flare of magic which shaped it and I ached to unleash my own magic upon the blaze despite having no idea how to do such a thing.

Sofia slipped through the crowd until she was walking at my side, offering a friendly smile as I glanced her way. *Nice to know I'm not a total pariah then.* Most of the other students were giving me a wide berth and I'd gotten the distinct impression that offending the Celestial Heirs had put me firmly on the shit list. At least I wouldn't have to worry about sending any Christmas cards as I wasn't likely to be receiving any.

"Well you certainly know how to make an entrance," Sofia said, the corner of her mouth hooking up in amusement.

I snorted. "Never did learn when to keep my mouth shut," I admitted. "Where I'm from I found out the hard way that this life will throw all kinds of crap at you, but the one thing you don't have to accept is other people's bullshit."

A few of the other freshmen heard that comment and edged away from me uneasily. I guessed they were concerned my status as persona non grata might be catching. And perhaps it would but Sofia didn't seem to mind the risk at least.

I kept thinking about Darcy, wondering if she was doing okay with the air Heir. Seth seemed like a bit less of an asshole than the other three on first impressions but it was hard to be sure. Birds of a feather and all that... I just hoped I'd be able to check in with her over breakfast and make sure she was alright. Our lives had never exactly been plain sailing but she'd never developed such a thick skin as me and the idea of those douchebags giving her a hard time without me there to back her up sent a shiver of anger coursing through my blood.

"Well I wish my balls were big enough to allow me to stand against the Heirs like you did and come out unscathed," Sofia said appreciatively. "Not that I have any reason to stand against them or any intention to find one."

"I wouldn't say I came out unscathed," I muttered, touching a finger to the tender skin on my neck where Caleb had bitten me.

Sofia's wide eyes followed the movement of my hand and she leaned closer to inspect the wound.

"Oh, I guess you didn't realise Caleb was of the Vampire Order when you provoked him?"

At the mention of him being a Vampire, a cold trickle of ice danced along my spine. Of course the word had come to mind after what he did to me but the idea of something so... *insane* existing just didn't want to line up in my brain. I wasn't sure why the idea of magical creatures was more difficult for me to accept than the idea of magic itself but it just seemed to go against every law of nature I thought I'd understood.

"I didn't know *anyone* was a Vampire before he attacked me," I muttered. "And he's bitten me now, so shouldn't that mean that I'm gonna start getting a thirst for blood or an appetite for toe sandwiches or something?"

Sofia laughed in surprise. "You really don't know *anything* about our world do you? All of your ideas about us come right out of a mortal fairytale!"

"So I'm not about to sprout fangs?" I confirmed, ignoring the subtle mockery. I could tell she didn't mean anything malicious by it. But I wasn't much of a fan of being the latest science experiment either.

"Nope. Vampires are just an Order of Fae. Each Order replenishes their own magic in different ways. The Vampires can't create their own so they have to take it from others by overpowering them. As freshmen we're all going to come under a lot of fire from them - we can't defend ourselves with our magic yet and trying to overpower them physically is crazy difficult. With your magic being as potent as it is you'll probably find that you get a lot of attention from the vamps while they're able to overpower you so you might wanna get used to it."

"Perfect. I always wanted to be a walking packed lunch," I said dryly, making a mental note to avoid all Vampires until I was strong enough to fight them off. Which would be a lot easier if I knew how to spot one. I eyed Sofia's teeth for a moment, wondering if I'd find any fangs.

She flashed me a smile at my joke and I was able to confirm no fangs. "Sometimes the strongest Vampires will lay a claim on a power source-"

"In this scenario am I the power source?" I asked.

"Err, yeah," Sofia shrugged apologetically. "But if Caleb decides he likes the way your power tastes he might want to keep you for himself and as he's one of the most powerful Vampires in the school the others would all bow to his dominance."

"Meaning he'd be the only one biting me?" I confirmed, just about understanding where she was going with this and not sure that I liked it one bit.

"Well, yeah. But look at it this way; if he *does* then you'll only have one Vampire to worry about instead of a whole Order of them. Besides, Vampires aren't even the most dangerous Order in this school; some of the creatures here could straight-up kill you if you caught them at the wrong moment. At least a Vampire needs you alive. *And* if I had to choose one Vampire to be pinning me up against a wall and putting his mouth all over me then Caleb Altair would be top of the list."

I let out a surprised laugh, wondering how I managed such a thing after the ordeal I'd just been through but I had to admit Sofia had a point. I didn't exactly relish the idea of any Vampire biting me but if I had to pick one then Caleb with his head of messy blonde curls, eyes as dark blue as the depths of the ocean and body cut straight from an Abercrombie and Fitch commercial would probably top the list. Or at least he would if he wasn't such a jackass.

Before I could voice my opinion on Caleb Altair's lack of personal boundaries and general aura of entitled douchebag, the crowd of students came to a halt and I gave my attention to what had stopped us.

As the hill was still sloping down, I was offered a view of the building that we'd reached although the term 'building' didn't seem to cut it.

An arching doorway was cut into what looked like a hulking rock but the clouds had drawn in over the stars and I couldn't see anything outside of the huge fire which blazed above the opening.

Most of the older students had headed on in and only the freshmen and ten of the older fire Celestials remained. Darius moved to stand before the doorway and the huge fire on the platform above it moulded itself into a giant dragon. The detail of the beast was insane; its body was darkest red with glimmering gold outlining individual scales and teeth which looked sharp enough to bite. The fire beast unfurled huge wings which spread out widely on either side of it as it opened its jaws.

My heart was pounding as I watched the display of magic and the dragon turned straight towards me. I knew the creature wasn't real but something about it felt like so much more than a mirage.

With a roar created from the crackling rumble of burning embers, the dragon blew a torrent of fire over our heads, low enough to make a lot of the freshmen shriek and duck aside.

I held my ground, tipping my head back as the heat of the fire warmed my skin and the power within me purred with appreciation. I already felt like some of what Caleb had stolen from me was returning and my magic seemed to rise to meet with the dragon's flames as if it were greeting an old friend.

"Fire is the most potent Element of all," Darius announced. "It brings light to the dark, warmth in the cold and can destroy everything placed in its way. Only those born with veins filled with the heat of the sun and hearts blazing with the true power of the flames can enter our House and claim their place amongst us."

I glanced at Sofia, wanting to ask her what this was all about but the hush that had fallen over the crowd of freshmen held me silent.

"So who wants to be the first to try and gain access to the greatest House in Zodiac Academy?" Darius called, holding his arms wide as he stood before the entrance like a monster guarding its keep.

The other students were all casting glances at each other, none of them seeming to want to volunteer to go first. More than a few sets of eyes drifted to me and I wondered if my title as the lost Vega Heir meant I was expected to go first.

As the idea occurred to me, Darius's eyes met mine through the crowd and the dare in his gaze was clear. My blood simmered with the urge to rise to the challenge and my feet began to carry me forward before I'd fully made the decision to face him.

The rest of the freshmen parted like a tide and I prowled forward with my best don't-screw-with-me look slapped on my face. A few years of hanging around Joey's bar had given me enough practice at dealing with dangerous men and rule number one in my book of survival was ringing in my ears.

Don't back down. Don't show weakness.

So despite my thundering heart and slick palms, I held Darius's eye and gave off an aura of mildly underwhelmed as I approached him.

"First one in always gets the toughest run of it," Darius warned. "Feel free to back down if your mortal upbringing has left you unprepared to face the gauntlet."

"We're all going in one way or another. I'd sooner get this over with quickly," I replied dismissively.

Darius's eyes flared with irritation at my tone and for a moment I thought I saw something shift within them. If Vampires weren't the most dangerous creatures in this school then what was exactly? Because I had the distinct impression that I was currently looking one in the eye and poking it. I swallowed the lump in my throat as I held his gaze and he took a step towards me.

"Maybe you should have picked an easier House to join," he warned. "I don't get the feeling you're cut out for the trials of this one."

"Well you made it in," I pointed out. "So it can't be that hard."

Before he could respond, I sidestepped him and headed into the mouth of the cave. My heart was racing so fast that I was almost convinced he would be able to hear it. But through some combination of rock hard willpower and sheer dumb luck, my bravado held out and I managed to enter the cave without descending into a trembling wreck.

As I stepped over the threshold, a strange sensation slipped along my skin and the light from the fire outside disappeared. I glanced over my shoulder, my heart leaping as I realised the entrance was no longer there. In its place was a solid wall which didn't so much as tremble as I reached out to touch it.

I blinked as I adjusted to the dim light which came from somewhere further along the tunnel around the next corner. The flickering quality of it coupled with the orange glow led me to believe there was a fire down there. *Of course there's a fire, this is the house of fire, if there wasn't it would be like going to a gingerbread house and finding brick walls.*

I stayed still for several more seconds, listening, squinting around at what little I could see. The walls and floor were black and pockmarked with thousands of tiny holes. Memories pricked at me as I recognised it as a lava tube. One of our foster parents had been obsessed with the discovery channel and the six months I'd spent living there had filled my brain with all kinds of random facts about the world.

As lava was like liquid fire, it suddenly made sense for this cave to be a part of the House of Ignis.

The entrance was gone and there was only one way on so I took a deep breath and started walking. I adopted a fast pace knowing that going slow wouldn't have any effect on what awaited me anyway. I'd heard plenty of stories about frat house hazing and the twisted things they forced their pledges to do but I tried not to let my mind linger on those. Whatever I was about to face couldn't be that bad...right?

As I rounded the corner, I came across the source of the flickering light.

A pit of burning coals barred the way on, glowing deep red with heat in the centre while burning freely towards the sides of the tunnel. They filled the space ahead of me for at least five meters and I knew there was zero chance of me making that jump.

I glanced down at my favourite boots with a pang of regret. I only had two pairs of shoes and I'd left my battered sneakers back in our apartment. These boots were just the right combination of practical and fashionable. They looked good *and* I could run, jump and ride in them. They'd been with me for every less-than-legal acquisition I'd made and had helped me keep a roof over our heads and food in our bellies...

Before I could get too lost in the misery induced by having to put my boots through the ordeal of the hot coals, a deep growl sounded from the tunnel behind me and I froze.

My breath caught as I looked over my shoulder and my lips parted in horror. There was nothing back there. I'd just come that way. And yet...

A shape burst around the corner and I screamed as I spotted the huge lioness. She roared at me as she charged forward and I scrambled into a sprint.

I pounded the final distance to the pit of coals and didn't slow as I raced onto them. They shifted beneath my feet and my arms cartwheeled as I struggled to maintain my balance while moving as fast as humanly possible. If I fell I had no doubt that the skin would be melted from my flesh just as the soles of my boots were already beginning to.

I sprinted on, the heat of the embers beneath me encasing my feet in an oven of burning leather. A lump of sole fell off and my bare foot hit the coals twice before I launched myself off of the pit and crashed to the cold floor of the cave beyond.

I rolled twice, shielding my face with my hands before jarring to a stop. A bloody graze drew my attention to my forearm as a hiss of pain left me. The lava rock was sharp and skidding across it was more than a little unpleasant.

I quickly looked back across the pit of coals to see the lioness prowling back and forth on the far side beyond the shimmering heat-soaked air.

My lips parted in shock as I stared at the impossible creature before me. First Vampires and now this? What the hell kind of place had we ended up in?

Warmth drew my attention to my left foot and I gasped as I spotted a small flame taking hold of my boot. I ripped the ruined leather off of me followed by the tattered remains of my sock then repeated the process on the right foot. Miraculously, I'd avoided any burns and I silently thanked my poor boots for their sacrifice.

With a twinge of regret, I tossed the destroyed items onto the coals and pushed myself to my feet. The sharp rock pricked at my soles as I headed on but I forced my attention to remain on the task at hand. The sooner I got through this, the better. I just needed to focus on taking one step at a time and I'd manage it. It wasn't like they'd just let students die down here... was it?

The tunnel started to decline in a twisting formation which didn't seem natural. Thankfully, the sharp rocks smoothed out and I was able to up my pace again as I stopped hobbling.

The cave was still dimly lit with an orange glow but every time I thought I was closing in on the source of it, it retreated.

Faint laughter called to me from up ahead and I stilled for a moment.

It came again and I began to wonder if the other students could somehow see me. I glanced around, trying to spot any cameras or anything like that but as far as I could tell, the cave was empty.

A chill was creeping up my spine, intuition urging me to up my pace. Those same senses had saved me from the cops more than once and I wasn't foolish enough to ignore them.

I started jogging then running faster as the light ahead tried to dance away again but I finally felt like I was gaining on it.

I rounded a corner and fell still as I found myself in a wide room. There was no furniture in sight but various weapons lined the wall, urging me to claim them.

On the far side of the room, three figures stood, hidden beneath deep red robes, their faces in shadow within their hoods.

Their attention was clearly on me and as I watched, three beings built from flame leapt to life in front of them. The figures were humanoid in shape though their arms hung down past their knees and their fingers curved with burning claws. In place of eyes they had black pits which stared at me hungrily.

I only had a moment to stare in fascination before the fire manikins sprang at me.

I cried out in alarm, launching myself at the collection of weapons. I ripped an axe from the wall and swung it before me as the first manikin reached me. The heavy weapon carved straight through the creature's chest but the flames quickly reformed around the hole.

I stumbled back, swinging again in a vain effort to keep the things away from me but they barely flinched beneath the might of my attacks.

I launched the axe at them and ducked aside, making it to the wall again and claiming a dagger. I threw it at the closest manikin but it sailed through it harmlessly.

Before I could claim a third weapon, the creatures moved too close and I cried out as a hot hand brushed against my thigh, singeing the fabric of my yoga pants.

I threw myself at the inch of space between two of them, clasping my hands over my face as the brush of flames caressed my bare arms.

I could feel my magic welling up inside of me, filling me to the brim and aching to be set free but I had no idea how to harness it.

I rolled across the smooth floor and jumped to my feet as I backed away. The three fire manikins came at me again as I eyed the wall of weapons behind them. There were swords, spears, bows, even a mace. None of them would do a damn thing against a creature made of fire.

They rushed at me and I backed up as fast as I could. My gaze fell on the three students who were controlling them and I was struck with the certainty that they should be my real targets. Behind them, a wide doorway stood open which must have been the way forward and I fixed its position in my mind as my escape route.

I tried to run for it but the manikins leapt into my path, forcing me to halt before the wall created by their flaming bodies.

I backed up quickly, my mind whirling with ideas as I tried to figure this out but they wouldn't let me think before coming for me again.

I threw myself aside, rolling across the cold floor then trying to regain my feet once more. A manikin was there to stop me, its flaming claws reaching for my face.

I screamed, slamming back down onto the ground and hitting my head.

I can't fight against fire! What I need is a bucket of goddamn water!

As the thought left my mind so did a flood of the liquid I desired. A torrent of water shot from my hands and slammed into the nearest manikin before drenching the students behind it too. The creatures were extinguished and I grabbed my chance without wasting time marvelling over what I'd just done.

"Hey!" one of the students moaned as I sped between them.

"She's only gotta get past," another replied. "There's no rules about *how.*"

I grinned to myself as I ran through the door and found a spiralling flight of stairs. I took them two at a time, sparing only a little attention for the burning sconces along the walls which pulsed in colours from blood red to orange, yellow and even blue.

At the top of the stairs was an arching doorway and beyond it sat a wide room filled with comfortable chairs and soft furnishings.

Darius looked up from the centre of a group of preening admirers as he heard me approaching and for a moment I could have sworn his eyes flickered with surprise.

He got to his feet before I could make it inside and the doorway suddenly filled with fire.

I fell still as I looked at it. There was no way around. The only option was to go through.

"Final challenge," Darius called from somewhere beyond the flames. "If you really want to be one of us, you're going to have to leave everything from your time with the mortals behind."

I frowned, wondering what he meant by that. Darcy was here with me and there had really been very little else in my life that I cared about enough to bring anyway. Did he imagine I'd left behind some great group of friends and family who I held some desperate urge to return to? Perhaps he thought that challenging me to release those bonds would be endlessly difficult for me but I had no such concerns.

His attempt at cruelty was falling flat and he didn't even realise it.

"You can step through the flames once you're ready to leave your mortal trappings behind. The fire will burn them all away but your flesh will remain unscathed," Darius sounded amused though I couldn't see his face and I couldn't help a small smile of my own. Leaving the mortal world behind was just fine by me. It had never seemed to care for me much anyway. And the feeling was mutual.

I blinked at the wall of fire, fearing that more than any separation to the mortals I knew. My adopted parents had died in a fire. And though I had no memory of the event, I knew Darcy and I were lucky to have survived it. That knowledge had always made me a little wary of open flames. But I wasn't going to let a little fear stop me.

I took a deep breath and stepped through the fire.

Heat enveloped me but instead of burning, I felt only the gentle embrace of it against my skin like a thousand tiny kisses.

The stench of burning filled my nostrils and my heart stuttered in panic as I clutched at my long hair but thankfully it was completely fine.

The warm carpet was a relief to my bare feet as I stepped into the room and I looked up at Darius, prepared to tell him just how little his last challenge had meant to me but everyone in the room started laughing before I could.

Darius was smirking at me, his eyes dripping over my body in a way that made me look down.

I gasped as I realised what he'd done; my clothes were gone, burned away by the fire he'd created so that I was left standing before them butt-naked.

I'd always liked my body and I'd had a few boyfriends and flings over the years so it wasn't like no one had seen it before but this was something else. Heat raced to my cheeks as I realised he hadn't been talking about leaving emotional ties to the mortal world behind - he'd been talking much more literally. He'd meant everything physical I'd brought, which meant my clothes and-

"Motherfucker!" I cursed as I took a step towards him angrily then stopped myself as I remembered I was as naked as the dawn. "I had nearly three grand in my pocket! Do you know how hard my sister and I worked for that money?"

Darius only smiled wider in response to my anger as he held out a key.

"Your room is on the third floor, end of the corridor," he said, completely ignoring everything I'd just said. "If you wanna go and find something to wear?"

I moved forward to snatch the key from him, refusing to try and cover my body. It was too late now anyway and the heat crawling down my spine wasn't going to lessen if I made a pathetic attempt to hide. My only defence against what he'd done to me at this point was in trying to pretend I didn't care. Though the blood which filled my cheeks must have been clear for everyone to see if they could tear their eyes away from my ass and breasts for long enough to notice it. Tears prickled the backs of my eyes but I bitch-slapped them down hard. I would *not* cry in front of this goddamn bastard.

As my fingers curled around the brass key, Darius used his hold on it to tug me a step closer.

"Of course, if you'd rather just come on up to my room, I can give you a *real* welcome to the House of Fire," he suggested as his gaze slid over every exposed inch of my flesh and embarrassment prickled up my spine.

A flutter grew in my stomach as I noted the heat in his gaze and I mentally cursed myself for giving even a moment's consideration to his offer.

I squared my shoulders, looking him over just as he had me. I took in everything from the way his jeans hung low on his hips to the swell of his muscles beneath his tightly fitting shirt. I eyed the tattoos which curved out of sight beneath his short sleeves and the biceps which cried out to be touched. His broad shoulders and towering height built a type of carnal need in me as I tilted my head back to look up at him.

A cocky smile pulled at the kind of lips that I could definitely make use of given half a chance and his dark hair fell forward just enough to make me think about fisting my hands in it.

Why did I always have to want the bad guys?

I shifted an inch closer as if I was going to share a secret with him but kept my voice loud enough to carry.

"I wouldn't come near you even if someone held a knife to my heart and told me that the world would end if I didn't," I snarled, snatching the key out of his hand. "So why don't you take a long, hard look while you can. Because I can promise you, you won't be seeing this again."

Darius's face dropped a fraction as the rest of the students in the room started laughing at him instead of me and I slammed my shoulder against his as I moved past him. It was kinda like walking into a brick wall but I managed to force him to move a little, mostly because I took him by surprise.

I stalked across the room to the stairs which led to the promised dorm, forcing myself to maintain a steady pace instead of sprinting.

Eyes followed my progress and whispers broke out around me but I kept my gaze fixed on my destination, refusing to look anywhere else. The tears were coming and I knew I was fighting a losing battle against time as I fought to hold them off.

Just a few seconds longer...

"You should be more careful about the kinds of enemies you make around here, *Roxy*," Darius called after me, a beat too late for him to pull it off as smoothly as he must have wanted. A sense of satisfaction filled me with the knowledge that I'd rattled him for a moment too.

I didn't bother to respond. Getting into a pissing contest with an asshole really wasn't my style and if I didn't get behind a closed door soon then I was pretty sure I was going to start bawling in front of everyone. If I could keep my chin high and my face blank then maybe I'd be able to leave this room with my dignity intact even if I had had to scrape it up off of the floor.

I made it up three flights of stairs and to the end of the corridor where my key thankfully opened the door.

I spilled inside and pushed it closed behind me a second before the floodgates burst and the tears fell.

I sank to the floor and buried my head in my arms as I drew my knees to my chest. Anger and humiliation washed through me and I gave them five minutes to have their way before I was going to lock them down again.

Tears never did anyone any favours, but sometimes they just needed to fall.

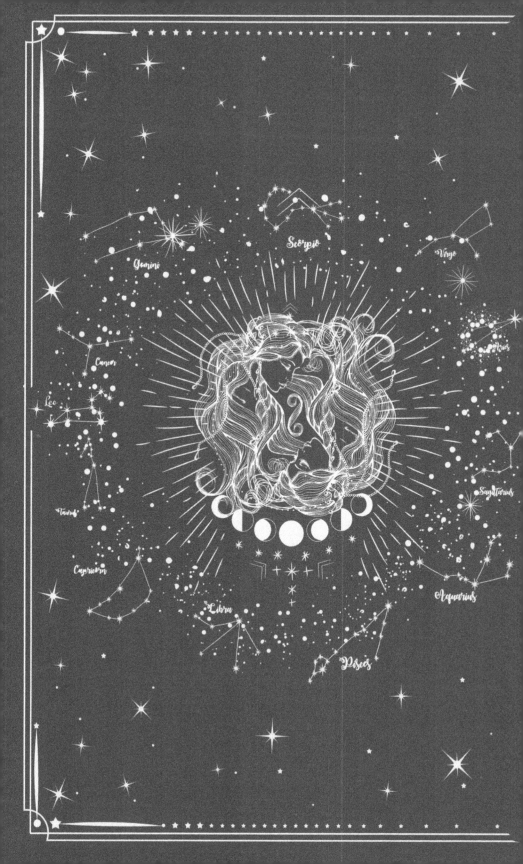

DARCY

CHAPTER SEVEN

The adrenaline was still thick in my blood as I used the power of air to get back inside, lighting up the symbol above the doorway and stepping into a circular chamber at the base of the tower. My fingers buzzed with the tingle of magic and I couldn't fight the giddy smile that pulled at my mouth.

I just jumped from the top of a tower and survived. Hair well and truly intact.

I gathered my wavy locks into my hands, having an intense emotional reaction to them. I'd started dying the ends blue a year ago. It wasn't some indie statement or a cry for help. It was, in my own twisted kind of way, a reminder of one of the darkest and most pivotal moments in my life which I was determined never to forget.

On one side of the atrium, the grey stone floor met with a white marble staircase. I moved to the centre of the space, gazing up at the incredible stairway circling high above me.

I took a slow breath, fear and anticipation washing together in my belly as I made my way up the stairs. My Converses hitting the steps was the only noise around me, but as I made it up several more levels, I found my way barred.

Seth stood alone, his arms folded, his eyes narrowed. The air between us was filled with static and I expected a thunderstorm to erupt from him at any moment. Instead, he thrust a hand out and in it was a silver triangle with a long key dangling from it. "Eleventh floor, room three."

My lips parted, but no words came out as I closed the distance between us and reached for the key. Victory sailed through me on a summer breeze.

I beat him at his own game.

"Congratulations," he purred, but there was no kindness to his tone. "You've survived day one in hell. Each day after this will be worse. Are you sure you don't wanna drop out of Zodiac yet?"

I took the key from him, my hand closing into a fist so the sharp metal dug into my palm. "Why do you care if I'm here or not? We're clearly not going to get along. So let's just stay out of each other's way." I tried to move around him but he side-stepped, planting his shoulder against the wall to block my path.

Irritation rattled through me.

He reached out, brushing his fingers through my hair, coiling a handful around his fingers.

"Why do you keep touching me like that?" I jerked aside, my upper lip peeling back.

He released a gruff noise in his throat. "Because I'm an Alpha, *babe*. And this is how I show you who's in charge. You need to forget about rising against me, because you won't win." He tightened his grip on my hair and I ground my teeth, refusing to let out a yelp of pain.

"I don't have plans to rise against you, Seth," I said as calmly as I could. "I just want to go to bed."

He grinned, tugging my hair extra hard then stepping back entirely, gesturing for me to go past. I pressed my shoulders back, marching past him, feeling his eyes on me all the way as I fought the urge to rub my sore scalp.

"You owe me your hair," he called.

Anger flashed through my body hot and fast. I quickened my pace to a jog, wanting to put as much distance between Seth and I as possible.

When I found my floor, I was thankful that there were no students around. I could hear panicked cries from somewhere high above though and wondered if the other freshmen had gotten off so easy after all.

I headed down the stone corridor which held ten doors, five on either side. I pushed the key into the door of room three and headed inside with a sigh of relief.

At my movement, a light came on above me and a smile captured my lips.

The room had a dark wooden floor with a single bed to one side of it made up with white sheets and fluffy pillows. The walls were the same grey stone as the rest of the tower and they swept toward the vertical window at the end of the room. It was taller than me and had two heavy shutters bolted across it. To my left was a long desk and above it were shelves of books and notepads. A line of white pencils lay on the desk and my fingers itched. It had been ages since I'd had the inspiration to sketch anything. But it had always made me feel better, forget the world. If I hadn't been so exhausted, I probably would have jumped on the opportunity after the night I'd had.

Next to the pencils was a slim device, sleek and white. It looked like an iPad only wider with a few rectangular buttons along the bottom of it and a digital pen attached to the side.

I brushed my fingers over the screen and a noise sounded like wind chimes as the symbol of Aer appeared in black on a white background.

A soft male voice emitted from it as the image dissolved and several rows of apps appeared. "Welcome to Zodiac Academy. This is your Atlas. Your profile has been added to our database. You can now call or message your friends throughout the entire school. Click through the apps to discover your timetable, school events, Pitball matches and scores, and find your full syllabus for the term. If you need assistance, just send a message directly to your House Captain and they'll help you with any problems you have."

"Yeah sure he will," I muttered, picking up the Atlas and finding my way to a long list of contacts. I typed Tory's name in at the top but it found no results. When I typed 'Vega' I found my name listed as Gwendalina and Tory's as Roxanya. I changed mine to Darcy and my finger hovered over Tory's original name as I thought about the people who'd given it to her. Could they really have been the king and queen of this unknown world?

I'd always thought we'd been orphaned, but now it was almost worse to know our parents had chosen to get rid of us. Orion had thought we'd been in danger, but from what? And if that were true, why swap us for some random human children and put them in danger instead? It was beyond cruel.

Seth had mentioned Solaria was better off without my father as king, but judging from the nastiness I'd witnessed in him tonight, I wondered if I could believe anything he said.

I gave up on trying to figure out the answers to the never ending questions in my brain. Tiredness took hold of me and as I checked the time on my Atlas, I found it was almost three in the morning.

I yawned broadly, kicking off my shoes and slumping onto the soft bed as I called Tory. I prayed she'd answer. I had so much to catch up on with her and I half-hoped her time in Ignis had been easier than my time here. But somehow, I doubted it.

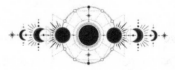

Windchimes were calling to me, ting ting ting-alinging. The noise grew louder and more persistent and I rolled over with a groan, finding I'd fallen asleep fully-clothed with my face squashed against my Atlas.

What Tory had been through sounded even worse than what I'd endured. She was strong as hell, but I always knew when she was quietly hurting. She'd sounded nothing but angry on the phone, but I wouldn't have been surprised if she'd let a few tears escape after what Darius had done to her.

In the end, we'd both agreed to try and make the most out of this incredible opportunity. A few idiot bullies weren't going to ruin a whole lifetime of possibilities for us. But we needed to start learning about this world as fast as we could if we were ever going to survive here. Claims to thrones and royal blood was all too much to take in without knowing a damn thing about what that meant. And the Heirs would soon realise we weren't here to steal anything from them.

With all that in mind, I was excited for my first lessons, to learn everything there was to know about my newfound powers. I couldn't wait to feel the kiss of them against my palms again.

The chiming persisted and I realised my Atlas was the source of the noise. I squinted at the bright screen as a notification flashed up on it.

Your daily horoscope is waiting for you, Darcy!

I clicked on the message and a night sky spread across the screen, shimmering brightly as words scrawled to life in silver lettering.

Good morning Gemini.
The stars have spoken about your day.
You've recently been through a transformative change, but now
that the dust has settled you're feeling strangely at home in your
new landscape.
The clouds are parting and you can almost see the sun shining
back at you. But don't be too hasty. Mars is still casting a

shadow over your movements this month and it looks like it's
here to stay for a while yet.
Between a Libra and an Aquarius, your day may become very
challenging but if you call upon your Gemini instincts, you'll
find a way to rise above the trials thrown your way.

I frowned. My Gemini instincts? I vaguely recalled my star sign described a Gemini as optimistic and today I felt I was lining up with that assumption.

Another message flashed up on the Atlas.

Your Cardinal Magic class starts in thiry minutes, Darcy.
Click here for a map.

I pressed the button and found a route laid out for me leading away from Aer Tower toward The Orb at the centre of the grounds. Ringing it were a group of buildings named after the planets and my lesson was located in Jupiter Hall.

I yawned broadly, getting out of bed and heading into my own private bathroom. The tiles were blue and white and a huge shower unit stood to one side of it. There was even my own toothbrush and a whole basket full of cosmetics for me to use.

I squealed like a kid as I washed in the waterfall-like shower then applied a sweet smelling moisturiser to my skin. Conscious of time, I rushed back into my bedroom and headed to a wardrobe which reached right up to the ceiling. I tugged it open, finding a uniform waiting inside for me. There were a few of them plus a bunch of yoga pants, shirts and sweaters with the Aer logo printed on them.

I pulled on my uniform, eyeing myself in the mirror inside the wardrobe door. The navy and white check skirt was pleated and brushed my knees, the white shirt crisp and figure hugging. I pulled on knee-high socks and some pumps then put my blazer over the top, brushing my fingers over the golden crest of the Academy which was ringed with each symbol of the zodiac.

I tamed my hair which ran loosely over my shoulders, the blue tips almost blending in with the navy blazer.

Today will be a good day, I promised myself then grabbed a leather satchel from the wardrobe and tucked the Atlas inside it alongside a few notebooks and pens.

I headed out of my room, locking the door before following the flow of students who were all descending the stairs. Some of them glanced my way and mutters were exchanged. None of them said hello. But it wasn't going to bother me. I'd proven my worth yesterday and I deserved my place here as much as them. In a few days, they'd probably forget I was a 'Vega Twin' and I could start making some friends.

Outside, the morning air was fresh and the scent of junipers carried to me on the breeze. As the wind washed against my face, my skin tingled as if the weather were bringing the Elements to life inside my veins. Anticipation rolled through me at the idea of using more magic and I wondered what it would be like to wield fire, water and earth too.

"Your majesty!" someone called from behind me and I turned curiously, spotting the burly girl who'd been one of the few students happy to see us in The Orb last night. She rushed toward me up the path, her eyes widening with joy.

Was she talking to me?

She came to a halt before me, bowing her head low. I frowned, taken aback.

"My name is Geraldine Grus and I am at your service. I wanted to let you know that you now have a loyal band of followers around you, the Almighty Sovereign Society. Do not fear the Celestial ruffians who call themselves Heirs. You and your sister are the true queens and they will accept that soon enough."

She bowed again and I sensed eyes on us as students headed by.

"Oh um…" I had no idea what to say. But I didn't like the attention she was drawing, or the way she referred to Tory and I as queens. "We're actually not really here for the throne. The Heirs are welcome to it to be honest."

"Sacrilege!" she gasped, her dark eyes rounding. "How can you say such a thing Princess Gwendalina?"

"Don't call me that," I begged. "It's Darcy."

"Of course, as you wish," she said with another flourishing bow.

Oh God make this stop.

"Geraldine!" a girl called. "Is that one of the queens!?"

I sucked in air as I spotted a band of people running up the path to meet us.

Nope. I'm out.

"I'd better get going," I said quickly. "I don't wanna be late to class." I gave her a polite smile then hurried away, relief flowing through me when she didn't follow.

"Remember the A.S.S love you!" she cried and several people who heard her started laughing.

Really? That was the name she went with? The *ass* club?

I didn't want to be ungrateful for her kindness, but I also knew there was a ninety nine percent chance I'd jump into the nearest bush the next time I spotted her coming.

I soon found my way to Jupiter Hall and gazed up at the towering, gothic building in awe. I filed inside with the rest of the students and entered a wide atrium made of white stone. A row of pillars held up a stairway on the opposite wall and I followed a group of freshmen up it toward the classroom on my timetable.

Everyone moved inside and I glanced over my shoulder, hoping to spot Tory at any moment.

The classroom was built of honey-coloured bricks and one side of the room held a long row of arching windows, allowing the sunlight to fall across the space in eight perfect shafts.

There were nearly a hundred students and the wooden desks were filling up fast. I jogged toward the nearest one, planting my bag on the one beside it for Tory when she showed up.

I was a few rows back from the front where a crescent-shaped oaken desk sat before a large electronic screen.

I pulled my Atlas out of my bag, finding a message glowing on it.

Welcome to Cardinal Magic, Darcy!
Click here to begin.

I tapped on it and a blank page appeared. I took the pen attached to the Atlas and scribbled on the screen to try it out.

"Hey!"

I glanced up, finding Tory beside me in her own Academy uniform, her eyes hooded with lack of sleep. She was much less of a morning person than I was but even I was feeling the pain of missed sleep today.

Sofia was a step behind her, smiling brightly as she took in the classroom.

"Did you manage to avoid the Fire Asshole this morning?" I asked Tory, tugging my bag off of the desk beside mine.

She dropped into the seat I'd saved with a laugh and Sofia took the one beyond that. "Yeah, not on purpose though. I'm not gonna hide from that jerk."

"We might have someone else we need to hide from," I said, filling her in on my encounter with Geraldine.

"She called you your majesty?" Tory asked in disbelief and I nodded.

"There's a fair few royal supporters in the school from what I heard," Sofia chipped in and I quietly hoped they weren't all as enthusiastic as Geraldine.

"Que pasa amigas?"

I turned at the male voice, finding one of the Aer pledges dropping down to sit at the desk on my other side. I vaguely remembered him from last night. He wore a black beanie hat with a white cross on it, his dark hair curling out from beneath it. He had a kind face, his skin deeply tanned but his eyes unusually blue.

He raised a dark brow at me as I gave him a blank look. "Oh sorry, I thought you guys spoke Spanish." He gestured at us in general. Our Latino looks had served us more than one occasion like this, but I was surprised to find it happening in a completely different world to ours.

"Are you from the er...mortal world?" I asked, feeling strange referring to earth as that.

He stared at me for a second then burst out laughing. "No, Solaria is a mirror world. The same but different, claro? So you've never learned our beautiful language?"

I smiled warmly, shaking my head. "Nope, we kinda missed out on learning since we were never in a foster home with anyone who spoke it."

"Although there was that one maid who always called Mr Harrison an hijo de puta," Tory chipped in.

The guy burst out laughing. "So the only phrase you know in Spanish is son of a bitch?"

"That's what that means?" Tory laughed.

"Yeah." He took out his Atlas and dropped his satchel on the floor. "I'm Diego."

"Darcy and that's-"

"Tory, I know," he finished for me with a sideways smile. "You're Los Gemelas Vega -sorry, the Vega Twins. Everyone's talking about you on FaeBook since what happened at The Orb last night."

"On...what?" I frowned.

"It's a social media site for the school. Here, look." Diego took my Atlas, tapping on a purple app with a circle connecting each of the star signs.

A social media page came up.

FaeBook? He's got to be kidding right?

I pressed my profile and found it had already been filled in for me. Star signs took the place of profile pictures and the Gemini symbol shone in pink on mine. I tapped onto the newsfeed and my mouth dried up as I spotted the most popular post at the top of the screen.

Max Rigel*:*

A big welcome to Darcy and Tory (let's call 'em Dory to make it easier). I'm so glad the Vega Twins showed up just in time to try and challenge us for the throne of Solaria because I've been dying to try out my latest elemental combo attacks on someone. #waterguns #wetterisbetter

Comments:

Marguerite Helebor:

PMSL

Milton Hubert:

Hahaha yeah get them wet!

Gary Jones:

BRUTAL BRO! Catch ya at Pitball practice later!

Milly Badgerville:

You're soooo funny Max!

Tory read it over my shoulder and blew out a breath of irritation. "Great, we're the butt of a joke on a social media site I didn't realise existed until three seconds ago."

I scowled, closing down the app. "Just ignore it."

"I'm not like those idiotas," Diego said gently. "I don't know anyone here, my family live way out in the sticks of Solaria. Most of the Fae here already have ties with each other. It's muy cliquey. So...if you wanna hang out sometime..."

The door opened and Orion strode in, kicking it shut behind him as he sipped on a mug of coffee. I glanced at the clock on the wall noticing he was ten minutes late.

He strode behind his desk and the class continued to chatter with one another. I spotted Kylie cross-legged on a desk as she spoke with a couple of boys in the back row, twirling a lock of sunshine hair between her fingers.

I chewed on the end of my digital pen as I waited for Orion to start the lesson, wondering what we were going to be learning about today. I couldn't deny I was curious. Our whole lives had been tipped upside down in the space of twenty four hours. And now I was sitting in a classroom in front of the hottest teacher I'd ever seen.

I'd always had a thing for older guys and that coupled with the fact that Orion had the sort of face that made me forget to blink, meant I was definitely distracted. What kind of teacher looked like that? In my last school the male staff all had various combos of handle-bar moustaches and shiny bald patches.

Orion planted his coffee cup on the table and grabbed a digital marker pen, writing across the board in large letters:

YOU DO NOT HAVE A PLACE AT ZODIAC ACADEMY.

Tory and I shared a look as Professor Orion swung around. I noticed his tie was undone as he took hold of it, taking his time as he fixed it.

"Do you always get dressed on your way to work, sir?" asked a boy in the front row, his words a clear jibe.

Orion gave him a sweeping glance, tightening the knot at his throat. "Name?" he demanded of him.

"Tyler Corbin."

"Well Corbin, you're not here to cast judgment on a single thing I do. In fact it's entirely the other way around. So if I want to show up naked five minutes before the lesson ends, I will."

A few of the girls giggled, Kylie included and a ball of heat grew in my stomach.

Orion pointed at Kylie. "Sit in your seat or you can stand on your desk for the rest of the lesson, Miss..?"

"Kylie Major," she sighed then fell into her chair, tossing her hair over one shoulder.

"Read this out, Major," he directed, pointing at the board.

She cleared her throat a few times and the pretty brunette beside her suppressed another giggle. "You do not have a place at Zodiac Academy."

Chatter broke out again and Orion folded his arms, his stare demanding silence. He got his wish, the cold look in his gaze daring anyone to disobey it.

When the silence was so keen it rang in my ears, he spoke. "You all have a mid-term assessment which will decide whether or not you continue here at Zodiac. We call it The Reckoning because it will decide the fate of your entire lives. Zodiac Academy is the most prestigious school in Solaria and we won't waste time on anyone who can't prove their worth. If you fail it, you're out. Back to whatever crevice of this world – or any other world -" he gave Tory and I a hard look, "-you came from. Is that clear?"

"Yes," we all said in unison and my gut tied into a tight knot.

"Yes what?" he demanded.

"Yes, sir," everyone corrected.

Orion pressed a button at the base of the board and the words vanished. "This is Cardinal Magic where I will attempt to give you a basic understanding of all practical magic, simple divination and astrology. Today, I'll be introducing you to the Orders of Fae. None of you will be casting a single spell in my classroom until you have a basic foundation of knowledge to work from, so pay attention."

A groan sounded from several of my classmates in response. I wasn't too bothered, more than happy to learn the basics as I had absolutely no grasp on anything in this world.

"Everyone will need to be at the same level of understanding by the end of term. Whatever you think you know, you will soon learn there is much more that you do not." He shed his blazer and my mouth dried up at the press of his muscles against his pale blue shirt. He tapped the board and a diagram appeared on it, giving me an excuse to look at something else. My Atlas flashed and I found the same image there with space around it for taking notes.

ORDERS OF FAE

TAENIA
(Parasitic Orders)
Vampire
Siren

MUTATIO
(Mutating Orders)
Dragon
Manticore
Griffin
Cerberus
Pegasus
Werewolf
Nemean Lion
Hydra
Caucasian Eagle
Chimera

DIVISUS

(Spliced Orders)

Minotaur

Medusa

Centaur

Cyclops

Sphinx

Harpy

I stared across the names in fascination, unable to believe all of these strange creatures really existed.

Orion turned to face us again. "You each have an Order, most of which will have been apparent since childhood. Let me have a show of hands who does not yet know their Order."

Tory and I slowly raised our hands and Diego did the same. I glanced around, finding a handful more joining us and I was glad we weren't singled out in something else.

Orion nodded stiffly. "Email me after class." He turned back to the board without further explanation. "The Taenia have just two divisions whereas if I were to write every Mutatio on this board we would be here until next week."

I gazed down the list, my mind boggling at the words Werewolf, Dragon, Medusa, Cyclops and all the rest.

Orion pointed to the middle column. "The easiest way to distinguish a Mutatio Order is that they will shift fully into a creature without humanoid characteristics. The Divisus Order can get confused with the Mutatio, but the easiest way to distinguish them is that the Divisus Orders maintain human-like characteristics when they have mutated into their magical form. The Taenia differ from the other two Orders in that they maintain human form at all times, except for one feature. Can anyone name the feature of a Siren which changes when they embrace their powers?" He looked to the class and I glanced around, finding many of the students with their hands raised.

Orion picked a girl at the back with long braided hair. "Sirens get scales." She twisted her hand in the air and a shimmer of blue and gold rippled across her skin. "They're tough as hell and perfect for swimming."

"Correct," Orion said and I jotted down the note on my Atlas under Sirens. "And what feature changes for Vampires?"

"Teeth," Tory offered in a sharp tone.

Some of the students snickered and the hairs on the back of my neck rose to attention.

"Correct, Miss Vega." Orion rested his hands flat on his desk and peeled his upper lip back.

My heart took a freedive into my stomach as his canines extended into sharp points. He grinned darkly, then ran his tongue across them as they retracted once more.

My heart pounded unhappily in my chest. He was a Vampire? Like Caleb?

My nose wrinkled as I stared at Orion, seeing him in a wholly different light. And not a good one.

"And what is the purpose of Vampire fangs?" he asked.

"To suck magic out of other Orders!" Kylie called out, seeming excited.

"Correct," Orion said with a hungry glimmer in his gaze. "Any volunteers?"

Nervous laughter rang out and my stomach twisted up.

"No?" Orion pressed, strolling casually into the aisles between the desks. "Because in Solaria, Fae don't tend to ask for what they want, do they?"

He paused beside Diego's desk and the boy's eyes widened.

"Name?" Orion demanded of him.

"Diego Polaris," he said. "And as a teacher, sir, don't you have to ask for blood?"

In answer, Orion snatched Diego's arm and dug his fangs into it.

My heart slammed into my throat as Diego released a yell of pain and I suddenly found myself on my feet.

"Stop!" I demanded and Orion extracted his fangs, wiping the blood from the corner of his mouth.

Diego seemed a little weak, blinking heavily as he held his bloody wrist as far away from Orion as possible.

"Problem, Miss Vega?" Orion asked, his brows arching as he assessed me.

I glanced over my shoulder at Tory and she shook her head to warn me off.

I sank back into my seat, my heart thundering in my ears. I didn't answer him, instead looking away in disgust.

Pig.

Orion marched back to his desk and dropped into the wide leather chair behind it. "You have ten minutes to describe the shifted forms of each Mutatio in the table. Go." He plucked up his coffee cup, drained it in one then sat back in his chair, thumbing through something on his Atlas.

"Great, we'll just sit here for ten minutes then," Tory said under her breath, folding her arms.

I nodded, pursing my lips.

A few minutes into the task we had no chance of completing, I glanced at Diego. "Are you okay?"

He nodded, seeming to have gotten over Orion's vicious attack. He dropped his eyes back to his Atlas and continued tapping away the answers.

My gaze drifted to Orion who was grinning about something he was reading on his Atlas. His eyes shimmered with a deep heat and I firmly reminded myself he was only a beast with a beautiful face. Just like Caleb.

"Orion is so hot," Kylie whispered, her voice carrying to my ears.

"Yeah and he knows it." The girl beside her smothered a laugh.

"He does know it, because he has Vampire hearing." Orion looked up from his desk, pinning them in his sharp gaze. "So if you don't want detention for the next week, I suggest you keep your petty thoughts to yourselves about me and any other member of faculty for that matter."

The girls' mouths dropped open and a snort escaped me.

"Oh come on Professor as if you don't love having a bunch of girls drooling over you," Tyler called out from the front row, shoving a hand into his blonde-tipped hair to mess it up.

Orion rose from his seat, wandering casually toward the boy with a smile that said he was thoroughly amused. The guy grinned from ear to ear as Orion reached out to him. In a surge of movement, he cracked Tyler's head against his desk and the entire class inhaled as his smile fell away.

Orion pointed a finger and swept it across everyone in the room who wasn't yet sporting a head wound. "To me, each and every one of you is just a pair of ears. Ears that are going to listen to me speak and no one else in this classroom. If you want to talk to your little *BFF* in the seat next to you, go ahead. But you'll join Frosted Tips here in detention tonight. And trust me when I say, detention with me is not a fun experience."

"Detention?" the boy gasped as he rubbed his forehead.

Orion's eyes narrowed on him with a do-you-really-want-to-backchat-me-right-now? look and the boy backed down, nodding quickly.

I released a breath I hadn't realised I'd been holding. That teacher had just physically attacked a student! What the hell kind of school was this?

Tory and I exchanged a glance and anger bubbled inside me. That was *so* not okay.

"This place is crazy," I whispered to Tory.

"Batshit," she agreed.

My Atlas pinged loudly and Orion's gaze narrowed on me in fury. I waved a hand in apology before he lost it and tried to find the mute button. My gaze snagged on the notification on the screen and I frowned.

You've received a private message on FaeBook, Darcy!

Overwhelmed with curiosity, I tapped the screen and navigated my way to the app. I found a single message in my inbox from someone called 'Falling Star' and their profile picture was of a crescent moon.

Falling Star:
He didn't tell you the whole story...

I glanced at Tory and found she had her own Atlas pulled in front of her. I realised she was in the chat box too and my brow creased as she looked to me in confusion.

She tapped out an answer and I glanced down at my screen as it popped up.

Roxanya Vega:
Who?

She seriously needed to change that profile name. I stifled a laugh, taking her Atlas and doing it for her. She mouthed me a thank you as I passed it back. I'd always been slightly more tech savvy than her when it came to computers.

A sharp ping sounded from my Atlas and I winced, my shoulders hunching as I locked eyes with Orion. If eyes could fire lasers, I would have been a puddle of guts right then.

"Miss Vega, are you entirely dense?" he snarled.

"No," I forced out with as much strength as I could.

"Then why are your Atlas notifications switched on in my classroom after I gave you a clear warning to turn them off?"

My throat closed up but I didn't want to let him see me flounder. I might have been ten (okay eighty) percent scared of this guy but he wasn't going to know that if I could help it.

"I didn't realise-" I started but he cut me off, his mouth twisting into a demonic smile.

"Don't ever lie to me," he growled and his tone lifted the hairs on the back of my neck. "Let's hear it then. What does this message say that is obviously important enough to interrupt my class?"

My breathing became shallow as I glanced down at the message on the screen. I traced the words with my eyes and my day took a seriously dark turn. It felt like reaching the top of a rollercoaster and realising your harness was unlocked.

"Out loud. Now," Orion demanded and I spotted Tory shaking her head in my periphery, clearing having read it.

Well, bye bye life, it was nice knowing you.

I cleared my throat as a few giggles sounded around me. Diego shot me a sympathetic look as I began to read it, every syllable enunciated, figuring I might as well enjoy the ride on the way to my doom.

"The lump of muscle who teaches your Cardinal Magic class. Just to be clear, you'll recognise Orion by the scent of bourbon on his breath,-" a big inhale sounded from the whole class, "-the permanent scowl stamped on his face and the general air of failed dreams about him since he lost his chance at playing for the Solarian Pitball League."

I lifted my eyes, my heart lodged firmly in my throat as I met Orion's could-melt-a-glacier gaze. The laughter was growing in the classroom and Orion looked like a volcano ready to blow.

"And which of your many, *many* friends sent you that colourful message?" he asked, deadly calm.

"I don't know. It's sort of... anonymous," I said weakly, offering up the Atlas.

He eyed it for a moment then looked to the class. "Everyone return to their work."

He settled himself back in his chair and I bit into my lip, the tension in my chest becoming unbearable.

There's no way I'm getting off that easy.

Orion returned to looking at his Atlas and I turned to Tory, a thousand words on my lips.

"Do you think we can trust this Falling Star person?" she whispered.

"I don't know," I said thoughtfully. "It's hard to know who to trust in this place."

Orion suddenly waved his hand as if he wanted me to get out of my seat. I frowned, glancing around for some kind of confirmation, but everyone was staring down at their Atlases with a steely determination.

"Miss Vega if you're not standing up in the next three seconds, you're going to regret it," Orion barked.

"Which Vega?" Tory asked, barely concealing her jibing tone.

Holy shit Tor.

Orion's eyes snapped to her. "The one who has tried to individualise herself by dying the ends of her hair blue. It has failed by the way."

I pressed my lips together at the insult, deciding not to budge.

You don't know anything about me, jackass.

"Stand up," he commanded.

"If I say no are you going to smash my head into the table?" I asked through gritted teeth. I might have been one-percent terrified to call his bluff but I also didn't want to be his next target. And it seemed everyone around here had to fight for their place in this culture. I wasn't going to be made into a weak link on my first day. And as I decided that, something innate came to life inside me like a planted seed suddenly growing a little shoot.

Hell, I really am Fae.

"I'll do it." Tory rose from her seat but Orion raised a hand.

"I didn't ask you," he snarled.

Tory pouted then dropped back into her chair, rolling her eyes. I didn't like that Tory always took bullets for me; she didn't always need to protect me.

I stood up and raised my brows as I waited for my sentence. Orion's mouth hooked up at the corner and a predatory glint entered his eyes. Fear trickled through me but I held his gaze, refusing to show my terror, though something told me he could taste it on the air.

"Tell me the qualities and abilities of a Nemean Lion." He did that creepy smile thing again. Like he was as happy as Larry. But I could see his tactic now. This was his way of intimidating people. Pretending to be the friendly type, like maybe he was on your side for a second then BAM he slams your face into a desk.

He knew I had no clue what a Nemean Lion was but he wanted to embarrass me. Just like every other asshole in this school apparently.

I shrugged. "I don't know."

"I thought not," he said quietly. "But while everyone else was working you thought it was a good time to speak with your equally useless sister?"

Anger flashed inside me and Tory rose abruptly from her seat. "Who are you calling useless?"

"Am I not speaking clearly enough?"

She pursed her lips and didn't answer.

He surveyed us for a moment then his eyes glittered with some idea. *"Both of you climb onto your desks."*

His sharp tone washed over me and I felt unable to do anything but obey. My heart hammered as I scrambled up onto my desk beside Tory and everyone in the room started chattering excitedly.

Orion moved to lean back against his desk, his hands in his pockets. He nodded to Diego. "Polaris, please explain loud and clear to the ignorant twins on your left what Coercion is."

Diego got up, his chair legs scraping across the floor with a screech. He adjusted his beanie hat, throwing us an apologetic glance before answering. "Coercion is one of the Cardinal magics gifted to all Fae without exception.

It's the ability to control those of weak mind and is particularly effective on mortals."

"Tell them why," Orion pressed, his eyes dancing with mirth as they remained on us.

My heart thundered as all of this information sank in. Anyone who could cast Coercion magic could *control* us.

Diego cleared his throat. "Because most Fae learn how to perform a simple shield on their minds to block basic Coercion from a young age."

"Thank you, sit down," Orion told Diego and heat built in my cheeks.

"We've never been taught any-" Tory started but Orion cut over her.

"*Quiet,*" he commanded her then looked to the rest of the class. "The Vega Twins need to learn how to perform a simple shield. To encourage them to do so, you are all assigned the task of Coercing them at any given opportunity from here on out."

Kylie squealed her delight and several more of the class laughed.

"What?" I gasped. "How are we supposed to learn to do something we've never even heard of before now?"

Tory was still struggling to open her lips after he'd ordered her to stay quiet, but she was working real hard at it.

Orion ignored us, pointing at Tyler in the front row. "Stand up, turn around, one command."

"Are you kidding me right now?" I blurted, trying to force myself to get off of the table, but finding myself unable to ignore the impulse to remain there.

Dammit.

Tyler grinned at us in excitement. *"Jump up and down and flap your arms like a chicken."*

My legs immediately complied as I started jumping and my arms swiftly followed suit, flapping madly beside me. Tory was still desperately trying to speak while she jumped up and down in time with me.

Heat slammed into my cheeks as laughter echoed around the classroom. Orion was grinning his head off too. "Who's next?" he asked and Kylie's arm launched into the air faster than a N.A.S.A rocket.

Crap!

"Go ahead." He nodded at her.

She stood up with a malicious expression on her too-pretty face and my heart raced with anger. I felt the previous compulsion wearing off of me and both Tory and I fell still.

"Screw this," Tory snapped, kicking her Atlas off of the desk. Orion's arm shot out and the Atlas stopped mid-air, floating back up to sit right back where it had been before on an invisible wind.

He opened his mouth to berate her when the classroom door opened and Principal Nova strode in. She surveyed the scene with a look of interest then smiled at Orion. "How is everyone's first lesson going?"

"Terrible," I muttered, but she didn't seem to hear me. Orion's eyes flashed my way, confirming *he* had. I dropped off of my desk, folding my arms as I glared at him. I didn't expect Nova to do anything, not after she'd stood idly by when Caleb had bitten Tory. But maybe the distraction would be enough to put an end to this madness.

"The twins are behind," Orion told her bluntly. "They don't know a thing about the Orders. Beyond that, they don't have even a basic shield against Coercion and I doubt against any other magic either. So they'll most likely be dead before the end of term."

My stomach scrunched up into a solid ball and in that moment, I hated him. He was talking as if it was *our* fault for being so under-prepared. We'd been here one day and spent our entire lives without any knowledge of Fae. How could we be expected to cast shields against magic we'd just found out about?

"Hmm." Nova glanced our way. "Well that won't do." She tapped her lower lip. "They'll have to have Liaisons for tuition once a week."

Orion nodded. "That's the least they need."

"They'll need the best for the job," Nova said thoughtfully.

"Right." Orion scratched the short beard on his chin, suddenly seeming disinterested in the conversation.

"So you'll have to tutor one of them and I'll elect another Professor for the other."

Orion's bored expression turned to a wall of fury. "I coach Pitball most evenings, I don't have time for that."

"Yes but you only coach for an hour, then you have the whole evening at your disposal," Nova said brightly.

"You're right, I'd *love* to give my private time up for this," he said dryly and Nova beamed as if she hadn't registered his sarcasm.

The Principal looked to me and pointed. "Tory, you'll be taught by Professor Orion and-"

"I'm Darcy," I corrected.

"I – er – of course you are," Nova backtracked. "So you'll be with Orion and Darcy I'll let you know-"

"I'm Tory," my sister huffed.

"Right er-" Nova started but Orion stepped in.

"Blue, you're with me." He pointed at me and I scowled at the nickname.

"Right," Nova said. "You should start tonight; they need to get on track as soon as possible."

"Great," he bit out and my stomach swirled with nerves. Me and him? *Liaising*? Please no.

"I'll leave you to it then." The Principal turned on her stilettos and headed out of the room, snapping the door shut behind her.

Orion sighed heavily, marching back to the board with tension in his posture.

"*Sir*?" Kylie moaned. "Are we not doing Coercion anymore?"

"No," he growled. "Sit down and shut up. That goes for all of you."

Tory and I sank back into our seats and my mood took an even darker turn. Spending my evenings in Aer tower with Seth and his friends had already seemed bad enough, but now it looked like it was going to get even worse. Me and Professor Bites-His-Students in a room together. It sounded like the universe was having a really good go at ruining my day. And as I recalled my morning horoscope, I wondered if Professor Orion was a Libra.

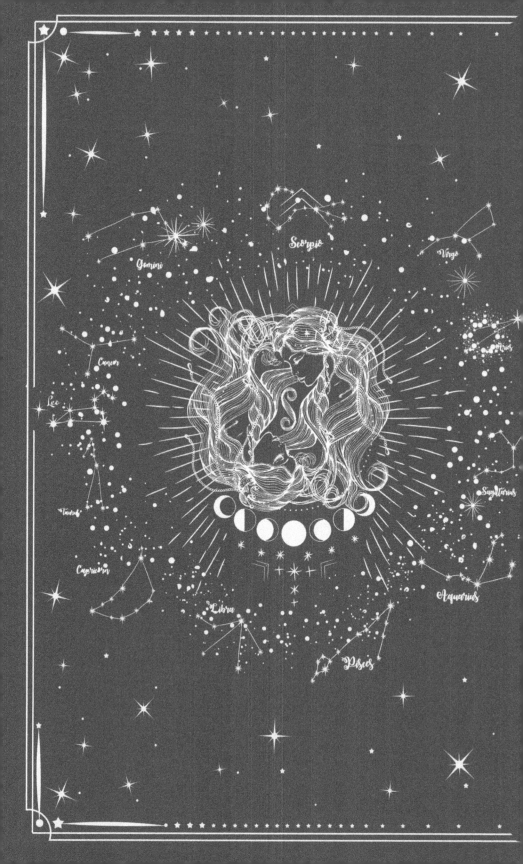

TORY

CHAPTER EIGHT

After our double Cardinal Magic class with Professor Asshat, we followed a trailing line of students towards The Orb for lunch. The glimmering golden building was even more breathtaking in the sunlight and I was so caught up in looking at it that I didn't notice the four Heirs standing by the entrance until we were almost on top of them.

Darcy muttered a curse beneath her breath as she spotted them, her fingers curling around my wrist in warning.

I exchanged a loaded glance with her and held my chin high as we drew closer. By some miracle, they didn't seem to have noticed us and the four of them headed inside before we were forced to pass them.

We merged into a group of excitable juniors who were discussing something called Pitball in loud voices and made our way to the lunch queue unnoticed. I wasn't going to hide from the Heirs but drawing their attention on purpose seemed like a stupid idea even to me.

"What do you think we should do about the messages from Falling

Star?" Darcy asked me as she chewed on her thumbnail.

"I dunno," I admitted. "It seems like everyone in this place is either threatened by us or wants something from us. And they already dropped us in it with Orion even if their assessment of him was pretty damn funny."

Darcy snorted a laugh. "I wonder if he really does stink of bourbon?"

"Well you can find out in your private class with him tonight," I joked and she winced.

We made it to a counter where so many meal choices lay waiting for us that I felt like I'd walked into a restaurant instead of a school cafeteria. A sign informed us that we could take anything cold from the display or order hot food for table service.

As I was deciding what kind of meal I'd prefer, a squeal of excitement caught my ear quickly followed by a cry of, "Your majesties! I've secured a table for you!"

I began to turn my head but Darcy yanked on my arm, making me duck into the group of juniors again.

"It's that crazy A.S.S. girl again," she hissed. "Let's just grab something and get out of here before the Heirs hear her calling us her queens!"

I snorted a laugh as Darcy grabbed a couple of huge subs for us and let her guide me through the crowd towards the exit.

I paused at a wide refrigerator which seemed to be made out of a huge block of ice and grabbed us a couple of drinks before glancing back into the room. A tall girl with long, brown hair was waving maniacally in our direction and I bit my lip as I ducked outside after my sister.

"The people here are all insane," Darcy grumbled as she picked a path at random and we began the hunt for somewhere to enjoy our food in peace. "They're either ecstatic to welcome back their long lost queens or furious at us for coming back to steal some throne."

"I know. It's like it never even occurred to them to ask if we want their stupid throne. I mean, the fairytale version of finding out you're a princess is great and all but in reality I imagine there's a hell of a lot of work involved with running an empire. And we have zero qualifications to take on that role."

"Yeah. Let the stupid Heirs keep their damn throne," Darcy agreed. "I just want my magic."

"And our inheritance," I added with a grin.

"Yeah, and that. Even more so since Darius burned everything we owned," she replied darkly and I had to grind my teeth to stop myself from stringing together yet another line of curses about the Ignis House Captain. Darcy had had to listen to over an hour of it last night anyway and calling him any more names wouldn't bring our cash back.

Darcy handed me the sub she'd snagged for me in The Orb and I swapped it for the bottle of pink lemonade I'd gotten her.

We ate as we walked and I couldn't help but groan aloud at the amazing flavour combination which danced across my tastebuds. There was cheese and salad and some kind of sauce that was sweet and salty at once. On our meagre income, meals were plain and semi-nourishing. The best food I'd eaten recently was the odd dinner Joey had offered up at the bar. And as much as I'd loved the greasy burger and fries at the time, it really couldn't hold a candle to this.

"Holy shit, I'd stay here for the food alone," I moaned as I licked the last of the sauce from my fingers and tipped the delicious lemonade down my throat to follow it.

"It sure puts Pete's efforts at sausage and mash to shame," Darcy agreed with a laugh. Our former foster parent had the skills to cook precisely three meals under his belt and the other two were frozen pizzas. If I never ate a sausage again it would be too soon.

Our walk had taken us into an area to the north of the Academy grounds which was marked as 'Earth Territory' on our maps. We were surrounded by every shade of green imaginable and stunning flowers blooming in every colour under the sun. The map showed the grounds were divided into four sections, one for each of the Elements and I was beginning to realise that the division was about more than just a name. The entire landscape was moulded by the Element which named it and stepping between them was like moving between different continents.

To our left, a sloping green hill filled with wildflowers curved away from us and I fell still as I spotted a creature swooping from the sky to land on the soft grass.

I grabbed Darcy's arm, unable to form a word as my lips parted at the sight before me. A whole herd of stunning winged unicorns landed before ambling through the meadow, their coats gleaming in sparkling metallic colours from silver to bronze and gold to pinks, yellows and even green. Their coats were sprinkled with glitter and their long, golden horns caught the sunlight like they were made from polished metal.

"No freaking way," Darcy breathed.

A small stallion looked up at the sound of her voice and we froze, worried we'd startled him but the beautiful, silver creature simply looked at us curiously.

My lips curved into a smile which grew uncontrollably. I mean, I wasn't usually a girly girl but this was a goddamn *flying unicorn!*

I had to stamp down on the squeal of excitement that was bubbling in my chest as the unicorn trotted towards us.

"Omagod," Darcy gasped as he came to stand directly in front of us.

I tentatively reached out a hand, wondering if the glorious creature would allow me to touch his sparkling coat.

The unicorn's eyes seemed to glimmer with amusement and he leaned forward so that my fingers swept over his soft nose and into his mane.

Darcy reached out too, running her fingers along the side of his face and down his neck.

The unicorn pressed closer, rubbing the side of his face against my chest and eliciting a laugh from me. He pressed his face against Darcy next and she grinned like a Cheshire Cat as she wrapped her arms around his neck.

A pink unicorn trotted close, eyeing us for a moment before whinnying at the stallion as he pressed his nose against my neck. The stallion snorted in a way that seemed weirdly dismissive and the pink unicorn stamped her foot before moving into the trees to our left.

"Stop it Tyler!" Sofia's voice came from the trees the pink unicorn had just entered and I flinched in surprise, wondering where the hell she'd come from.

The silver unicorn pushed his face against my chest again and I ran my hand along his neck.

"They don't know what you are!" Sofia said angrily as she stomped out of the bushes with her skirt on backwards and her shirt only half done up. She continued buttoning it as she stalked towards us barefoot, glaring at the silver unicorn like he'd done something to offend her.

"Be careful you don't scare him," I began but the unicorn beside me let out a snort which sounded annoyed before suddenly lurching towards me and turning into a boy with frosted tips in his hair and a huge grin on his face. He also happened to be butt naked which apparently didn't faze him in the slightest. My hand, which had been pressed to the unicorn's neck, was now planted on his chest. I snatched it back with a cry of disgust and Darcy let out a scream, jerking backwards and falling on her ass.

"Well now we've gotten the foreplay out of the way, are you girls going to be coming back to my room?" Tyler asked me and Darcy with a wink.

"You were a unicorn!" Darcy yelled in confusion as my brain struggled to comprehend what had just happened.

"Pegasus," Tyler corrected. "And you two were all over me." His grin was widening if that was even possible and I suddenly caught on to what he was saying. The beautiful creature we'd just been petting had actually been *him*.

"Did you *nuzzle* my chest?" I asked in disgust.

"Yeah," Tyler replied, dropping his gaze to my breasts which were thankfully hidden beneath my shirt.

My fist snapped out on instinct and I caught him unprepared, hitting him in the jaw and sending him stumbling back.

"Shit!" he swore, clutching his face.

"What the hell is wrong with you?" Darcy demanded as she regained her feet and moved to stand shoulder to shoulder with me.

"Hey, how was I supposed to know that you didn't realise what I was?" Tyler asked as he started to back up. "You seemed just as into it as me."

"That's because we thought we were stroking a wild animal not getting molested by some horse-faced weirdo," I snarled.

Sofia snorted in amusement at my dig and Tyler kept backing away as Darcy raised her hands at him threateningly.

"Okay, okay, I'm sorry," Tyler said placatingly. "I'll get out of your hair."

He lurched forward like he was going to fall over but before his hands could hit the floor they turned into hooves and the rest of his body transformed into the beautiful silver Pegasus again.

I couldn't help but stare as he trotted up the hill towards the rest of the herd and Sofia offered me an apologetic shrug.

"Sorry about him," she muttered. "Shame you can't choose who gets to be in your Order."

"You were the pink Pegasus?" I asked in realisation and she nodded shyly.

"Yeah. We replenish our power by flying through the clouds and I was just charging up before our Fire Elemental Class next," she explained, like turning into a goddamn flying unicorn was no big deal.

I struggled for something to say about that but I just couldn't think of a damn thing.

"Actually, I think we'd better get going," Sofia continued, breezing past our shock like she hadn't noticed it. "We've only got twenty minutes until class begins and the Fire Arena is all the way at the south end of the grounds.

"I don't have Fire next," Darcy said as she glanced at her timetable on her Atlas. "I've got Air. I think Diego said he'd be there too though."

"That's good. At least there are two normal people in this place for us to talk to," I said, although as Sofia headed off to find her socks, shoes and blazer in the bushes, I had to wonder if normal really applied to someone who spent their spare time with hooves.

Darcy gave me a knowing smile as she pulled up the map to her next class on her Atlas and she said goodbye to Sofia and me as she took a path that led to the east of the grounds. I was a little disappointed to be heading in separate directions for our very first real magic class but it was one of only a few where we would be separated.

Sofia fell into step with me as we headed towards House Ignis and the Arena beyond it where we were about to have our first Elemental lesson.

It took a while to cross out of Earth Territory and into Fire Territory in the south, but Sofia kept me amused with facts about her Order as we went and I slowly recovered from my shock.

The midday sun shone down on the home of the fire students as we drew close to it and my lips parted in surprise. Last night it had been so dark that I'd only really seen the entrance to the building with the multiple fires ruining my night vision and blocking my view of the rest. What I hadn't realised was that from the first floor up, the building was entirely made of glass in varying shades of yellow, orange and red which all blended together to give the impression of a huge, glimmering fire.

"From above it looks like a star," Sofia commented, noticing my attention on the building.

"How did they create such a thing?" I asked in wonder. No doubt magic was involved but I just couldn't picture the amount of work that had gone into it. The design alone boggled my mind.

"Fire magic of course, and I think there was probably some dragon fire involved too. We'll learn more about magical infrastructure in our sophomore year."

"You mean we'll learn to make things like that?" I asked eagerly, unable to tear my eyes away from the magical building. As we walked, the sun caught on different pieces of the glass and it almost looked like it was truly burning.

"Well creating *that* might be a little ambitious," Sofia laughed. "But we will learn to use our Elemental magic more subtly for creation, yeah."

I couldn't help but grin at the idea of that.

We passed Ignis House and followed the path around through the Fire Territory where the landscape was rocky and dry. I hadn't had time to explore Air or Water Territory yet but I had glimpsed a huge forest to the east and a sweeping lake to the west on my way to Cardinal Magic earlier.

A creeper filled with bright red flowers clung to a wall of black lava rock to my right and I noticed more plants peppered around too. Although the fire landscape seemed barren at first, the harder I looked, the more beautiful it became.

We moved along a crevice cut between two rock faces which glimmered with yellow and gold minerals.

"That's brimstone," Sofia said, noticing my interest again.

"You're a walking talking encyclopaedia, you know that?" I teased, not that I was complaining. I had zero idea what I was dealing with in this place and her knowledge was invaluable to me.

"I like facts. I'm a Sagittarius which helps; we love learning new things and are usually pretty intelligent," she replied with a smirk.

The serious way she said that made me attempt to squash the snort of disbelief which wanted to be set loose. I guessed I was going to have to try and open my mind to all this star sign stuff if I wanted to fit in here.

"Is that so?" I asked, trying to keep my scepticism at bay.

"Yep. And I have a damn good memory too which should help me ace the tests and make up for my lack of power somewhat."

"Are you lacking power then?" I asked delicately, unsure if that was okay to say but she was the one who'd brought it up.

"Yeah. My family are pretty low on the rankings when it comes to power. If you imagine yourself as a ten I'd be like... a three I guess." She shrugged. "Our world is all about power so it means I'm kinda destined to stay at the bottom of the food chain but I don't really mind. I mean, at least I don't have to worry about seizing and holding my position for the rest of my life, you know?"

"Not really, but I think I'm going to find out pretty soon whether I like it or not."

"Err yeah, I'd say so. Your whole life is going to be a power struggle," she said with a grin.

"Perfect," I sighed. "What if I were to say I don't want whatever power it is that I'm supposed to claim? I just want to use my own magic for my own purposes and have nothing to do with any birthright or throne or Heirs-"

Sofia's laughter cut me off and I raised an eyebrow at her.

"I wasn't joking," I said firmly.

"Oh god, Tory," she said, reining herself in a little. "You really don't know anything about our world. I'd love to say that you could just run off into the sunset but... that's *never* going to happen."

"Well damn," I replied half heartedly. I still had no plans to do any of the things that were expected of me but at least I had my answer about one thing. There was no way I was going to be able to just bow out of the running for power and avoid the attention of the other Heirs as I'd hoped. Maybe I could talk to them and tell them that I didn't want their power though. They couldn't be completely unreasonable...

We exited the crevice filled with brimstone and the scent of sulphur assaulted my nostrils.

I looked around until I spotted curling tendrils of steam rising across the land to our right and the glimmer of water in the distance.

"Is that hot springs?" I asked eagerly.

"Oh yeah. That's where fire meets with the territory of water. I've heard it's the best place to go for a swim and relax. We should head over after class one evening and try it out!" Sofia replied enthusiastically.

"I don't have a bikini," I said with a shrug, though the idea of a swim in the springs was definitely tempting. So long as the water wasn't too deep; a few years ago I'd had a traumatising accident and ever since then, the mere thought of deep water gave me the creeps.

"Didn't you bring one from home? I'm sure it was on the list of recommended-"

"The only things I brought from home were the clothes on my back and a pocket full of cash and Darius saw to destroying them last night," I replied darkly.

"Oh, yeah, I *might* have heard about that after I made it through my initiation last night. It sounds like he went a bit far with you..."

"So he didn't burn the clothes from your body then?" I asked, figuring I already knew the answer. That particular trial had been specially designed for my benefit.

"Umm, no. But then I'm not very powerful, like I said. So I wouldn't really expect him to take any notice of me anyway." Sofia dropped her gaze to the path beneath her feet as I let out a huff of irritation.

"Trust me to get on the wrong side of an overgrown, entitled prick within half an hour of arriving," I muttered.

Sofia gasped, glancing around to check if anyone had heard me. "You might want to keep that opinion to yourself if you don't want it getting back to him. The Heirs have a lot of fans and I wouldn't trust anyone to keep quiet on your behalf."

"I'm fairly sure Darius and his bromance crew know exactly what I think of them without me needing to worry about hiding it. Besides, if he asked me I'd happily tell him to his face that I think he's a jumped up little ass wipe

132

who needs to get a new hobby which doesn't involve tormenting people."

Sofia's mouth fell open and I could tell she was caught between shock and laughter. I was glad when a giggle finally escaped her.

As we came to the end of the path, a huge building rose up ahead of us. It looked a bit like the Colosseum where the gladiators had fought in Ancient Rome but the brickwork was all black.

Our conversation stalled as I stared up at the stone dragons and gargoyles who glared at us from their positions along the wall above our heads.

We moved beneath an arch and found a female Professor with short red hair and deep bronze skin waiting for us.

"Come along girls, you need to get changed and out into the arena," she commanded, not bothering with introductions. My timetable had informed me her name was Professor Pyro and I offered her a faint smile as I hurried to comply with her instructions.

Sofia and I made it into the girls' changing rooms where a row of hooks held bags with our names written on them. I lifted the one with Roxanya Vega scrawled across it, my nose wrinkling at the name I refused to accept as my own. There must have been someone I could talk to about changing everything official to say Tory. I could cope with the Vega thing if I had to but Roxanya was a girl who should have grown up in this strange Fae world and I wasn't her. Tory had been my name throughout everything that had shaped me into the person I was today and I had no interest in shedding that persona now or in the future.

I opened the bag and pulled out a matching pair of deep red leggings and a long sleeved shirt. The material felt almost silky but it was stretchy at the same time. I swapped my uniform for it and eyed myself in the mirror for a moment as I adjusted my black hair.

The outfit was skin tight and accentuated my curves in a way that somehow drew more attention to them than it would have done if more skin was on show. Though as I'd literally paraded around naked in front of most of the members of House Ignis last night, I didn't imagine it mattered.

I pulled on a pair of white sneakers last and waited while Sofia finished changing too.

Some more girls were arriving and I noticed more than one hostile glare aimed my way as I glanced between them. Not wanting to engage in any further altercations with my classmates, I quickly hurried out into the arena with Sofia.

"I'm so excited about this class," she admitted as we moved out into an open stadium filled with sand.

My first impression of thinking it looked like the Colosseum was only compounded as I looked up at the stands which ringed the arena. Around the walls, four plinths were lit with crackling fires and alternated with four gurgling water fountains.

As I took another step, the ground beneath my feet lurched and I almost fell flat on my face. I wheeled my arms to steady myself and the earth shuddered again.

I tipped backwards, wondering what the hell was happening to me just as strong arms caught me.

"Thanks, I-" I cut myself off as I looked up at my saviour and found Caleb Altair grinning down at me, his mess of blonde curls making him look almost angelic in the midday sun. But I knew he was no angel.

"You wanna watch out for that. The ground around here can be mighty unpredictable," he purred and I suddenly remembered that he was the leader of House Terra; the earth house. No prizes for guessing who'd made the ground shudder beneath my feet.

Sofia shuffled away from us but I couldn't blame her for wanting to avoid the attention of the Terra Heir.

"Right. I'll be sure to do that." I snatched my arms out of his grip and tried to step back but the earth lurched beneath me again and I was knocked to the ground.

Tittering laughter rang out around me as some of the other students drew close to watch and I scrambled to push myself upright again.

Before I could, Caleb dropped down, straddling me with a wicked grin which revealed his lengthening canines.

"Oh for the love of god," I snarled as I slammed my palms into his chest. "You'd better not be about to-"

He caught my wrists in an impossibly strong grip and shoved me back down to the ground as he buried his teeth in my neck.

I let my sailor's mouth loose on him, cursing him with every foul name I could think of and adding a few colourful new creations to the mix as well. I could feel my blood and power shifting out of my body and into his and it made my stomach roll with disgust.

The laughter around me grew as I tried to buck him off but he was like a goddamn ton of bricks. Superhuman strength in a superhuman leech.

"That's more than enough, Altair," Professor Pyro muttered, her tone bored instead of reprimanding. "She needs *some* energy left if she's going to be able to perform in my class today."

Caleb removed his fangs from my neck and I watched in morbid fascination as they withdrew into normal looking teeth again. He licked the last drops of my blood from his lips as he looked down at me, amusement flickering in his eyes.

"You have no idea how good you taste," he said without a hint of shame and I scrunched my nose up in disgust.

"You've got what you wanted from me so why don't you just get the hell off of me?" I snarled, yanking at my wrists again as he kept them pinned in the sand.

Caleb tilted his head as he regarded me and a slow smile spread across his face. "You know, I'm not sure I've ever fed from anyone who hates it quite as much as you do," he said, almost to himself. "The other Fae have grown up knowing about my kind and they just accept this as part of the chain of power but you..."

"Yeah, I hate it," I snarled. "So why don't you get your kicks feeding off of someone who enjoys your twisted brand of creep and leave me alone?"

Caleb released me and jumped up, leaving me scrambling in the sand at his feet.

"This girl is my personal Source," he said loudly to the group who had gathered around us which I realised had grown to at least fifty people. "If any other Vampire wants to feed from her then they can take it up with me, spread the word."

A weight built in my gut as I managed to regain my feet and I glared at him.

"I'm not your personal anything," I snapped.

"Feel free to try and stop me, sweetheart," he mocked. "But until you manage it, you can consider yourself my own personal juice box."

A deep laugh drew my attention to my left and I noticed Darius goddamn Acrux watching this interaction with amusement. Why did he have to be here to witness this? Why did there have to be four of them at all? I just wanted to keep my head down and get on with my own business but I was beginning to realise that the Heirs had zero intention of letting me or my sister do that.

"Well if all of the Vampires are fully replenished, I'd like to get on with my lesson," Professor Pyro announced, putting an end to any further discussion about the ownership of my blood.

I simmered with rage as I forced my attention onto the teacher, firmly turning my back on Caleb and Darius. A deep growl emitted from one of them and the hairs along the back of my neck stood on end. I remembered what they'd said yesterday about turning my back on them being an insult but I didn't give a rat's ass. If they were content to torment me then the last thing I'd be doing was showing them any respect.

"As it's the first class for the freshmen, I want the rest of you to pair off and take some time reacquainting yourselves with the techniques you learned at the end of last year. You should have been practicing over the summer and

I'll be coming around to look for improvements once I've got these guys going." Professor Pyro shooed the older students away but Caleb and Darius stayed where they were, their gazes fixed on me.

"What are you still doing here boys? The last I checked, you were sophomores," Pyro said as she fixed the Heirs in her penetrating gaze.

"We just wanted to see how powerful the new Heir really is," Darius said and a wave of discomfort filled me as I realised they planned on watching my first attempt at wielding fire magic.

"Well unfortunately for you, ogling the new girl isn't part of the syllabus," she replied dismissively, shooing them again and a little of the tension left my spine as the Heirs retreated.

Darius cast one last look at me as he walked away and I cursed myself for noticing the way the tight outfit clung to his muscular body before turning back to my teacher.

"So. The task for today is simple. I want you to bring a flame to life in the palm of your hand and maintain it. If you can manage that then I want you to form it into an orb. The tighter you wrap the power, the hotter it will burn. Don't get sloppy - your suits will protect you from burns but your hands and faces are vulnerable. It's down to your control over the flames to keep them from turning on you. If anyone is having trouble summoning the power from within yourself then you may draw it from the sconces to conserve energy. Miss Vega, if your power has been too depleted by Mr Altair to cast your own flame then you'll have to use the sconces too."

My rage increased as I realised what she meant; Caleb might have weakened me enough to hurt my ability to perform in this class. *Asshole!*

With a flicker of anger I thrust my palm out in front of me and willed a flame to life. My hand burst alight so quickly that I had to flinch back as the flare of fire almost claimed my eyebrows as trophies. The beam of red flames shot right up into the sky and lit the low clouds with an orange glow before I snapped my fist shut in surprise, extinguishing it.

"Holy cow," Sofia muttered and I glanced at her with wide eyes.

Professor Pyro snorted a laugh. "Looks like we don't have to worry about your power being too diminished after all," she said appreciatively. "You're going to have to work on your control if you've got that much to offer while you're only at half capacity."

A satisfied smile pulled at my lips as the flood of power faded from my veins. Sure, that had scared the crap out of me but it had felt damn good too. I could feel the Heirs looking at me again and I hoped my show of power was enough to make them leave me alone.

"Keep working on trying to build and maintain an orb," Pyro commanded as she began to move between the students and I tried to focus my mind on the task she'd set me.

I took a deep breath, holding my hand out again as I willed a flame to life. This time, my whole hand was engulfed in a fireball as big as a labrador and I squeaked in surprise as I tried to rein it in. It shrank to a cocker spaniel then lurched right to bull mastiff before I was forced to extinguish it.

Professor Pyro approached me once she'd made a round of the other freshmen and watched my attempts with a keen eye.

"Do you feel tired at all? Like you're starting to consume a lot of your reserves?" she asked with interest.

"I don't think so," I replied. If anything, the longer I practiced, the more my magic reserves seemed to swell within me.

"Okay. Let me see if I can help you to guide your power." She moved close to me and took my left hand in hers. I looked at her in surprise and she gave me a reassuring smile. "We have to maintain contact skin to skin to be able to guide and channel another's power. My influence will only work on your magic while that contact is maintained."

"Okay," I agreed. "So you want me to try and create a ball again?"

"Yes. Whenever you're ready."

I tried to ignore the fact that I was holding her hand and focused on my other palm instead as I held it out before me.

I took a breath and focused on creating the smallest amount of fire as possible. An inferno blazed to life instantly, creating a spear that hit the sand at my feet and shot up way above my head at the same time.

Professor Pyro's grip on my hand tightened and I could feel the sway of her magic as she tried to coax mine under control. I attempted to copy what she was doing, wrapping my will around the unruly Element as I gave all of my attention to creating a ball.

Slowly, the flames began to shrink as the Professor and I worked together to wrangle the beast which was my power.

Finally, a ball of fire no bigger than a baseball sat above the palm of my hand and I grinned at it triumphantly. It burned a deep red colour and I knew without having to touch it that it was as hot as the depths of a volcano.

Professor Pyro dropped my hand and stumbled back. I lost control of the fire as I turned to her in shock and it flared brightly before I managed to extinguish it again.

"I'm okay," she said ruefully as she stepped further away from me.

"What happened?" I asked, my brows pinching together with concern.

A fine layer of sweat lined her skin and her hands were trembling slightly. "Nothing that a good dose of sunlight won't fix. Don't worry, my dear."

"I don't understand." I could tell that she wasn't feeling well at all but the way she was trying to shrug it off made me feel like I'd been the cause of whatever was wrong with her. "Did I hurt you?"

"My own arrogance is what hurt me," she said with a shrug. "I thought to guide the power of an Heir with my magic. When guiding someone else's power, my own is drained too. Think of it as trying to wrap a king sized bed in a toddler's sheet."

"So your magic is gone?" I asked.

"For now, I find myself depleted," she confirmed with a nod. "I had thought that after your run-in with Mr Altair, your stores would be low enough for me to contain. I won't be making the same mistake twice."

"So what now?" I asked. I hadn't been making any progress until she'd guided me and I wasn't sure how easily I'd learn to harness my power if I wasn't able to work on it that way again.

"Now..." Professor Pyro tapped her forefinger against her lips as she considered my options. "There are two possible courses of action which could work. We could invite Mr Altair to drain your energy to a much lower level so that you have less to deal with-"

My features skewed with horror at the idea of requesting such a thing and the Professor's lips quirked with amusement.

"On second thought that would only help in the very short term anyway," she admitted and I sagged with relief as she seemed to go off the idea. "You need to be able to wrangle your powers at full strength. Which means you need a tutor who is strong enough to handle you..."

Her gaze wandered away from me and I turned to see what she was looking at.

On the far side of the arena, Darius and Caleb were locked in a battle of fire which looked like something out of a movie. Darius directed a huge fire dragon to take potshots at hundreds of fire snakes which were under Caleb's control.

Though the dragon was much bigger than the snakes, the sheer number of them which Caleb had created made it difficult for Darius to maintain the advantage. It almost seemed like a game and both of their faces were lit with smiles but in their eyes raged a fierce competitive streak which made it clear they were both playing to win.

As I watched, a second dragon sprang to life, clambering out the water fountain which was nearest to them before diving headlong into the swarm of vipers. The fire creations didn't stand a chance and as they spluttered out of existence, Darius gave a whoop of triumph and the two dragons did a victory lap of the arena.

"Always the cheat," Caleb mocked, folding his arms.

Darius started laughing and Caleb shot forward at a speed which didn't seem possible.

The two of them collided and started throwing punches. I looked at the Professor in surprise, expecting her to step in but her gaze had fallen back on me.

"There are only a few people whose power would be strong enough to keep yours in check," she said thoughtfully and my stomach dropped as I realised where her train of thought had taken her. I did not want her to get off at this stop but I had no idea what I was supposed to say to prevent the words from leaving her lips. "Caleb is good but you might as well be taught by the best so it'll have to be Darius."

"But I..." I what? *What?* Professor Pyro was staring at me and my mouth was opening and closing like a goldfish as I hunted for something, *anything* to say which would turn her from this idea. The last thing I wanted was to be indebted to Darius Acrux. But the cogs in my brain were turning too slowly and the only thing I could think to say was 'but he's mean to me and I don't like it' which would have made me seem like a pathetic little girl even though it was the truth. "Principal Nova is assigning me a Liaison to help me catch up and I'm sure a teacher would be the best person to help me-"

"Your Liaison will be guiding you in a more practical role, teaching you about our world and how to live up to the standards expected of you. As strange as it may seem to you after spending a lifetime in the mortal world, the amount of power we each hold is something that we are born with. There are no teachers here strong enough to handle guiding your magic this way. Only the other Heirs can rival you with your power. And even then, as twins born to Gemini who each hold all four Elements, I'd wager they'll have their hands full." Her lips quirked for a moment and I got the impression that that idea amused her.

My mind whirled as my only argument hit a dead end and I scrambled for another excuse. "I just... feel bad asking him to waste his time working with me while my level of understanding is so much less-"

"Nonsense," Professor Pyro waved me off as she beckoned for me to follow her across the arena towards the two Heirs who were still wrestling on the ground, their fight getting increasingly violent. "This will be good for him too, melding your power with another Fae's is a skill that is hard to master so it'll be a perfect opportunity for him to flex those muscles. It takes a lot of concentration and it can be really quite intimate as the two of you will have to strive towards a level of trust so that your magic can work in harmony with one another."

Intimate? Gross - though not as gross as I was trying to convince myself. And trust? She was insane if she thought I'd ever trust him. I'd sooner trust a monkey with a bunch of bananas than believe anything good of him.

We came to a halt beside the Heirs as Darius pinned Caleb to the ground, his hands tight around the other guy's throat. Caleb was thrashing, trying to get up but he didn't look likely to succeed.

Darius snarled and the sound was so animal that I almost flinched. He was a predator taking down his prey and at any moment I could imagine him ripping into Caleb's flesh.

Professor Pyro merely watched the interaction with a faint level of interest as Caleb's lips started to turn blue.

I opened my mouth, wanting to step in. I mean, Caleb was a total dickwad but it was starting to look like Darius might kill him and that was probably going a bit too far. Before I could say anything, Caleb smacked his hand against the ground three times and Darius released him with a smirk.

Caleb started laughing and Darius got to his feet, offering the other Heir a hand so that he could pull him up too.

"I'll get you next time," Caleb announced as he slapped his friend on the back.

"You said that last time," Darius teased and for a moment they both seemed... well not nice but not entirely loathsome at least. Or they did until their attention moved to me.

Darius's face dipped into a scowl instantly and Caleb tossed his curly hair back as he eyed my neck hungrily with absolutely zero shame about the fact.

"I have a new assignment for you, Mr Acrux," Professor Pyro announced and my heart sank like a stone as I realised there was no way out of this.

"Yes, Professor?" Darius asked, his face set with a look suggesting that he couldn't think of anything better than doing whatever she requested of him.

"I'd like you to give Tory here some one on one tutoring to help her learn to harness that tempest of power within her. I tried to guide her myself but she needs someone more powerful than me and as the most accomplished fire weaver in the Academy, you were the obvious choice."

Darius's eyes darted to me and I felt like he'd just plunged a dagger through my chest as the sharpness of his gaze hit me.

"Of course, Professor Pyro," he agreed smoothly. "Only, I do have a full timetable at the moment so it may be better for her to choose someone else."

"Okay," I agreed with a smile that let him know this hadn't been my idea in the first place. "Never mind." I began to turn away from them but Professor Pyro stopped me.

"That's not a problem," she said firmly. "You can train her on Thursday evenings after dinner and we can add Mondays if necessary."

Darius's gaze darkened as she stole his evenings from him and I had to force myself to keep my chin high.

"Yes Professor," he agreed finally and she smiled with satisfaction as she led me away from him.

I hadn't said anything but I didn't think my input would do anything other than possibly make a bad situation worse.

As I made it back to where the other freshmen were practicing, I couldn't help but glance back over at the Heirs. The two of them were looking at me and

I almost flinched away from the ire in their gaze.

Perfect. This day was just getting worse and worse.

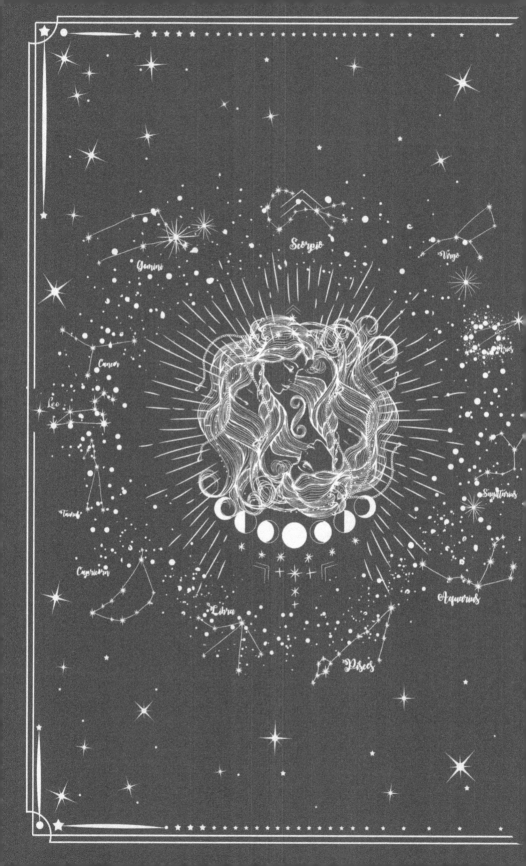

DARCY

CHAPTER NINE

I lay on my bed, reading over the notes from the day on my Atlas. My air Elemental class had been incredible; Professor Perseus had brought us to the cliff at the eastern edge of Air Territory and we'd cast wind down onto the turquoise sea. Eventually I'd been able to direct it at specific waves and send the spray flying up the side of the cliff. So much power was difficult to harness precisely, but he'd seemed content to let us unleash everything we had on the ocean.

I was still buzzing with the excitement of it all, but as seven o'clock neared, my excitement finally gave way to nerves. I had my first session with Professor Orion tonight. And I was still reeling after seeing him bite Diego without a care in the middle of his classroom.

What if he tries that with me?

I brushed my fingers together, a light breeze dancing between them. After releasing the full force of my power on the sea, I felt slightly more confident. But I didn't fancy my chances up against an opponent yet. Especially one who had razor sharp teeth and was built like a fortress.

I picked up the banana I'd grabbed from The Orb earlier, wishing I'd taken something more substantial now. Tory and I had plans to meet up after my Liaison session anyway, so I'd survive.

When I'd finished my fruit, I changed into my sports kit in favour of my uniform which I'd been in all day. There was nothing else to wear and I half wondered about that stipend Orion had mentioned. If he'd been more frank back at our apartment, I could have brought some more clothes with me.

I tugged on my Converses at a quarter to seven and slung my satchel over my shoulder. My heart was bouncing with anxiety as I headed out of my room, locking it before jogging toward the stairwell.

The tower was quiet and I suspected most of the Aer students were hanging out in the common room upstairs or eating at The Orb.

As I circled down to the ground floor, a ping sounded from my Atlas. I took it out, finding a notification flashing up on it.

You've been mentioned in a FaeBook post, Darcy!

I frowned, tapping on the app even though I imagined I was about to regret it.

Kylie Major:
Great first day, I am so blessed to be here at ZA! It must be harder for girls like Darcy and Tory – they don't even have basic Coercion defense. Be careful out on campus girls. #loveya #besafe #girlssticktogether

Comments:
Lois Hargreeves:
Not even a basic shield??? Hahahahaha

148

Jillian Minor:

OMG hun you're so sweet :)

Yewande Rubel:

Are you really going steady with Seth Capella, Kylie??

Milton Hubert:

YESSSSSS!!!

I bit into my cheek so hard I almost drew blood. Everyone in the entire Academy would see this and over a hundred people had already liked it! It was practically painting a neon target on our heads. And I didn't have a single doubt that Kylie knew *exactly* what she was doing.

Girl code my ass.

I glanced over my shoulder, feeling overly cautious of being pounced on.

Being in Orion's office suddenly didn't seem like the worst fate in the world. I checked the map, heading out of the tower onto the grounds. Iron lanterns lit the path as the evening drew in and I quickened my pace along it as I took a shortcut through The Wailing Wood.

The winding path led me into the trees and a cool wind gusted over me as I stepped onto a dirt track. Goosebumps bristled along my arms. The further I walked, the quieter the world seemed. The leaves rustled above me, some of them licked with the first colours of fall.

The deeper I delved into the woodland, the closer the trees seemed to gather, arching overhead to create an endless tunnel before me.

The lanterns had become more sparse and the amber glow of the next one seemed to shrink and flicker up ahead.

Should have taken the longer route. This place is creepy as hell.

My foot caught on a root and I stumbled, nearly hitting the ground before catching myself at the last second. I muttered curses at myself as I hurried on, wanting to get out of this place without a couple of scuffed knees. Honestly, I should have grown out of it by now. But I fell over more times in a week than was normal for a toddler, let alone a grown woman.

I took the Atlas from my satchel, double-checking the way and found a FaeBook message waiting for me.

Falling Star:

The Shadow draws closer to you, Darcy!

Stay in the light!

My heart thrashed in my chest as I reread the words. Who the hell was this Falling Star and what was that supposed to mean?

I ignored the twisting sensation in my gut and checked the map. The paths had forked a few times but luckily I'd stayed on track. Forcing Falling Star's eerie message from my mind, I continued on.

As I arrived at the circular glow cast by the next lantern, I tilted the map and a little star blinked, marking my spot amongst the thick wood.

Relief filled me as I realised that I was nearing the exit. Then it was a straight shot right up to Jupiter Hall where Orion's office was located.

A twig cracked somewhere behind me and I stiffened, turning to stare out into the darkness beyond the ring of light around me.

I squinted at the shadows between the trees and my heart pattered wildly in my chest.

It's nothing. Keep walking.

As much as I didn't want to leave the illusion of safety in the light of the lantern, I forced myself to move, quickening my pace to a half-jog.

A shiver darted up my spine and the sense of being watched cascaded over me like ice-cold water. Footsteps padded along the path behind me, soft and swift, as if someone were trying to remain quiet.

I spun around as fear lodged a jagged lump in my throat.

It was probably just another student, why was I getting so terrified over a few shadows and noises? Falling Star's message had unnerved me. But they were probably just trying to mess with me too. I had to rise above it.

A flash of blue light made me freeze, every muscle in my body becoming a solid thing. It had only been for a moment, but for second I thought I'd seen a hulking form out there in the trees. Deep in the wood...a beast.

Everyone in this school is a beast. It's just a student. Just someone in one of their Order forms.

I tried to steady my rampant heart, telling myself I was overreacting. But something in my gut told me I should be afraid.

A force of energy crashed into me from behind and a pitchy scream escaped me as I hit the ground, rolling over and holding up a hand in defence. "Get away!" I yelled, the dark silhouette shifting closer.

Fire flared in his palm and Darius came into view with a wide smirk on his face. "Whoops didn't see you there, Vega." He held out a hand with a deep chuckle. I took it rather reluctantly, still shaking.

"Was that you out there trying to scare me?" I demanded as he pulled me to my feet.

"Out where?" he asked lazily, releasing my hand to sweep his fingers through his dark hair.

"Over there." I pointed into the trees, shifting toward Darius, unable to help clinging to the comfort of company. But after what he'd done to Tory I was far from trusting him.

"Dunno what you're talking about," he said lightly. "See ya." He went to move and I caught his arm which was firm with muscle beneath my fingers, my pride dissolving before my eyes.

"Would you mind maybe...just walking me out of the woods?" Shame washed through me but I did *not* like this place one bit and the idea of getting turned around in here when I'd seen some huge beast sniffing about didn't appeal to me. Even if my girl power had to take a significant hit.

Darius snorted. "You scared, Vega?"

"*No*," I said indignantly, giving away that I absolutely was. I cleared my throat. "I just don't want to get lost in here. I've got a meeting with Professor Orion in five minutes."

"Pfft, he'll be late anyways, you're not in any hurry." He tried to shake me off but I held on tight.

I sucked up the last of my pride like a hoover and said, "Please."

He sighed heavily then turned around and yanked me along at a fierce pace. I didn't care. I just wanted to be planted outside of these woods and move on with my life. Right now it felt like I was never going to escape the darkness and the feeling of being hunted. And Darius might have been an asshole but I was happy to use him in my moment of need.

"Bro!" a voice howled then Seth burst out of the darkness wearing a white sports kit splashed with mud. The symbol of Aer was stamped on the chest of his shirt which was half torn off of him. "Who's your date?" He stepped closer then scowled as he realised it was me. "Don't tell me you're hanging out with a Vega?"

I ground my jaw, not needing this right now. An orb of golden light lit up above Seth and floated there to illuminate us all.

"She's scared," Darius said in a dry tone that sent embarrassment washing through me.

"I'm not scared," I insisted but I sounded more like a child than an adult with her shit together. *Dammit.*

Seth's eyes lit up and he clawed a hand through his unkempt hair. He looked as happy as if Christmas day had come early.

Seth moved toward us, petting Darius's arm then moving forward to nuzzle my hair with his face. I lurched sideways.

Damn animal.

"I'll walk you out, babe." He clutched my arm, trying to steer me away from Darius.

I looked to the Fire Heir for any semblance of mercy in his eyes but he gave me nothing but a cold stare.

"Wait," he said with a dangerous smile as Seth tried to guide me away under his arm. "She needs to give me a proper goodbye first."

Seth shoved me toward Darius with a laugh and Darius smiled cruelly. "*Kneel*," he commanded, using Coercion on me and I winced as his order claimed my body.

I dropped to the ground before him, cursing his name between my teeth.

"*Kiss my foot.*" He barked a laugh as my back bent and I grimaced as I tried to force myself to stop. My mouth met his fancy shoe and I rued the moment I'd asked this twisted asshole for help.

Why can't I just be more like Tory with her unwavering backbone?

Seth laughed raucously. "Let's make her dance for us," he said eagerly. "Max and Caleb should be here any second, they'll lose it when they see her doing the cha-cha-cha."

My heart hammered angrily. "Don't you dare."

Darius took my arm, dragging me to my feet with a vicious smile. "I have a better idea."

"Get off of me," I snapped, trying to pull away. My heart stumbled as I stared into the fiery pit of excitement in his eyes.

He released me and I glanced between him and Seth, their beautiful faces dancing with shadows under the glowing orb above.

Falling Star's message circled in my head: *The Shadow draws closer.* But it must have been a coincidence.

Seth licked his lips and the sight was so sexual I couldn›t help but stare at his mouth for a second.

"*Run*," Darius ordered and my legs moved before I realised what was happening.

Seth howled his excitement behind me as I tore away along the path. I moved as fast as I could, my arms wheeling back and forth beside me, half glad Darius had told me to run because I'd always been quick. And he may have just unknowingly given me an advantage.

Their footsteps pounded behind me and fear sliced into my belly as I started to doubt my chances against them.

What are they gonna do if they catch me?!

Lights twinkled through the trees, the promise of the main campus lying just at the edges of this never-ending path.

My heart pounded and sweat poured down my back. My hands suddenly heated with power and the wind skipped between my fingers. I focused on it as Professor Perseus had taught me and guided it toward my back. The air was suddenly my greatest ally, driving me forward at a tremendous speed.

A whoop of excitement escaped me as the end of the path came in sight.

I was almost there. I was gonna win.

Twenty feet.

Ten.

Five.

Two figures darted into my way and I crashed into them at full force. The scent of something sharp and deadly hit my senses as Caleb's arms wrapped around me, steadying me.

"Woah there horsey." He pushed my hair back from my neck and his eyes sparkled with hunger.

Oh no.

I backed up and bumped into Max with a sickening lurch of my stomach. I had to crane my neck to look up at him, his height immense and his mohawk adding an extra couple of inches.

"Out for a moonlit stroll?" he asked, his voice deep and probing like it was trying to draw something intimate out of me.

Darius and Seth came to a halt before us and I was suddenly surrounded. A deer at the end of four hunters' guns.

My hands curled into fists as I tried to keep control of the breeze around me, praying it would be enough to keep them back. But deep down, I knew I was royally screwed.

"Let me past," I demanded in my strongest voice, stepping toward Caleb who was firmly in my way. He pushed me back and another set of hands steadied me from behind. Seth's arms curled around my shoulders like he was hugging me. His mouth ran over my ear and a deep heat mixed with the fear in my belly to create a deadly cocktail.

He rubbed his rough chin against my temple and I tilted my head sideways to try and avoid his overt touches.

"I need to go," I growled. "I have a meeting with Professor Orion."

"Orion?" Caleb snarled, snatching my arm and tugging me out of Seth's arms into his again. "Is he getting blood from you already? Private meetings just for you and his teeth, huh?" He opened his mouth, baring his fangs and a gasp escaped me as I shoved him back, trying to will air into my palms. A sharp gust slammed into his chest and he released me with a grunt.

I glanced over his shoulder, ready to try and escape this circle of hell.

Caleb scowled. "Lucky for you I filled up on your sister earlier."

I made my move, darting for the gap that had opened up between Caleb and Max. As one, they closed in, surrounding me in a tight circle of muscle and heated man bodies.

"Power of four?" Max suggested with a grin, leaning toward me and making my heart stutter.

"Brilliant idea. That'll stop Orion feeding from her tonight," Caleb said eagerly.

"What the hell are you-" Before I could finish that sentence Max raised his hands and water fell down on me in a torrential rain shower, soaking me from head to foot.

My white t-shirt turned transparent and I raised my hands to cover myself, my breath halting in shock. Caleb wielded the ground beneath my feet and mud splashed up around me in a ring. I was suddenly caked in freezing cold sludge and my heart was screaming with rage and embarrassment.

I wiped the back of my hand over my eyes to try and remove the filth, my pulse hammering in my ears.

As I regained my sight, I found Darius and Seth side by side before me. Seth blew a harsh wind over the top of a fire burning in Darius's palms. The combined effect was like being blasted in an oven and I gasped in horror as the sticky substance coating me dried to a hard, impenetrable second skin.

No no no!

I clawed at it, but it wouldn't budge. My hair hung in thick chunks and my face felt like it had been pasted with the biggest mud pack ever.

"Argh!" I shouted in fury, a fire in my veins. "Get this off of me!"

A flash of light told me a photo was being taken then they all fell about laughing. After a few more seconds they tore away from me into the woodland, their hysterics carrying back to me.

I trembled as I stood there, so angry I didn't know what to do with myself.

I picked at the compacted mud on my arms but it wouldn't budge. Tears of embarrassment stung my eyes as I realised what I had to do.

I stomped toward the edge of the woodland like a swamp monster, emerging onto the pathway that led up to the ring of buildings surrounding The Orb.

A group of girls were heading my way, their conversation falling dead on their lips as they spotted me walking toward them. The word embarrassment was not even close to what I felt right then.

"Is that an Order?" one of them murmured.

"No I think it's a Vega," another said in glee, snatching her Atlas out to take a picture.

"*Make a sound like a donkey,*" a girl commanded, her eyes alight with mischief. The Coercion washed over me and I slapped a hand to my mouth to try and stop the noise escaping. It tore free of my throat and a shameful and horrifyingly loud, *"EEH-OOHR!"* burst from my lips.

I ran past them as their laughter poured over me. Embarrassment stabbed at my cheeks as I desperately tried to avoid more photo ops, making a beeline for Jupiter Hall as I cupped my hands over my head.

Just keep running. Don't stop.

"Mud monster!" a boy shouted at me as he exited The Orb and the girls around him ran about screaming and giggling.

Tears burned my eyes as I was consumed by the utter shame of this situation. And the worst was yet to come. Because I had to ask god-damn Professor Hot-As-Shit Orion to help me while looking like the beast from the bog.

Inside Jupiter Hall, I found my way to his office by following a long corridor. I clutched the door handle and hesitated for several long seconds.

Please swallow me up, ground. That would be really great right now.

I turned the handle, but found the door locked. I frowned, pulling my Atlas out to check the time. I was five minutes late so where the hell was he? Had he given up waiting already?

"I hope that's not a fashion choice, Miss Vega." Professor Orion appeared in jeans and a white shirt, his hair damp as if he'd just showered – *it's alright for some.*

His obsidian eyes dragged down me from head to toe and his mouth pulled up at one side, revealing the dimple in his right cheek.

"Oh yes, I just *love* rolling in mud in the evenings," I deadpanned, trying my best to front this out. But it was pretty hard when all I could see in my periphery was clumps of mud.

He stepped right into my breathing space, pushing his key into the door. He headed inside, leaving the door open for me to follow and I trailed in after him, feeling like an ogre in a ballroom as I took in his lavish office.

A crescent-moon desk built from cherry wood sat at the heart of it, behind which was an archway of shelves filled with leather-bound books. A closed door in the arch stopped me from nosing any further in that direction so I stared around at the rest of the room. The tall window to my left looked over The Orb and the sound of laughter and conversation carried through the cracked-open window. I was almost certain I heard someone mentioned my name and pig-shit in the same sentence. A ping from my Atlas told me all I needed to know. My photo was now live and waiting for me on FaeBook for the entire school to see.

My insides withered and died.

I stood awkwardly on a deep crimson rug as Orion dropped into his large Ottoman chair, pulling something from a cupboard in his desk. He placed a crystal glass on the surface followed by a large bottle of bourbon. *I guess Falling Star's assessment about him was true.*

He continued to ignore me as he poured himself a measure than sat back in his chair, tipping the contents down his throat. He smacked his lips, placing the glass down and moving to refill it.

"Excuse me?" I interrupted his rudeness.

Orion's eyes flicked up. "Yes?"

"Well, it's just that apparently I'm standing in your office looking like a swamp monster and watching you get drunk."

"That does appear to be happening, yes. Very observant, Blue. Or perhaps I should call you Brown now?" He nearly choked on his laughter at his own joke.

God this guy was a piece of work.

I placed my hands on my hips and he tried to rein in his laughter as he stared at me – he did *not* manage it.

"Right, screw this." I marched toward the door, done with this day and every bastard I'd encountered during it. How could I have thought for one second that this teacher would help me? I had to remember the faculty in Zodiac were as heartless as the students.

As I grabbed the door handle, the mud on my skin heated with a punishing warmth. I winced as it was scraped off of me inch by inch then washed away by a stream of water that wrapped around my skin like a film. The combined magic dragged the mud from my flesh and it sailed right out of the window.

Relief swept through me as my body was cleaned of the muck and my hair fell about me in a soft fan of blue and black.

As I turned to Orion to thank him, a harsh wind forced me back against the door. I had to shut my eyes against the onslaught of air and my heart raced as I was held in place.

When the wind died away, I blinked a few times and found Orion standing before me. The scent of bourbon floated from him. He was frighteningly tall and all those muscles made me weak, but he was still just another asshole with a pretty face.

"Thank you," I forced out.

"Your gratitude isn't what I want." He snatched my arm and in one, single heartbeat I knew what he was going to do. My thoughts went haywire and my body tumbled into panic mode. Before I realised what I was doing, my hand smashed against his face and a loud clap filled the room.

Oh holy shit I just slapped a teacher.

The moment following my strike lasted for two whole eternities. Orion stared at me and I stared right back. His cheek was pinking with the imprint of my hand and he lifted his fingers to touch the mark as if he was unsure whether it had actually happened.

My tongue was a desperately dry lump of flesh but I managed to speak in a hoarse voice. "Don't bite me."

He leaned down so he was nose to nose with me and the heavenly scent of cinnamon sailed from his skin, tangling with the sharpness of bourbon on his breath.

His lips pursed and all amusement fled from his expression. "How are you going to stop me?" he asked as if he genuinely wanted an answer out of me. I suddenly felt like I was in a quiz.

I took a slow breath, the proximity of him making my thoughts harder to grasp than usual. "I know how to wield air. I can push you back."

"Are you sure about that?" He shifted closer, opening his mouth to reveal the sharp points of his fangs.

I shook my head. "Honestly? No. But I'm asking you not to and I'm telling you I'll try to fight you if you do." My voice barely quavered and I gave myself a mental pat on the back considering the night I'd had. Small victories and all.

Orion stepped away, a thoughtful glint in his eyes. I tried to move around him but he snatched my arm and sliced his fangs into my skin. I gasped in horror, bringing up my other hand as I tried to will magic into my fingers. But I couldn't focus and the second my hand got close, he slammed it against the door behind me. The hard plain of his chest flattened me to the wood and I winced as his bite deepened, my heart hammering like a rabbit's.

A draining feeling tugged at my insides and power flowed in a channel toward my wrist. My magic was being taken from me, swallowed by this ruthless creature.

His hands on me were unyielding and as hard as I concentrated, I couldn't conjure so much as a gentle breeze against him. Now he was drinking from me, he seemed to have my power in his grasp and it was all moving toward him, the well inside me emptying out.

He released me at last and my head spun, darkness momentarily curtaining my vision. A stream of the vilest swear words in my vocabulary swarmed through my head as I clutched the two bloody pinpricks on my wrist.

Orion gave me an even stare. "Everything in Solaria is about power, Miss Vega. Don't forget that. Everyone takes what they want. It's our way. And if you don't start taking it yourself, you're going to fail at this Academy before you've even attempted to pass The Reckoning."

My heart pounded out of rhythm as his words sank in.

I am Fae. And I need to embrace the darkest part of me if I'm ever going to survive here.

Orion sailed away from me, dropping into his chair with a satisfied sigh. "Sit down." He gestured to the seat opposite him.

My heart crumpled with frustration as I moved to take the chair, refusing to show him how rattled I was. Part of me wanted to run back to my room and hide under a blanket, but that wasn't exactly constructive...or dignified.

I eyed the ends of my hair, the blue tips feathery and smooth since Orion had essentially put me through a car wash with his Elements of air and water. I supposed I had something to thank him for. Though he'd taken plenty in return for it.

He poured himself another glass of bourbon and I frowned. "Isn't this supposed to be a lesson?"

"Nope. I'm supposed to be providing guidance for you. But I'm doing so on my time. And on my time, I like to have a drink. So here we are."

"Right," I said through tight lips. "So what exactly am I going to learn here while you're enjoying yourself?"

"Trust me, I'm not enjoying myself." He planted his glass down, giving me a hard stare. "Hand," he commanded and both of my hands curled up in refusal.

He half rolled his eyes. "Don't make me Coerce you. It's rather draining and I just added a nice chunk to my own power."

"You mean you sucked out my magic like a mosquito."

"Sure." He shrugged. "Whatever colourful analogy soothes you." He grinned, sipping his drink slower this time. "Hand, come on, we've only got forty more minutes of my life to waste."

I pressed my lips together, thrusting my right hand at him.

"Flat on the desk, palm up," he instructed and I did so. "Is this your dominant hand?"

I nodded.

"Good, I'm going to do an assessment."

"What kind of assessment?" I asked.

"Of your power."

"Okay..."

"Don't move. And don't giggle – for the love of the sun I hate the gigglers." He took my hand and heat stroked my veins as he brushed his fingertips over my palm. It tickled like hell and laughter bit at my throat.

He glanced up at me as if judging whether I was going to be one of his hated gigglers. I gave him a straight face, refusing to let it out.

He traced his thumb across the line at the centre of my palm and my skin tingled with sensitivity. Heat dug a needy pit at the base of my stomach and I tried my absolute best to ignore it.

Why are the hot ones always jerks?

"In palmistry mortals usually have four lines on their palms." Orion pointed them out from top to bottom. "Heart, head, life and fate. Fae, however, have a fifth line. A power line." He pressed his thumb to the middle of my palm again and I shifted in my seat as my body reacted much too keenly toward Professor Asshole.

Curiosity got the better of me and I leaned in closer to see the line he was pointing out. It stretched right across my palm and had little prongs running off of it.

"Most Fae have shorter lines here." He rolled his own hand over, showing me his palm and I noticed that on his wrist he had the triangular symbol of air tattooed there. "Mine extends two thirds of the way. Yours, however, is a complete line." He gave me a once over and I sensed he was somehow angry about that, but I couldn't understand why.

"The strength of each particular Element is defined by these intersecting lines." He plucked a small ruler off of his desk and laid it on my palm.

He fell into a rhythm as he noted down the length of each line, working across my palm. The brush of his rough fingers and the repetitive movements were making me heady and I tried to focus on anything else in the room besides his touch.

Orion eventually released me and a breath of relief passed my lips. He started jotting down numbers on his pad, totalling up those he'd written down, doing some complicated calculations. Finally, he had four numbers underlined at the bottom of the page: Seven, eight, nine and ten.

"These are your power rankings." His eyes were dark as he pushed the numbers in front of me. "Ten is the strongest you can be in any Element. To put it in perspective, Miss Vega, even a seven is considered high."

I stared at the numbers in awe, unable to believe what he was saying. That I was this powerful in a world that had been a mystery to me forever. "Your weakest Element is fire, although I use the word *weak* very loosely. You're an eight in earth, a nine in water and a ten in air."

A breath got trapped in my lungs as I glanced up at him, trying to comprehend all of this. "And we're this powerful because...our parents were royal? The king and queen?" It sounded so mad coming from my own tongue. But that was what everyone kept telling us. That we were essentially princesses.

"Yes. Your father was the most powerful Fae in Solaria. He held three Elements: fire, water and air. Your mother had just one Element: air. She was a Gemini like you and was named the most beautiful woman in Solaria. That was after he returned with her from a faraway land his army had invaded. King Vega married her, disregarding tradition. The powerful families tend to breed with their own kind; it keeps bloodlines pure and usually produces offspring of the same Orders. The purer the line, the more powerful their magic."

"And not doing that is...bad?" I asked, trying to understand.

"No, just foolish. Their children are more likely to be weaker but...that is clearly not the case with you and your sister. Your mother and father have produced two of the most powerful Fae to ever walk in our world." He leaned back in his chair, swilling the amber nectar in his glass.

"What were they?" I breathed, wishing I had someone more reassuring to discuss this with but he was all I had. "What were their Orders?"

For a moment, I was almost certain an ounce of pity entered his eyes but it fizzled away just as fast. "Your mother was a Harpy and your father was a Hydra."

My skin prickled at the mention of a Hydra. My Greek mythology knowledge came pretty much entirely from Disney's Hercules, but that serpentine beast had stuck in my mind.

"Hydra?" I whispered, my blood chilling. "Like the monster with multiple heads?"

Oh God please don't let me be one of them.

"Yes," he said quietly. "They are one of the rarest Orders in the world."

I took a slow breath as I tried to process it all. "So what do you think me and Tory are, sir?" I asked, nervous of the answer.

He drummed his fingers on the desk then swallowed the last of his drink. "Trouble," he muttered and I stiffened.

"That's not fair. It's not like we asked for this."

"What's not fair, Miss Vega, is that you and your sister now have a stronger claim to the throne of Solaria than the four Celestial Heirs who have been training their entire lives to rule." He slammed his empty glass down on the table and a jolt went through me. "When your parents died, the Celestial Council claimed the right to rule together. But now you have returned, it is our law that you be placed upon the throne if you can prove yourselves strong enough to claim it. Which is just our damn luck." He pinned me in place with a knife-sharp stare and my heart fluttered madly at his words. "Do you have any idea of the dangerous times we're living in, *Blue*?" he demanded and heat scolded my neck as he eyed my hair with disdain.

"No, but maybe if you'd tell me-"

"Tell you what? Even if I relayed the entire history of Solaria to you, do you really think that would be enough?" He released a dry laugh. "The world has already fallen out of balance and now you and your sister have shown up to tip the scales even further into chaos. Whole families are turning up dead. Powerful ones too. Your parents were the first but not the last and it's only a matter of time before-" He halted himself mid-sentence, seeming to think better of finishing his line of thought.

"Are you saying my birth parents were murdered?" I asked in horror, the knowledge dripping through me like melting ice.

"I'm not saying anything." He cleared his throat, pouring himself another glass of bourbon.

It might have been a Monday night but if it was loosening his tongue, I sure as hell wasn't going to remind him of that.

"Anyway," he grunted. "Your Order will emerge sooner or later. Your power source will give you a clue as to what you are so pay attention. Different Orders' magic is replenished in specific ways. A Werewolf draws their power from the moon, a Medusa draws from mirrors, and if you hadn't guessed it yet, a Vampire draws powers from others through their blood." He flashed his fangs at me and I shuddered.

"Well I'm definitely not like you," I said coldly and his brows pinched for a moment.

He glanced down at his Atlas, his lips tight as he tapped something on it. "If your magic swells try to focus on what is in your immediate vicinity that you could be drawing power from. It could be the sun, the shade, a goddamn rainbow for all you know, just keep your mind sharp. In the meantime, I'll sign you up to all of the Order Enhancement classes. Those who develop late tend to evolve under the influence of their kind."

A notification pinged on my Atlas and I took it out, finding I'd been enrolled in several more lessons on my timetable. And tomorrow I was due to hang out with the Werewolves. My stomach dipped as I thought of Seth and his touchy-feely ways. That wasn't like me at all. There was no way I was one of them.

I looked up, preparing to tell Orion that but the glacial look on his face stopped me.

"You and your sister won't pass The Reckoning," he said if he was stating the truth. "The world doesn't need two ignorant girls in power right now. And as much as most of the Celestial Heirs piss me off to no end, they at least know how to deal with the Nymph population."

"Nymphs?" I questioned, trying to ignore his insulting tone and latching onto the nugget of knowledge.

He cursed, pushing the glass of bourbon away from him. "They're another race, don't worry about it. You'll be long gone before they become relevant to your life."

I folded my arms, growing tired of his tone. "Professor, I know you think I'm useless because I don't know anything about magic or Fae, but I'm not stupid. I can learn. Isn't that what these classes are supposed to be for? Guiding me? Catching me up on everything I've missed out on? So at least give me the chance to prove myself." I wasn't quite sure where the determination had come from, but being dismissed so easily just rubbed me the wrong way. It wasn't like I thought I was fit to run a kingdom I'd never even heard of until two days ago, but I at least wanted to be given a chance to learn about my supposed birthright.

His brows arched and a soft smile brushed over his mouth. "I suppose that's only fair, Miss Vega. And as a Libra, I'm a sucker for fairness," he said and my mouth parted in surprise.

So he is *the Libra my horoscope mentioned this morning. And apparently being fair didn't extend to being nice.*

He glanced at a large brass clock on the wall. "We›re almost out of time and I have somewhere to be." He rose from his seat. "I›ll send reading materials on Coercion to your Atlas. You will have a lesson with me every Monday evening. I expect you to have a basic grasp on shields by our next one. There *will* be a test." He smirked and I suspected he was the kind of teacher who loved springing pop quizzes on his students.

I got up, lifting my chin as I internally accepted the challenge with all my heart. "I plan on getting an A."

I headed to the door and he whipped across the space in double the speed. My heart rushed at the sudden display of his powers.

He wrenched the door open. "I don't do grades. With me, it's always pass or fail." He snatched my Atlas from my hand, tapping something on it and signing off my lesson with the digital pen. He passed it back then held the door wider and I moved to step through it, surprised by the gentlemanly act.

In a surge of movement he passed me by and the door swung closed in my face.

Oh.

TORY

CHAPTER TEN

An irritating kind of jingling noise called me from my sleep and I pushed myself upright with a jerk of surprise as I frowned around at the unfamiliar surroundings. I'd been awake late again talking to Darcy about the screwed up family history lecture she'd been given by Orion and trying to figure out how the hell I should feel about all of it.

I kicked off my red duvet, scrubbing the sleep from my eyes as I glanced at my dorm. It was going to take a while to start thinking of this place as home. Even longer to stop expecting Darcy's smiley face first thing each day.

At least I don't have to endure the cheeriness of a morning person while I drag myself out of my sleep-induced coma.

Though as that thought passed through my mind, I realised I actually missed her incessant morning chatter and whistling. Well, maybe not the whistling. But I definitely missed the mug of coffee she always offered to tempt me from my pit.

The jingling started up again and I located my Atlas, flicking the screen to shut the alarm off. No way that was staying. I needed something with a much lower pitch to rouse me, especially if I was supposed to be waking up at - I checked the time - *six thirty??*

"What, the actual, *fuck*?" I cursed. I only ever saw that time of day if I still happened to be awake from the night before. I never made it out of bed before eight and even that was being generous. Nine was more my style. Ten my preference. Eleven a luxury I afforded for myself most weekends... *well shit.*

Yesterday I'd been too tired to check the time when the alarm had woken me and now I knew why.

I stepped out of my single bed, which I'd quickly come to realise was the most comfortable bed I'd ever slept in, and ran my fingers through my long hair to tease out the worst of the tangles.

My bare feet met with gloriously warm tiles which were heated from beneath. Everything in Ignis house was kept warm by the fire that gave it its name and I sure as hell had no complaints about that. The apartment we'd left behind in one of the shittiest parts of Chicago had no heating and a window which let in way more than a little draft. I hadn't been looking forward to surviving winter in that place and even if the only good thing about this whole magical academy business turned out to be this bedroom it still made it worth staying put.

The plaid pyjamas I wore were not to my taste in any way and I plucked at the flannelette material, adding a mental note to my slowly increasing shopping list. Bikini, pyjamas, boots, underwear that was anything other than the Bridget Jones specials they'd given me alongside the matching breast-flattening crop tops which apparently served as bras. And as if the design of the underwear wasn't disgusting enough they'd decided to go for nude as the colour of choice. I mean, was there a woman alive whose skin was actually that god-awful shade of anaemic peach? Because it sure as hell didn't come close to matching my bronze skin tone and the effect of it against my flesh was really quite gross looking.

I needed to have a word with someone about that promised stipend and a trip to the local mall ASAP. Not that I had any immediate plans to be flaunting my underwear at anyone but you never knew when a hot guy might present himself. And so long as he wasn't of the over-privileged, self-indulging, sadistic, devastatingly attractive Heir variety, I could be tempted.

Luckily, whoever had gathered toiletries for me hadn't had such horrifying taste as the underwear selector, who I could only imagine was a seventy year old virgin nun. I'd even been provided with a makeup bag stuffed full of more cosmetics than I ever could have afforded before I came here. Not to say that my own collection hadn't been as impressive - makeup was one of the simplest things to claim a five finger discount on at the local store. But it was a novelty to be given a collection that had actually been paid for.

I made quick work of applying my war paint, ready to face whatever today had in store for me from behind the safety of a generous supply of eyeliner and a sweep of plumb lipstick.

A single chime sounded on the Atlas and I glanced at it as a message flashed up.

Your daily horoscope is waiting for you, Tory!

Just what I've been waiting for - a vague set of sentences which might just relate to my day if I skew the meaning to fit whatever random things actually occur.

Good morning Gemini!
The stars have spoken about your day.
Today, you may find yourself on a collision course with a Sagittarius. Though this altercation may bring you peace of mind for a while, try not to forget the true obstacles in your way.

Today could well send you spiralling down various paths so be sure that each decision you make is one you want to stick with.
Whatever stance you choose to take today will set the dice rolling and take the control out of your hands.

I rolled my eyes as I tossed my Atlas aside dismissively but it instantly started up its merry tune again. I grabbed it, jabbing it vaguely in an effort to shut it up permanently. *That's a strong hell no to your jingly morning bullshit.* My efforts were rewarded as it fell quiet but I also somehow managed to open the FaeBook app.

I hadn't really given it a look yet aside from a quick glance when Diego had told us about it. Social media participation insinuated the user had a social life and as of yet I could claim no such thing here at Zodiac Academy. Aside from Darcy I'd only really had semi-decent interactions with a few students and we certainly hadn't made it to the pouting for the camera, taking a selfie stage of our relationship yet. Not that I'd ever really been the type for that anyway.

I gave the newsfeed a quick scroll and my heart leapt as I spotted a picture of my bare ass as I stood in the middle of the common room after Darius's initiation prank. I guessed it would have been too much to hope that no one had thought to snap a pic while I was exposed like that but I'd spent every second since my exposure trying to pretend it had never happened and being confronted by it again made my pulse quicken.

There were three hundred and fourteen reactions and ninety-five comments and the post had only gone live an hour ago. I glanced at the name of the student who'd posted it. Milton Hubert. The name meant nothing to me. My finger hovered over the comments tab. I knew I shouldn't tap it. It was better off not to know. *Just close the page and forget it even exists.* I tapped it. *Idiot.*

Milton Hubert:

Things got hotttttt during the Ignis hazing! #wouldntsayno

Comments:

Marguerite Helebor:

Looks like the unwanted Heirs are already learning their place at the bottom of the pecking order. #whoresgohairless

Damian Evergile:

Are you saying you're a hairless whore or are you hiding a full bush beneath that pleated skirt, Margeurite?

Marguerite Helebor:

As if you'd ever get beneath my skirt to find out, Damian Douchebag.

Damian Evergile:

Not a whore then. Just sporting a vagina sweater. #muffscruff

Marguerite Helebor:

Shut your face Damian! #basicbastard

Terrance Bonnerville:

If both Vega girls look that good naked then I've just found my latest fantasy threesome. #idtaketwofortheteam

Barry Gurra:

Nice on Damian!

Tyler Corbin:

Next time he'll get her on her knees too. #gaggingonit

My lips parted in a mixture of disgust and outrage as I read through more of the comments discussing me like I was a piece of meat. There were plenty of scathing and mocking responses from girls as well as the many, many lewd comments from the male students. There was more than one mention of a threesome including me and Darcy which made my lip curl back. Why did guys think that would be hot? If I told them to start making out with their sibling they'd be disgusted but because we were twins that somehow made that twisted idea of a fantasy okay?

I was a little surprised to see that none of the Heirs had commented, though I noticed Darius had given a laughing reaction to the comment about getting me on my knees. I guessed they thought they were above adding comments to other people's posts.

My fingers poised above the comment bar as I tried to figure out whether or not I should respond. I knew deep down that anything I said would only stoke the flames but sitting back and taking this crap was just so not me...

Before I could make the decision, the post and all of the comments that went along with it suddenly disappeared. A message flashed up in its place and relief spilled through me.

FaeBook Admin:
Students are reminded that this social media site is not intended for sharing pornography.
Milton Hubert you have been docked ten house points for Ignis. In future, please share naked photographs privately and not on the public page.

I blinked at the message. Ten house points? That was all the teachers were going to take from the boy who had posted a naked photograph of me for the whole school to see? And there was no mention of punishing Darius for the hazing. That was it. In fact, as I read it again, I realised they weren't even telling him not to share that photograph - just to do it via personal message.

Screw that.

I grabbed my uniform out of the closet, pulling it on as fast as I could before jamming my books into my satchel. I picked up the Atlas again and tapped on Milton Hubert's profile picture so that I could get a look at him. He was a jock type, well built with a prominent brow and thick eyebrows that almost ran into each other.

I shoved the Atlas into my bag and headed out of my room before marching straight downstairs towards the common area.

No one noticed me as I arrived and my gaze was snagged by a large group in the centre of the room. Darius was leaning back in an armchair beside the fire which apparently never went out. His black hair was dishevelled in an I-just-rolled-out-of-bed way that should have made him look like shit like it did for the rest of the population but instead made him look hot as hell. If he wasn't such a grade-A asshole I would totally be okay with waking up to his bed hair. But as he was, the sight of it just pissed me off more. An ugly soul deserved to be housed in an ugly vessel.

A girl with vivid, blood red hair and legs that went on for days dropped into his lap and claimed his attention with a kiss that crossed the line from uncomfortable into inappropriate as she began dry humping him in front of the whole room.

Ergh.

I quickly scanned the faces of his fan club while they still hadn't noticed me and a savage smile pulled at my lips as I spotted Milton Hubert to the left of the group.

I knew I had very little chance of matching anyone in this room in a straight fight but with my anger burning hot and fast in my veins, I could feel my power raising its head like a prowling beast readying to strike. And with the element of surprise coupled with the raw brutality of my power, I was hoping to teach this douchebag a lesson.

As luck would have it, his Atlas was sitting on the table beside him which meant that photo was within reach too.

Magic flared inside me as I strode into the room and I felt Darius's posse turning their attention my way but I didn't spare them an ounce of attention. My gaze was set on Milton Hubert and his monobrow raised in surprise as he realised it.

"Oh hey, it's Tory, right?" he asked but he'd forfeited the chance for an introduction when he'd plastered a naked a picture of me all over the internet.

My magic rose to my fingertips and I grinned as I realised I'd summoned water. Of course I had, what better way to punish a fire-hungry masochist than by giving him an ice cold shower?

I raised my hand and a torrent of water slammed into him, knocking him flying back off of his chair and crashing to the floor. I increased the pressure of the water bursting from me, rolling him across the wooden floor and pinning him to the wall.

The rest of Darius's crew all leapt up in shock and the redhead practically fell out of his lap as Darius stood too. But to my surprise, no one stepped in to intervene on Milton's behalf. I guessed their screwed up Fae way of doing things meant that these kinds of disagreements were handled personally and I tried not to show my relief at that fact.

Milton was shouting something between gargling on the water which pummelled his face and I lowered the deluge a fraction so that it slammed into his chest instead, making sure I pinned his arms down so that he couldn't aim any magic back at me.

"Delete the picture," I snarled, grabbing his Atlas and holding it out towards him with the hand that wasn't directing my magic.

The power inside me purred with satisfaction and I couldn't deny the swell of pride that came with holding my own like this.

"Piss off," Milton snapped.

With a flick of my fingers, I switched the water for air and Milton was lifted and slammed against the wall upright by a gust of wind so powerful that even his bushy eyebrows were fluttering in it. I wasn't subtle, I was just using the full force of my power to immobilise him but that was fine by me. It got the job done.

I stalked forward and jammed his thumb down on the Atlas to unlock it before quickly opening up his photo album and locating the picture of me. There were actually over twenty of them, though he'd chosen the clearest one to share on FaeBook and luckily for me, his position in the room had only offered him a view of the rear. I deleted all of them, double checking the trash folder before tossing his Atlas at his feet.

I released my magic and he stumbled forward, raising a hand at me. Before he could recover enough to attack me, I threw my power at him again, this time summoning earth though I hadn't planned it. Milton was wrapped tightly in vines which sprang to life as my rage channelled itself into the shape that came most naturally. I didn't know what I was doing but my magic seemed to. The vines pinned his arms to his sides and encircled his mouth to make sure he stayed quiet. Milton fell to the ground with a resounding crash and I finally let my magic fall still. The swell of it within me felt a little less full than it had but I still had plenty to go around.

"You need to learn to respect women," I snarled, resisting the urge to kick him while he was down.

I turned and headed for the exit but Darius's voice halted me.

"He sent me copies of those photos, you know," he said calmly.

I turned to look at him, my teeth clenching as I forced myself to meet his dark gaze.

He didn't make any move against me and I wasn't foolish enough to attempt anything myself. I may have just taken down Milton but I knew full well that without the element of surprise, I couldn't have done it. And Darius was an entirely different kind of beast. I knew my chances against him ranked at less than zero even if I snuck up on him while he was blind drunk and fast asleep.

"Teach her a lesson, baby," the redhead cooed and I offered her a moment of my attention. Suddenly her face clicked together with a trout-pout picture I'd seen on FaeBook as I trawled through my most vocal haters and tried to put names to faces.

"You're Marguerite right?" I asked, my face making it clear that her angular features and pouting lips weren't going to intimidate me. "Or do you go by muff scruff now?"

More than one of the onlookers laughed in response to that and for half a second I thought that Darius had to suppress a smile too. But as my gaze fixed on him again I was sure I'd imagined it. There was nothing in his expression beyond a bored kind of loathing.

Marguerite's eyes flared with rage and she made a move towards me but Darius flicked a hand at her, making her back down like a little whipped puppy. How pathetic. She needed daddy's permission to play with me and he wasn't giving it.

"So are you going to try and make me delete my copies?" Darius pressed, holding his Atlas out as if he were offering it to me.

My heart thumped steadily in my chest and I let out a breath before replying.

"Keep them," I said dismissively. "If you're that desperate for material to jerk off to then be my guest."

"As if he'd be turned on by pictures of you!" Marguerite spat as Darius scowled, clearly irritated that I wasn't going to try and reclaim them. At this point they were probably all over the school anyway. Anyone could have saved copies and I'd punished the guy responsible for distributing them. There was no point in me trying to hunt down each and every copy so I was just going to have to make my peace with the fact that those images were out there.

"Don't worry, Marguerite," I said soothingly. "It's not your fault that he needs them to get his motor going. I'm sure your hairy bush does it for him once you start bouncing about on his lap."

Marguerite looked about ready to scratch my eyes out but Darius still hadn't given her permission to act. "You jumped-up, two cent alley-whore!" Marguerite screeched at me but Darius cut across her before she could go on with what was shaping up to be a beautiful rendition of mean-girl hysteria.

Top marks for making more friends, Tory.

"I can have any girl I like. Why would I be interested in looking at images of *you*?" Darius growled, his deep tone sending a shiver down my spine.

I raised my hands in mock surrender. "Hey dude, you're the one with naked photos of *me*, not the other way around. And you can't have *any* girl you like. Because that's a hard no from me. But you may as well enjoy the fantasy you're creating with those images because I can assure you that you've got zero chance of getting your hands on the real thing."

A couple of the guys sniggered in amusement before quickly schooling their expressions.

Darius's lips pressed into a thin line and I backed out of the room before he decided to burn my clothes off again or humiliate me in some other way. *Did I actually manage to get the last word there?*

I ran down the steps with a smile tugging at my mouth and headed straight out into the sunshine before heading for The Orb where I was set to meet Darcy for breakfast.

When I arrived in the huge bronze dome, I looked around until I spotted my sister sitting at a table slap bang in the middle of the room. It was to the left of the huge fire pit while the Heir's favourite red couch sat to its right. For a moment I wondered why the hell she'd chosen that spot then noticed the tall A.S.S. girl sitting beside her.

Darcy smiled knowingly as she noticed me, her usual morning perkiness a welcome reminder of all the breakfasts we'd always shared. She beckoned me over to join her and I navigated the sprawling layout of couches and tables which filled the circular space.

Sofia and Diego sat with her, the latter wearing his trademark beanie hat and I couldn't help but wonder why he was allowed to couple it with the preppy uniform.

The A.S.S. girl perked up as she spotted me coming and suddenly I was surrounded by a flurry of scraping chairs as people at all of the surrounding tables scrambled to their feet.

I fell still behind the chair across from my sister, frowning at the group of around thirty students who now all stood staring at me.

None of them seemed inclined to do anything other than stare and I slowly sank into my chair, looking to Darcy for an explanation.

As soon as my ass hit the seat, the onlookers all sat down again too.

"What the-"

"I'm Geraldine Grus," the tall girl gushed, lowering her head as she reached for my hand across the table. "And I am so delighted to meet you Queen Roxanya!"

I withdrew my hand before she could claim it. "Oh hell no," I began but she cut me off again.

"The Almighty Sovereign Society just want to make sure that you are afforded the proper respect and courtesy as you navigate your return to the Fae world," she explained, her voice prim and proper despite her muscular build which could give a lot of men a run for their money. "If you need anything at all, you need only ask."

"Right." I offered her a tight lipped smile before raising an eyebrow at Darcy.

My sister smirked knowingly before pushing a plate she had filled for me across the table. It was piled high with croissants and fruit and I reached for it with a groan of longing. I decided I'd ignore our current company in favour of demolishing my food.

"I dunno if I tell you often enough how much I love you, Darcy," I said.

She smirked, pushing a mug of coffee my way too and I descended on it, sighing in total bliss.

"You know you make sex noises over your food, right?" Sofia teased.

"No I don't," I countered as I placed my mug down and lifted a pastry to my mouth. "I'm a lot louder than that in bed."

Diego spluttered on his coffee, hacking his guts up as Darcy laughed. Geraldine seemed caught between looking scandalised and smiling but my opinion of her went up a notch when she released a snigger.

"Too much information, Tory," Diego said in disgust once he'd recovered and I laughed.

"I could put that information to the test if you like?" a voice came from behind me and Sofia looked over my shoulder with wide eyes.

Before I could turn to face him, Caleb's hand landed on my shoulder, his fingertips walking up my neck.

I jerked away from him, facing him with a scowl.

"Let me guess, the leech is here for breakfast too?" I snarled, trying to front him out despite the trickle of fear that his touch elicited. A rustle of tension went through the A.S.S. crowd around me but they seemed unsure about getting involved with the Heir.

"Tempting." Caleb brushed my hair over my shoulder delicately and I pointedly ignored the shiver which danced over my skin as his fingertips caressed me.

He leaned down and I refused to flinch away as his lips brushed my neck and he inhaled deeply. There was no point in me trying to fight him off despite how much I wanted to, he'd only pin me to the ground in front of everyone again. As I'd turned this situation over in my mind last night, I'd come to the decision to weather his attacks with as much dignity as I could muster. I'd put up with him biting me until I could figure out how to stop him for myself. Until then, running or trying to fight him off only made me look stupid.

"But I'm still full from yesterday," he breathed before placing a kiss against my skin. I flinched at the weirdly intimate gesture and turned to glare at him as he stayed put in the space three inches away.

"If you're not after my blood then why are you still here?" I asked icily, pinning his dark blue eyes with mine.

"I just didn't want you to think I'd forgotten you," he purred, patting my neck like I was a good pet. "Keep it warm for me. I'll leave you outcasts to your meal."

Caleb walked away and we released a collective breath of relief.

"I half expected him to flip the breakfast table up or something," Darcy muttered as we watched Caleb weaving his way between the crowded space. Everyone moved aside for him. Some people even bowed their heads in deference. What the hell was up with that?

"I don't think that's his style," I grumbled. "He just wants us to be afraid of him. To remind us that we're at his mercy."

"Well let's hope we get the opportunity to give his toothbrush the Pete treatment," Darcy suggested and I snorted a laugh.

"What does that mean?" Diego questioned. Him and Sofia had practically shrunk into the shadows when the Terra Heir had arrived but I could hardly blame them. I wouldn't have chosen to be on his radar either given the choice.

"I'd just like to give it a dip in the toilet, that's all." Darcy shrugged innocently.

Sofia opened her mouth, seeming unsure whether to laugh while Diego gave a bark of laughter before quickly checking around to see if anyone had overheard.

We demolished our breakfast like a pack of starving beasts and I couldn't help but feel happy about the food in this place. Months of surviving on essential items and basic meals had left a lot to be desired and the cooking in The Orb was exceptional. If I didn't watch out I knew I'd be gaining weight pretty quickly.

When the bell sounded to tell us to get to our first class of the day, Darcy and I said goodbye to our new friends and the A.S.S. and headed towards our first

Water Elemental lesson.

Geraldine had told us she'd be in our class, but luckily for us she'd forgotten something in her room so we wouldn't have to walk there with her.

After Darcy's run-in with the Heirs last night, I could tell she wasn't looking forward to taking a class with some of them present but there wasn't much we could do about it. And at least this time we'd be facing them together.

We followed the directions on Darcy's Atlas which led us to the west of the grounds. We began to follow a winding stream before crossing over a stone bridge into an area filled with burbling brooks, ponds and swaying reeds. The path weaved between the various water sources and the sound of dripping and gurgling filled the air alongside a heavy layer of moisture which misted against my skin.

We passed by Aqua House on the lake and I eyed the floating island made up of glass pods with interest. There was a symbol above the entrance stopping anyone without the Element of water from entering but that wouldn't keep us out. The urge to explore the building filled me and I filed it away for a later expedition.

The path drew us on, passing over more bridges with iron railings and moss clinging to the stonework.

At the end of the trail, we found ourselves looking at a waterfall which fell over a tumbling rock face. The path disappeared beneath it and I glanced at Darcy in confusion.

"Is this some kind of mistake?" she muttered, looking at the map on her Atlas again. A flashing star indicated that we were standing right outside our classroom but there was nothing here aside from the waterfall.

"Come along girls, no time to dilly-dally. The rest of your class have already headed in," a deep voice came from behind us and I turned to find a man striding towards us. Although 'man' wasn't exactly the right word to describe him. He only wore a pair of super small black shorts to cover his junk and every inch of his exposed, muscular body was covered in iridescent blue scales.

He stepped towards us, placing a hand on each of our shoulders as he looked down at us. "I'm Professor Washer," he said kindly. "Are you worried about the class today?"

"I am a little," I admitted, immediately wondering why I'd been so forthright with this stranger. The place where his skin met with mine beneath the fabric of my uniform felt warm and oddly comforting and it tingled a little at my admission.

"And how are you girls settling in? I heard the other Heirs have been giving you a bit of a hard time?" he said, concern lacing his voice.

I was so surprised to hear one of the teachers acknowledge the awful behaviour of the other students that I didn't even know how to respond but Darcy beat me to it anyway.

"They're horrible," she admitted, her voice catching a little. "It's so much to take in, we've been ripped out of the life we've known and we're struggling to figure this place out and fit in. And then on top of that to have to deal with the four of *them*..." Darcy trailed off, looking like she was going to cry and I felt tears spring to my eyes too.

"There, there," Professor Washer said as he pulled us both into a hug.

It should have felt weird to embrace a teacher who was wearing skin tight, tiny trunks and had scales covering his flesh but it was oddly comforting.

I pressed my cheek to his bare chest as I exhaled deeply, letting go of a whole host of the anguish which had been building up inside me since our arrival.

I could feel a strange tugging sensation in my chest, kind of like I was using my power reserves somehow but that didn't make any sense.

Darcy squeezed Professor Washer tightly beside me and I smiled at her tear-stained face as she glanced at me.

A bark of laughter pulled me to my senses and Professor Washer released us with a smirk. Max Rigel was looking at us with a highly amused expression on his face and my cheeks flushed with embarrassment as I realised he'd just seen us cuddling our nearly nude teacher. *What the hell just got into us?* To make matters worse, Darius Acrux sauntered up behind him, his face falling into an amused grin as his gaze turned our way.

"Thanks for that girls," Professor Washer said, his voice a little mocking. "Anytime you need a shoulder to cry on, you can come my way."

I frowned in confusion as the sense of safety and warmth from his embrace abandoned me and I suddenly realised that I'd been hugging a half naked stranger in the middle of the path.

"What was that?" I demanded, feeling sure that we'd just fallen prey to something but unsure what.

The Professor only chuckled, parting the waterfall with a wave of magic as he headed beneath it, leaving us alone with Max and Darius.

"You two really don't know anything about our world, do you?" Darius asked, his disgust at that fact clear. "How can you expect to rule over a people you know nothing about?"

I frowned at Darcy in confusion. All this talk of Heirs and birthrights and claiming power was great but no one had actually asked us what *we* wanted to do.

"The Professor is a Siren like me," Max explained in a tone which suggested he was talking to a pair of children. "We draw energy from our hosts by feeding on their emotions. So I wouldn't go feeling all mushy over him caring about you. He just drained a shit-load of your power while you cried your little eyes out for him."

"You steal people's energy by sucking out their pain?" Darcy asked.

I hugged my arms to my chest feeling slightly violated by what had just happened to us.

"Any emotion will do it so long as we're maintaining physical contact." He stepped forward suddenly and I tensed as he reached out to grasp Darcy's arm. She tried to jerk back but he held her firmly. "*I* quite like the taste of fear," Max said darkly as my sister's eyes flickered uncertainly.

"Get off of her," I demanded but he ignored me, shifting his grip on her so that his hand brushed across her chest for a moment.

"Lust will get the job done too," he added with a smirk.

"In your dreams," Darcy snapped, batting his hand away.

The two Heirs started laughing as they turned away from us, heading into the space beneath the waterfall, parting the gush of water with their magic just as Washer had.

"Well that's screwed up," Darcy muttered, rubbing her hands over her arms as if she was still trying to banish the feeling of our Professor's embrace.

We stepped towards the waterfall and I raised my hands hopefully, trying to make the water part at my command. For a moment nothing happened then suddenly a spray of water slammed into us. I squealed in surprise, jumping back as I stopped trying to harness the magic.

The waterfall resumed its normal course and I turned to Darcy, laughing as I noticed how drenched she was.

"Well at least I'm making a habit of this," she said ruefully. "Maybe I'll make it my signature look."

"It definitely makes for a change," I agreed, swiping my wet hair back out of my eyes.

"Shall we just run through as we're already soaked?" she suggested.

"May as well," I agreed, offering her my hand.

She took it with a grin and we ran beneath the water together, screaming as we were doused with the freezing flow. We emerged in a cave on the other side and I released my hold on Darcy as we headed for the patch of light at the far end of it.

Professor Washer was waiting for us as we squelched out of the cave in our soaking uniforms. "Minus five points for Ignis and Aer for failing to navigate the waterfall. It'll be the same every time you two fail to make it to my class dry. Although those transparent shirts will give the boys a thing or two to look at..."

I arched an eyebrow at him. Turned out Mr Touchy-Feely wasn't one for genuine emotional connections. He'd taken what he wanted from us and fallen straight into pervy douchebag mode. It kinda reminded me of a few guys I'd dated who seemed great all the time that they were trying to get in my pants and then turned out to be straight-up assholes come sunrise. *Note to self, no more emotional donations to Siren Dickwad.*

"Are you staring at me for a reason?" he asked. "Because if you want another cuddle I'm up for it."

"Ergh, no thanks," I said, not bothering to hide my disgust as Darcy recoiled beside me.

Washer's mouth fell into a thin line. "Well then, if you're not changed and in the pool in three minutes that'll be five more points off each."

We hurried past him, entering a door to his left which led to the female locker room. A couple of girls were leaving as we entered and I upped my pace as I realised we were the last ones.

Once again bags hung on the hooks with our training outfits awaiting us and I quickly shed my saturated uniform for a deep blue bathing suit with the Aqua symbol emblazoned across the midriff. It had a plunging neckline which showed off way more cleavage than seemed appropriate for lessons and rode high over my hips as well as revealing a good chunk of my ass.

"Do you think the Professor chose this uniform?" Darcy asked, wrinkling her nose in disgust as she attempted to cover her chest with her hair.

"I think I've worn bikinis with more material," I agreed.

"Thirty seconds!" Washer's voice came from outside and we ran from the locker room before he could dock us any more points.

I slowed as we emerged outside. The 'pool' was in fact a huge area filled with crystal blue water interspersed with caves, islands, bridges and even slides. It looked like something from a luxury holiday brochure and yet seemed weirdly natural too, the banks lined with bright green plants and trees swaying around the outskirts.

Professor Washer was standing in the water, his blue scales glimmering wetly as it lapped around his shins. The freshmen were lined up along a sandy shore before him and we hurried to join them as he began to speak.

On the far side of the pool, the older students were practicing wielding their water magic and I watched them firing bursts of liquid at each other and creating shapes which danced across the surface.

Geraldine spotted us and bowed so low that her face ended up underwater. I wasn't sure whether to laugh or cringe and I quickly gave my attention back to the Professor.

"Today we are going to focus on building your understanding of our Element," Washer was saying. "In many ways, water is the most unpredictable and changeable of all the Elements. When subjected to different temperatures it can range from solid to liquid to gas and each of these forms can be used in multiple ways." He began to explain the various ways that those forms could be put to use but my attention was snared by two figures who were scaling a cliff face at the rear of the pool.

The cliff was sheer and rocky and I couldn't quite work out how they were managing to climb it. I nudged Darcy to point them out to her too and a slight frown pulled at her face as we watched Max and Darius make it to the top. Even from this distance I could tell that their bathing suits left as much to the imagination as ours did and the tight shorts clung to their flesh in an indecent way which gave my imagination plenty of ideas. *Ideas based on a fantasy of them having decent personalities and not being utterly abhorrent.*

They stood at the top of the cliff and started wrestling with each other. My heart skittered at the idea of them fighting so close to the edge and I couldn't tear my gaze away as I waited to see what would happen.

"They're going to fall," Darcy breathed.

"Maybe they'll do us a favour and hurt themselves badly enough to be forced to leave the Academy," I joked.

As we watched, Max managed to get the upper hand, slamming his shoulder into Darius's stomach and making him stumble back. He lost his footing on the cliff edge and fell, his arms cartwheeling and a whoop of laughter leaving his lips. He somehow managed to flip himself around so that he hit the water feet first, disappearing beneath the surface with a huge splash.

A second later, Max took a running jump and dove from the cliff too. He entered the water like an Olympic diver, barely raising a ripple and I couldn't help but be a little impressed.

My attention was snagged by the freshman class as they began to move into the shallow water and my sister and I hurried to follow.

It was surprisingly warm and I smiled as I waded out, running my fingertips across the surface as my power called to the liquid that surrounded me.

I wasn't sure what exactly we were supposed to be doing after I'd let my attention waver but I was more than ready to begin.

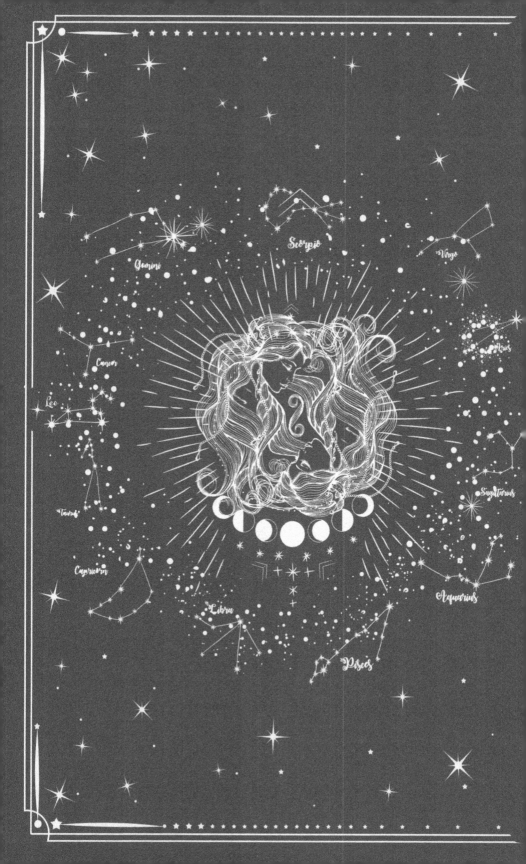

DARCY

CHAPTER ELEVEN

Ting-aling-aling.

    I rolled over with a wide yawn, reaching for my Atlas with a sleepy smile. Birds were singing beyond the window, the bed seemed to hug every inch of my body and the morning was calling to me.

    I clicked on my horoscope with fascination. My last two had been damn accurate and this time I wanted to try and look out for the warning signs. If they could help me avoid another run-in with the Heirs, then I had to try and read between the lines.

Good morning Gemini!
The stars have spoken about your day.
With the world falling into chaos around you, you will have to remain vigilant and let the steady path of the sun keep your grounded. It may seem like a lot to take in, but you're doing better than you think.
With the world falling into chaos around you, you will have to remain vigilant

and let the steady path of the sun keep your grounded. It may seem like a lot
to take in, but you're doing better than you think.
Be wary of those around you. Even the friendliest of dogs can bite.

I read it over a couple of times then checked my timetable. I had Order Enhancement with the Werewolves today. One guess who I needed to be concerned about biting me...

I got out of bed, taking a shower and dressing in my uniform for the day. When I returned to my bedroom a clamour of voices and pounding footsteps carried from out in the tower.

I slung my satchel over my shoulder then caught sight of the sketches I'd done last night on my desk. They were just of the grounds and buildings in Zodiac but I was always overly self-conscious about my art. Even *I* felt uncomfortable looking at them. I stuffed them in a drawer and headed out of my room, locking it quickly before walking onto the stairway.

Students were running about, many looking tense, others chattering excitedly. They were all heading downstairs as if they'd just departed from something important in the common room. Curiosity got the better of me and I headed up, despite the fact that I always avoided hanging out up there. Since the photo of me looking like I'd lost an argument with a sewer had gone viral, I was trying to make myself as invisible as possible to the four walking-talking six-packs who ran this school. But I didn't want to hide forever.

When I arrived in the circular room of grey stone, filled with cream couches and armchairs, my eyes fell on a large screen on one wall. A news reporter with long dark hair was relaying an event which had happened yesterday evening in a town called Tucana.

"-the body was discovered by a student at Zodiac Academy whose name is being kept anonymous. Just this morning, the head of the Fae Investigation Bureau has confirmed that the culprit of the murder was a Nymph who is currently still at large. The residents of Tucana should be extra vigilant during dark hours and report any sightings of the creature to the FIB. The Fae who was killed has been named as Ferris Pike and held two Elements: fire and earth-" The television went blank and I frowned, my heart hammering as Seth stood up from the ring of chairs before it. Kylie jumped up beside him as he tossed the remote on his seat.

He had a taut look on his face and as Kylie tried to take his hand, he shook her off. He jogged through the room, barely sparing me a glance as he disappeared out into the stairwell with intention in his stride.

Kylie tossed her sunbeam hair over her shoulder, moving to join a couple of the girls from Aer. "Who cares about some old dead man anyway?" she moaned to her friend, flicking open a compact to check her doll-faced reflection.

Someone touched my arm and I jolted back to my own space, turning to find Diego there. He gave me a terse smile.

"Did you hear?" he asked.

"Yes but..." I bit my lip guiltily. "What's a Nymph?"

He blew out a breath of laughter, glancing over my shoulder at Kylie and her gang of preening barbies before drawing me toward the exit.

He didn't answer until we were walking down the stairs, away from prying ears. "Nymphs are another race. They live in the shadows of Fae. They're our enemies."

"Why?" I whispered, sensing this conversation needed a quiet voice.

"Because..." He glanced over his shoulder then linked his arm through mine to draw me nearer. "Nymphs aren't born with Elemental powers. But if they kill a Fae, they absorb all of their magic. Every last drop and then they can use it against us." His eyes glowed at me, unblinking as he delivered this news.

"That's..." I didn't have the words so I just shook my head.

"Yeah." He nodded. "Sick. And it means the Nymphs are always a danger. They hunger for magic even more than a Vampire does. And do you know how they take it?"

My mouth became parched as I shook my head.

"They have the gift of the shadows, able to drain a Fae of its power. They do it using these probes...their fingernails grow all long and drive right into the hearts of Fae and suck out all of their power." Diego seemed to have a morbid fascination with the idea of it but it just made me sick to the stomach.

"That woman on the news said a student found the body," I said in horror.

Diego nodded slowly. "Yeah, they won't say who though. My guess is they're having their memory removed right about now. Who could forget a sight like that, you know? It would totally mess you up."

"Memory removal is a thing?" I hissed, my chest tightening at the idea.

Diego glanced around again, lowering his voice even further. "Not exactly. It's advanced Coercion. Forcing the Fae to forget. It's completely illegal, but there's a lot of conspiracy theories about the FIB which say they do it on the sly."

"And you believe them?" I guessed.

He grinned at me. "If you knew the dodgy stuff that went on in law enforcement, you'd believe it too. And not just the FIB, Darcy, this very school. There's even rumours about some of the faculty practicing dark magic on the sly."

My mind spun as we stepped out of the tower and the sun shone down on us, the air cool and the clouds sparse.

"Have you got tarot this morning?" Diego asked, changing the subject as we made our way to The Orb for breakfast.

I nodded, my gaze snagging on Seth up ahead. His band of followers were around him, brushing their hands over his back and nuzzling him – what was with the nuzzling?! - but he barely responded.

As we arrived at The Orb, he headed away from them, making a beeline for Darius, Max and Caleb who were already on their usual couch, surrounded by a ring of excited fans who were running back and forth from the canteen to bring them food and coffee. The Heirs barely took any notice of them, the four of them falling into a tense conversation the second Seth joined them.

"Darcy?" Diego nudged me and I dragged my gaze away from them. "You coming?" He pointed over at our new spot at the heart of the room. Geraldine had laid a wide spread of food across the circular table which looked fit for King Arthur and his Knights. I fought a groan at the sight of the Almighty Sovereign Society gathered there. Tory was actively trying to avoid a conversation with them by engaging Sofia in never-ending chitchat.

I nodded, following Diego over to join them and the guy sitting beside Tory leapt out of his seat and bowed low. "I kept it warm for you, your majesty."

"Right, thanks," I said, smiling as I tried to hide my discomfort at his display.

Geraldine swooped on me before my ass touched the chair. "The croissants were going cold so I had another batch sent from the kitchen." She wafted a mound of them under my nose and the sweet, mouthwatering scent was too good to pass up.

I took one with a word of thanks and Geraldine hurried around to her seat opposite my sister and I. Diego had forced a chair in beside Sofia but his shoulder was firmly squashed up a brutish girl in the A.S.S who seemed intent on remaining where she was. He stole a croissant from Geraldine's stash while she was talking to a girl beside her in hushed whispers.

"Did you hear about the Nymph attack?" Sofia asked, her eyes bulging as she leaned forward to look at me across the table.

"Yeah," I said, glancing at Tory. "And have you noticed how weird the Heirs are acting this morning?"

"*Everyone's* upset," Sofia said.

Tory glanced over her shoulder at the four guys, her brows pulling together. "No, Darcy's right. Something's going on with them."

"They're Heirs," Diego said through a mouthful of croissant. "They have to take an interest in Nymph murders, it's their job. Or at least, it will be when they rule."

Sofia sounded her agreement and I nodded, figuring that made sense but wondering if that meant Tory and I would be expected to take an interest in them too.

The tension in the room was at an all time high as people discussed the mystery student who'd discovered the body.

The girl Geraldine was speaking to seemed to be getting herself in a complete state over the attack. "It's happening all over again just like-"

"Shh!" Geraldine hissed, casting a look at us. She forced a laugh when I caught her eye then snatched her friend's arm and dragged her away from the table.

"What was that about?" Tory asked me and I shook my head in confusion.

"Hey Vegas!"

We both looked up and I spotted the fire asshole with the unibrow, Milton Hubert, standing on a table surrounded by a group students, gazing at him excitedly. "*Make out with each other.*"

His Coercion slammed into me and I shrieked in horror as Tory and I angled toward each other. Diego sprang from his chair, forcing himself between us before we even got close to committing the vile act.

"For the Queens!" Geraldine sprang out of the crowd, launched herself onto a chair and propelled a rocket of water at Milton so quickly he wasn't remotely ready for the impact. He flew halfway across the room and slammed into a group of freshmen, taking several of them to the floor.

The Coercion ebbed out of my body as laughter rang through the room. I shuddered, pulling back from Diego. "We've got to stop this from happening," I groaned as Tory fixed Milton with a death glare as he walked sullenly back to his friends, dripping wet. The Heirs had barely looked up to acknowledge the drama, still stuck in an intense-looking discussion.

"I'll teach you to shield yourselves," Sofia piped up, her eyes shining. "We'll start tonight and spend every moment we can until you've got it."

"Thank you," Tory sighed and I smiled gratefully at her. Well that was something.

By the time we headed to Tarot Class in Mercury Chambers, my heart was still pounding with all the adrenaline of the morning. It was only a short walk from The Orb and we soon arrived at the ancient-looking building with high walls that were painted with strange murals. One appeared to be a man hanging from a tree, another a jester. We headed into the gloomy interior with faded stone walls, the low lighting giving the place a creepy feeling. A dark stairway led down to another floor and a silver sign directed us that way toward Tarot.

"My grandma was a Tarot reader," Sofia said as we followed the other freshmen down the steep staircase. "She taught me about the cards but I was never that good at it."

"What *are* you good at?" Kylie asked as she shoulder-barged past her, tossing her hair back to slap Sofia in the face.

Tory scowled at the back of Kylie's head as Sofia dipped her head, her cheeks reddening. Diego rested a hand on her back and she glanced at him with a small smile.

I glared after Kylie in anger.

Bitch.

"In you come," a hoarse voice called from up ahead.

A hazy purple light guided us forward and we soon arrived in a vast room that resembled a cellar. A circular wooden table filled nearly the entire space and the centre of it was completely hollow. Within the ring the table created was a tall man with a long grey moustache which hung right down over his chin. His almond eyes swiftly landed on us and a glimmer in his gaze told me he knew exactly who we were. But then again, who didn't?

"Take a seat," he instructed as we filed around the edges of the table and the four of us dropped down to sit together.

"I'm Professor Astrum and today I'll be giving you an introduction to Tarot: the telling of fates through the mystical cards of the stars." He reached into the pocket of his tweed blazer and produced a deck, fanning them out between his fingers with perfect skill.

He threw them into the air, waving his hand so they spread out in a wide circle around him on a mystical wind, the images facing the class. They started spinning in a slow circle and I gazed across each of the cards in fascination.

The Professor spent the first half of the lesson naming each of the twenty one cards and describing their meanings. I had my Atlas propped up on my desk and my notes sprawled around each of the cards' images, enthralled by everything I was learning.

Sofia knew all of them by heart and Astrum called on her more than once to explain the meanings behind each card. She might have thought she sucked at this but it seemed like she was an expert to me. My mind was boggling by the time he finally let us do a prediction. And I couldn't remember which card meant what beyond a few of them.

Astrum passed out decks and split us into pairs. I turned to Tory as she shuffled our deck and laid them in a fan between us as the Professor had instructed.

"That's it, now one of you pick a card and interpret it using your notes," Astrum said, twirling one end of his moustache around his finger.

"Do you wanna go first?" Tory asked and I shrugged, slowly moving my hand above the cards as the Professor had taught us.

When I felt an instinctive tingle in my fingers, I plucked up the card I'd paused above.

I turned it over and Tory leaned in close as we gazed at it. The High Priestess. She was sitting in a golden throne, her body clad in blue robes with a veil over her face.

"What does that one mean?" I asked, thumbing through the notes on my Atlas.

"Err...it means..." Tory scrolled through her own notes.

Sofia pressed against my shoulder, leaning over to look at my card. She gasped sharply and I turned to her in alarm.

"What?" I demanded.

She shook her head apologetically, plucking the card from my hand. "This means someone's being dishonest with you or withholding information." She turned the card over then grabbed my hand, placing it flat against the back of it. "What do you feel?" she whispered, her tone making goosebumps rise on the back of my neck.

"Ummm..." I looked to Tory who was trying not to laugh.

"What do you mean, Sofia?" I hissed, trying to pull my hand away but she was weirdly strong for a beanpole. Several other students were turning to watch and my cheeks flushed with heat.

I glanced at Diego for help but he was gazing glumly at his own card. Death.

"Shut your eyes and feel it," Sofia pressed. "Sometimes the cards can give you a sense of who they're referring to."

I shut my eyes and heard Tory cluck her tongue with disbelief. But I had to have an open mind. With my horoscopes seeming more accurate every day, how could I deny that this was possible too?

I focused on the card, the back of it cool against my heated palm.

Light danced at the edges of my vision and the noise in the room suddenly fell away. Strange whispers replaced the sound of my classmates but I couldn't catch anything they were saying.

My blood turned icily cold as I got the strangest feeling I was being watched. It was like yesterday in The Wailing Wood. Eyes on me. Darkness pressing in. Then fire licked at my feet and closed in all around, burning,

burning, burning-

"Darcy!" Tory shook me and my eyes flew open. She gazed at me in alarm and I found my mouth desperately dry and sweat beading on my brow.

The room had fallen quiet and all eyes were on me. Professor Astrum drew closer. "Did the card show you something, Miss Vega?" His gaze was hopeful.

I nodded, then shook my head. Because it hadn't. Not really. "It was more of a feeling." I shuddered, rubbing my fingers together as warm air tickled my palms.

"What feeling?" Sofia asked, her tone dramatic.

"Just the feeling of being...watched. And then there was fire." I didn't like the attention of the whole room on me and I saw Kylie lean in to her dark-haired friend Jillian beside her, cupping her mouth with her hand as she whispered something. They both fell into silent giggles and my neck grew hot with irritation.

Astrum frowned, directing the other students to get back to work. I was relieved when they all returned to talking with each other and Astrum stepped closer, eyeing my card.

"May I hold your hand a moment, Miss Vega?" He reached out, his fingers long and spindly. I hesitantly took his palm and his eyes fell blank and his shoulders slumped.

The cool clamp of his hand was iron tight and I didn't think I'd be able to pull mine free if I tried. Astrum gasped, releasing me as he stumbled back with a look of horror on his face.

"What is it?" I demanded, not liking how pale he suddenly looked.

He cleared his throat, brushing down his dark robes. He dropped his voice to a deadly whisper, leaning closer. "Beware of your enemies, girl. They are made of fire and shadow." He turned away, moving to help another pair of students while I was left to stew on what he'd said.

"This is all bullshit," Tory said, elbowing me. "Don't look so freaked out, Darcy."

"How can you say that?" I sighed. "After everything we know to be true now." I loved Tory but she was too cynical for her own good sometimes. We were in a classroom for magical lessons, on the grounds of an Academy in a world of Fae and she'd shot magic at one of Darius's cronies just yesterday. But she was still intent on denying the possibility that horoscopes, tarot and any magic beyond the physical could exist too.

"It's fairy tales," she said but she didn't seem as convinced this time. "I can see the fire in my hand, but this is just a card which can be interpreted any way anyone wants to."

"What about the vision I just had, are you denying that happened too?" I arched a brow and she frowned in apology.

"Of course not. Are you alright?" Tory asked more gently and I nodded.

"Just freaked me out a bit," I murmured, burying the sensation deep inside me. I laid the deck out before her with a grin pulling at my mouth. "Alright, your turn. Let's see if this can make you a believer."

She beamed with the challenge, holding her hand above them as Astrum had taught us. A moment later, she picked out a card and turned it over.

The High Priestess glared up at us and my heart jolted at the sight.

"I'm gonna do it again." Tory immediately shoved the card back into the deck, shuffled it several times then laid them out once more. My throat constricted as I watched her run her hands across the pile then pluck out the card on the far left.

She flipped it over and The High Priestess stared back at us. Tory shuddered, placing it down on the desk and pushing it away from her.

"So someone's lying to us," I whispered and Tory nodded, belief filling her eyes as she finally bought into the art of Tarot.

Tory and I headed toward The Howling Meadow, following the directions on my Atlas to our Werewolf Order Enhancement Class. Sofia headed off to join the Pegasus group and Diego had been sent to the Griffins to see if they could bring out his own Order.

As we wound through the path in Air Territory, the scent of the sea washed over us and the crash of waves beyond the eastern cliff soothed my anxiety. The Tarot class had creeped me out, but now I was out of the cold room with the sun shining down on my back, it didn't seem so frightening. More than half the students in Zodiac were probably withholding crap from us. Especially the Heirs who didn't want us anywhere near their precious throne.

As we cut through a corner of The Wailing Wood, we stepped out into the sprawling meadow where we'd had our Awakening. Yellow and purple flowers swayed in a gentle breeze, the grass almost up to our knees as we carved a path through it to where a large group of around a hundred and fifty students were gathered.

Many of them were howling, bouncing up and down on their heels, some tussling in the grass.

"I don't know why we have to do this," Tory said, pursing her lips. "I know I'm not a dog."

I nodded in total agreement.

I am not like Seth.

"Right!" the Professor barked loudly from the centre of the group. The students ringed around her, some jogging on the spot in anticipation.

We hurried to join the group and the Professor beckoned us forward. She had a long black ponytail and a wide smile on her face. She caught us both by the arm, tugging us toward her, her hands immediately sliding into our hair. "These are our new pups, take good care of them. They're trying to work out what Order they are so no shifting too close to them, no biting, no scratching, no being an asshole, alright?"

The class hollered and howled in answer and I spotted Seth amongst them, eyeing us with a devilish expression that made my gut prickle.

"I'm Professor Canis." She leaned in close to Tory, breathing in deeply. "Don't be shy," she said as Tory flinched away.

"I'm not shy, you're just so far beyond my personal boundaries right now I can't even see them anymore." She stepped back and the Professor laughed loudly then pushed us forward to join the group.

"Don't we have like...a lesson plan or something?" I asked her, but she answered by pulling her shirt off.

What the actual crap?

"No plan," she said brightly, her neon pink bra all I could look at in that second. "Just run free."

"Holy shit," Tory breathed as everyone around us started stripping.

"What is happening?" My eyes travelled to Seth as he pulled his shirt over his head and the sun gleamed on the hard muscles of his body. He looked like temptation embodied with his ripped stomach and the sharp V which cut a path beneath his waistband.

Warmth spread through my cheeks as over a hundred students dropped their pants and I shielded my eyes as I saw way too much of my classmates and Professor.

Seth's trousers were hanging open, riding lower over his hips as he cupped his hand around his mouth and started howling to the sky. Every single person in the valley but Tory and I joined the chorus, the noise a cacophony pounding into my skull.

Seth tugged off his pants and boxers, turning away at the last second before we got an unwanted eyeful. Tory started laughing and I looked at her, shaking my head as a bubble of laughter escaped me too.

Seth started running down the hill and one hundred and fifty naked students sped after him. The Heir leapt forward in a sudden movement and his whole body changed as he pounced. White hair spread across his skin, fluffy ears, a brush of a tail and four huge paws hit the ground in his place. My mouth fell open and my pulse quickened at the startling sight.

Behind him everyone was changing too like a ripple effect, all of them turning into enormous wolves, twice the size of any normal beast.

Fear and excitement battered my heart as I watched the incredible display.

The huge mass started splitting off into packs, dividing across the meadow and darting into the trees at the verges. There were only a few white wolves amongst them and Seth was the largest of all the animals, meaning I could keep my eye on him the entire time.

He led a group of nine along the edge of The Wailing Wood, moving like the wind as he circled around, his ears flattened to his head. The ground shook as all ten of the massive beasts bounded our way led by the pure white beast at the front of them.

Tory and I backed up and my hands raised on instinct as I willed power into them but Seth came to a halt before I needed to even attempt to defend myself.

He released a soft whine, moving forward, eye to eye with me with his massive size. He bumped his wet nose against my cheek then did the same to Tory. She tentatively reached out, brushing her fingers over his ears. He nuzzled into her so hard that she fell on her ass and she laughed as I pulled her back up. In that moment, I pushed aside the fact he was an Heir, too fascinated by his beautiful transformation and the inviting look in his wolfish eyes. The magic of this place and the students in it was just too wonderful to ignore. And I longed more than anything to know what my own Order was.

Seth suddenly dropped to the ground, turning his head as he gestured toward his back.

"I think he wants us to get on," I said in alarm.

Tory looked to me with a grin and excitement tore through my body like wildfire.

At least Seth can't talk in this form. So what the hell?

I ran my hand down his velvet soft neck and swung a leg over his shoulders, not placing my weight down until I was sure this was what he meant. When he didn't react I settled into place, wrapping my hands in his fur to try and get a good grip.

Tory moved to get on behind me but another black male dropped down next to Seth and barked at her in encouragement. She bit into her lip as she hurried over and clambered onto his back.

"This is crazy," I laughed as Seth rose beneath me and my belly swooped.

I clung on for dear life as his nose angled toward the trees far across the valley. He threw his head back, howling loud enough to make me wince, then lurched forward in a burst of speed.

I cried out in alarm as the wind tore at my hair and I nearly lost my grip on his silky smooth fur. I clamped my knees tighter around him, slipping back an inch as I clung on for dear life.

Laughter burst from my throat and I whooped as adrenaline bled through me. Seth bounded toward The Wailing Wood, charging into the trees down a long path. He immediately turned off of it into the thicker woodland and I ducked my head in time to avoid the low-hanging branches. The crash of heavy paws sounded behind me and I threw a look over my shoulder, spotting Tory grinning her head off as she clung to the wolf beneath her.

A chorus of howls carried from more packs throughout the forest and my heart raced as one of them charged across our path, making Seth swerve violently to the left.

The trees whipped past me in a blur of green and we were soon so deep in the forest I didn't think I'd ever get out without the wolves' help.

Seth finally slowed, padding down into a clearing where a large pool of shimmering water lay. It was surrounded by tall reeds and shaded by the low-hanging fronds of a willow. The sunlight fell in shafts over the beautiful spot and dust and pollen spiralled within the golden rays.

Seth padded straight into the pool and I gasped as he sank deep into the icy water. I slid off of him and he swam under the surface, disappearing into the depths. A moment later he resurfaced in his human form, smirking at me.

"Did you like riding me?" he asked suggestively.

"I prefer you as a wolf." I splashed him, but a smile tugged at my lips.

Several of the wolves dropped to the ground around the pool, rolling in the dust or resting in the shade. A few of them joined us in the water, changing back into their human forms and baring all to the world. Seth's eyes followed a girl with curves to die for as she swam across the rippling pond. Tory dismounted from her ride and the guy changed back right in front of her, making her bristle as he leaned in too close. She eyed the pool with concern, taking a measured step away from it and my heart went out to her. She hated deep water and even a bunch of handsy naked students weren't going to chase her in here.

I moved to swim back to shore but Seth curled an arm around my waist, tugging me close. I surveyed the water droplets running down his chiselled face, unable to help tracing the angles of his cheeks as I debated whether to run away. His hair was a mane of damp hazel and his eyes were penetratingly dark. I wanted to push him back but something kept me in place as I fell captive to his animalistic aura. There was something about him in that moment that made me feel like I was a part of something. Maybe it was a pack thing. Like he was always trying to bond, but at the same time keeping me under his heel. Perhaps I was a Werewolf after all...

The stressed look I'd seen in his gaze this morning seemed to have dimmed, but he was clearly less on form today. Words rose to my lips and I let them fall free as I hoped the softness I saw in his eyes now would stay a while longer. "You seemed upset this morning," I said, cocking a brow and his eyes narrowed.

"You been spying on me, babe?" His muscular arm folded tighter around me and he dragged me against his hip.

"No," I whispered. "It was plain to see." My knee brushed against his thigh and a deep noise left his throat.

He released a heavy breath. "It's nothing to worry yourself with, Vega." He released me then splashed a wave at me in the same movement.

Bastard!

I spluttered, lurching back as he swam away toward a huge rock jutting up from the middle of the pool. I headed back to shore, rejoining Tory, annoyed with myself that I'd tried to make some effort with him.

"You okay?" I murmured, not wanting to draw attention to the fact Tory wouldn't go anywhere near the deep pond. I didn't want to give wolf boy any more ammo against her.

She nodded, a smile etched into her cheeks that only I had the laser vision to see through.

"There's only one sure way to know if you're a wolf!" Seth's sharp tone sent a tremor through me.

He stood up to his waist at the far edge of the pool, an inch away from giving the whole woodland a glimpse of his magic wand.

"What's that?" Tory called, folding her arms.

"Both of you howl," he commanded, pointing to the sky.

Tory and I shared a glance and we both remained silent.

"Shut your eyes and howl with all your might," Seth commanded, but neither of us were ready to make a fool of ourselves like that.

Shall we dig holes and sniff each other's butts too?

Seth shrugged when we didn't respond. "Fine don't bother. But howling can bring out the change so it's up to you." Seth turned and strode up the bank, his bare ass staring me in the face as he marched out of the water.

Tory sighed. "*One* howl."

Seth didn't answer.

Tory cupped her hands around her mouth and I mimicked her, gazing up at the wide blue sky beyond the treetops.

"A-wooo!" we called together.

Some of the wolves joined in and we continued on despite the fact it felt pretty ridiculous. I didn't sense anything wolfy happening to me so I looked down at Seth who was stood near the edge of the clearing.

"You're not wolves," he growled dismissively. "So you don't run with my pack." He leapt toward the trees and morphed into his beautiful white form once again. My heart stuttered as the rest of the pack tore after him, those in human form shifting into wolves as they charged away into the forest, their pounding footfalls rumbling through the air.

My mouth fell open and my heart stuttered to a halt as they left us in the middle of the The Wailing Wood who knew how far away from the meadow.

"Asshole!" Tory shouted after him as we gathered up our satchels.

I retrieved my Atlas, locating us on the map with a groan. "We're practically off campus."

"Great," Tory sighed as she stalked off ahead of me into the trees. "Just goddamn great."

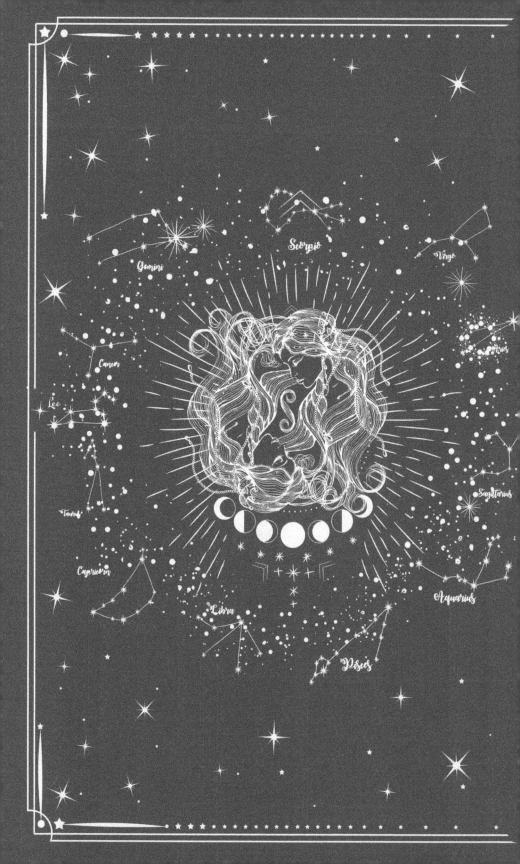

TORY

CHAPTER TWELVE

I sat across from Professor perfect-manicure Prestos who had been assigned as my Liaison while she tap, tap, tapped away on her keyboard. We'd had a thirty-five second conversation during which she had let me know that she intended to conduct this relationship via email after this meeting. She had zero interest in giving up her personal time to me a couple of evenings a week and was confident that sending me worksheets and corresponding online would be more than sufficient to bring me up to speed.

Aside from the fact that I was clearly not invited to spend more time with her than absolutely necessary, she did seem to know what she was talking about and had been forthright, if a little short, with the answers to every question I'd had.

She was currently in the process of sending me at least fifty emails containing information on everything from the history of Changeling Fae to news articles about our birth parents to resisting Coercion and even casting it: If I could learn to Coerce some of the asshole students in retaliation to their efforts against Darcy and me then I was definitely up for that and Prestos had encouraged a fighting back attitude which I appreciated.

From the example sheet she'd given me to peruse while she worked, I got the feeling that this was going to work out well for both of us. Though she clearly didn't want to be directly involved with me more than absolutely necessary she was more than happy for me to contact her with any questions - strictly online - and the information she'd provided was thorough and easy to understand. I just needed to stop by her office every now and then so that she could sign off on our lessons together so that it looked like I'd physically attended. Simple.

She'd even given me a credit card with access to my sizeable stipend, emailed me a map and shuttle bus timetable for the local town and thrown in some advice on the best shops there for free. And judging by her outfit, her advice was well worth taking.

We were going to get on just great.

"Okay then, Tory," she said with a flourish as she hit send. "I'll have a meeting with you after The Reckoning once you earn your official spot in the Academy and we can discuss the new classes which will be added to fill in your timetable then. Other than that, I have a date in town and I'm already running late."

She got to her feet and I followed suit as we moved towards the door.

"Well I hope you make him work for it," I said, eyeing the tight fitting black dress she was wearing with a smirk.

"I always do, don't worry," Prestos replied with a grin before locking her door and strutting away from me in her three inch heels.

Well that was a lot less painful than I expected. What to do with my evening of freedom?

After spending half the afternoon traipsing back through the woods soaking wet and missing most of our following class, I had no desire to face The Orb for the dinner rush where no doubt all of the Heirs would be holding court and laughing about Seth's prank.

I made my way down the steps of Neptune Tower where the brief meeting with Prestos had been held and looked up at the sky where the sun had begun to set. It was just eight-thirty and I wondered if I should try to contact Darcy. We'd had a Coercion practice session with Sofia after our last class of the day and I already felt slightly more confident at fighting it off but now I wasn't sure what to do with myself.

The campus was massive and there were countless places we hadn't seen yet. I opened my satchel to search for my Atlas to call my sister but after a good few minutes of rifling through I had to accept that I'd forgotten it back in my dorm and I gave up with a sigh.

The evening was warm, a breeze filled with the memory of summer washing around me.

I crossed the path which led back towards The Orb and headed the other way, following the curve of the hill into the trees which marked the edge of The Wailing Wood.

I hesitated, after spending so much of the afternoon in those trees I wasn't exactly keen to go in again but if I went the other way I'd have to pass The Orb and all its merry occupants. Where we'd grown up there was very little in the way of forests or any kind of nature at all. It was all stone and steel, urban and boring, the idea of heading into the silence beneath the trees was tempting enough as an alternative to any further interaction with my classmates today.

I glanced over my shoulder, making sure no Heirs or anyone else were coming my way but the path behind me was totally clear.

I moved further into the trees and followed the winding path up a hill which grew steeper the further I went. This would be a good place to run just as soon as I bought some workout clothes with the credit card which was burning a hole in my pocket already. Running always helped me clear my head and I could definitely use a bit of clarity these days. There was a huge leisure centre beside The Orb with every workout machine known to man but the one time

I'd popped my head in there I'd spotted the Heirs lifting weights and decided against it. Besides, I'd always liked running in the fresh air.

As I made it to the top of the hill, I noticed a thin trail which led away into the woodland.

In all of my years in foster care I'd never had the opportunity to spend a lot of time in the great outdoors. And though I was a city girl through and through, the joyful cries of the birds heading to roost filled me such a sense of peace that I found myself wanting to just sit and admire it for a while. Besides, my only other option was returning to my room for the night and it was still so early that that idea was practically tragic.

I stepped off of the path, following the trail until I came to an open patch of ground on the top of a rock face which overlooked the campus below.

The dirt beneath my feet was well trodden and I could tell that this was a spot favoured by other students. There was a ring of tree stumps in the widest part of the clearing which had been set up as a seating area but I ignored them in favour of a more sheltered spot. There was no sign of anyone nearby so I took a seat by an uprooted tree at the far left of the space, away from the well-used area where I could look out over the view with my back pressed to its trunk and just hide from the world for a little while.

The view over the valley was beautiful. It was an endless sea of green treetops with countless birds swooping back and forth. As I watched, a huge eagle burst out of the trees, shooting high into the sky with a cry of triumph. My heart leapt as I realised it wasn't just an eagle - it had the hind legs of a lion which kicked out behind it as its powerful wings lifted it higher and higher into the sky.

My lips parted as I watched the Griffin circling above the forest and my brain struggled to accept the unbelievable sight. I guessed that it must have been one of the students who had shifted into their Order form but learning about such things and seeing them in the flesh were insanely different. That creature defied nature and yet as I watched the movements of its powerful body, I couldn't help but appreciate the beauty of it too.

After around half an hour, the Griffin grew tired of circling the treetops and descended out of sight again. The last rays of the sun sent a glimmer of light dancing from the top of The Orb in the distance and the temperature began to drop.

The sun slowly sank out of sight and I began to wonder if I should leave before the light was stolen entirely and I was forced to navigate the trail out of here in the dark.

I pressed my hands to the cool ground beside me and began to push myself upright just as the sound of laughter reached me.

A shiver raced down my spine as one of the voices was raised above the others in a mockery of a howl. I had the feeling I knew exactly who was heading my way and they were the last people I wanted to meet while I was alone in the woods. I'd presumed that Darcy meeting the four of them here had been an unlucky coincidence but maybe it wasn't. Maybe this was where they liked to hang out, away from all the other students.

I glanced around at the small clearing and shuffled further into the hidden spot behind my fallen tree. Unless they came right around it they wouldn't see me and as much as I hated to hide from a bunch of bullies, I knew that I didn't stand a chance against any of them alone, let alone all four together.

I shifted so that I could peek out into the clearing between the roots of the upturned tree while remaining concealed by it.

"I heard something pretty interesting today, Darius," Seth cooed as he stepped into the clearing, dropping down on a stump which formed part of the circle. He'd tied his long hair in a bun at the nape of his neck and it brought out the angles in his face more noticeably than usual.

"Hang on a second," Max said as he entered the clearing alongside Darius. "If you're going to get emotional over this then I want in on your pain."

"If you must," Darius said, giving a half-assed attempt to seem irritated about it as they took two more of the stumps for themselves and Max threw an arm around his shoulders.

After what he'd told me about Sirens, I guessed he was planning on feeding on Darius's power and I was surprised that the Ignis Heir was allowing such a thing so casually.

"Well," Seth said, pausing dramatically. "I heard that you've promised Marguerite a meeting with your parents the next time they come for a visit."

Darius snorted a laugh as he leaned forward, resting his elbows on his knees and Max was forced to shift with him to maintain the contact between them. "Well she can certainly come up with some creative stories even if she's less imaginative than a potato in the bedroom."

Seth barked a laugh which actually sounded half bark and Max grinned.

"Still all set to marry your cousin then?" Caleb teased as he emerged from the trees, rearranging his fly in a way that made me think he'd just been taking a piss. *Lovely.*

Darius released a noise that was more of a growl than anything else and the others all laughed.

"I'm not marrying my fucking cousin. Besides, she's my second cousin," Darius muttered and it sounded like this was something they'd discussed plenty of times before.

"Okay then, are you all set to marry your *second* cousin? And did she ever manage to get rid of that growth on her face?" Caleb jibed.

"What growth on her face?" Darius asked, his lips twitching with amusement.

"No, Caleb. That growth *is* her face. Remember?" Max said and the three of them fell about laughing while Darius tried to maintain the pissed off vibe for several seconds before caving to the laughter too.

"Ah, your joy tastes so much better than your rage," Max commented with a grin as he tugged Darius closer, pulling him into a headlock.

"I swear on all the stars I've never seen an uglier girl," Darius chuckled as he shoved Max off. The Siren shifted his grip but didn't let go, clearly not done feeding on his emotions yet. "And I'm *not* marrying her. I'd sooner give up my claim."

I couldn't believe they were all sitting around discussing him getting married like it was a genuine possibility in the near future. He was a sophomore for God's sake. Why the hell would his family be trying to marry him off?

"I'd argue with you on that but I've seen her and I think I'd give up my claim to save you from that marriage too," Seth snorted. "So maybe you *will* be presenting Marguerite as an alternative after all?"

Darius rolled his eyes. "No chance of that. Can you really see my father going for a Sphinx as an alternative? They're ten a penny and half useless in combat, plus she's only a level six in fire. No secondary power at all. Besides, I prefer my women to present more of a challenge and she's far too... ordinary to make the cut long term."

As far as I was concerned, Marguerite was a grade-A bitch but I still didn't think it was particularly classy of Darius to be slating her behind her back while he was clearly screwing her.

"I can't feel my left butt cheek," Max complained. "Can one of you make these stumps more comfortable if we're going to be sitting here?"

"Don't look at me," Seth said. "I'm tapped out until the moon rises." He glanced up hopefully but there was no sign of it in the sky. I guessed that meant Werewolves replenished their power beneath the light of the moon.

Max turned his gaze on Caleb hopefully but the Terra Heir shook his head. "No can do, I rinsed my power in training tonight. Unless one of you wants to donate to the cause?"

"Not me," Max said. "I'm still getting my own fix."

Seth shrugged, already having confirmed that he didn't have any to spare and Caleb shifted his gaze to Darius hopefully. It was weird to hear them discussing the idea of this so casually. Caleb usually just took what he wanted but he clearly wouldn't attempt that with his friends. And I didn't think it was because he couldn't manage it. The four Heirs seemed fairly evenly matched and I was sure he'd at least have had a good shot at taking power from one of the others by force as he did to me. No. This was about respect. He cared about his friends and he would only take power from them if they offered.

"I'm already feeding one parasite tonight, you're not seriously going to ask me to feed two are you?" Darius asked. It wasn't a flat out refusal though. I got the feeling he'd give in if Caleb pushed for it which seemed more than strange as it was clear he didn't really want to. I never would have expected Darius Acrux to give in to anyone.

Caleb sighed dramatically as he finally dropped down onto a stump. "I *had* planned on topping up from my Source at dinner but the Vegas never showed."

I smiled to myself, glad that I'd managed to grab an early dinner before my Liaison meeting and avoided that particular run-in.

"You could bite any idiot in the school," Darius said, rolling his eyes. "Why didn't you just get your top-up elsewhere?"

"You know I like my power how I like my spirits," Caleb replied dismissively. "Top shelf or nothing. I enjoy the way Tory tastes, she's got more power in her blood than even you assholes."

The other three shifted uncomfortably at that comment and Caleb shrugged, running a hand through his blonde curls.

"There's no point in denying it," he said. "We all know what their potential is."

"Which is why we need to make sure they fail The Reckoning," Max growled.

A shiver ran down my spine at the malice in his tone. Did they really think Darcy and I wanted their stupid throne so badly? Why hadn't any of them even bothered to talk to us about this instead of just blindly fixating on getting rid of us.

"It's all in hand," Seth shrugged. "We can come up with some more ideas back at King's Hollow. I think tomorrow should be a big day for those twins. And if you wanna come for a run with me at midnight then I'll let you feed on me," he added to Caleb.

"Or you can meet me at Ignis House in the morning and wait outside Tory's room to surprise her," Darius suggested with a smirk and I ground my teeth angrily. "If we get really lucky we might find out that she sleeps naked."

"I'm surprised you haven't found that out already," Max said suggestively and Darius's mouth hooked up into half a smile which made me bristle and flush red at the same time.

"Yeah... I might just take you up on that," Caleb replied, his own smile widening.

"Why don't we all show up," Seth said enthusiastically. "We can give her a wake up call she'll never forget."

Thanks for the heads up, pricks. I know exactly where I won't be tomorrow morning.

"Sounds good to me," Darius said, getting to his feet and knocking Max's arm from his shoulders. "I'm going to head to bed."

"You're not coming to the Hollow?" Max asked, looking disappointed.

"Nah, I'm beat. I'll see all of you in the morning then? Wanna say six? She never gets up early."

Stalker much? Was he really paying that much attention to me?

"Alright, we'll work on something special for our Vega fun," Seth agreed.

He shifted forward and pulled Darius into a hug, brushing his fingers through the back of his dark hair for a moment before heading back out of the clearing. Darius accepted the Werewolf's tactile behaviour with an air of understanding that said he was used to it even if it wasn't the way he'd choose to behave himself. Again, I was surprised that he would alter his natural behaviour to please one of his friends but it was clear that these four were more than willing to adapt their natures to come together as a group. I had assumed their bond came from being in the same position as each other as Heirs but

219

there was more to it than just responsibility and expectation. They seemed almost like family.

Max and Caleb both clapped Darius on the arm before they headed out of the clearing too and Darius hesitated a moment, pulling his Atlas from his pocket as he waited for them to go.

A couple of minutes ticked by as I waited in silence for him to leave and he finally dialled a number on the device in his hand before clipping on an earpiece.

Darius ran his fingers over his jaw as he waited for the call to connect and his brow dipped into a frown.

"Took you long enough," he growled when the person on the other end finally answered. "I need to talk to you in person... No, not tomorrow; *now.* This situation is going on too long, we should have dealt with them by now. I think we need to escalate the plan... Just stop. I'm coming to yours now."

Darius killed the call and got to his feet, the rising moon throwing his features into shadow beneath his scowl. A prickle ran along my spine as I tried to figure out who he'd been talking to and what it was about. He said he wanted 'them' dealt with. Could he have been talking about me and Darcy?

He moved out of the clearing and I slipped from my hiding place, watching as he reached the path. Instead of turning left and heading back towards Ignis House, he turned right and set off at a fast pace.

I crept onto the path behind him, watching his silhouette slip away between the trees. Why had he lied to his friends about what he was doing? And who had he been talking to if it wasn't one of them? If there really was a chance that he was plotting something against me and my sister then I needed to find out what it was. But if he caught me following him then God only knew what he'd do to me.

I hesitated and he moved around a bend, slipping out of view. I made a snap decision which I hoped I wouldn't regret and hurried after him.

I'd been stealing bikes since I was fifteen and one thing I knew how to do better than anything else was move silently and stay hidden in the shadows.

I adopted a careful jog to catch up to him, following the path as he strolled away from me. His long stride and obvious desire to get to his destination meant that he was moving quickly but he also wasn't making any attempt to check for possible tails. Rookie mistake. Rule number one where I came from: always make sure no one is on your ass. Be it a cop or another thief hoping to cash in on your hard work, you can never be too careful about watching your back.

I crept closer, slipping into the cover of the trees once I made it within a few meters of him. I was too exposed on the path should he look back and I had zero interest in incurring the wrath of Darius Acrux.

I'd never been on this side of the campus and had no idea where we were. We were deep into Earth Territory but I couldn't see anything other than trees. It occurred to me that without my Atlas and no other souls in sight I could easily end up lost again in these woods tonight.

I shoved that thought aside and firmly forced it from my thoughts.

It's a bit late to consider that now, Tory.

When he made it to the edge of The Wailing Wood, he hesitated before a wide clearing and I shifted through the trees to try and get a look at what was out there. Darius straightened suddenly, turning to look back into the trees and I flattened myself to a hulking trunk as his gaze swept over my hiding place.

My heart raced but I kept my breaths even. This was where holding my nerve would count the most. When you knew someone had caught on to you your body would always try and urge you into action but the only solution to this situation was complete and utter inaction.

I froze and my magic coiled within me like a living thing as he tried to spot me in the dark. He may have felt my eyes on him but there was no way for him to be sure. Nine times out of ten this was when the mark would dismiss their bad feeling as paranoia and carry on. It was the one out of ten I worried about. Someone with the right instincts would catch me. But I had the feeling that Darius was just arrogant enough to believe that no one would dare to follow him like I was.

But then I'd never been the kind to let fear rule me. Was I afraid? Hell yes. Would I turn back? Hell no.

Darius turned away from the trees and headed out into the clearing beyond. I shifted closer slowly, darting from trunk to trunk and using the deep shadows to hide me.

He crossed a clearing and approached a gated complex of apartments with a wide swimming pool in front of them. A sign had been thrust into the grass a few meters from the edge of the trees and I squinted to read it in the moonlight.

Asteroid Place.

Faculty Accommodation Only.

Strictly no students at any time.

Failure to comply with this rule will result in serious consequences.

My interest piqued as Darius cut through the distance to the complex before heading off around the right hand side of the wrought iron fencing. Whatever he was doing it was shady as shit and it looked like it involved a teacher.

My mind snagged on Professor Prestos in her perfectly presented glory and I wondered if I'd just followed him all the way out here for the sake of some sordid affair. She was definitely attractive enough and if any student was going to catch a teacher's eye it would be Darius Acrux with his unnaturally rugged run-your-hands-all-over-me perfection. Not that I'd noticed.

But as I thought back to the conversation I'd overheard, I knew that that wasn't right. Whoever he was here to meet didn't really want to see him. And their business didn't sound like fun.

I glanced up at the moon, wishing it would take a break from its position in the clear sky above me then darted out into the clearing. I raced to the fence and hurried after Darius as the soft grass bent beneath my feet, muffling my approach.

I kept going, wondering how he planned to get inside the complex before finding out as I reached a patch of the thick fencing which had been melted to create a hole more than wide enough to admit me.

Subtle, Darius.

I slipped inside, carefully avoiding the melted iron which still glowed red with the heat he'd created to destroy it.

For a moment I stalled, unsure of where to go then the sound of angry voices drew me between the houses to my right and around the back of them.

As I drew close, I forced myself to slow, pressing my back to a cold, stone wall as I slid down a narrow alley and took cover behind a low hedge.

"-I told you not to come here!" Orion snarled as he stepped right up into Darius's face and snatched hold of his grey t-shirt, bunching the expensive fabric in his fist. "If someone were to see you-"

"I think you're forgetting who you're talking to, *sir*," Darius snarled, shoving Orion's chest so hard that he stumbled back a step and was forced to release him.

They glared at each other for several seconds as the promise of violence danced on the cool wind before fading away.

"You know how much I care about this," Orion bit out. "I just don't want us to fuck it up when we're so close."

"So why are we waiting? We know where they are. We could go there now and find them while they're sleeping - end this once and for all," Darius pressed, his voice low with anger which seemed ready to burst free at any moment.

"Not yet. If we're wrong we could end up taking innocent lives," Orion insisted. "It's too hard to be sure with the information we have. Just give it a few more days. I'll see her again, I'll confirm our suspicions."

"In a few days they could be even more powerful. You've seen what's happened since the start of term. The longer we give them to adjust to their power, the more chance we have of them figuring out how to harness it and turn it against us. If you're afraid that you aren't up to the job then let me call on the others for help. You know they want to destroy them almost as much as we do."

Orion ran a hand over his face, shaking his head. "It's too risky. Seth can't keep his mouth shut, he'd tell every member of his pack before sunrise and Max's powers soften him to others no matter how much he might deny it's true."

"What about Caleb then? Or is your petty rivalry too keen for you to look past, even with the threat we face here?" Darius demanded. He started pacing and I shrank back as my heart pounded. Were they talking about us? It sure sounded like it but why were they so threatened by two girls who didn't even know how to harness our powers yet?

"It's not about rivalry," Orion spat. "It's about strength. You know him better than me but I'd judge him to be too impulsive for this. If he were to strike too soon then all the work we've done to get to this point will have been for nothing. The same goes for if *we* try to kill them now. While we still aren't sure. What if we fail and they manage to escape us? Or we succeed but we miss something vital and it sets something greater in motion-"

"You've been consulting with those damn bones again," Darius snarled.

"I have," Orion agreed darkly. "And though they aren't revealing many answers to me, one thing is clear. This is *not* our moment."

Darius fell still, releasing a long breath through his nose as he fought to rein in his temper. "Sometimes I wish we didn't live in a world where everything was mapped out for us as if our lives are nothing more than pieces in some greater fucking puzzle and we get no say at all."

Orion sighed, moving closer so that he could place a hand on Darius's shoulder. "Is this about your father? Is he still putting pressure on you to-"

"Of course he is. It's all he ever thinks about. It's like he hasn't even noticed that the world we live in could be teetering on the edge of chaos." Darius shook his head before shrugging Orion's hand off of him. "Don't worry about my father, I'll bear the brunt of his wrath as always. Once the other Heirs and I sort out that situation, he'll back off anyway. You just focus on confirming everything so that we can act."

"I'm meeting with her again in a few days. I'll do a reading. Make sure that we have every piece of the truth," Orion replied with a firm nod.

"And then?" Darius pressed, seeming to need an answer before he'd allow himself to be turned from the path he'd pictured.

"And then... well then we'll do what we have to before anyone finds out it was us."

"Good," Darius replied and his face lit with a smile sharp enough to cut glass.

He didn't bother with farewells before turning and striding away from Orion. My heart leapt as I recoiled further into the shadows but thankfully he chose a different alley and I waited as his footsteps beat a path away from me.

Orion stood there in the moonlight for several seconds, his gaze locked on the alley Darius had taken long beyond the time when he must have moved out of sight.

Eventually he released a curse beneath his breath before turning and marching away too.

I let the minutes tick by as I hid in the shadows. There was only one way back to the Academy from here and I wasn't going to risk bumping into Darius on the way. If he found out that I'd followed him, he'd probably incinerate me on the spot.

By the time I eased out of my hiding place and crept back into the woods, Darius was long gone. I hurried back along the twisting paths as quickly as I could, aiming for my bed and my Atlas so that I could call Darcy. I wasn't sure exactly what I'd just overheard but one thing was clear. Darius and Orion were keeping secrets. And if there was even the slightest chance that they involved my sister and I then I intended to get to the bottom of them.

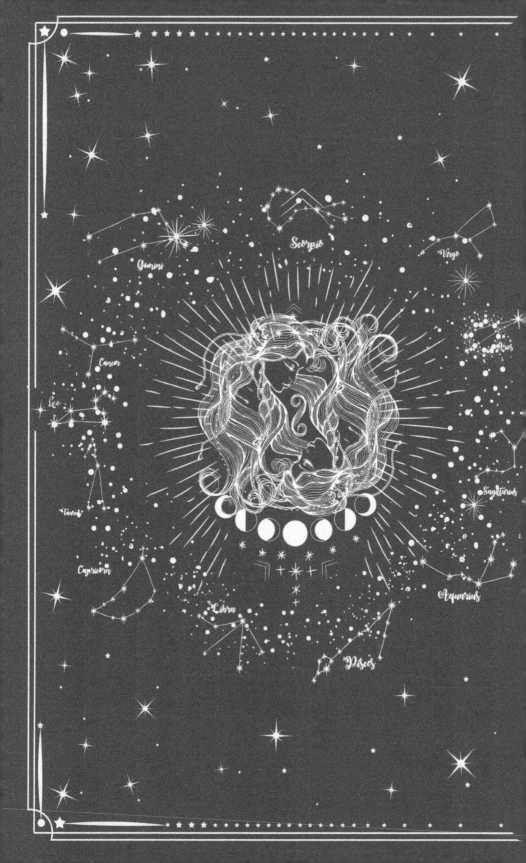

DARCY

CHAPTER TWELVE

I was just drifting off to sleep when my Atlas starting pinging. I took it from the nightstand, finding Tory calling me.

My heart beat harder as I tapped the screen to answer, fearful that something had happened to her.

"Tory, are you alright?" I asked.

"Yeah, I'm good. But can I come stay with you tonight? I heard the Heirs plotting to jump me in the morning and...well there's something we need to talk about too."

"Sure I'll meet you outside Aer Tower," I said, sitting up with a yawn.

"I'm already here," she said with amusement in her tone.

I grinned, springing out of bed as the line cut out. I grabbed my sports sweater and pulled it on, heading quietly out into the corridor. My bare feet grew cold against the hard stone floor and I started tip-toeing to save my heels from its icy touch.

Moving into the stairwell, I hurried down at double speed, the tower achingly quiet around me. I made it to the ground floor, only receiving two glares from a couple of students on their way to bed. *Win!*

I tugged the large iron door open and stepped outside, searching for Tory as the chilly night air blew around me.

"I'm here," she said, stepping out from behind a bush that clung to the wall. She gave me a frown that said something was bothering her. "If Seth catches me, the game's up."

"He won't. Come on." I raised a hand, casting a gust of wind at the Aer symbol above the door to open it again. I led the way inside and Tory kept on my heels as we hurried up the spiralling staircase.

I nearly tripped over a step as I veered into my floor, muttering a curse at myself as I hurried along the corridor to my room. I jammed the key in the lock and a second later we were safely inside.

I gave Tory a triumphant smile but she didn't return it.

"Darcy, something really weird is going on," she said, dropping down to perch on my bed and planting her bag by her feet.

"What do you mean?" I grabbed the desk chair and turned it around to sit before her.

She pulled her hair over one shoulder, knotting her fingers in it. "I followed Darius tonight. He split up from the Heirs and was acting all shady so I went after him. And he led me right to Orion."

"Orion?" I breathed in confusion. "Why?"

"They were hiding something." Tory relayed everything they'd said and my mind snagged on the worst of it all. That it very much sounded like Darius and Orion wanted us dead.

I chewed on my lip as I willed my heart to settle. "Maybe you misunderstood?" I tried and Tory nodded slowly.

"Maybe...but I'm pretty sure."

"Then what do we do?" I asked.

"What about Falling Star?" she suggested. "Didn't they say something about Orion? That he wasn't telling us everything. Maybe they have the answers."

I frowned, my gut knotting. "We don't even know who they are. They could be an Heir messing with us for all we know." I didn't like the idea of placing our trust in some unknown source. "What if we're just playing into the Heirs' hands by responding to that account?"

"Seems like a weird game to play," Tory encouraged. "They haven't exactly said anything to hurt us. Just...confuse us."

I remained quiet, lifting a hand to wrap my hair in my fingers.

Tory's brow wrinkled as she looked to me and a flash of pity entered her gaze. "You don't have to trust them, Darcy. Just see what they say."

I nodded, giving in as I took my Atlas from my bag. I jumped onto the bed with her, sitting cross-legged as I lay the device on my lap.

I brought up the chat window and tapped out our question to Falling Star as my heart hammered violently beneath my ribcage.

Darcy Vega:

You said there were things we didn't know about Orion. Care to explain?

We waited in tense silence and I wondered if we shouldn't expect an answer until tomorrow. It was past midnight and most students were in bed by now.

A moment later, three dots appeared at the bottom of the screen, telling me Falling Star was writing a reply.

I shared an anxious look with Tory as we waited in tense silence and finally the message came through.

Falling Star:

I don't like the company he keeps.

Darcy Vega:

Do you mean Darius?

My heart was fit to burst as we waited on their reply again.

Falling Star:

Yes.

"Holy shit," Tory breathed in my ear.
I tapped out another question, my teeth clenched together.

Darcy Vega:

Do you know what they're up to?

Falling Star:

No.

I sighed, lowering the Atlas when another message came through.

Falling Star:

But I do know this…
Anyone in allegiance with the Acrux family is bad news.
Don't trust them.

Darcy Vega:

But why?

Tory's shoulder pressed against mine as she leaned in closer, both of us
hanging on their reply. I was now convinced this couldn't be the Heirs messing
with us.

The three dots taunted us as we waited with bated breath.

Falling Star:

I believe the House of Acrux was involved in the death of your birth parents.
And I have my suspicions that the other Heirs' families assisted.

I turned to Tory in alarm. "Do you believe this?"

Tory gazed at me, her eyes wide as she thought on it. "I don't know. We don't even know who this Falling Star person is."

"But if they're right and Darius and Orion are coming after us then..." Fear crackled in my chest.

"Then we're so screwed," she whispered.

My Atlas pinged as another message came through.

Falling Star:

I can't share all of the findings through FaeBook. It's not secure.
But read this and I'll be in touch soon.

A link came up beneath their message and I clicked on the site, finding myself looking at what appeared to be a news report printed the day after the deaths of our real parents. Heat rolled down my spine as I started reading it.

King Hail Vega, his wife Merissa and their two children, Roxanya and Gwendalina, were found dead in their palace beds at 7:08 yesterday morning. King Hail, termed The Savage King during his reign, and his two children were the last living heirs to the throne of Solaria. Their deaths have now been declared as murder and the evidence points to a calculated Nymph attack involving two or more of the creatures.

With the kingdom already in turmoil, the four Houses of the Celestial Council

(Acrux, Rigel, Altair and Capella) have stepped up to rule in King Vega's place.

Lord Lionel Acrux was the first on the scene in an effort to help his life-long friend King Vega when a distress call was reportedly sent to him. Unfortunately, his arrival came too late and the Nymphs in question still remain at large. The offending Nymphs now possess the magic of the royal line and are the most powerful and dangerous of their kind ever to have existed. A mass hunt has begun in an effort to destroy the creatures before they have time to harness their newly absorbed powers.

The news has been taken with a mixture of grief and celebration since the reign of King Vega was one of hardship and turmoil. Professor Astrum of Zodiac Academy was quoted as predicting what he termed as 'the bloody decades' through Tarot and star charting before the King's ascension. Though dismissed previously, his words have since been adopted to describe the reign of The Savage King and are now printed on banners across the City of Lunar in protest to the millions of aurums being spent on a funeral organised by the royal supporters.

One lead advocate of King Vega and his family, Hamish Grus, demanded that the throne be handed to the nearest royal bloodline. But with only distant cousins remaining in the Vega family, the four houses of the Celestial Council are in opposition to this proposal. They are currently petitioning for the throne to remain empty until an appropriate ruler can be found. Royal blood or not. In the meantime, the four houses will rule together - a motion which has been greeted with open arms by many in Solaria.

I dragged my eyes from the article with a heavy breath and Tory flopped back onto the bed beside me.

"Falling Star could be right," she said and I nodded.

"The Heirs' families had motive to kill them," I agreed with a sickly taste in my mouth. "But this report says Nymphs did it. And Diego was telling me they do something weird like... stab you in the heart and suck out the magic with their claws."

"Ew," Tory breathed. "There would have been evidence of that."

"Yeah..." I desperately wanted to rule out the possibility that the Heirs' families could have been involved. That one of them was coming after us. And Professor Orion was helping them. Because if it was true, I didn't know how we'd ever escape.

I sat in Cardinal Magic with a tightness in my chest. Orion was late. And I kept glancing at the door, half-expecting him to march in with a machine gun to take out Tory and I.

Stop getting carried away.

Besides, he wouldn't need a machine gun, he could cut you to ribbons with his cheekbones alone - not to mention his fangs...

After everything we'd learned last night, I'd barely gotten any sleep. And I'd been dreading this lesson all morning.

Diego looked between us, his pale blue eyes twinkling with concern. "Everything bien? You guys look like the undead today."

I forced out a laugh but it didn't sound very convincing.

"I missed you last night," Sofia whispered to Tory. "It's not the same in Ignis without you."

Tory gave her an apologetic smile. "The Heirs were out for my blood. I had to lay low."

Sofia sighed, painting a circle on the table with her finger. "I wish they'd back off."

Kylie was parading through the room, handing out bright pink leaflets as she danced between the aisles. "Fresher's party in The Orb next Friday!" she said brightly, arriving at our row.

She clutched the leaflets in her hand as she glanced between Tory and I, her rich amber eyes moving between us like a viper about to strike. "Oh I suppose you guys won't be coming." She waved a leaflet in front of our faces with a mock frown.

"Why?" Sofia took the bait.

"Because no one wants you there," she said with a poison ivy glare and I bristled with unease.

The door swung open and Orion strode in, causing my heart to clench into a hard ball. He took one, sweeping glance at the classroom then at the leaflets in Kylie's grip.

"*No,*" he snarled, waving a hand so every single leaflet in the room swept toward him on a violent breeze then slammed into the trash can beside his desk.

Kylie froze, looking to him in alarm, turning as pale as a sheet. "Sir, I-"

"Miss Major if you ever hand out garbage in my classroom again you'll be banned from attending a single one of this year's formals."

Kylie's mouth dropped open and I couldn't help the little thrill I got at seeing her knocked down several pegs. Even if it was by a potential psycho.

"But sir!" she gasped.

He flicked his hand and the remaining leaflets were snatched from her grip and torn to shreds, cascading over her in a shower of pink confetti.

Oh my God he could probably do that to me if he wanted to.

Then why hasn't he yet?

Laughter rang out around us and a small snort escaped me as Kylie turned bright red and rushed back to her seat.

Orion slammed his coffee cup on the desk and the room fell quiet as he glared across the sea of faces before him. His eyes lingered on me for half a second and I lifted my chin.

You don't scare me.

Except crap, maybe you do.

Orion turned to the board, writing on it with his digital pen.

YOU ARE NOT UNIQUE.

I blew out a breath. *Man* did this guy know how to give a pep talk...

He snapped around to face us, seeming extra pissy today (which was saying something). "Every star sign in the Zodiac holds its own attributes. Good and bad. They can influence your nature. But they do not make you different or special. They make you Fae." He tapped on the board and my Atlas flashed up with the first image in our lesson notes. The Zodiac appeared: a beautiful circle in which all of the star signs interconnected.

"All Fae are a part of this," he continued, his tone suddenly softer. "And we all share two defining celestial beings in common." He pointed at the centre of the Zodiac. "The sun and the moon. They bind us. And no Order, no eyeliner, or blue hair-" he gave me a pointed look as he stepped into the aisles and I pursed my lips. "Or beanie hat." He took a swipe at Diego's hat but he grabbed hold of it, glaring up at Orion in a challenge.

The Professor smirked, "Makes you different," he finished. He headed deeper into the classroom and I kept my eyes on the board as he continued.

"There are twelve signs, I expect even our royal Vega Heirs know what they are. So let's hear them." He was suddenly behind us, a hand on each of our shoulders.

My skin tingled from the imprint of his palm and I refused to turn my head to look at him. "Go ahead, Miss Vega," he commanded.

"Which one?" Tory and I said at the same time.

"Blue." He tapped me on the shoulder. "Vega number two can come with me." He nudged Tory and she rose to her feet with a frown, casting a look my way. I gave her a sympathetic glance as Orion led her to his desk and sat down in his chair. "Palm," he ordered and she hesitantly placed her hand in his. He started doing a reading and I wondered if it was the same one he'd done on me the other night. "I don't hear Zodiac Signs filling my ears."

I ground my teeth at his rude tone and the sound of giggles carrying from Kylie and her friends.

I called out the names to him in a flat tone. "Aquarius, Pisces, Aries, Taurus, Gemini, Cancer, Leo, Virgo, Libra, Scorpio, Sagittarius, Capricorn."

"Good, five points to House Aer," Orion said and I could have sworn my jaw nearly hit the table.

Maybe he's covering his tracks. When they find my mutilated body Kylie will say, "He can't have killed her Principal Nova, he gave her five house points just a few hours ago!"

Orion jotted down notes as he read Tory's palm and she squirmed uncomfortably under his touch. Her posture alone told me how much she hated him.

He finally released her hand and passed her a slip of paper. "These are your Element scores. The higher the number, the stronger your power. Your principal magic is fire."

"Oh...right." She nodded, moving to walk away but he caught her wrist and dragged her forwards.

A wave of horror crashed into my chest as he dug his fangs into her wrist.

She gritted her teeth, sagging forward as he drained her power and stopped her from using her magic to throw him off.

"Oh my God, sir!" Kylie gasped, but he ignored her, continuing to feed from my sister.

"Stop it!" I snapped at him, raising a hand in a wild act as I prepared to slam a blast of air into his face to push him off. Tory threw me a look, shaking her head in warning and I released a noise of distress.

When Orion finally released her, she staggered away from him with a dark expression. He rose to his feet, seeming in a better mood as he continued to chat about star signs.

As Tory walked back to her desk, my attention was snagged by a notification flashing up on her Atlas.

You've been mentioned in a FaeBook post, Tory!

My heart stammered as I clicked on my own Atlas, tapping on the app to find the post. Tory dropped into her seat at the same moment as I found it.

Kylie Major:
Looks like Professor Orion is tapping in to someone else's Source.
#sharingiscaring #hairsgonnacare

Attached to the post was a picture of Orion feeding from Tory's wrist. My sister shot a vicious look at Kylie over her shoulder.

Comments popped up at the bottom of the post and I bit into my lip as I pointed out the top one to Tory.

Comments:
Caleb Altair:
W.T.F???????????????????????????

Ranjeep Shan:
@Calebaltair – this is not okay bro…

Tyler Corbin:
Had a front row seat for it. #Orionwentdeep

Laughter started ringing out in the room and Orion halted mid-sentence as he spotted all of us staring at our Atlases.

He looked like he was about to murder every one of us when the door flew wide open and Caleb sprinted into the room, diving over Orion's desk. He slammed the Professor against the board and a collective inhale sounded around me. My heart took a freedive as Orion shoved him off with a blast of air and Caleb's head slammed into the desk, sending a crack up the middle of the wood.

Caleb snarled like a beast, slashing at Orion's face with a hand full of flames.

"Enough!" Orion bellowed before Caleb could land the strike. The Terra Heir paused and it felt like everyone in the class had turned to stone.

Tension rippled through the air as Caleb extinguished the flames in his palms, a low growl emitting from his throat. "She's my Source. Touch her again and you're dead. Professor or not."

Orion snatched the front of his shirt, pulling him within an inch of his face. "Get out of my classroom."

"Not until you swear it," Caleb spat, wheeling a hand around to point at Tory. "She's mine. Keep your teeth out of her."

"I don't belong to anyone!" Tory snapped and I nodded my agreement.

When Orion didn't respond, Caleb pushed the Professor off of him so hard his back smashed into the board.

Tense mutters broke out in the class and I realised I was clutching the edge of my desk, my knuckles turning white.

"Fine," Orion said in a deadly tone. "But the other Vega Twin is mine."

"Excuse me?" I gasped, but they continued to ignore us.

Caleb grumbled something, starting to stalk back and forth before him like a caged lion. "*Deal*," he finally forced out then marched from the room, slamming the door behind him.

Orion straightened his shirt then turned back to the board. "Aries are ruled by Mars so they can be particularly impulsive and often aggressive when..." He went on and I turned to Tory in absolute shock as Orion continued as if nothing had just happened.

"Don't we get a say in this?" I hissed to my sister.

"Not unless we can fight them off," Tory said, her brow creasing with rage.

"Which you won't be able to do unless you listen in class!" A book slammed into our desk and Tory and I sprang apart to avoid it hitting us. Orion glared at us, the clear perpetrator. "One more word out of either of you and you'll be in detention for the rest of the year."

I pressed my lips together as fury bubbled and steamed inside me.

Is he serious right now?

He stared at us, waiting for either of us to talk back. We remained silent and he returned to teaching.

"When you're Awakened, you will always obtain the Elemental power linked to your star sign. For example, as a water sign, all Pisceans are gifted with the Elemental magic of water. Those who gain more than one Element are usually gifted this way because they are linked to more than one constellation." Orion tapped the board and a chart appeared which showed every constellation in the sky. "As you can see, there are hundreds of combinations. The powers gifted to you by the stars are very elusive. Little is known about how or why some Fae are born with more than one Element. But we do know that genetics play a roll and so does your Order." He gave us a pointed look and I gave him a cold stare back.

You literally just claimed me as your blood bag, you jackass! How can you go on with life as if nothing just happened!?

He approached me with a smile that made my chest hollow out. "Can you name some of the constellations which aren't linked to a Zodiac sign, Miss Vega?"

Why was he always picking on us? There were nearly a hundred people

241

in this class. And he knew for a fact that my sister and I had the least knowledge here out of everyone.

I thought back to my youth, lying under the stars beside Tory. Our foster mother at the time had laid with us, pointing out the few constellations she knew. She'd been a kind woman, but her husband had never wanted us there. In the end, she chose him and we were cast out. *The story of my life.*

One of the constellations had stuck in my mind from those long-ago days. "Um..." I cleared my throat. "The little bear?"

"Correct." He pointed at Diego beside me. "Which is also known as?"

"The little dipper, sir," he supplied.

"I bet Diego's got a Little Dipper," Tyler Corbin snorted from the front row.

"Five points from Terra," Orion snapped at him and Tyler huffed.

"And the Latin name?" Orion pointed at Sofia who turned pink-faced as she answered.

"Ursa Minor?" she squeaked.

"Ten points to House Ignis." Orion strode away and Sofia beamed from ear to ear. I didn't know why she doubted herself so much, she knew more than Tory, Diego and I combined.

Orion started writing on the board again. "So if you are an Aquarius but are also linked to Ursa Minor which has the power of earth, you will possibly be gifted with two Elements."

"Possibly, sir?" a girl with a long braid of raven hair asked from the second row.

"The stars can be unpredictable," Orion explained. "Their nature must compliment ours for everything to align." Orion folded his arms. "So, what does your Zodiac Sign mean for you personally? Does anyone know?"

A few hands rose and he picked out a boy in the row behind us. "It tells you your nature."

"Inaccurate," Orion said. "Try again."

"It er..." the boy glanced around for help but no one had any to offer. He cleared his throat then shrugged.

"Anyone?" Orion asked in annoyance.

"It influences your nature, sir?" Sofia offered.

"Correct," he said brightly, moving to lean back against his desk. He pointed at the dark haired beauty Jillian who was always in Kylie's shadow. "Miss Minor, what are the other three things that influence a Fae's nature?"

She turned the colour of a beetroot, looking to Kylie who sighed dramatically.

"Order," Kylie offered for her.

"And?" Orion pressed.

"Er...genetics?" she guessed.

"Correct. And?" he demanded.

She fell quiet and an answer sprang into my mind, hovering on the tip of my tongue.

"Anyone?" Orion asked, gazing over us all in clear disappointment.

Oh what the hell?

"Life experience, sir?" I'd been through enough in my life to know exactly how shaped I'd been by everything I'd endured. If he disagreed that experiences didn't affect the way we were, then I was ready to dispute it. My hair was one example.

To most, blue meant cold or sad, the sea, the sky. To me, it was something else. And that reason was why I wore it in my hair. As a constant reminder of that meaning. *Don't. Forget.*

"Correct," Orion said, seeming surprised. He strode down the aisle, halting in front of my desk and I raked my eyes up his athletic body to his penetrating eyes. "Also known as?"

"Nurture," I said, my tongue parched.

"Good. See me after class." He marched away, leaving me in the wake of that A-bomb with my heart rattling in my chest.

Tory gave me an alarmed look and an ice-cold creature slithered up my spine.

Crap.

Tory waited until every last person had filed out of the classroom before she left me alone with Orion.

"I'll wait outside," she whispered and I gave her a smile that I hoped soothed her worries as she headed through the door. But it didn't do much to soothe mine.

Orion was gazing at something on his Atlas, resting back in his chair as the door swung closed behind my sister.

I stood awkwardly, adjusting my satchel over my shoulder as I waited for him to explain why he'd kept me back.

"How's the Coercion shield coming?" he asked, not looking up from his Atlas.

"Better. I've been practicing with friends."

He nodded, seeming satisfied with that. "You should be spending every free moment on it." He swung around in his chair, snaring me in his onyx gaze. "It's imperative that you can throw off basic Coercion. Do you understand how vulnerable you are while you're unable to?"

I nodded, thinking of all the embarrassing times I'd succumbed to it in the past couple of days. My insides crumbled into dust at the memories.

"Yes, sir." I surveyed him closely, wondering why he would try to help me out with this if he was plotting to kill Tory and I.

Could be a cover...but for who? There was no one in this room but me.

"Good." His hard mask broke into a soft smile and I was completely taken aback by it. "So, I wanted to be clear about what it means to be my Source."

"I don't want to be your Source," I said immediately, my skin itching at the mere idea of it.

"Until you manage to stop me, I'm afraid that's not your decision." He gave me a bemused look and I scowled at him, tempted to shout, *is it just my magic you want or is it my life too?*

Orion stood, moving around his desk to stand before me. I swallowed against the lump in my throat, gazing up at him and refusing to let him see my fear.

"You will tell me if any other Vampire bites you. That is non-negotiable, Miss Vega. I will make it known to the Academy that you're mine and that should save us any more incidents like today. I am not likely to be challenged by anyone except Caleb, but now that has been settled we should have no more issues. However, if another Vampire happens to take a liking to you ...you *will* tell me."

He didn't Coerce me and I had to wonder why. Maybe he wanted me to agree to this on my own terms. And an internal battle took hold of me as I thought about what he was demanding. At least this would stop other Vampires taking a bite out of me in the corridors. But that was about the only plus side I could see.

"How often do you expect to feed from me?" I folded my arms and his brows lifted.

"Once or twice a week." He shrugged. "But if I become drained then it may be more."

I nodded stiffly, knowing I didn't have a choice anyway. I'd take the small benefit of not being bitten by other Vampires and in the meantime I'd work my ass off to harness my magic.

I lifted my chin and the air became thick between us. "One day, Professor, I'm going to be strong enough to fight you off."

He took a measured breath and I felt like he was sucking something vital out of my body that I wasn't sure I'd ever get back.

"I know," he said, his eyes glittering. "But until that day, you're mine, Blue."

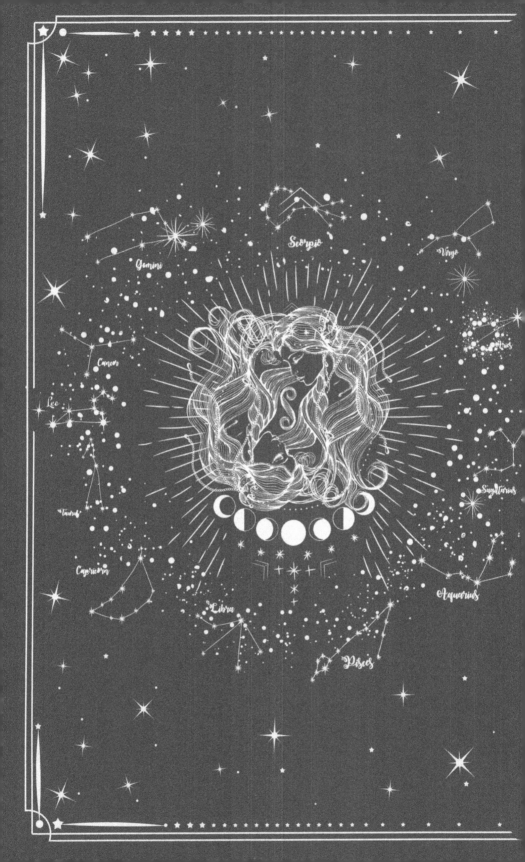

TORY

CHAPTER THIRTEEN

Avoiding the heirs for a whole day had put me in an amazing mood and even after I'd wrenched my ass out of bed at five thirty this morning to make sure I escaped any repeat attempts at whatever hellish wake-up call they'd planned for me, I still felt pretty damn good about it. Of course that was all going to end today because I had my first Earth Elemental lesson this morning and I would have to endure Seth and Caleb's company throughout.

I hadn't actually spoken to Caleb since he'd burst into our Cardinal Magic class yesterday, assaulted my teacher and effectively pissed all over me like he was a dog and I was his favourite lamppost. He'd been angry as all hell and I was more than a little nervous about how that interaction would go when I was forced into his company again today.

I could only hope that being segregated into the freshman training with the Professor would afford me a little bit of safety from the Heirs, but I had resigned myself to the fact that I'd be getting bitten either way.

In the meantime I had an errand to run and avoiding The Orb during the breakfast rush meant that I was at least delaying the inevitable a little longer.

I'd woken up to my usual horoscope nonsense which involved something about invoking the ire of a Taurus and an Aquarius but I'd quickly dismissed that in favour of the much more exciting message beneath it. My online order had arrived which meant I was about to claim a little piece of myself back in the form of clothes. I was beyond sick of spending all of my free time in my uniform or sports kit and I was overdue some outfits which actually reflected who I was.

I made my way to the Pluto Offices where all of the admin clerks who organised the school worked. I guessed students' post was delivered via unicorn farts or whatever their version of a postie was.

The racks and racks of shelves filled with letters and parcels towered to the roof in a room so tall that it must have spanned three floors. I craned my neck, wondering how the hell I was supposed to find my deliveries amongst all of it. There was no labelling system to speak of and the guy on the front desk had been less than helpful, only pointing me toward this room with a single finger and not even bothering to say hi.

"-if you really feel it's necessary then fine. But I assure you I have it all in hand."

I swivelled around at the sound of that voice, cursing my luck as I prepared myself for whatever I'd have to face now. The door swung open and Darius eyed me with a faint glimmer of surprise as he listened to whoever was on the other end of the call he was taking. I hadn't seen him since I'd stalked him in the woods the other night and I had to wonder if I was standing face to face with my potential murderer. My pulse spiked accordingly and I eyed the exit, unsure if I should try to bolt.

"As you wish," he said, his attention on his call but his eyes locked on me. I half considered slipping out of the room while he was occupied but I still hadn't retrieved my parcels and I refused to go running for the hills every time

I was faced with him or one of his friends. "I'll get it done. Is Xavier there?...
Hello?" Darius shot a look at his Atlas before releasing a breath of irritation
and shoving his earpiece into his back pocket. I wondered who had had the
balls to hang up on him and silently applauded them for causing that scowl to
fill his features. Or at least I *did* until I realised it was now firmly directed at
me.

"Just get it over with then," I said with a sigh. There was no point in me
trying to run and my progress with my magic had barely even gotten started so
fighting was out too.

"Is this where you've been hiding then?" he asked, ignoring what I'd
said as he tapped something on his Atlas.

"What do you mean, hiding?" I asked innocently. I hated that I'd been
avoiding them rather than facing them but I hadn't been wasting my time.
I'd devoured everything that Professor Prestos had sent me on Coercion and
Shielding and had been giving every free moment I had to trying to build up
my defences. If there really was a chance that Darius and Orion were after me
and Darcy then I intended to be as prepared as humanly possible to face them.
Though as I stood face to face with the guy I suspected of plotting my murder,
I began to doubt that that was the case. Here I was, alone and at his mercy and
the only thing he'd done was poke fun at me. Hardly seemed like the actions of
a serial killer. But then again maybe trying to off me in the middle of the day
wasn't the smartest move.

"I haven't seen you at the House or The Orb since Tuesday," Darius
replied, his gaze trailing over me suspiciously before he returned his attention
to his Atlas.

"I didn't realise you were so obsessed with me," I quipped. "Am I
expected to run all of my movements past you? Or are you just disappointed
that your cunning plans to surprise me when I woke up yesterday with your
little friends didn't work out?"

Darius's gaze snapped up to mine in surprise and I offered him an insolent smile. "How did you find out about that?" he asked, not even bothering to deny it.

"I'm used to looking out for myself. Not all of us grew up with Daddy's money keeping us safe and warm at night-"

"You don't know shit about my father or the way I grew up," Darius snarled, taking a step towards me.

My heart leapt and I was struck with the desire to run as fast and as far as my legs would take me but I forced myself to hold his eye instead, raising my chin as I looked into his dark eyes.

"Just like you don't know the first thing about *me*," I replied. "I've met much meaner bastards than the four of you before and come out swinging. And I've learned a thing or two about the way basic bastards like you operate; you're not very original. And you don't frighten me," I said, my tone miraculously level despite my thundering heartbeat. I was lying and it was pretty clear we both knew it. Yes I'd dealt with my fair share of dickwads and biker dudes with a superiority complex but I doubted any of them came close to rivalling the Heirs in strength or brutality.

Darius eyed me for another second before releasing a breath of laughter.

"You've got balls, I'll give you that," he muttered, before dropping his eyes to his Atlas and hitting a button on it.

The shelves before us suddenly began to move and I looked around at them in surprise as they shifted left and right, up and down, making way for a compartment which had been near the roof to slide down before us. The movement ground to a halt and Darius stepped forward to claim the contents of the shelf for himself.

He flicked through a handful of envelopes before stuffing them into his blazer pocket.

He turned for the door without bothering to do anything else to me and I counted my blessings that he seemed to be in too much of a hurry to torment me today.

I looked back at the shelves before me, frowning in confusion and pulling my own Atlas from my bag as I tried to figure out how he'd just gotten his deliveries to present themselves.

Darius sighed heavily and pulled my Atlas out of my hands. I looked up at him in shock, reaching forward to snatch it back but he ignored me, pulling up an app on the third page and quickly selecting 'Post Retrieval' from a list of options. He caught my hand and the warmth of his skin surprised me almost as much as the fact that his touch was gentle.

My traitorous heart fluttered at the contact and I tried to stop my eyes from trailing over the strong line of his jaw and the set of his mouth but failed miserably. He was just too damn good to look at.

"It needs a thumb print," he explained in his deep voice as I tried to resist his directions. I relaxed marginally, letting him press my thumb to the screen and the shelves beside us started moving.

Darius released me, tossing my Atlas back to me so that I was forced to catch it before it ended up hitting the floor.

A big compartment stopped before us, stuffed full of bags and boxes containing new clothes for me and Darcy.

"Thanks," I muttered as I pushed my Atlas back into my satchel and stepped forward to claim my hoard.

Darius beat me to it and pulled a box from the top of the pile which was emblazoned with the slogan of a lingerie company.

"Looking to burn even more of my clothes?" I asked, wondering if I was about to watch everything I'd just bought go up in flames.

"I could be persuaded not to," he replied, his mouth hooking up at one corner and making my heart leap. I had no idea what he was going to demand of me but I knew exactly what the answer would be. There was no way I was going to start dancing to his tune.

"Just do what you've gotta do, dude. I can't stop you." I folded my arms and waited him out. I wasn't going to beg.

"You're really sucking the fun out of this, you know that, right?" he asked. "How about you give me a fashion show wearing the contents of this box and I'll let you keep your new wardrobe?"

I rolled my eyes and turned to leave the room, abandoning my new clothes and resigning myself to ordering all of it again. At least our stipend was stupidly generous; I wasn't in danger of running low on funding any time soon.

Darius caught my wrist before I could make it to the exit, tugging me back to face him again. My skin flared beneath his as my heart leapt in either fear or excitement and I wasn't entirely sure which. I yanked my arm out of his grip and he smirked at me.

"Keep your shit, Roxy," he said in a tone that suggested I was boring him. "Ruining your clothes was last week's fun. I can do better than that next time."

He tossed the box of lingerie into my hands before sauntering out of the room like he thought he owned the place.

"Pleasure seeing you as always, asshole!" I called loud enough for it to carry to him before heading back to claim my deliveries.

I stacked my arms up with the various bags and boxes before running them all back to my room. I sent Darcy a quick message, urging her to go on ahead rather than waiting for me. Thanks to Darius, I was running late for my first Earth Elemental lesson and I was going to have to run across campus to reach it, following the directions on my Atlas with one eye while making sure I didn't fall with the other.

I jogged down a path which skirted the edge of The Wailing Wood before swinging a right and heading along the side of a tall rock face covered in vines and moss.

The path finally led me to the mouth of a wide cave which delved beneath the ground and I hesitated a moment before heading inside. Rough steps were hewn into the stone at my feet and I descended quickly, following the tunnel until I reached the bottom. To my right were the locker rooms and I headed on in, finding it full of girls getting changed and a bag of clothes waiting for me again. Irritatingly, it was still labelled Roxanya which instantly made my mind go to Darius's stupid nickname for me. I made a mental note to email Professor Prestos about changing it when I had the chance.

Darcy was waiting on the bench, already dressed for class and I muttered a quick hello to her as I tried to catch my breath after my run to get here.

The Earth class uniform was deep green and consisted of a pair of skin tight shorts and a tank top decorated with the symbol for Earth. The thick heat of the cave was the obvious reason for the thin outfit and I moved towards the exit to discover what this class would entail.

"Freshmen, gather around!" a soft voice called and I moved towards the girls at the far end of the locker room, craning my neck to get a look at our Professor. She was a short woman with a brown pixie cut and wide eyes which made her seem almost fragile, like a child. "I'm Professor Rockford and I'll be instructing you on the use of your Earth Element. For today's class I'm not going to set you up with any specific work. I just want you to explore the cavern and let your magic do whatever comes most naturally. I'll be observing and assessing but there's no right or wrong way to wield the power of Earth. By its very nature, our magic grows like a budding plant, so the best way to learn to wield it is to go with the flow. So head on out when you're ready and let's see what you've got." She smiled encouragingly as she opened the door and I fell in at the back of the group of girls as they made their way into the classroom.

A huge cavern opened up above my head as I stepped out and I couldn't help but stare up at the vaulted ceiling in amazement. Intricate patterns had been carved into every inch of the stone and soft green and yellow orbs of light hung all around the space.

More caverns and tunnels led away from the huge central chamber and I noticed lines of precious metals and gemstones sparkling along the rough walls.

"Wow," Darcy breathed beside me and I turned to her with a grin of my own.

"These people might all be crazy but they sure do know how to make school interesting," I said as we started walking towards the other side of the cave beneath the glow of green lights.

"Holy biscuits! Your majesties!" Geraldine's voice caught my ear and I suppressed a sigh as I turned to face her. She was flanked by six of her A.S.S members who were all giving us that creepy doe-eyed look that they reserved just for us.

As a group they all bowed their heads and I exchanged an uncomfortable glance with Darcy.

"We keep asking you not to do that," Darcy muttered.

"We only want to show our respect to the two true Heirs," Geraldine said proudly, puffing out her chest. Her eyes were rimmed with dark eyeliner which looked suspiciously similar to the way I did mine, though she'd gone a little too heavy on it. And she'd coupled it with a pale pink shade of lipstick like the kind Darcy favoured which didn't really match up.

"Well as your rightful rulers or whatever, we're asking you to stop it," I said firmly, glancing about to see how many people had witnessed their little act of devotion.

A few girls were muttering to each other on the far side of the cavern and shooting glances our way but luckily no one else seemed to be paying us much attention.

"I'm so sorry if we've displeased you, your maj-"

"Don't call me that," I snapped before Geraldine could finish her sentence. I was a foster kid from the rougher part of town. I'd never even had dreams of being a princess like the other little girls who put on Cinderella dresses and plastic tiaras as they pranced around the local mall. My dreams had always contained a lot more grease and oil and an open road leading me to freedom. Even as a little kid I'd been more interested in watching Speedway races than Disney cartoons.

"Right. Sorry your... Tory," she said, lowering her head like I'd whipped her. I knew she was only trying to be nice but I didn't want a fan club.

I glanced at Darcy for help; she was always the more diplomatic one. My mouth ran away from me with all the speed of an ill mannered gazelle. I tended to speak first and think later and I was getting the feeling that brash wasn't the best approach for our fan club.

"We just don't want to be seen any differently to the rest of you," Darcy explained, saving me. "We aren't looking for any followers."

"Oh." Geraldine's face dropped and for a moment I was worried she might burst into tears. Darcy caved to that slapped puppy look and hastily offered an olive branch.

"But maybe we could try being friends?" Darcy said with a warm smile.

If a kid woke up on Christmas Day and found out that Santa had brought them their own personal Disney World resort complete with actual real-life talking bunnies, their face wouldn't have lit up as brightly as Geraldine's did with that suggestion.

"I would be boundlessly honoured to even be considered as a candidate for your friendship!" she gushed, rushing forward to embrace my sister. Darcy patted her on the back a little awkwardly and I failed to stifle a laugh.

"Perfect," I said through a grin. "Now that we're all friends, I'm just going to go for a little explore."

I backed out of the circle as the rest of the group pressed forward to join the hugathon and smirked at Darcy as she remained trapped in the centre of it. She rolled her eyes at me but her face was set with amusement so I knew I'd be forgiven for abandoning her to the masses.

I crossed the cavern and let my magic simmer to the surface of my skin, trying to do as Professor Rockford had suggested and give it the chance to pick what it wanted to become.

One of the side tunnels drew my attention as a sense of warmth emanated from it and I headed inside to explore.

It was darker down here than in the main cavern, the glowing lights reduced to pin pricks of blue which twinkled intermittently along the high roof. I followed the trail, the warmth growing stronger as I went and my magic rose up inside my chest as though it was soaking it in.

A hand landed on my shoulder and I flinched as Seth Capella pushed his face into my hair, inhaling deeply.

"Where have you been hiding, little Vega?" he asked, the arm around me tightening as I tried to push him off.

"I think we've established I'm not of your Order," I growled as I shoved him away more firmly. "So how about you cut the touchy-feely stuff with me?"

"You know, I could take offence to that," he said, catching the hand which I was using to push him back and linking his fingers through mine for a moment. "Order shaming isn't cool."

I extracted my fingers and managed to pull out of his grip as I offered him a scowl in the dim light. "It's not Order shaming. I just prefer to keep my body to myself unless *I'm* the one choosing to share it."

"Is that an offer?" Caleb purred behind me and I didn't quite manage to hide my flinch as his cool fingers brushed down my arm.

"No, it wasn't," I snapped, sidestepping so that I was no longer stuck between the two Heirs.

They moved to stand side by side, Seth brushing his arm against Caleb's as the pair of them towered over me.

"What do you want?" I asked, taking a step back warily.

"We've been looking for you," Seth said. "Poor Caleb has practically starved to death without his little lunchbox on tap. You really should have come begging for his forgiveness after letting Orion put his mouth all over you like that."

"Forgiveness?" I scoffed shifting my gaze to Caleb as he waited expectantly. Did he really think I was going to apologise? "You can be assured that I have zero interest in *any* Vampire feeding from me but if I do decide to let a man put his mouth on me, I won't be asking permission from *you* for it. You don't own me."

"Wrong," Caleb said darkly. "I claimed you. Which makes you mine, we're bonded you and I. It's your responsibility to remind any *lesser* Vampires of that fact if they try to feed from you again. And if you don't want to agree to that then we could always try out the old fashioned way of marking you as my Source."

Seth chuckled as my brow furrowed in confusion. "What's that supposed to mean?"

"Years ago Vampires would mark their Sources with a tattoo right in the centre of their forehead." He reached out to poke me between my eyes and I flinched. "It helped them to avoid little accidents like your run-in with Orion. If I can't trust you to make other Vampires aware of my claim then maybe I should consider it," Caleb said thoughtfully.

"If you come anywhere near me with a needle I'll drive it through your fucking eye," I snarled.

"So can I assume that I have your word to announce my claim to any other Vampires who show an interest?" Caleb pressed, his gaze lighting excitedly.

"Fine. So long as you keep any ideas about permanently marking my body off of the table I'll tell all your little buddies that my blood is spoken for." *At least until I figure out how to fight you off.*

"You do realise that there are a lot of people who would kill for your position, don't you?" Seth asked as he seemed to sense my continued disgust for this situation. "Being the Source of Caleb Altair is an honour."

"Well they're welcome to have it. By all means, find another girl or guy to suck on and I'll be on my way." I made a half-assed attempt to sidestep them but they closed ranks, stopping me.

"I own you. I wanna hear you say it, Tory," Caleb said, his voice rough.

259

"Who do you belong to?"

"Go screw yourself, I don't belong to you." I considered the dark look in his eyes for a moment and decided to throw him a bone in the hopes of saving myself some grief. "But the Tory blood-bar is closed for all other business and I'll pass the message on to any parasites who come my way."

Caleb grinned at me and I sighed as I resigned myself to where this was going.

"Fine. Bite me then if you have to," I said, holding out my wrist with the faint idea that he might take it rather than biting my neck again.

"It's not as much fun if you just accept it willingly," Caleb complained.

"Well why don't you find someone else to suck on if you're looking to get your kicks from fear? And I can assure you I'm *not* willing, I'm just practical. I can't stop you so I just have to endure it."

"You're making it sound so boring," Caleb muttered. "But you are right about one thing. You *can't* stop me."

"Yet," I replied icily and the word hung between the three of us in the silence of the cave for a moment.

"Confident little thing aren't you?" Seth murmured as he took a step towards me.

I held my ground despite the fact that every fibre of my being was urging me to run. The green glow of the central cavern was still visible beyond them and I couldn't help but glance that way, wondering if I could make it back.

"I think this little Vega needs reminding who she's up against," Seth purred, running his hand down Caleb's back.

Caleb's deep blue eyes sparkled with excitement and I half considered yelling for help. Geraldine and the others were still out there with Darcy and the Heirs had waited for me to isolate myself from them before they'd pounced. Perhaps The A.S.S would be able to help me escape this situation but I hesitated before I could form the word. Screaming for help like a damsel in distress was just so not me. I wanted to face off against these assholes and come out on top, I just couldn't figure out how.

Before I could decide on how much my pride meant to me, Caleb shot forward and wrenched me off of my feet. He tossed me over his shoulder like a sack of potatoes and raced further into the tunnel as if I didn't weigh a thing.

I cursed and hit him, trying to make him put me down as he shot along with the unnatural speed of his Order.

We made it into a wide space that glowed with blue and silver light and Caleb came to a halt. I could hear Seth howling with excitement back in the tunnel we'd left behind but Caleb's speed had separated us from him.

Caleb set me on my feet with a boyish grin that almost could have made me believe he wasn't a total bastard. *Ignore the dimples, Tory, he's an award winning dickasaurus.*

"You're stupidly strong," I grumbled as I pushed myself out of his grip and glanced at the cave he'd brought me to. We were standing on a ledge high above a sea of sparkling stalagmites which looked sharp enough to impale anyone unlucky enough to fall the ten meters down onto them. I shifted away from the edge uneasily.

"I am," Caleb agreed, smirking like that was meant to be a compliment. "And that's only my second best attribute."

"What's your best?" I asked automatically, wondering why I was even bothering to get into a conversation with him.

"That would involve us ditching our clothes," he said, his voice dipping in pitch suggestively and making my traitorous blood flare with heat for a moment.

I glanced at his broad shoulders and mischievous eyes for all of half a second before I turned away, refusing to be blinded to his asshole nature by the pretty shell which housed it. *Why do I have such terrible taste in men?*

"Well I won't be putting that claim to the test," I assured him dismissively. "Why have you brought me here?"

"I thought you might like a look at the view," he said, prowling towards me with purpose in his gaze.

I glanced at the dizzying drop of doom beside me and shifted further from it again. "Er, yeah. It's great, thanks. But I really should be getting back to my lesson."

"Don't you want a closer look?" Caleb pressed, closing the distance between us once more.

"I can see it just fine from here," I insisted, trying to keep my tone level.

Running footsteps approached and Seth burst from the tunnel behind us with a howl which echoed off of the cave walls so loudly that I glanced up at the stalactites which hung from the roof with concern.

"Like the view, little Vega?" he asked, shaking his long hair around his head like a dog driving water from its fur.

I looked between the two Heirs for any hint that they might be about to back off but the excitement which danced between them gave me my answer.

"I think she needs a closer look," Seth said, stepping forward.

"Yeah, you can't really appreciate it from way back here," Caleb agreed.

Holy shit on a starfish.

My mind whirled with some way out of this but before I could think of a single thing, Caleb shot towards me, shoving my chest so that I was thrown towards the edge.

I fell backwards, a scream escaping me as the sea of razor sharp rocks winked at me with promises of my death.

Two hands caught mine before I could tumble to my doom and my heart leapt as my sneakers scrambled for purchase on the crumbling lip of the ledge. They didn't pull me up but laughed as I hung at their mercy, my back to the terrifying drop below.

"Pull me up," I demanded but my voice came out like more of a plea as fear sped through me.

They grinned at me with twin smiles of beautiful devils and I clung to their hands with all of my strength as they held me in limbo.

"Solaria has been much better off since the Vegas left the throne to the Celestial Families," Seth growled. "Since our parents took up the throne that yours left cold, our world has been a better place. We don't need you to come back here and claim it for yourselves. We don't want you to."

"We didn't ask for this," I breathed, my heart pounding at the thought of the drop beneath me. "We don't want it. You can keep your stupid throne and your power!"

"That's a beautiful offer, sweetheart, but it doesn't change the facts," Caleb said, his tone suggesting we were having a casual chat and no one was in imminent danger of death. "Your blood-right means the throne belongs to you so long as you prove yourself capable of taking it. And there are enough people who would support your claim to cause a civil war over it."

"But we don't want it!" I spluttered, trying and failing to keep my cool. "How can anyone seriously expect us to rule over a nation we know nothing about? It's insane!"

It could have been the dim light in the chamber but for a moment I could have sworn that Caleb's features softened a little. I hurried to continue while there was a glimmer of hope that he was listening to me.

"Look, all we want is to learn how to control this magic inside us and get our inheritance. That's it. We grew up with no one and nothing. Before we came here we weren't even sure if we were going to be able to keep a roof over our heads for the winter! I swear we have zero interest in claiming any throne or taking your places."

Seth and Caleb exchanged a look but I couldn't read what they meant by it in their expressions.

"I say we drop her," Seth said with a shrug of his powerful shoulder which made me lurch beneath him.

My grip on them tightened with panic and my magic swirled like a tempest within me. But if I wanted to attempt to use it, I was going to have to release my grip to free my hands and there was no way in hell I was taking that risk.

Caleb's lips twitched with amusement and panic engulfed me as I began to wonder if they might truly let me fall. No one had seen them take me down here. They could leave and pretend they'd never seen me, let someone else discover my body dashed to pieces on the rocks below.

But I wasn't going to let them rule my fate like that. I was born a fighter and if there was even the slightest chance that I could get myself out of this then I was going to do it.

I drew on everything I'd learned about Coercion during my practice sessions with Darcy and Sofia. Sure, I'd only managed to execute a handful of simple commands and I'd never even attempted to batter my way past mental defences as strong as the Heirs were sure to have but it was my only shot. And hopefully they wouldn't even be expecting me to try. I took my fear and helplessness and coiled it into a desperate little ball which I imbued with my utter need to escape this situation. The words pressed against my throat, brimming with power just aching to be set free as I opened my mouth.

"Pull me up," I demanded, my tone fierce and imbued with power.

To my complete and utter shock, Caleb and Seth heaved me up over the edge to safety.

Adrenaline coursed through my veins and I scrambled away from them as their faces fell in shock at what I'd just done.

"Shit," Seth muttered, eyeing me like he didn't know whether to attack or retreat.

"I told you how strong they were," Caleb growled, his navy eyes glowing with the new challenge I presented.

"Stay away from me," I said, my tone dark.

They both hesitated, exchanging a loaded look before Caleb's mouth hooked up to one side.

"Nice try sweetheart, but you aren't going to slip past our defences so easily a second time." He shot towards me before I had the chance to respond and his teeth slid into my neck as he drew me against his body.

I tried to pull my magic to me again so that I could fight him off but as soon as he started feeding, I couldn't lay claim to it. I was at his mercy once more but at least I'd managed one act of defiance against them.

Seth moved closer and brushed his fingers against my arm for a moment. As soon as his fingers touched my flesh, a deep growl sounded from the back of Caleb's throat and his grip on me tightened.

My heart leapt and Caleb's fingers knotted in my hair as his other hand gripped my waist, dragging me against the hard lines of his body. My own hands had made it to his arms, the tight press of his biceps unyielding beneath my fingers. It was almost like we were locked in an embrace, if I could just ignore the teeth which were lodged in my throat. Which I really couldn't.

"Sorry," Seth said with a smirk, taking a step back.

Caleb relaxed marginally as he finished feeding on me and finally stepped away.

"Don't touch my Source while I'm feeding," Caleb muttered irritably, shooting a dark glance at Seth.

Seth grinned at the challenge in his tone and I felt like a bone being fought over by a pair of dogs. The idea of it made me grit my teeth in anger.

"I'm still here, assholes," I snapped, though I instantly wondered why I'd thought that drawing their attention back to me was a good idea.

"You know I'm not going to bite her, what's the big deal?" Seth asked innocently, ignoring me.

Caleb flexed his muscles for a moment and I felt like I was looking at the raw essence of their differences. They may have been bonded like family but rubbing along together despite the differences in their Orders was obviously an issue now and then. I wondered if there was any way that I could use that against them but before I could give it any real consideration, Caleb cracked a smile.

"I just don't want your paws all over my food while I eat," he teased, bumping his shoulder against Seth's in a way that was mostly playful but still knocked him back a step.

"Wanna go finish this lesson with a contest?" Seth asked excitedly, his eyes flashing with a challenge.

"Only if you don't mind getting your ass whipped," Caleb countered.

The two of them ran off through the tunnels without even sparing me another glance and I stared after them in surprise as Seth's howls echoed off of the walls around me.

Somehow I'd managed to escape that interaction fairly unscathed and I could only hope that I could say the same next time.

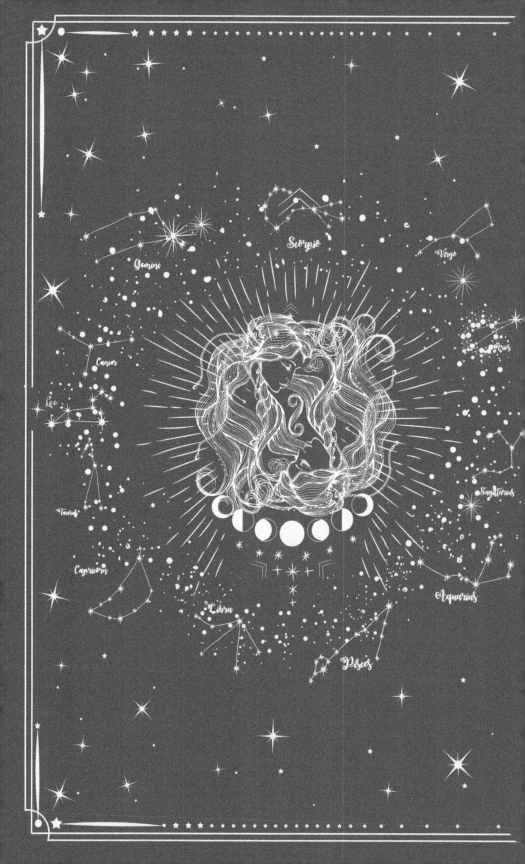

Darcy

CHAPTER FOURTEEN

It was our first Friday night at Zodiac and it felt like the entire school had plans. I watched from my floor-length vertical window in Aer Tower as students wound along the paths, laughing and talking as they headed who-knew-where for the evening. Probably somewhere better than here.

Sofia was sat at my desk re-reading her lesson notes from the day while Diego sat against a wall playing some depressing music on his Atlas. Tory was slumped on the bed, looking as bored as me.

"I wish we could go out," I complained. "I feel like all we ever do is avoid the Heirs."

"Agreed." Tory sat upright with a sigh. "Plus they've probably got better things to be doing on a Friday night than hunting us down so it's not like we have to hide tonight."

"So where can we go?" I pleaded, bouncing on my heels at the idea.

"The Orb?" Sofia suggested, looking up from her Atlas.

Tory threw herself back down on the bed with a dramatic groan in answer.

"We could go off campus?" Diego suggested, killing the morose tune which had made me wanna jump out of the window since he'd started it.

"Off campus?" I asked, my stomach fluttering at the idea.

"How?" Tory demanded, her eyes bright.

"I have a car." Diego shrugged and I jumped up and down.

"Yes! Let's go." I ran forward, grabbing his hand and leaning back as far as I could to make him get up.

He grinned, adjusting his beanie hat as I released his hand. His unusually blue eyes glinted with excitement. "I'll go get the keys."

"Give us like....half an hour?" Tory said, springing to her feet and hounding toward Sofia. She pulled her dark blonde hair away from her shoulders and grinned conspiratorially. "Make-over time."

"What?" Sofia squeaked.

I beamed, moving to the wardrobe where the beautiful clothes Tory had ordered me were hanging.

I tossed out some jeans and tops as Diego shook his head at us and opened the door. "You'd better mean half an hour and not two hours."

We were so excited to go, we were knocking on Diego's door twenty minutes later. Tory and I both wore jeans and heels – hers were way higher than mine. I was as clumsy as a brick but the occasion called for the slingbacks and besides, it felt like summer had returned for one last evening before fall and I wanted to go all out for it. The floaty black cami I wore and lacy bralette felt so good after a week in uniform.

Tory's deep blue cami was low cut and she had a grin on her face that said she was in party mode. Sofia was smiling from ear to ear, her slim figure looking incredible in a navy maxi dress I'd leant her. She'd kept her school pumps on as I hadn't had shoes in her size and she'd let us style her hair. It was flicked edgily about her shoulders and her wide eyes looked even bigger now they were painted with eyeliner.

Diego opened the door dressed in a blue flannel shirt and jeans, his beanie hat still in place. His fair eyes bypassed Tory and I, landing on Sofia instead. His mouth hooked up at the corner and she turned bright pink.

I shared a look with Tory and we started grinning as Diego cleared his throat and stepped into the corridor. "Let's go then, chicas," he said, leading the way.

We headed across campus and I soaked in the last of the sun as it sank toward the horizon, casting amber tones across the entire sky.

Someone whistled at us and I glanced over my shoulder, spotting a group of guys grinning at our asses. "Hey Vegas, wanna come sit on my throne?" one of them called.

Tory put her middle finger up and I snorted a laugh, turning away from them.

"This school is full of assholes," Diego muttered, shooting a glare at them over his shoulder.

"What does that make us?" I teased.

"Losers?" he suggested and a laugh escaped me.

"Well I'd rather be a loser than an asshole." I shrugged.

I'd never had many friends in my old schools anyway. We'd moved around too much when we were younger and I'd learned not to get close to anyone after a while. It was always a doubly whammy. Our foster parents would give us up and we'd get hauled out of school and dumped in the next town over. Tory had always dealt with it better than me. But my heart had been on lock-down for years. I didn't want to get too comfortable in one place, knowing I'd be ripped away from it soon enough.

We wound down the path toward The Orb and a squeal announced Geraldine's arrival before I saw her.

"Oh no," I breathed.

"Don't tell her we're going out," Tory hissed.

"Jiminy Christmas!" She pounced on us and her hair flew about her in a fan – *wait, is that blue dye in the end of it???*

"Are you going out?" she asked excitedly. "I was just about to catch the shuttle, we can all go together!"

"Er...actually we were just going to The Orb," I said, feeling a bit shitty about lying.

Her eyes cast down our clothes to our high heels. "Oh, well you look amazing. Maybe I'll catch you tomorrow? Breakfast at seven thirty?"

"Well-" Tory started but Geraldine waved a hand.

"It's no bother, see you then your majesties!" She jogged away along the path and I sighed.

"Seven thirty on a Saturday?" Tory huffed. "No chance."

"Come on, let's go before she realises we lied." Diego turned left, swerving past Jupiter Hall and into Earth Territory.

We headed through The Wailing Wood, following a paved path all the way out to the edge of campus. A glint of light caught my eye between the trees and we followed Diego toward it into a clearing.

The parking lot rose up several levels inside a glass dome that reflected the tones of the colourful sunset. I caught glimpses of the gleaming cars peeking out beyond the glass walls and anticipation inched into me.

Diego gained entry to the building by tapping something on his Atlas and the glass door slid open.

Inside, the air smelled like new leather and car fumes. The lot circled up in a perfect spiral and we soon arrived in front of a massive black jeep with tinted windows.

"Woah is this your car?" I asked.

"Um no," Diego said awkwardly, stepping past the huge vehicle and pointing.

We moved around the jeep and I bit down on my lip as I spotted the beat-up, rusted red hatchback before us. "Oh, well this is great too," I said, trying to save face.

Well done, idiot.

"At least you don't have to worry about anyone stealing it." Tory tried not to laugh and I poked her in the ribs, a giggle escaping me.

"It will get us from A to B." Diego shrugged, but the crease on his forehead said how embarrassed he was.

"That's all we want," I said brightly and Sofia nodded keenly, brushing his arm.

He muttered something inaudible as he dropped into the driver's seat and I took the passenger one beside him.

Sofia and Tory sat in the back and we waited as it took Diego a couple of painful tries to get the car going.

"If you want, I can take a look at your engine sometime?" Tory offered. "I'm not as great with cars as I am with bikes but-"

"It's fine," Diego said through his teeth and the engine roared as if his embarrassment had sparked life into it.

We circled out of the lot and headed onto the road that led off-campus. We curved around the edge of a jagged mountain, rising up high toward the twilight sky. I caught a glimpse of a huge iron door set into the side of it with the symbol of earth above it and my heart beat a little harder. Students were milling about outside the Terra House and some of them pointed at us, laughing as they noticed the car which was making a loud clunking noise.

I pressed my lips together in irritation. "At least we *have* a car," I muttered, but that didn't seem to cheer Diego up.

The engine protested as he pressed his foot down and we started to gain speed, but not much. I rolled the window down, letting in the evening breeze as the sun said its final goodbye and dropped below the tree line in the distance.

We headed to the furthest regions of campus and finally reached an enormous steel gate, flanked by a fence which stretched off for miles in either direction. A guard nodded to us from a stone booth and the gates swung open as he flicked his hand.

We trundled onto the road and a weight lifted from my chest as we left Zodiac Academy behind.

A night of freedom called to me. And I wanted to make the most of it. No Heirs. In fact, no shitbags period.

We sped along a vast road that stretched on forever, cutting through a thick forest of pine trees which reached up high on either side of us. The moon was rising above them, the shimmering crescent a perfect jewel amongst a bed of stars.

The road soon dropped steeply down into a valley and nestled at the heart of it were the twinkling lights of a town.

"That's Tucana," Sofia said, leaning forward to poke her head between the front seats. "I grew up juuuust over that hill." She pointed to the far side of the valley.

"It's beautiful." I smiled as we drew closer and closer to the town then drove through the bustling streets. People sat outside bars beneath the amber light of lampposts, drinking and eating.

I stared out at the ancient buildings with their weathered stone faces, utterly fascinated by the place. Cafes, bars, restaurants. It was nothing like Chicago. In fact, it reminded me of a holiday brochure I'd seen of Italy once. Everything was quaint, the main streets intersected by cobble alleyways and stone archways. The itch to explore overwhelmed me and I soaked in the buzzing atmosphere as the clamour of voices sailed through my open window.

We were clearly on the main street now and there were people everywhere enjoying the evening. I recognised a few students from Zodiac milling along the sidewalk, but the town was big enough that we'd probably be able to avoid them. The last thing I wanted was to bump into any one of our many enemies from the Academy.

"Pull over here," Sofia instructed, pointing.

Diego parked outside a restaurant/bar on the corner of a street. The windowsills were painted red and a rainbow of flowers hung from several baskets around the doorway.

"The food here is great," Sofia said, hopping out of the car.

We followed her onto the sidewalk and I gazed up at a worn sign above the door, naming it as Andromeda's Place.

We headed inside and a smiley waitress hurried over to seat us. The space was brimming with people and the lights were dim throughout. Low-hanging bulbs lit booths and tables and to one side was a long wooden bar with the Zodiac's symbols printed all over it in silver.

"Isn't that Professor Orion?" Sofia asked and my heart lurched upwards.

I located him in less than a nanosecond.

On the far side of the bar Orion was sitting knee to knee with a leggy brunette who looked like beauty on speed.

"Could be." I shrugged, turning in the opposite direction as I forcibly ignored the strange reaction my body was having to seeing him here. And the raging pit of death in my chest definitely had nothing to do with the Victoria's Secret model sitting opposite him.

"This way," the waitress said brightly and we followed her to a table with a perfect view of Orion. It was as if the damn waitress *wanted* me to stare at him all night. I was too slow to grab a seat facing away from him and couldn't voice my complaints to the others in case they questioned me on it.

I sank into the seat beside Diego and took a breath.

He's just a teacher, who cares if he's here?

You apparently.

I picked up my menu, determinedly eyeing the list of sodas on offer.

"Rum and coke," Diego ordered from the hovering waitress and she nodded as if that was completely okay.

Didn't she realise we were freshmen?

"I'll have the same," Sofia said brightly, a daring look in her eye. Sofia looked the youngest of us all. Even with the makeup we'd painted on her, she still barely passed for a day over sixteen.

"And for you girls?"

Tory gave me an excited look. "Tequila sunrise?" she asked, seeming to expect the waitress to refuse but she jotted it down without a word, looking to me.

A thrill hummed through me. Tory and I had had fake I.Ds back in Chicago, but even they had failed us occasionally. "Whiskey and coke?"

She smiled and walked away to the bar.

I glanced at the others. "How did we just get away with that?"

"Get away with what?" Sofia asked casually as she perused the food items on the menu.

"Err, the alcohol?" Tory supplied. "We're only eighteen."

"And your point being?" Diego asked, looking between us in confusion.

"Don't you have like...legal drinking ages in Solaria?" I asked with a frown.

"There's no laws against drinking here," Diego said with a laugh, lifting a hand to tug on one side of his beanie. "You just have to have the gold to buy it. Which kids tend not to."

"That's crazy," I said as the waitress arrived with our drinks.

"My kind of crazy," Tory said brightly, taking her cocktail.

I sipped my whiskey and coke and had the prickling feeling that I was being watched. My eyes snagged on Orion and I found he was looking right at me; it felt a lot like looking down the barrel of a gun. My throat constricted and I choked on my drink, placing it down as I tried to rein in my coughing. With a noise like a dying goat, I managed to gain my breath and Tory shook her head at me with an amused smile.

Well that's just great.

Diego patted my back. "Are you alright?"

"I'm fine," I said airily, glancing over at Orion and finding he'd returned to talking with his date anyway. Hopefully that meant he hadn't just witnessed my choke attack.

What had my horoscope said this morning? Oh yeah, *the universe is out of sync with you today. Be prepared to ride out the storm.*

I'd ridden the storm all week, so how much worse could it really get?

The waitress returned to take our food orders and I jumped on the opportunity of a distraction, ordering a pizza from the menu.

When she walked away, I took a slower sip of my drink and decided to pointedly ignore Professor Jerk-Face's presence. But it was pretty difficult considering Tory and I were fairly convinced he wanted us dead.

A group of professors walked in the door and Diego scowled. "Is this the teachers' hang out or something, Sofia?"

"Er...maybe. I didn't realise," she said, her cheeks lining with colour.

Our water Element teacher, Professor Washer was wearing a tight-fitting flowery shirt with way too many buttons undone and a roguish smile. He cast his eyes our way and shot us a wink. I would have guessed he was about forty and looked like he'd spent way too much time crisping himself up under the sun.

"Ew," Tory hissed and I shuddered.

Our Tarot teacher, Professor Astrum, led him away by the arm firmly and his lips pinched tightly together in disappointment.

"Washer is a total perve," Sofia whispered then giggled as if she shouldn't have said it.

"Is that why we have to wear bathing suits that barely cover our asses in his class?" I asked, my nose wrinkling.

"I'd bet on it, chica," Diego laughed, nudging me in the ribs.

Our food soon arrived and we ate every last bite as we ordered more and more drinks. By the time the waitress cleared our plates, my head was a little swimmy and I'd forgotten all about Orion and hadn't at all noticed that his hand was currently placed on his date's knee.

"Shots!" Diego announced, rising from his seat.

"Yes!" Sofia hooted, her hair dancing around her shoulders as she swayed in her chair.

Tory and I laughed as Diego strode away to the bar.

"Oh no," Tory said suddenly, sinking low in her seat.

"What is it?" I followed her line of sight to the window behind me.

Geraldine was crossing the street with a paper bag in her grip.

"Hide," Tory begged, grabbing up a menu and burying her face in it.

I pulled my hair over my shoulders, knowing the blue ends were a giveaway but a loud knocking on the window said I'd reacted too late.

"Just ignore her," Tory hissed as I fought the urge to turn around. Sofia raised a hand to wave and Tory took a swat at her with her menu.

"We can't," I said, a pang of sympathy rolling through me.

I couldn't resist the urge to look and found Geraldine pressed up against the window, her hands cupped around her eyes so she could see in.

I looked away again and Tory stole a glance over her menu. "Shit."

"What?" I whispered, staring resolutely forward.

"She's coming in," Tory said through her teeth.

I fought a groan as Geraldine appeared, grinning from ear to ear as she pranced across the restaurant to our table. "Well bless my cream crackers! I thought you were staying at The Orb?" She looked between us, ignoring Sofia, her face plastered with confusion.

"We changed our minds," I said innocently.

"Oh." Her confusion melted into a bright smile. "Well why didn't you call me?" She dropped into Diego's chair, placing her paper bag on the table. "You're going to *love* these, I just got them made."

She tipped the bag up and a pile of sparkly silver badges fell onto the table with the letters A.S.S inscribed on them in black. *Holy...shit. Does she not realise what that spells? Is she actually going to walk around campus with one of them on!?*

"They're for the Almighty Sovereign Society – aren't they just the gnat's pyjamas?!" Geraldine leaned right across the table, pinning one on Sofia's dress before she could refuse. Sofia gazed at it in abject horror and I drowned my laughter by taking a sip of my drink.

"Wonderful," Tory said dryly but if Geraldine noticed her sarcasm, she didn't let it show.

My gut sank as Geraldine pinned one onto her denim jacket and started dancing in her chair.

If the Heirs see those they're gonna rip her apart.

"Um Geraldine," I said gently, feeling it was my duty to save her from a host of abuse at the Academy.

"Yes?" she asked brightly, shimmying her shoulders back and forth so the badge caught the light as she admired it.

"It's just...that acronym, it kinda spells *ass*."

Tory snorted into her drink.

Geraldine stared at me for a long moment and I wasn't sure if she was about to flip out. Laughter erupted from her throat and she petted my arm. "Don't be ridiculous! No one but *you* would have noticed that, Darcy." She shook her head at me as if I was so amusing and my heart floated down to the base of my stomach.

Well I tried.

Diego returned with four bright green shots and frowned as he spotted Geraldine in his seat. She lifted a hand as if to take one of the shots and he moved them out of her reach.

"Isn't that your gang out there?" he asked, nodding to the window.

Geraldine wheeled around then gasped as she spotted a bunch of the royal supporters walking up the street.

"Oh sweet raisin bran!" She gathered the badges into her bag, practically panting as she leapt from her seat then curtsied at us. "Your majesties, forgive me but I must go."

"You're forgiven," Tory said brightly.

Geraldine checked her watch. "I can be back in one hour! Then we can all go dancing together." Geraldine shot out of the restaurant before anyone could reply, waving her bag at the group in excitement. I watched for one gut-churning second as they all pinned the ass badges onto their chests.

"Asses," I breathed in horror. "They're a group of *asses* and they don't seem to realise it."

"Oh man I can't wait for the Heirs see those." Tory started laughing.

"*Tory*," I snorted. "You can't say that."

"At least it will get the attention off of us for five minutes." Her laughter descended into fits and I pressed a hand to my mouth as I tried to stifle my own.

Sofia took hers off and placed it on the table with a giggle. "Sorry guys, I won't be an *ass* member no matter how much I love you both."

Diego dropped into his seat with a sigh of relief. "Who needs a drink?"

"I do." Sofia leaned forward, grabbing a shot and swallowing it in one. Before we could lay a hand on the rest of them, she downed them all in quick succession with a wild laugh.

"Sofia!" Diego gasped.

I stared at her in surprise. She was usually so quiet, what had gotten into her?

"Sofia's a secret party girl," Tory jibed as Sofia tossed a lock of hair out of her face with a shrug.

"I wouldn't say that, but I can handle my drink," she said with a coy smile and Diego stared at her with a frown.

I grinned, rising from my seat. "I'll get us some more."

The others nodded keenly and I headed to the bar, moving into the only free gap which unfortunately placed me behind Orion and his date. I was one percent curious about what they were saying and couldn't help but strain my ears as the woman leant in to speak with him.

"It's all moving so fast. We should do something about it tonight."

She squeezed his arm and I tried my best not to hate her.

She's on a date with a hot guy, why wouldn't she want to jump him?

Orion cocked his head. "No. It's too soon. We have to wait."

My eyebrows arched. Did this asshole actually have an ounce of gentleman in him?

"It will get out of control, Orion. It has to be tonight. I can't wait any longer," she begged.

Woah, desperate much?

"That's not what we planned," Orion hissed. "If we try to kill them now we'll draw attention to ourselves."

My heart slammed into my ribcage. This conversation was *not* about sex. The girl looked up and her eyes widened as they landed on me. I tried to casually walk away, but the barman pointed at me to get my order and suddenly Orion had hold of my arm. His grip was painfully tight as he dragged me against his thigh. Heat surged everywhere, powerful and terrifying. The scent of cinnamon and something entirely man washed over me, permanently becoming my new favourite smell despite the origin.

"What did you hear?" he growled and I gasped, trying to prise his fingers off of me.

"*Orion,*" his date warned and he released me.

"I didn't hear anything," I insisted and my heart tripled its pace as I darted away, escaping into the women's bathroom.

I clutched onto a basin, taking in a shuddering breath, well and truly rattled.

Was that woman in on the plot to kill us? How far did this go? How many people wanted Tory and I dead?

The few drinks I'd had helped keep me calm as I turned over what I'd heard, trying to work out what to do.

The door swung open and I realised with a horrifying clarity I'd just made a terrible mistake. Orion stepped into the room, shutting the door behind him and the lock clicked loudly through the air.

I backed up, my pulse drumming in my ears.

Run.

Scream.

Do something!

I opened my mouth to call out for help but he flicked a hand and the air in my throat halted, refusing to let out any noise.

My heart pounded a frantic tune as I continued to back up until my spine hit the far wall. I raised my hands, ready to force every ounce of magic into my palms to stop him. Whatever it took; I wasn't going to die here in some bathroom.

"Stay back," I hissed, my voice only allowing a whisper. He was controlling the airflow in my damn throat!

"What did you hear?" he growled. *"Tell me everything."*

His Coercion was powerful and no matter how much practice I'd had with Tory and Sofia, it wasn't anywhere near enough to throw off his magic. My tongue loosened and I couldn't hold the words back. "That you're planning to kill someone. And I know it's us. You want us out. You don't want me and my sister ruling Solaria, but you can't really think you'd get away with killing us in a restaurant do you?" My voice was barely above a whisper and I cursed him for the power he had over me. Fear rattled my heart, but my blood was pounding with alcohol and adrenaline too.

Maybe I could run – get past him. But I knew it was impossible. I wouldn't make it two steps in the direction of the door before he disabled me.

Attack him then!

I lifted my palms higher, preparing to do whatever I had to to survive. I willed magic to my fingers and they tingled with a deadly heat. Fire had come to my aid. And I would unleash the pits of hell on him if he made one move to hurt me.

Orion waved a hand almost lazily and my arms were suddenly clamped to my sides as he wielded the air around me.

Oh crap.

"That's it?" His voice was calmer as if it was entirely normal that he'd be planning my demise.

"Yes," I spat as my heart crashed into my chest. "Isn't that enough?"

He blew out a laugh, staring at me for a few painful seconds, his eyes two black holes which sucked at everything I was and tried to swallow it whole.

"Go home, Blue." He unlocked the door and stepped out of the room, leaving me with a chasm of rage spitting venom in my chest.

I glared at the door for one long moment before marching toward it and heading back into the restaurant. I didn't look his way as I strode back to the table and dropped into my seat, my pulse everywhere.

"Where's our drinks?" Sofia slurred with a pout but Tory shushed her, looking at me intently.

"What happened?"

Call it a twin thing, but we could tell when the other was upset. No matter how hard we tried to hide it. Not that I was trying that hard right then.

"Orion," I said in answer and quickly rattled off an explanation, leaving out the part where my knees had trembled like I was in a grade five earthquake.

Sofia laughed. "Come onnnn, he's a teacher. You guys are getting *waaay* too caught up in conspiracy theories."

Diego shook his head, his expression serious. "They could be right. The evidence points his way." He shot a glare at Orion and I spotted him leaving the restaurant with his date. Who maybe wasn't his date after all.

Relief spilled through me as he left and I glanced over at the cluster of Professors on the other side of the room. Of course he wouldn't have attacked me here in a public bathroom. How could I have thought he would? *Because he had his psycho eyes in place, that's why.*

I didn't know Orion, for all I knew he could be the type of guy who chopped people up in women's bathrooms on a regular occasion.

"Do you want to go home?" Tory asked me, frowning in concern.

I ground my jaw, shaking my head. "That's what he wants."

"Well we can't do that then," Tory agreed with a grin and my mood brightened by a mile.

"He's gone now anyway," Sofia said, standing and starting to dance to the background music playing in the bar. She started dancing provocatively with her chair and my mouth parted.

"Sofia!" Diego gasped, looking alarmed and Tory cracked a laugh.

Sofia stumbled into the table and knocked over a small vase at the heart of it. Diego cast a gust of air from his hand to direct the water away from pouring all over us.

Tory steadied her, glancing at us. "I thought she said she could handle her drink," she teased.

"I caaaaan," Sofia slurred, clutching onto Tory to stay upright.

"It was only a few shots," I said in confusion.

"Maybe she doesn't drink often," Diego said, rising to his feet. "I should take her home."

"No." Sofia planted her hands on her hips. "I'm fiiiine."

Diego looked to us. "I think it'd be best. There's a shuttle bus that runs back to the Academy at the end of the street. Do you mind catching it home?"

"Yeah that's fine," I said as Sofia reached out, trying to grab hold of Tory's arm while Diego led her away. She quickly gave up and clutched onto Diego instead, looking up at him with dreamy eyes. "Your hat...I like your hat. Can I wear it?" She reached for it and he chuckled as he caught her hand in his, holding it as he led her out of the door.

The waitress appeared, planting two glasses of some bright pink cocktail down in front of us. "From your friend over there." She pointed at the group of professors and Washer grinned at us, licking his lips and wiggling his fingers. He was jammed up against Astrum who threw us an apologetic smile.

I couldn't even disguise the disgust on my face.

Tory clucked her tongue.

"Ergh Washer is such a pig," she muttered, but picked her glass up and held it out to me anyway. "From this point on, this night is going to be about having fun without any creeps."

I grinned, picking up my cocktail and clinking my glass to hers. "To no creeps."

She whooped. "To no creeps!"

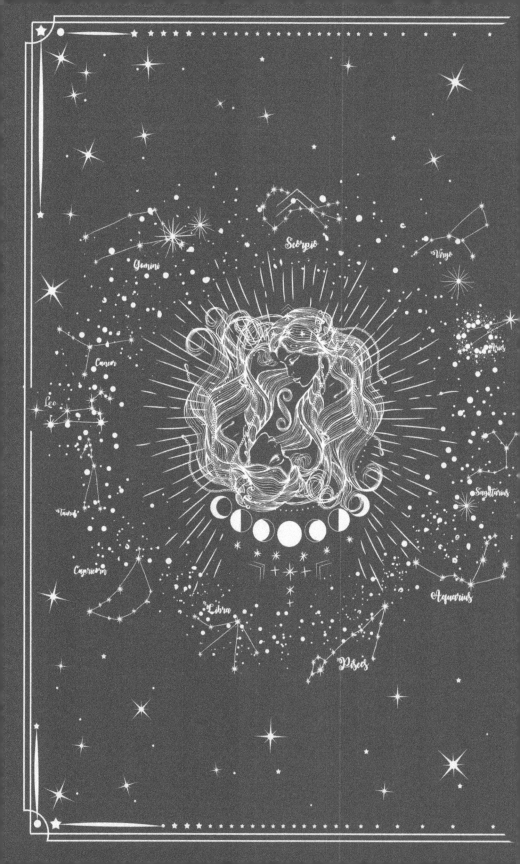

TORY

CHAPTER FIFTEEN

A tell-tale vibration came from my clutch and I pulled my Atlas out, hoping it was Diego letting us know that he'd gotten Sofia back okay.

Falling Star:

New information has come to light.
Can we meet?

I raised an eyebrow in surprise and nudged Darcy to draw her attention away from trying to summon the barman again.

"Why are they so keen to meet us all of a sudden?" Darcy asked curiously.

"Only one way to find out, I guess," I replied as I tapped out a response.

Tory Vega:

When?

Falling Star:

Ten minutes.

There's an alleyway behind the bar.

I'll see you there.

A shiver raced along my spine as I read their response and I snapped my head up, scouring everyone around us to see who had their Atlas out. Whoever Falling Star was, they knew where we were, which meant they were here somewhere. The restaurant was thronging with people and plenty of Zodiac students had come and gone.

Was it a coincidence? Or was Falling Star following us? The idea gave me the creeps.

"Are we sure we should trust this stalker?" I muttered as I narrowed my eyes at a group of sophomores who were laughing loudly in a booth behind us.

Darcy cast her eyes around the restaurant too. "I don't know. But they seem like one of a very few people who are actually trying to help us in this place. Even if they are annoyingly cryptic."

I bit my tongue, glancing down at the message again. Was it completely insane to trust an anonymous stranger who wanted to meet us in a dark alley at night? Yes, probably. But was I curious enough to take the risk? Apparently so.

"I want answers from this weirdo and I don't think we're going to get any unless we meet them. So I say we do it," I said firmly.

"Are you sure that's a good idea?" Darcy asked hesitantly.

"Honestly? No. But I still think we should do it."

"Okay," Darcy agreed, chewing on her lip. "I'll order us some Dutch courage."

I grinned as she finally snagged the bartender's attention and ordered us a round of drinks.

As it drew nearer to our arranged meeting time, I tried to keep an eye on anyone who was getting ready to leave but it was pretty hard to say. Quite a few of the students were heading on to some of the other bars down the street now that they'd finished their meals. I guessed we'd be finding out soon either way.

"Are you ready?" I asked as I placed my empty glass down on the bar.

We'd planned to head onto another bar soon anyway, neither of us mentioning the fact that Geraldine was meant to be coming back to meet us. I felt a little guilty knowing we were ditching her but I only had to think about those goddamn ass badges and I knew that it had to be done. No way I was spending my time hanging out with people who happily branded themselves as an ass.

"Let's see what they've got to say for themselves," Darcy agreed as she pushed her stool back and got to her feet.

She led the way outside and the cool evening air washed around us, making promises of the winter to come. I should have worn a jacket but I'd been tricked by the warmth of the sun before it had set. I wrapped my arms around myself as my thin cami did nothing to protect me from the Elements and wondered why I always sacrificed my comfort for fashion choices.

We headed along the sidewalk, falling into silence as we reached a narrow alleyway between the bar and a dark store which occupied the space beside it.

I offered Darcy a reassuring smile before taking the lead into the alley.

The music from the bar faded to a muffled thump of bass as we delved into the darkness and goosebumps rose along my skin. Yep, we were definitely heading into a serial-killer's wet dream and I couldn't help but question our sanity a little as we failed to turn back.

Behind the bar, the alley widened out and a row of dumpsters kept company with a questionable puddle. There was no one waiting in the shadows and a sense of unease settled on me as we glanced about.

"This seems like a pretty shady place for a meeting," Darcy muttered, eyeing the alley we'd used to get here in a way that suggested she wanted to go back.

"Agreed," I said, rubbing my hands up and down my arms to try and coax a little warmth back into them. "So how long are we going to wait for our mystery man?"

"Or woman," Darcy added and I nodded vaguely, though our current position in a darkened alleyway definitely had me imagine a hulking man coming for us, jagged knife in hand, backpack full of rope and duct tape...

"I don't like this," I breathed. "Maybe we should just leave?"

My Atlas buzzed again and I quickly pulled it out.

Falling Star:

The Shadow is moving closer. I can't risk a meet now.
You should find a way to safety before the darkness claims you!

Darcy leaned close to read the message too and I cursed our stupid mystery messenger for leading us out here for nothing.

"We should get out of here," Darcy said, her voice low as she glanced around.

"Come on," I agreed, taking a step towards the alley we'd used to get here.

A dark shadow moved to block the light from the street beyond and I fell still. Darcy bumped into me as she failed to notice that I'd stopped and I caught her arm to prevent her from falling.

"Who's there?" I called hesitantly, wondering if Falling Star had decided to turn up after all.

The silence echoed for several long seconds then a deep rattling noise came as the shadow drew closer.

My magic flared in response as I backed up a step, driving Darcy back with me. She tried to move to my side to get a better look but I wouldn't let her, keeping my body between her and whoever the hell was blocking our exit.

Ice trickled through my veins and I tried to draw on my magic to light a fire in my palm.

Heat swelled along my fingertips just as that rattle sounded again, deeper this time, louder.

My magic stuttered. A small flame sprang to life then died as if someone had sucked it away.

My heart lurched with panic as the figure took a step closer and we took another step back.

I could feel my magic swarming like a tempest beneath my flesh but I couldn't draw it out.

"I can't summon my power," Darcy breathed, her voice tinged with fear.

"Me either," I whispered.

Was this whole thing some trick? Were we about to be surrounded by the Heirs, ready to spring some new horror on us?

The third rattle was so loud that my limbs trembled in response to it. I didn't know what it was but it felt like it was forming a cage around my power and locking it up tight. The next step I took felt weighted with lead and I sucked in a sharp breath as I realised that the noise was starting to harness my limbs too. If we didn't get out of there quickly, I was sure we wouldn't be able to escape at all.

"Run!" I yelled, snatching Darcy's hand in mine and spinning in the opposite direction.

We broke into a sprint, our stilettos made it difficult but we refused to let them slow us.

Darcy's grip on my hand was tight as we shot past the row of dumpsters and that rattle sounded again. For a terrifying moment we slowed despite our intentions and the sound of pounding feet closed in behind us.

I released a scream, throwing every inch of my resolve into placing my feet down as fast as I could.

Darcy stumbled and I caught her arm, righting her as I shoved her ahead of me. I whirled towards the nearest dumpster and snatched a large sack of trash from the top of it before launching it back towards whoever the hell was chasing us just as that rattling started again.

The noise cut off with a muffled grunt as I managed to hit my target and power surged in my fingertips.

A rush of air slammed past me as Darcy unleashed her magic. The wind carved around me like it was made of stone and barely even pulled at my hair before crashing into our stalker with the strength of a tornado.

The shadowy figure was thrown back and I staggered to Darcy's side with my eyes wide as I tried to draw on my own magic to join with hers.

Before I could, the rattling came again and all access to my power was snatched away once more.

The figure stood again, shadows seeming to cling to them as if they were drawn by a magnet. It concealed everything about them apart from the certainty in my gut that there was something horribly *wrong* with them.

Darcy whimpered as she caught my arm and dragged me back.

We started running again, fear lending strength to our limbs as we raced down darkened alleys, one after another.

I could feel the shadow drawing closer with each step, imagine their breath on the back of my neck.

The rattling began again and I clapped my hands over my ears, not understanding what the hell it was but knowing that it was doing something to me each time I heard it.

Darcy staggered as the force of the rattle hit her but I urged her on and we managed to sprint even faster as adrenaline spiked through my limbs.

A warm light illuminated the end of the alleyway ahead of us and relief spilled through me as I spied the exit.

We leapt forward and ran straight out onto a well lit street before a busy bar. Tables were sat outside it full of students who were laughing and drinking.

I was too afraid to care about the surprised looks they were shooting us and we darted straight across the street to join the safety of the crowd without slowing at all.

As soon as we were surrounded by warm bodies I spun back to face the alley, my eyes wide as I attempted to spot whoever had been chasing us.

Darcy leaned in close beside me, her arm brushing against mine as my galloping heartbeat thundered in my ears.

The alleyway was empty. Just a dark space between two innocent looking buildings. But the fear knotting my insides was real.

A hand landed on my shoulder and I flinched as I looked up to find Max Rigel smiling at us. He was dressed in the kind of flashy shirt which probably cost more than a week's rent in our old apartment and his mohawk was slicked back stylishly.

"What's got our two little Vegas so worked up?" he asked kindly and I could feel the call of his power urging us to divulge our fears to him.

I glanced at Darcy, unsure whether or not to tell him. On the one hand, letting him take some of this fear from me didn't sound like the worst idea in that moment. On the other, I was probably only terrified at all because one of his dumbass friends had been chasing us.

But as that thought crossed my mind, I spotted the other Heirs lounging at a table to our left. They all had drinks underway and showed every sign that they'd been sitting there for a while. Besides, I still hadn't taken my eyes off of that alley and no one else had emerged from it.

"There was someone chasing us," Darcy murmured, giving in to the call of the Siren's power.

"Really?" Max asked with interest, sliding his arms around us so that we were pulled closer to him. I knew what he was after but I definitely felt safer here than I had in that alleyway. And considering the fact that we were currently surrounded by a bunch of douchebags who I knew wished us harm, that was saying a lot.

"They were trying to hurt us," I muttered, feeling the pull of Max's magic as he drew some of mine into himself alongside a sliver of my fear. Sirens would probably make a killing as psychiatrists; who wouldn't like someone to suck the misery out of them every now and then?

"That sounds like a good story to be told over a drink." Max steered us between the crowd of students towards the other Heirs. I threw a concerned glance at Darcy and her eyes widened but before we could voice any objections, we found ourselves at their table.

The other Heirs looked up at us in surprise and I frowned, wondering why the hell I'd let Max drag us over here.

"Look who I just found running from shadows," Max announced with a wide smile, his hand dropping down my back until it was in danger of skimming my ass.

I shrugged him off before he could manage it.

"We weren't running from shadows, someone was chasing us," Darcy said defensively as Seth leaned forward with a wolfish smile.

"You really must be scared if you thought we were a better option," he said.

"They are. I can taste their fear," Max said enthusiastically. "And they were just about to tell me all about it."

Caleb released a breath of laughter as he ran a hand through his tightly curling blonde hair, his eyes darting between my sister and I.

Max dropped into the only free chair at the table and yanked Darcy down into his lap, pulling her against his chest as he leaned close to her ear.

"What was the worst part?" he asked and I could feel his power tugging at me even though he wasn't touching me anymore. Darcy was snared in his magic and her lips parted to answer his question automatically.

"They kept making this horrible noise," she replied. "Like a growl or a rattle..."

Darius leaned forward, his brows lifting with interest as he surveyed my sister and me.

"We aren't staying," I said sharply, leaning forward to pull Darcy out of Max's grip so that we could make our second escape of the evening.

"Hold on a moment." A large hand encircled my wrist before I could pull her to her feet and my blood raised in warning as Darius kept hold of me. I turned to meet his dark eyes and couldn't help but skim my gaze over his white shirt which was almost too tight over his muscular frame. "What if we call a truce on our issues? For one night only," he offered.

"Why would we believe that?" I asked dismissively.

Darcy was frowning, trying to push her way out of Max's grip half heartedly like she was vaguely aware that she didn't want to be there. He unleashed a wave of reassuring power which brushed against me as Darcy relaxed again.

"We just want a fun night," Caleb piped up. "We can leave our political situation out of it."

"Our political situation?" Darcy echoed with a frown.

"Yeah, you know. The little issue we have with you rocking up out of nowhere to steal our birthright and upset the balance of power in the entire kingdom," Caleb teased.

"We don't want your stupid birthright," I muttered.

Darius still hadn't released me and I tried to reclaim my hand by jerking it back. He smirked at my effort then tugged me forward so hard that I fell into his lap.

He wrapped an arm around my waist and shifted me into a more comfortable position with a deep laugh that sent heat flooding my limbs.

"Drink with us," he insisted, waving at the bartender through the glass window beside us despite the fact that the bar was packed and they were clearly run off of their feet. "I swear we won't lay a finger on you unless you want us to."

"Well I didn't want you to drag me into your lap but that didn't seem to stop you," I muttered, though I was fairly sure that me still sitting there weighed against my argument somewhat.

Darius laughed again and I could feel the deep tone of it where his chest was pressed against my side.

Caleb shifted closer on my right and brushed his fingers against my arm, raising goosebumps along my skin. "I'll even promise not to bite you tonight if you want?"

I caught Darcy's eye and she offered me a shrug to let me know she was as unsure as I was. Max sent out another wave of relaxing energy and I felt my resolve shattering.

"I guess we could stay for one drink," Darcy said hesitantly as Max stroked her arm, the press of his influence skittering through the air. We were surrounded by smiles that sent my heart fluttering and my gut plummeting in equal measures.

I was almost positive that this was a terrible idea but the tequila in my system, the Siren's call and the table filled with gorgeous men were working hard against my better judgment.

"One drink then," I agreed finally just as voluptuous bartender appeared with a smile and a notepad ready to take our order.

"Better make it a big one then if you'll only stay for one," Seth teased as he ordered for all of us.

Darius leaned back in his chair, pulling me closer as he brushed my hair away from my ear and I internally kicked myself as I moved nearer to hear what he was going to say. Guys like him were always a bad idea for me. It was like I had a magnet inside me which drew me towards the most ruthless kind of asshole despite the fact that I knew how it would end. And I'd never met one guy who could even begin to rival Darius Acrux's dark and mysterious vibe let alone his devastatingly handsome features. I was powerless to stop my traitorous body from shifting against his, especially when his fingertips skimmed along my bare shoulder.

"Do you want to tell me about what happened in that alley?" he asked.

I couldn't suppress the shiver that ran down my spine as I thought back to the shadowy figure who'd been stalking us.

"Is this the part where you laugh at us for falling for some prank you set up?" I asked, refusing to answer his question. "Was that one of your friends back there? Did you get someone to send the messages too?"

His dark gaze flickered for a moment and he seemed to stop himself from saying something.

"I don't need to recruit anyone to do my handy work," he replied dismissively. "Maybe I'm concerned for your wellbeing."

I snorted in disbelief, shifting back so that I was no longer touching his chest. Yes he was stupid hot but he was also damn horrible when he wanted to be and I wasn't going to fall for his Prince Charming act just because he'd decided to switch it on for me.

I turned away from him and found Caleb eyeing us with interest as the bartender returned with a tray full of drinks.

Darcy was telling Max about the fright we'd gotten in the alley as his arm stayed firmly around her waist, drinking in her fear like a big old leech. I wondered again why we'd let them convince us to join them and shifted my focus to the drinks as the bartender placed them down and Darius pressed a wedge of notes into her hand. It looked like way too much money to me but no doubt she'd earned the tip with her push-up bra.

The drinks were all the same; some tall mixture of liquor and coke and I took mine before anyone else reached for theirs. Caleb was still looking at me and I held his eye as I emptied the contents of the glass in one long drink. It was stupidly strong and I could feel it burning all the way down my throat where it joined the tequila I'd consumed earlier for a warm little party in my stomach.

"There you go," I announced. "One drink." I pushed out of Darius's lap and he looked up at me in surprise, reaching out like he thought he might pull me back again but I stepped aside, offering him a flat smile.

Darcy smirked at me she got to her feet too, not even bothering to touch her own beverage. "See you later, guys," she agreed as she walked away, clearly hurrying to break free of Max's power before he upped the voltage again.

I made a move to follow her but Caleb stood and shot into my path using his Vampire speed. I arched an eyebrow at him as his eyes ran over me.

"I guess your word means shit then?" I asked as his gaze landed on my neck for an extra moment and I prepared for him to bite me.

"No. I said I won't bite you tonight and I meant it," he assured me with a teasing smile. "I'm just wondering where you're going now?"

I considered his question for a moment. The night was still fairly young and we hadn't had any immediate plans to head home before our run in with our mystery tormentor. Darcy had made it to the bar's entrance and was waiting for me, throwing Caleb a scowl for good measure.

"Dancing," I replied simply as I brushed past him, my hands landing on his toned waist for a fraction of a second as I guided him out of my way. "You can always join us if you think you can keep up."

Why did I just say that?

His navy eyes sparkled for a moment and I couldn't stop a small smile from pulling at my lips. I let my gaze run over him for all of half a second then turned away to join my sister. Tequila always made me a sucker for a hot guy with asshole intentions and there were way too many of them about tonight.

I fell into step beside Darcy as we entered the bar and I looked around at the grey walls which sparkled with silver glitter in the dim light. The place was heaving and a huge dance floor took up the space at the far end of the room.

"Let's find some nice men to buy our drinks," Darcy said with a grin as she began to eye up the possibilities and we fell into our familiar night out routine. We'd never had spare money for our own drinks but it was usually just a matter of time before one or both of us could catch someone's eye. Of course with our new-found wealth I guessed we didn't need to do that anymore but why break the habit of a lifetime?

It didn't take Darcy long to spot a couple of guys looking her way and she took the lead as we moved to stand beside them at the bar. They looked a few years older than us and I was pleased she'd found guys who didn't go to school with us and wouldn't have any opinion on the whole Heir situation to taint our interaction with them.

The blonde guy led the way over as we super casually pretended not to notice them coming and I offered him a 'surprised' smile as he moved into our space.

"Hi," he said all smiles with his red haired friend seconding the grin from his left. "I'm Peter, this is-"

"No," Max said loudly as he elbowed his way between our new friends and us.

"Not happening," Caleb agreed forcefully, giving blondie a glare that made him back up.

I sighed dramatically. "Really?"

"Now you're going to put a stop to our free drinks?" Darcy asked with an air of resignation.

"Why are you drinking at the bar when we have the VIP section to ourselves over there?" Caleb asked, pointing at a roped off area beside the dance floor.

"I think you just answered your own question there, Caleb," I muttered, rolling my eyes.

Max chuckled at his friend's expense and I raised an eyebrow at him in surprise. "You're going to have to work a lot harder to get into this one's pants, mate," he teased.

"Never going to happen," I said before Caleb could reply.

"Come on, Tor," Darcy said, ignoring the Heirs entirely. "If we aren't drinking then we should be dancing."

She caught my hand and turned her back on Max and Caleb with a flick of her blue-tipped hair. I turned from them too, a little thrill running through me with the knowledge that they hated that as Darcy led me up to dance.

The music was familiar and I wondered why they listened to human tunes. Maybe Fae had no songwriting skills? Or perhaps Miley Cyrus was part Fae too? Whatever the reason, I was more than happy to lose myself to something familiar for a change. Dancing on a Friday night seemed to transcend the mortal/Fae divide and that was just fine by me.

I closed my eyes and lost myself to the music as I danced with my sister and we pointedly ignored the feeling of the Heirs watching us from their fancy table beyond the rope. Who wanted to go out drinking and then hide themselves away behind a barrier anyway? Wasn't the whole point of this exercise to cut loose and socialise a bit? If being an Heir meant spending my life segregated from everyone else then I was doubly sure I had no interest in it.

A set of hands landed on my hips and my eyes flicked open as I found Darius holding me, his fingertips brushing the line of skin between my waistband and the hem of my shirt.

My heart stuttered with surprise for a moment and I had to work hard to keep the emotion from my face. Instead I offered him the faintest half of a smile which I hoped translated into 'truce' as I let him pull me closer. And as much as I would have liked to deny it, being held against Darius Acrux's broad chest really wasn't the worst place a girl could find herself.

I turned in his arms as we kept moving to the music and spotted Darcy receiving the same treatment from Seth. He'd wrapped his arms around her from behind and was pushing his face into her hair in his wolfy way which in that particular moment didn't seem to be a problem for her at all.

I smirked at her as she gave me a 'when in Rome' kinda look and I shrugged in acceptance as I moved my body with Darius's. If I closed my eyes I could even pretend he wasn't such an asshole but then I couldn't look at his face or his mouth, or the way his muscles were trying really hard to fight against the confines of his shirt... *damn* I was definitely going to be in trouble with him if I didn't watch out.

Darius turned me to face him again and I looped my arms around his neck as my chest brushed against his.

He caught me in his gaze for a moment that stretched a little too long and I bit my lip as I tried not to let my imagination get carried away. His eyes dropped to my mouth and the heat in his gaze sent an ache of longing right through me. I couldn't forget who he was or what he'd done but there were certainly a few parts of me that wished I could.

He leaned an inch closer to me and the space between us burned hot with raw energy for a moment and I suddenly felt like I was caught in a hunter's snare. The worst thing of all was that I didn't even want to break free. He had me and in that second we both knew it.

His grip on my waist tightened and my body was pulled against his in a way that demanded a hell of a lot less clothes be present. My breath caught in my throat and one of his hands slid up my back, a line of fire following it.

"Drink!" Caleb demanded from beside us and I pushed away from Darius to accept the shot he was holding out for me.

Darius kept his gaze locked on me as he consumed his own shot but I took another step back. I wasn't going to fall into his trap again. This was the guy who'd burned my clothes off and circulated naked pictures of me. He was rude and arrogant and full of himself. There was no way in hell I'd be ending up in his bed tonight. I was at least sixty-seven percent certain of that.

"Orion's looking for you," Caleb said to Darius, pointing back over to the bar where our teacher stood watching us. My gut plummeted and I shot a concerned look at Darcy but she was too caught up with Seth to have noticed. "Something about an assignment you haven't handed in. I told him to chill the hell out and enjoy his drink but he gave me that look, you know the look where you're not sure if he's trying to set you alight with the power of thought alone or if he's just super constipated, so I said I'd tell you."

I snorted a laugh, knowing exactly what look Caleb meant and I eyed Orion over the top of my glass. He scowled at us in a way that made me think he'd heard us and I realised that with his Vampire abilities it was possible he had. For a moment I felt like a kid being told off in school and I frowned at the weirdness of that situation. I was out in a bar for God's sake, why was I being chastised by my Professor? If I'd ever spotted my old English teacher hanging out at Joey's in her loose fitting slacks and glasses on a string I'd have bust a gut over it. Although I guessed Orion didn't exactly look like your standard teacher. He didn't even stick out amongst us. It was more that I knew what he was that made it feel odd.

"I guess I'd better see what he wants," Darius said, sounding resigned. He cast a final look at me but I pretended not to notice as I moved away and shoved my empty shot glass down on an abandoned table.

Caleb was where I'd left him when I returned to the dance floor. I followed his gaze as he threw a scowl at Orion's back as he and Darius headed out of the bar to talk. A shiver raced down my spine seeing them together like that and I was forced to wonder about what I'd overheard the other night again. Could the guy I'd just been dancing with really be out to hurt me and Darcy? Orion had gotten Darcy alone back at the restaurant and hadn't laid a finger on her. But he hadn't denied it when she'd accused him of wanting to hurt her either...

I glanced at my sister again to find that she was still definitely okay with Seth's tactile ways. I smirked at her as she leaned into him and he ran his hands down her back.

Caleb continued to scowl from his position in the middle of the dance floor as I made it back to him. A group of girls were dancing provocatively, casting less than subtle looks at his general hotness but he was ignoring them.

I caught his hand and placed it on my waist as I snagged him for a new dance partner. I might have been a little overfamiliar thanks to Mr Jack Daniels but I pushed through any concerns about being forward with an air of I-don't-give-a-shit. As his attention shifted to me, I tiptoed up to speak in his ear over the thumping music.

"Did you hate Orion before he tried to poach my blood or is it all about me?" I teased.

Caleb snorted a laugh, pulling me closer as he leaned in to reply. His hands slipped around me, drawing me closer before he spoke and earning me a heap of scowls from the hopeful girls.

"It's a Vampire thing. We're always driven to secure the best Source available. We have a hierarchy that's determined by power but his position as my teacher makes our relationship a little more strained than most. I should respect him because he's a professor at my school and is technically my superior but I'm more powerful than him so... it causes a little tension." Caleb shrugged before a playful smile captured his lips. "Do you like us fighting over you then?"

I rolled my eyes and slid my hands up his chest before linking them behind his neck. "Well if either of you wanted anything other than my blood then maybe I'd be flattered. But as I'm rather against the whole concept of being a walking juice-box I'll have to go with no."

"What if I *did* want something other than your blood?" he asked suggestively, his breath dancing across my neck.

I lifted my eyes to meet his, my body pressing closer without me really intending to do it. I shifted my hands a little higher, my fingertips pushing into the short hair at the nape of his neck before trailing up to brush against his soft curls.

"Like what?" I asked, adopting an innocent tone which I really doubted he was buying. How much had I had to drink? Why was this starting to feel like it might not be the worst idea I'd ever had? Hadn't he hung me over a ravine and used me like a chew toy since my very first day? Why didn't that seem quite so awful to drunk Tory? And why was I asking myself so many questions when he'd just run his thumb down the centre of my back and my skin was lighting up beneath his touch?

Caleb's eyes glimmered with amusement. He pushed my hair back over my shoulder as he leaned down, his lips brushing my ear and sending a little shiver down my spine. "What if I wanted to-"

The music suddenly cut off and the overhead lights flared to life, filling the dance floor with way too much reality for my fuzzy head.

I squinted at the bright lights, releasing Caleb and taking a step back as I looked around, trying to figure out what was going on.

Professor Astrum's voice blared over the loudspeaker. "Would all students of Zodiac Academy please make your way to the student shuttle buses for immediate transportation back to your Houses!"

I looked up at Caleb in confusion. "Is that normal?" I asked.

He shook his head vaguely in response, obviously trying to figure out what was going on.

A chill crept up my spine and I shifted away from him to find Darcy. She moved to join me too, pulling her Atlas from her clutch with a frown and holding it out as she spotted a message there.

Falling Star:

I should have warned her too.

"Who is he talking about?" I demanded.

"I dunno. Do you think something has happened or-"

The doors of the bar flew open and Marguerite burst in, her blood red hair flying around her and her eyes wide with an excited kind of fear. "Geraldine Grus has just been attacked! They're saying she might die!"

A cold stone dropped into the pit of my stomach at her words. We'd left that other bar without waiting for Geraldine to show up. What if she'd been hurt because she was alone, or was looking for us? I mean, the girl irritated the hell out of me with her devotion to our lineage but I never would have wished any harm to come to her.

"We have to find out if she's okay," I breathed, looking at Darcy in desperation.

"Come on," she agreed, snatching my hand and dragging me towards the exit.

A tide of students and the other bar patrons had already come up with the same idea and we were stuck at the back of them, unable to force a way through. My attention snared on the kitchen entrance behind the bar and I towed Darcy towards it. My light-fingered ways had taught me to suss out escape routes on the run and I got the feeling that the staff entrance was going to be a lot less busy than the front door.

I hopped over the bar and Darcy followed right behind me as I led us straight through the kitchen to the exit which dumped us in an alley.

The cold air slapped me in the face and helped drive a little bit of the alcohol fuzz from my head.

A sleek black superbike was parked up in the alley and for a moment I couldn't help but stare at it. I knew there were way more important things going on right now but that bike was top of the line, stupid beautiful in a way that just purred *ride me*. If it had been any other circumstances I'd have found a way to do just that but right now we needed to find out what had happened to Geraldine.

Goosebumps rose along my skin at the memory of the last alley we'd found ourselves in and we ran back to the street where a crowd had formed.

I shoved my way between the bodies and my gaze caught on a pale arm dangling from a stretcher as Geraldine was loaded into the back of a blue and grey ambulance. I fought my way to the front and released a breath of relief as I heard her voice.

She was mumbling about her family, asking for her mom and her skin was sickly pale but she was okay. She was alive.

The paramedic closed the door once she was loaded in and Orion was revealed, leaning against the side of the ambulance.

His sleeves were shoved back and his forearms were stained with blood. His skin was pale and he had bags under his eyes like he hadn't slept for a month which I could have sworn hadn't been there earlier.

"You saved her life," the paramedic said to him seriously. "It's a good thing you found her before her attacker could finish the job."

"I was only just powerful enough. I haven't got a drop of magic left," Orion muttered and I realised with a jolt what that would mean.

I tried to shove Darcy back into the crowd before he noticed us but my movement had the opposite effect and drew his attention. My heart leapt as he shot forward with his unnatural speed and Darcy released a squeal of fright half a second before his teeth pierced the flesh of her neck.

I caught her hand in mine, squeezing it reassuringly as I waited for him to release her but instead of stopping after a minute or so like the Vampires usually did, he held her more firmly. A whimper escaped her lips as he continued to suck her power from her veins and anger built in me as I was forced to watch.

"Hey," I snapped, shoving him roughly to try and force him off of her. "That's enough!"

Orion released a growl like a goddamn animal which was a clear warning to back off but I sure as shit wouldn't be doing that. Darcy's magic might have been pinned down by this parasite but mine wasn't.

I drew fire to my hands as I shoved him again and he finally staggered back with a curse, two hand prints burnt right through the fabric of his shirt and his flesh seared beneath.

"You've had enough!" I snarled, daring him to test me again as he glared at me, baring his fangs.

"Maybe you want to donate to the cause then?" he asked angrily and for a moment it seemed like he'd actually lost control.

A heavy arm landed around my shoulders as Caleb appeared and he released a deep growl in the back of his throat. "You might want to rethink that statement, *Professor.*"

Orion stared at us for a few seconds then shook his head to clear it. He released a heavy breath and his features softened a little.

"I haven't been drained that low in a long time. I shouldn't have tried to take so much all at once," he muttered. Not an apology but I doubted he was capable of more than that.

"Well feel free to just steal all of mine then," Darcy spat icily, clutching her neck.

The ambulance pulled away and Orion glanced about as if he were looking for someone for a moment before returning his attention to us.

"Come on, I can drive you girls back in my car," he offered.

My lip curled back on instinct. He was a psycho who'd just attacked my sister and was half covered in Geraldine's blood. He was obviously claiming to have saved her life but what if he'd been the one trying to hurt her? He was certainly capable of acting like a monster and he'd left the bar right before it had happened.

"We're not going anywhere alone with you," Darcy replied bitterly.

"Don't be ridiculous," Orion snapped, stepping forward like he intended to grab her arm. I moved to intercept him and Caleb joined me too.

"You don't fucking touch her again," I growled.

Orion narrowed his eyes at me, looking like he was going to object again but he hesitated as he glanced at Darcy.

"*Bastard*," she hissed, looking woozy.

"Come on, girls. The bus is gonna leave soon," Caleb said, tugging me after him but I dug my heels in, waiting for Darcy.

My sister moved first and I threw Orion one more filthy look before heading after her down the street. Caleb kept his arm around my shoulders as he led the way and I hurried to keep up in my towering heels which I was beginning to daydream about taking off.

There were two buses parked up by the side of the street and a huge crowd of students waiting to get on. I moved to join the back of the queue but Caleb rolled his eyes, guiding us past all of the people who had gotten there first and climbing the steps onto the closest bus.

Max and Seth were sitting in the back row and Caleb told three other kids to get off and wait for the next bus so that we could join them.

I almost wanted to protest his rudeness but my bed was calling to me and I just wanted to escape the madness in this town.

The bus rumbled to life as the doors shut with a hiss and we started off down the road. My brain was still fuzzy with alcohol and I leaned my head back as I closed my eyes, waiting for the journey to be over.

Caleb drew me against him but I shrugged him off, the moment of madness where I'd almost forgotten what he was had been well and truly left behind with the sight of all that blood.

I tried to relax and enjoy the ride back to the Academy but as the bus bumped over a pothole I realised one person had never reappeared amongst all the mayhem. And the last person to see him was now covered in blood and had been discovered at the scene of a crime.

So where was Darius Acrux?

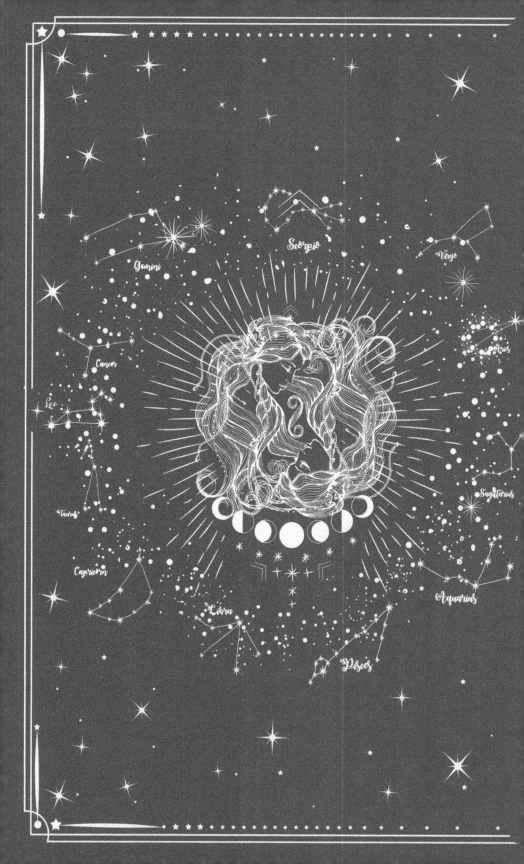

Darcy

CHAPTER SIXTEEN

I woke to a war drum in my head and a desert in my mouth.

The hangover from hell begins...

I groaned, rolling over and praying I wasn't about to find an Heir in my bed. It wasn't really my style but after the vat of alcohol I'd consumed last night, anything was possible.

There was no one there.

A sigh of relief preceded a wave of anxiety.

I replayed the events of last night, trying to fit everything into place like a puzzle with missing pieces.

I remembered the creepy alley, the bar, the dancing – *oh God the dancing* – then Geraldine -

"Shit!" I sat bolt upright, my hand flying up to my throat where Orion's teeth had dug into me and taken nearly every ounce of magic I had.

Geraldine had been hurt and Orion...he'd been covered in blood and completely drained of power.

I got up, pushing a hand into my tangled mane of hair, trying to pull it out of the nest it was determined to stay in. Strands of blue hovered over my face and I knew I resembled the undead even before I caught sight of myself in the bathroom mirror. Mascara and eyeliner were smudged under my eyes but I'd managed to put on the top half of my pyjamas before passing out which I was counting as a win.

I stepped into the shower, letting it run cold to help realign my thoughts.

Orion had been talking about killing someone.

Then Geraldine had shown up hurt and he'd been the first on the scene. It was too damn suspicious.

I had to speak with her. I had to know for sure. But *why* he'd attack her, I couldn't figure out.

I left my hair to air dry as it hung wet around my shoulders then pulled on a black sweater and jeans. I put on some thongs, my feet aching too much to bear being confined to any shoes.

I pulled the door open and my heart lurched as I came face to face with Seth, his fist raised to knock.

He looked disgustingly good for someone who'd been out as late as me last night. The flashbacks hit me in a wave. Me and him dancing. My ass grinding up against his...*oh dear god.*

"Morning, babe." He smirked, his eyes shining with all of the memories which were currently haunting me.

"Hey," I said tersely, tucking a damp lock behind my ear.

"Let me help you with that." He raised a hand and hot air pushed into my hair, wrapping around it until it was perfectly dry.

He stepped forward, pressing his nose into it with a sigh. "Cherry, my favourite. Speaking of cherries, has yours been popped yet?" He threw a suspicious glance into my room and I jammed my shoulder against the door to keep him out of my private space.

"That's none of your business." And it was *especially* none of his business that it was popped last year by a guy named Austin who'd been the perfect gentleman for three months up until the point he'd gotten what he wanted. And that was the not-so-funny punchline of my relationship history. The mere memory of the horrible day he'd dumped me bordered on the edges of my mind and I blocked it out as hard as I could.

"Can I make it my business?" he purred, wrapping his large hand around my back and yanking me into his chest.

"What the hell are you doing?" I pressed him back as my fragile hangover heart had a meltdown.

"I thought we were cool now...you know, after you sucked on my lower lip then whispered dirty things in my ear."

"I don't recall any whispering." I blushed because I *did* recall the other part. Vividly. And as I gazed at his mouth, heat coiled in my stomach.

He chuckled darkly. "Do you remember this bit too?" He moved his mouth to my ear and was half a second from biting it the way he had last night when I yelped and forced him back. He let me move him, stepping back with a wicked grin. I shut my door, locking it tight as I moved into the hallway.

Run or fight?

"Come on, I'll walk you to breakfast." He slung his arm over my shoulders and I tried to duck away. He held on firmly and that familiar, enticing scent sailed from his skin and planted twisted thoughts in my head.

"Why are you pretending to be nice to me? We've played this game before and I'm not falling for it, Seth."

"*Fuck*, do that again," he said, biting down on his fist.

"What?" I stared up at him in confusion.

"The part where you say my name like you're mouth-humping it."

"That's not a thing." I shook my head, making another attempt to escape and failing.

What the hell was happening right now?

"I need to go and see Geraldine," I said anxiously, glancing at him in

313

case he might have any news on her condition.

"Yeah, sounds like the poor chick got seriously messed up."

"Lucky Orion was there to help," I said dryly.

"Woah." Seth turned me to face him, his eyes as sharp as a razor.

"What?" I gasped.

"We have a serious problem, babe."

"What is it?" I asked, frantic. Did he know something about the attack? Had he seen Orion do it?

"You just mouth-humped another guy's name," he accused, deadly serious.

My lips parted and heat rushed up and down my spine. "Are you kidding me right now?"

"This is no joke. You know you can't date teachers right? Them's the rules. And I'd appreciate if you didn't mouth-hump his name in front of me."

"Can you please stop saying mouth hump? It's not a thing."

"It is a thing." He said with a shrug. "I just made it a thing."

"You're impossible," I sighed, turning and marching away from him. I needed to lose Dog Boy, find Tory and go and see Geraldine. I wasn't going to waste air talking nonsense with him any longer.

"Wait up," he called, his joking tone gone. He caught my hand, winding his fingers between mine. "Look, I know I mess around a lot and I've been an ass, okay?"

I turned to him in utter shock. Was he seriously about to do what I suspected?

He took a deep breath. "I'm sorry, alright? For your first night...for trying to make you cut your hair off and then covering you in mud with my mates and posting it online....and then leaving you in The Wailing-"

"I got it," I cut over him. "I remember it all pretty clearly."

I tried to pull my hand free but he wouldn't let go.

"I just thought...after last night." He cleared his throat - *was that actually a look of vulnerability in his eyes?* "I just thought things had changed. But clearly I was wrong." He released my hand and I assessed him, trying to work out his angle but I couldn't see one.

"Last night we were drunk," I said, my heart pounding like mad as I prepared to shoot down one of the most popular guys in school – *but surely this is some prank anyway?*

"I know but..." He shrugged. "So what? I still know how I feel this morning, don't you?"

I didn't answer. Because how *could* I answer? I didn't think I even had an answer. This guy had been my arch nemesis yesterday and a few overly handsy dances weren't going to change that.

I shook my head and he gave me the saddest puppy dog look I'd ever seen. Guilt weaved through my stomach.

"I don't trust you," I admitted. *Or anyone. But especially not an Heir.*

His eyes brightened as if I'd just given him the tiniest sliver of hope he needed.

"Can I try to make you trust me?" he asked.

I pressed my lips together and brushed my fingers through the blue tips of my hair.

The most important thing I'd learned in life? You can't trust people. And you especially can't trust boys with wicked smiles and equally wicked intentions. He'd already gone too far. Ridiculed me, made my first week at Zodiac as difficult as possible. So what more evidence did I need to stay the hell away from him?

"No," I whispered, the hurt of my past suddenly too close for me to breathe. I kept walking but he planted himself in my way and made me meet that begging expression of his again.

I can't actually agree to this can I? To let Seth try to make things up to me?

It was insanity to trust him. But now he was looking at me like *that* and

315

I swear his eyes were getting bigger and I was totally melting under his Puss-in-Boots face.

"Ergh *fine*," I gave in just to rid myself of that expression.

He grinned from ear to ear. "Kiss?" he asked.

"No!" I gasped as he leaned in for one. "Are you crazy?" I shoved him back and he started bobbing on his heels.

"Crazy for you."

"That is the cringiest thing I've ever heard," I laughed.

"Yeah actually, don't repeat that to anyone, babe. Street cred and all." He winked, snatching my hand again and tugging me along.

"You're not coming with me," I said, wanting to set firm boundaries here.

We moved into the stairwell and I spotted Diego heading down from his floor. He looked tired and I hoped Sofia hadn't given him too much trouble last night. His eyes landed on Seth's hand around mine and I immediately tugged it free.

"See ya," I shot at Seth with a firm 'stay away' stare.

He ran his tongue over his lower lip then headed off down the stairs, leaving my stomach in knots.

"Dios mio, tell me you didn't sleep with that mutt," Diego gasped as I met him on the stairs.

My cheeks flamed. "Of course not."

"Then why's he all over you?"

"Apparently he wants to be friends," I said, my disbelief of that fact obvious.

"Pfft, lucky you," Diego laughed. "Just don't buy into any of his bullshit, okay?"

"I won't," I swore. "So how's Sofia?"

"She's still sleeping." He gestured in the direction of his room and I raised an eyebrow.

"Oh nothing happened! I slept on the floor. But she didn't wanna be alone so..." He shrugged then gave me a frown. "I heard about Geraldine. What exactly happened last night? The rumours going around are locos, I don't know what to believe."

As we descended the stairs I explained everything, leaving out the part where I'd ground up against Seth for over an hour. *Gotta stop thinking about that.*

We headed outside and I regretted not bringing a coat as a heavy drizzle beat down on me. My Atlas buzzed and I took it out, finding a message from Tory.

Tory Vega:

Are you up?
If so, meet at The Orb in ten?

I tapped out a quick reply and headed toward The Orb with a yawn dragging at my mouth. I reached up to the bite marks on my neck, but my fingers ran over smooth skin. I'd recently learned in Cardinal Magic that Fae healed quicker than mortals once their power was Awakened but that seemed extra fast after I'd nearly been drained by Orion. Even now, the well of power inside me felt almost empty and as I didn't know my Order I had no idea how to replenish it.

I ground my teeth, furious at what he'd done. He hadn't just humiliated me in front of my friends and made me feel about as small as a peanut, he'd damn well left me vulnerable for who knew how long.

As I caressed the skin he'd bitten, a hazy memory came back to me on the bus. I'd been half asleep leaning against Seth's shoulder when he'd healed the wound, his magic brushing over my skin like a whisper.

Oh.

We arrived at The Orb and I anxiously waited for Tory to appear, glad to have someone who was in the same boat as me. The way she'd been dancing with Darius and Caleb last night had practically been pornographic and I didn't think she was going to live it down any time soon.

She appeared jogging down a path from the direction of Fire Territory, her leather jacket flapping out behind her and her face a picture of discomfort.

"Arghhhh," she groaned as she arrived, resting her hands on her knees. "I feel like death. But like if death was a puddle of shit."

I blew out a laugh, resting my hand against her shoulder for a second. "I feel your pain."

"The Heirs," she whispered like it was a horrible, horrible secret we shared. And in all fairness, it was.

Diego shook his head at both of us as if he was our disappointed father. Probably the first time we'd ever had one of those.

"Oh don't look at me like that," Tory said. "Blame the tequila."

"And the rum...and the whiskey. Remind me never to mix drinks again." I rubbed my head, sure a headache was going to make a fun appearance soon. For now, I was stuck in the wishy-washy hours before I truly sobered up. After that...it was all downhill.

"How's Sofia?" Tory asked Diego.

While he filled her in we made our way into The Orb to ask about Geraldine. Though who we were going to ask, I didn't know. I gazed across the gossiping sea of students and spotted Professor Washer on the other side of the room, tucking into a large cooked breakfast.

"Great," Tory huffed.

"It's him or a student," I muttered and from the nasty looks we were getting from the surrounding sophomores, I guessed it was best to ask Washer. No matter how much he made my skin crawl.

"Come on, he can't perve on us while he's eating," I said.

"Wanna bet?" Tory laughed and we headed across the room, halting in front of his table.

He looked up at us, clearly as hungover as we were. "Ah here's the tall drink of water I ordered with my breakfast." He glanced over at us appreciatively while Diego held back, looking scathingly in his direction.

"Er right," I said. "We were just wondering where Geraldine is? Is she in a hospital?"

"No she's in Uranus," he said around a mouthful of food.

"Excuse me?" Tory blurted. "Our friend has been hurt and you think it's an appropriate time to start throwing jokes around?"

"No," he said innocently. "She's in Uranus Infirmary, next to Neptune Tower?"

"Oh." Tory turned red and I burst out laughing as she stalked away.

Washer beckoned me closer with a grin and I felt his Siren power seeping over me. I drew nearer as a flood of warmth filled my chest. "Uranus is my favourite building," he whispered.

Diego snatched my arm, yanking me away as lust leaked into my body.

By the time I was halfway across The Orb with Diego, Washer's power left me and I shuddered violently. "*God* that guy's a creep. He makes everything sound filthy."

As we headed toward the exit, I noticed Tory had come to a halt before a group of girls. I increased my pace, frowning as I joined her and discovered Kylie standing there with her hands on her hips. Her friends surrounded her and a sea of pink lipgloss smirks were cast our way.

"Wanna explain *this*?" Kylie lifted her Atlas, playing a video on it for us to see.

Heat invaded my body as I watched a snapshot of Tory and I dancing with the Heirs. And it was *so* much worse seeing it replayed in the flesh. My eyes were hooded as I clasped Seth's neck and he wrapped my leg around his thigh. Tory was locked around Darius in much the same way, his hand riding up the back of her cami and caressing her skin.

Tory gazed coolly at Kylie, her shoulders squared. "And your point being..?"

Hell my sister had balls. I tried to conjure the same strength but words were failing me. I was the one draped over Kylie's supposed boyfriend in that video. But even as I thought it, a shriek of indignation hit my ears and Darius's girlfriend, Marguerite, appeared, shouldering past us to join Kylie's ranks.

Flames burst to life in Marguerite's hands as she glared at Tory. "Do you think he's actually interested in you? He was drunk and grabbed the nearest thing with a pulse."

"Well if that's Darius's standard now I understand why he's with you," Tory said airily and I couldn't help but exhale a laugh.

A crowd was forming around us and at Tory's words a chorus of ooohh's went up.

Diego had been jostled away from us by a few of the larger seniors and was trying to elbow his way back.

I lifted my palms and only a small trickle of power met my fingers.

Damn you to hell Orion!

"Bitch!" Marguerite snapped at Tory, stepping forward with a menacing glare.

Kylie glowered at me, looking more emotional than Marguerite. "Did you screw him?" she whispered, her lower lip quivering.

"No," I said earnestly. "It was just a dance, that's all." My heart twisted. I could see how hurt she was. I wanted to blame whiskey on the fact I'd shamelessly dry humped her boyfriend, but I supposed I had to take some responsibility for it too.

Kylie's hand whipped sideways and a blast of air smashed into my face in the hardest slap of my life. Pure poison poured from her eyes as if a venomous snake lived within her.

"Hey!" Tory barked as I cupped my stinging cheek with a wince.

"It's fine," I said through my teeth, looking back at Kylie. *Guess I deserved that one.*

The look in all of their eyes said they weren't close to done.

"Excuse me! Move move move!" Principal Nova's voice called from behind the group as she tried to get into The Orb.

The crowd disbanded and Tory and I made a break for it, darting through the gap. Tory snatched some energy bars from the hand of a shell-shocked A.S.S member who smiled like it was the best thing that had ever happened to her as we jogged out onto the path.

I glanced back at the doors, unable to spot Diego following but not wanting to remain there any longer.

Tory handed me a bar with a mischievous grin and I released a laugh, the tension in my chest disbanding.

"Hey! We're not done with you!" Kylie's voice followed us.

"Wanna fight 'em?" Tory asked with a manic smile and I was very almost caught up in that mad idea when I remembered something crucial.

"Can't, I'm running on fumes."

Tory sighed. "Fucking Orion. Let's run for it then."

We started jogging, the wind tugging our hair back and the thrill of escape dancing around us on the air. Laughter broke free of my throat and Tory joined me as we sped away from The Orb and every angry witch within its walls.

We followed the circling path all the way to Uranus Infirmary. The huge building looked more like an old manor house than a hospital ward and as we headed inside I noticed signs pointing to different classes. The place was home to Healing and Restoration magic and I wondered when we'd get to start learning skills like that. It would seriously come in handy on a campus full of beasts, half of whom seemed to be out for our blood.

In the foyer was a large fireplace with two staircases splitting off to the east and west wings. We followed signs to the ward, jogging past rows of gilded framed portraits on the stone walls. The eyes of past healers watched us go, all of them wearing blue robes and a white sash across their chests.

We headed deeper into the building, the way lit by flaming torches. My skin prickled with heat and a deep tingle flooded my body. "I hope Geraldine's alright," I said then chewed anxiously on my lip.

"She's tough," Tory said firmly. "She'll be okay."

We reached a long corridor of doors and I spotted a woman in full length blue robes stepping out of one of the rooms.

"Excuse me?" I hurried toward her and she looked up. "Is Geraldine Grus here?"

"Oh, yes, she's in here. She's been through the healing process overnight and has just woken up. She's still a bit drowsy, her injuries were quite extensive," she said sadly.

"What happened to her?" I whispered, my heart lurching uncomfortably in my chest.

She glanced up and down the corridor. "I can't talk about it. I'm bound by Healer confidentiality."

"Can we see her?" Tory asked and the woman gazed between us uncertainly.

"I'm not supposed to let anyone in until the Fae Investigation Bureau have spoken with her." She glanced over our shoulders then leant closer, rolling her lapel back to reveal a shiny A.S.S badge. "Her friend gave me one of these this morning. I know it's not the time but...I'm so humbled to meet you both." She bowed her head and I glanced at Tory awkwardly. "Just a few minutes," the Healer whispered with a conspiratorial smile, pushing the door to the room open.

"Thank you," I said brightly, heading inside. For once, being a Vega Heir had paid off.

The room was dark and smelled of a sickly sweet incense. Warmth washed over me from a fire behind a grate on one side the room and seemed to rush under my skin with its intensity. The thick curtains were drawn and the room looked more fitting for a Downtown Abbey character than an injured student.

Geraldine groaned, rolling beneath the crimson sheets, her hand falling to hang over the side of the bed.

"Hi Geraldine," I said gently, pulling up a wooden chair beside her.

Tory perched on the bed, giving her a sad smile.

Geraldine rolled toward us and her pale face was revealed between the nest of sheets.

"Gambolling gooseberries!" she gasped. "What are you doing here, your majesties? Surely you haven't come to see me?"

"Of course we have," Tory said firmly, patting her wrist.

"Ohhhh!" Geraldine wailed. "I feel so tired."

I frowned, my chest tightening as I gazed at her. "Are you okay? Do you remember what happened?"

She nodded, pushing herself upright and revealing the old fashioned white nightgown she was wearing. I wondered whether it belonged to her or the infirmary and I had a feeling it was the former.

"I took a shortcut down an alley toward the Odyssey bar, I figured that's where you would have headed. But as I was walking, I heard this terrible noise. A sucking, rasping, rattling noise. And I got such a fright I dropped all of my badges. So I knelt down, gathering them all up when this horrible dark shadow fell over me." She shuddered, gazing between us and guilt wrapped my stomach in knots. She took a measured breath, shutting her eyes for a second. "Then something cut into me right between my shoulder blades. Like a knife or -or a pitch fork, I'm not sure. But the pain was unbearable. Then everything fell dark and someone was kneeling over me and my magic was draining away so fast like it was being sucked right out of me. And all I remember is this scent... cinnamon." She shook her head as if she'd gone mad but my heart beat harder and harder. I looked to Tory and her brows pinched in a question.

"We'll leave you to rest, Geraldine," Tory said gently, rising to her feet.

"Yes, perhaps when I'm better we'll have breakfast again soon?" she called as we moved toward the door.

I glanced back at her, nodding firmly. "It's a date."

She squealed, raising a hand in goodbye as we stepped out of the room. The corridor was quiet and Tory immediately looked to me, her eyebrows hiking up. "What is it?"

"It's Orion," I hissed. "He smells like that." Heat crawled up my neck at the fact that I knew that. But it wasn't worth hiding out of embarrassment. "And if she felt drained, maybe he bit her?"

"He said he helped Geraldine," Tory whispered, but her face was painted in doubt.

"But what if he didn't? And what about Darius? The two of them left the bar together. And whoever it was must have been after us before. We heard the same weird noise."

"How can we be sure?" Tory asked, pushing a hand through her hair.

"We confront them," I said, my tone surprisingly fierce. "The next time we see them." My heart thumped a mad tune at the idea of me saying any such thing to Orion. But for the sake of Geraldine, I'd do it. We'd let her down by leaving her alone last night. And I was determined to try and make it right. Even if that meant facing my Cardinal Magic Professor in his foulest mood.

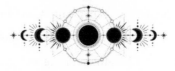

My magic returned. I wasn't sure how or when, but Sunday morning I'd noticed the keenness of its presence and was fairly sure it had replenished at some point on Saturday.

By Monday, I was growing even more anxious about facing Orion. I had my Liaison meeting with him that evening and it seemed like the perfect opportunity to broach the subject.

The FIB were currently visiting Geraldine and I was anxious to hear their latest report. After Friday, the news had been vague, not revealing many of the details. But today they were expected to announce their findings. And I hoped that meant arresting the perpetrator. Preferably Orion before I had to face him one on one.

I was gifted no such luck.

I stood outside his office at a quarter past seven in the evening, my throat tight as he appeared. Late as always. He wore a black sports kit with all four Elemental symbols printed on the front of it in white. He was splattered in mud and soaked through from the rain which had been descending on campus all day. His face was carved with stern lines and my heart beat a warning tune in my ears.

Oh shit, he's gone full asshole. I was joking when I said I'd face him in his foulest mood, universe. Give me a break!

He didn't look at me as he jammed his key in the lock of his office, pushing it open and stepping inside without a word.

I ground my teeth as the door swung closed in my face, taking a measured breath.

I am Darcy Vega. Heir to the throne of Solaria apparently. And I'm not going to be phased by a moody teacher.

Who might also happen to be a psychotic murder.

Holy crap.

I steeled myself and shoved the door open. A gust of wind left my palm in the same moment and the door slammed back into the wall.

Woops.

Orion didn't even seem to notice as he dropped into his ottoman chair and proceeded to siphon the mud off of himself with a wave of his hand.

I cleared my throat, wanting some damn acknowledgment before I started throwing around accusations.

He lifted a hand, whipping it sideways and the door slammed shut just as hard as I'd flung it open. My pulse went from nought to a million.

Should not have come here alone. Terrible plan. Abort abort.

"*Stand on the desk,*" Orion suddenly commanded, his voice dripping with Coercion.

The power of it slammed into me and I threw up a mental shield at the last second, just as I'd been learning to do all of last week. The command tried to burrow through my walls and I shut my eyes as I focused on keeping it out. My leg muscles twitched but I didn't budge, fighting the order with all my strength until eventually it fell away.

I released a breath that had been trapped in my lungs, opening my eyes and gazing triumphantly at Orion.

He clucked his tongue. "Good. Let's get on with tonight's session." He glanced at his watch. "All thirty five minutes of it."

I fought an eye roll, dropping into my seat opposite him, trying to muster the nerve to accuse him of murder.

Maybe I should build up to that.

"Geraldine's doing better," I said, eyeing him closely for a reaction.

"Yes, thank the stars," he said hollowly. "She can go back to annoying us all by preaching about the 'True Heirs'." He actually air-quoted it and I pursed my lips.

"Any idea who attacked her?" I asked airily.

"Whatever I know or do not know about that incident is none of your business." He stared me down and I refused to budge.

I'm not done with this conversation, douchebag. No matter how intimidating you are.

I scrunched my fingers up in the black skirt I was wearing, trying to decide on my next line of questioning.

"So, how is Order Enhancement coming along?" He leaned back in his chair, threading his fingers together and stacking his hands on his stomach. His t-shirt rode up to reveal a line of dark hair leading below his waistband and some unholy part of me squirmed with desire.

I forced my eyes up to meet his and didn't miss the flicker of amusement in his gaze.

"Well I know I'm not a Werewolf," I said with a shrug.

"Yes, a great way to figure out if you're a Werewolf is dancing with one of them like you were paid for it." He gave me a long, hard stare that pulled at my insides and unravelled them like twine. He'd seen me with Seth. Of course he'd seen me with Seth, he'd been at the bar. And I suddenly felt too hot and this seat felt too hard. I shifted nervously, his ridiculing tunnelling through my body.

I didn't have an answer to that, unsure exactly what he wanted me to say. Deny it? Couldn't. Confirm it? Wasn't necessary.

He picked up a pen and rolled it between his fingers, swivelling side to side in his chair. His eyes never left mine like he was trying to drill his way into my mind and pick out all of the information he wanted. "And screwing him didn't bring out the wolf in you either?" he asked calmly, rationally, like he had the right to ask that. Like he wasn't my damn teacher and it wasn't so inappropriate I wanted to scream.

My lips were pressed so tightly together I didn't know if they'd even allow me to answer. "I didn't," I hissed. "And it would be none of your business if I did."

He scooted forward in his chair and his bare knee brushed mine. I dug my heels in, inching backwards as my heart jolted from the contact.

He leaned forward and I held his gaze. "It's my business as your Liaison to look out for you. The Heirs will chew you up and spit you out, Miss Vega. Just a friendly warning."

Nothing about his face said friendly. In fact, if I looked up the exact opposite of friendly in the dictionary, there'd be a picture of him.

I rested my palms on the desk, leaning in rather than leaning away like I wanted to. My heart was frantic and begging me to run for the hills. But I wouldn't run away. This guy needed to know I was onto him. And there wasn't a damn thing he could do about it inside his own office. He couldn't incriminate himself like that. At least, that was what I was banking on.

"Funnily enough, sir, I've taken an interest in *your* business too lately."

I let the energy of that impending thunderstorm crackle over him.

He cocked his head, his mouth twisting up at the corner. "Well don't keep me in suspense, Miss Vega. I'm dying to hear the speech you've written for this occasion." He smirked darkly and in that moment, I knew that he knew what I was going to say. Because I'd already reacted like a kicked puppy when he came hounding into the bathroom after me on Friday night. He knew I was afraid of him. He knew I suspected him of coming after Tory and I. So he'd already put two and two together and realised I suspected him of attacking Geraldine too. But he didn't know *how* I knew.

I folded my arms and abandoned my speech because *dammit* he'd been right about that, I'd been rehearsing it all day. So I decided on being entirely blunt instead and laying out all of the facts.

I raised a hand to count them off. "You and Darius have been against Tory and I since we stepped in the door. You meet up in secret and you talk about going on killing sprees like it's completely normal. You chat with some stupidly hot model in a bar who is apparently in the know about your killing sprees and then you corner me in a women's bathroom like a psycho. *Then* later that evening both you and Darius go conveniently missing just before Geraldine turns up almost dead in a strange attack. Oh and who happens to be the first on the scene? You. Covered in blood and smelling like cinnamon."

Orion's brows had raised during my list and now he was grinning, his dimple out in full force. "Cinnamon?"

"Yes," I said firmly. "Geraldine smelled it and that's what you smell like so..." I waited for his outburst. A fierce denial, or him falling to his knees and begging me not to go to the FIB. But he just sat there watching me like I was his favourite TV show.

"And how many people have you told this, Miss Vega?" he asked calmly. Too damn calmly.

"Enough that if you lay a hand on me, the whole school will know what you're up to before midnight." Triumph scored a path through my body but something about his expression told me I hadn't quite won yet.

"Well it seems you've been spending a lot of your time spying on me - and smelling me apparently. But I'm still waiting for you to plant the evidence on my desk?" He gazed at my hands, mock-expecting me to produce something as my gut shrivelled into a prune. "No?" he questioned tauntingly. "No video, photo, audio recording? No evidence at all?"

I remained totally still, refusing to back down. I might not have had evidence but it was only a matter of time until the FIB caught on to him.

Orion calmly took his Atlas out of his bag, placed it under my nose and brought up a news report which had been published less than half an hour ago.

Wounds on Zodiac Academy Student Now Confirmed as a Nymph Attack.

Underneath it in bold were the words:

Professor Orion (the head of his field in Cardinal Magic at Zodiac Academy) is expected to be awarded the Noble Crest after his act of bravery saved her moments before her death.

"Oh," I breathed as the world crashed in around me.

"Yes – *oh*. Now can we return to your session or do you have any more wild accusations you want to throw around? Is Principal Nova dealing drugs under the bleachers at the Pitball Stadium? Or is Professor Pyro starting fires in The Wailing Wood?" He chuckled at his own words and I rose to my feet, knocking my chair over in my haste.

"You know what? I'm done with these sessions. I know what I heard, *sir*. And maybe you didn't attack Geraldine but I know you're up to something." I strode toward the door but Orion flew in front of me, his Vampire speed propelling him into my way.

My heart got jammed in my throat as he gazed at me.

"Don't bite me," I snarled, stepping back in a rage. "You took almost everything from me the other day and I've only just got my full power back."

His eyebrows knitted together. "You got it back? How?"

I shook my head. "I'm not sure."

"Well pay attention next time." He stepped forward and I slammed a hand to his chest, my heart screaming.

"Don't," I commanded.

"I wasn't going to bite you," he said and my shoulders sagged with relief. He stepped back and pointed to my chair, flicking a finger to force it upright. "Stay. Finish the session."

I glanced at the door uncertainly, unsure what to believe anymore. "Will you answer something for me first?"

"Depends what it is," he said in a gravelly tone.

"Do you want me and my sister dead?" I pinned him with my hardest, most unwavering stare. For Tory. For me. I had to hear his answer, even if it was a lie.

His eyes softened, running over my face with the faintest of frowns. "No, Blue. I don't."

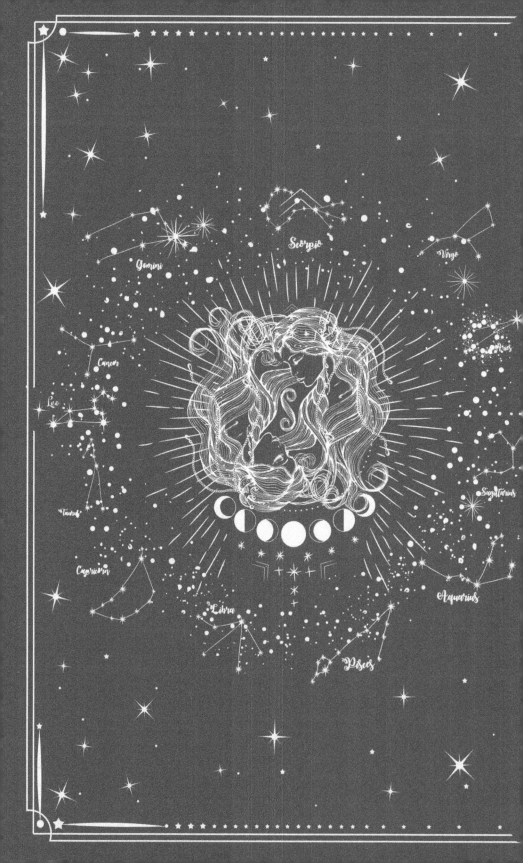

TORY

CHAPTER SEVENTEEN

The whole academy was buzzing with excitement for the dance this weekend and I couldn't help but get a little caught up in the idea of it too. Apparently the Professors always went all out to try and beat the previous year with impressive magic to decorate the place and fulfil the theme which was going to be 'fall' this time to match the season.

I was a little apprehensive about attending a party with our classmates who ranged from the weirdly obsessed A.S.S. to the outright hostile mean girls and quite possibly murderous Heirs. But I was trying to convince myself that the presence of the teachers and the general desire to have fun would mean that Darcy and I could enjoy it too.

After the arrival of my new clothes, I finally had some running gear and I was burning off a bit of nervous energy with a workout before I had to meet my least favourite Heir.

I jogged down to the Fire Arena wondering if Darius would actually show up for our tutoring session today. He'd skipped the one that had been arranged for last Thursday and Professor Pyro had bought into his blatant lies about getting caught up helping out some other students saving a cat from a well with a glowing look in her eyes that told me she was firmly Team Darius. *I* on the other hand had been told off for not rearranging the lesson myself even though I'd actually shown up and hadn't heard a word from Darius to excuse himself.

I was a little nervous about spending time with him one on one especially as I definitely had a few fuzzy memories of his hands trailing all over me on the dance floor the last time I'd gotten close enough to speak with him.

Each time I'd caught a glimpse of him in the Ignis House common room or The Orb since, I'd received glares from Marguerite which were toxic enough to cause physical harm. But she needn't have bothered; I had zero interest in approaching the possible-murderer/constant tormentor/crazy-hot asshole who had appointed himself king of the Academy. In fact if I had it my way I wouldn't even be heading to this session with him but Professor Pyro had made it clear that *I* would be held responsible if we missed another one and it would have a negative affect on my Reckoning. And despite all the glaring reasons for me to be running as far from this damn Academy as humanly possible, I wanted to stay. I wanted this magic that ran in my veins and I wanted the knowledge to wield it. And I wanted my damn inheritance too.

How many people could say that they'd had two sets of parents up and die on them? And what had our reward been for surviving those two tragedies? We'd lost our birth-right, grown up amongst people who had no idea what we were and had never had anyone to call mom or dad. We deserved that money for our suffering alone. We were owed a better life. And I'd survive a few years of torture if that was what it took to claim it. Hell, I'd already taken eighteen years of emotional neglect and uncertainty, what were a few more years to add to my sentence?

I reached the Fire Arena and forced myself to keep my head held high as I strolled straight in. As I'd run before having to face this meeting I chose to stay in the pair of tight fitting red yoga pants and grey sports bra for our session rather than changing into the Elemental lesson outfit.

I could never mention it to Professor Pyro but I'd been growing to hate that fire-proof outfit. I felt almost certain that it was making me struggle more with my fire magic rather than helping to protect me from the flames. I wasn't afraid of my own power hurting me no matter what form it took; it was such an intrinsic part of me that I just didn't believe it could. And something about the material designed to protect me from the flames felt more suffocating than I could explain. I'd taken the chance at summoning fire without it on a few times and had had much more success at controlling the flames in my hands.

Whether it was in my head or not, I wasn't sure but while she wasn't here to tell me otherwise, I was going to attempt this class without the outfit. I doubted Darius could give a shit what I wore and I guessed the only thing I had to worry about was the chance of someone else's flames burning me. But as Darius was only supposed to be helping me contain my own magic and not using any of his, I had to hope that wouldn't be a problem.

I looked around at the wide arena as I arrived and unsurprisingly didn't see Darius anywhere.

I resigned myself to waiting for him and eyed some of the other practicing students with interest.

The more I watched them creating different shapes and aiming their flames at various targets, the more my own magic seemed to build within me, aching to join them.

I glanced around a little guiltily, hoping I wasn't about to lose control again before easing my palm up in front of me. I bit my lip as I focused on the size of the flame I wanted to summon and suddenly it appeared.

I stared in surprise at the handful of fire as I held the magic steady. It didn't grow or shrink or reshape itself without me wanting it to. I felt... in control. A satisfied laugh escaped me as I banished the flame and I wondered if my theory about the Elemental lesson's outfit had some merit to it. Or maybe it was just not having an audience that worked in my favour. Whatever the reason, I was feeling a lot more hopeful about this session. If Darius ever turned up...

"Excuse me, your majesty?"

I glanced up as a tall guy with dark hair pushed back in a carefully styled kind of way walked towards me. He stopped about a meter away and bowed - fucking *bowed* - to me.

"Don't do that," I snapped, looking about to see if anyone had noticed him.

"Apologies, your majesty, I didn't mean-"

"And don't call me that either!" I said with exasperation as I eyed the shiny silver A.S.S. badge on his chest with distaste.

"Oh, err, apologies again, Roxanya I didn't mean-"

"Don't call me *that* either," I practically snarled. What was with these guys? What part of just treat me like anyone else and don't bring up that royal bullshit was so hard for them to compute? If they really did think Darcy and I were their sovereigns then shouldn't that mean they'd do what we asked them to?

"Right... Darcy?"

"*Tory.*" I frowned at him thinking go-the-hell-away-from-me thoughts but he didn't pick up on them despite the shouty barrage going on in my head. I probably wasn't any breed of psychic Order then...

"Tory," he agreed finally. We were two minutes into this conversation and he'd only just landed on a damn name for me, how long was it going to take him to get to the point?

"My name is Justin Masters," he announced and I kinda got the impression that that was supposed to mean something to me but my blank look encouraged him to go on. "I'm a senior. But my family served yours loyally right up until the devastating fall of your bloodline. I just wanted to tell you how deeply sorry I am for the tragedy your family befell."

"Oh. Well, thanks. I mean, we were babies so it's not the freshest wound but I appreciate the sentiment. Was that it?" I knew I was treading the line of bitch but the last thing I needed was for this guy to still be standing here when Darius finally arrived.

"No, actually. I was hoping that you might consider allowing me the honour to escort you to the dance this Friday?" he asked, his gaze holding mine as he awaited a reply.

I was so surprised that for a moment I could only stare at him. He was good looking, tall, well put together and clean shaven. In a nutshell he looked like the kinda guy your momma would love for you to bring home and your daddy would affectionately call son. Nice, clean cut - so not my type at all. He also clearly didn't know the first thing about me and was sporting that super shiny ass badge.

I leaned forward conspiratorially and lowered my voice a fraction. "Are you hoping to get into my pants, Justin?" I teased.

The heat that filled his cheeks at my suggestion was more than enough of a confirmation of my assessment of him and the spluttering response filled with words like 'escort' and 'propriety' and 'duty to protect' urged me to interrupt him.

"I'm just teasing you, Justin," I said soothingly. "But in all honesty I don't think we would be very well suited for a date. Perhaps you should see if Geraldine is free? If she's recovered by Friday I know she'd love to come to the dance and I get the feeling the two of you have a lot in common."

To his credit, Justin didn't seem upset about my refusal or even surprised. He merely thanked me for my time and excused himself with another bow.

I shook my head and gave my attention back to my solo practice session, keeping one eye on the entrance as I awaited my reluctant tutor.

I checked the clock. Multiple times. It was gone half past. At this point he wasn't just late; he'd left me waiting thirty-seven minutes. And as much as I wanted to think that maybe he'd just forgotten or wasn't good at time keeping, I knew better. He wasn't coming. And that left me with a conundrum. Of course I could just count my blessings, thank whatever forces that were working in my favour to save me from the torture of an hour in his company and leave it at that. But if I did, I knew I'd hear about it from Professor Pyro. She wanted me to work on my fire skills and she'd told him to tutor me and even though *I* was the one who had actually shown up, I knew I'd be the one to take the blame for this non-lesson if it didn't go ahead.

I released a breath of irritation and got to my feet, crossing the Fire Arena quickly as the other practicing students followed my movement with their ever-watchful stares. Nosey fuckers. No doubt everyone would be talking about Darius standing me up tomorrow if I left it at this but that wasn't what I was going to feed the rumour mill. No. It was time that lazy, entitled asshole got a taste of *my* fire.

I crossed the Fire Territory quickly, not giving anyone the chance to come at me on my journey. I drew on my power as I went, reinforcing my mental shields to the best of my ability in case I happened across any of Marguerite's posse.

My gut churned a little at the idea of confronting Darius. Who knew what way he'd take this but I wasn't about to just accept being stood up. If I challenged him over it and he flat out refused then Professor Pyro would have no choice but to assign me another tutor. Which I was hoping would be the case.

Only one way to find out.

I started up the stone steps which spiralled through the middle of Ignis House, ignoring the corridors which led to the various accommodation floors and heading straight for the common room.

A few people looked up curiously as I stormed in, wearing my irritation like a badge of pissed off right across my face. Luckily none of my regular tormentors appeared to be present and I used my momentum to carry me towards a group of three girls I didn't know. Their eyes widened as I stopped before them and I wondered if they knew who I was. The return of the Vega Heirs had certainly caused enough impact to have our names thrown around the masses but I wasn't quite conceited enough to believe my fame preceded me. Darius however was known by everyone.

"Hi," I said, not quite throwing enough saccharine into my tone to come off sweet and friendly but oh well. "I'm looking for Darius, has he been in here recently?"

"Not tonight," one of them replied slowly, her eyes narrowing as she tried to figure out why I wanted to know.

I turned away from them with a huff of irritation. He could be anywhere. Where was I supposed to look next?

"He's in his room," a guy offered from the couch beside me. He was big enough and sultry enough to be a Shifter but I wasn't sure what kind.

"Care to elaborate there pal?" I asked with a sigh. "It's a big building."

He raised an eyebrow at my tone then rolled his eyes as he decided to let it slide. "Top floor, all the way at the end of the corridor. Best room in the house."

"Of course it is," I muttered. "Thanks."

I turned away from him and headed straight to the stairs while my anger was still running hot in my blood and my nerve stayed strong. This could well be a terrible idea but I wasn't going to back down now.

I marched to the top of the stairs and all the way along the corridor. Beside his bedroom door a floor length window stood wide open and I resisted the urge to pull it closed as I looked at the dizzying drop below. It looked like the perfect place to toss someone who had disturbed you uninvited and I just had to hope that Darius didn't end up with the same idea.

The thump of a heavy bass reached me through the door to Darius's room and I ground my teeth as I recognised one of my favourite songs. *Thanks for ruining it for me, asshole.*

With a steadying breath, I lifted my hand and knocked on the door.

"It's open," Darius called, his tone casual, clearly expecting one of his friends. "Come in."

I hesitated, taken aback by the friendly tone and wondering what the hell I was letting myself in for by coming to invade his personal space. But I was here now. I'd knocked on the goddamn door so I couldn't back out. Besides, what was the worst he could do?

I steeled myself and pushed the door open. A huge space greeted me, at least four times the size of my own room which was in no way small. In fact I'd probably have gone so far as to call it more of a penthouse than a dorm.

He had goddamn king sized bed which sat beneath sprawling yellow and orange windows with a view out over the Fire Territory beyond. There was even a couch to the right big enough to seat four people, sitting beneath a huge TV hanging on the wall.

Aside from the extravagant size of it, the most eye catching thing about the room was the choice of gaudy decorations. Everything that possibly could be was made of gold and it didn't look fake either; the bed posts, coffee table, bedside cabinets and wardrobe doors were all heavily gilt. There was an alarm clock, picture frames, coasters, even a small trash can, all of which seemed to be solid gold. At the foot of his bed a chest stood with the top open to reveal the fact that it was half full of gold coins and gemstones as big as goddamn eggs. More of the same treasure was spread across his bed where he was currently laying, surrounded by the stuff and glaring at me like I'd just grown a second head. He was only wearing a pair of jeans and for a second I couldn't help but stare at the thick muscles which lined his chest but my attention was quickly snagged by the treasure again.

"What the hell do you want?" Darius snarled, pushing himself up to a sitting position so that he could throw the full weight of his scowl at me.

"Do you have a pirate fetish or something?" I blurted, eyeing the coins and gold with confusion.

"What?" he asked, his scowl somehow defying the laws of physics and finding a way to deepen.

"Well you're half naked in a bed full of coins so either you're doing something with them or putting them somewhere... *inaccessible* while fully dressed or I missed the memo about your enrolment in Captain Silver's new fleet."

A beat of silence passed as his gaze dragged over me.

"You really don't know anything do you?" he asked. "This is how my kind regenerate our power; from gold."

"Oh." I frowned at the coins again as I processed that. "So are you Order of pirate then? Do you transform into a one legged man with an eyepatch, a hankering for rum and a pet parrot?"

Darius stared at me for several long seconds and I began to wonder if he might just be about to crack a smile when he spoke again.

"What the hell are you doing in my room?" he demanded.

"Why do you think I'm here?" I bit back instantly. He knew full well that he'd been scheduled to meet me for our tutoring session and there was no way that I was going to allow some bullshit excuse about a kitten to spring from his lips this time.

"The only possible reason I can imagine for you to be stupid enough to come bursting in here would be that you've finally come to realise who really deserves to rule Solaria. And that being the case, I imagine you're about to bow down low and praise me and the other Heirs as your kings," he said, the casual tone of his voice possibly suggesting he truly thought I might be here for that reason.

"Keep dreaming," I muttered. "I'm here because you missed yet another one of our tutoring sessions, as I'm sure you're aware."

"And what if I am?" he asked, rising to his feet suddenly and sending a little cascade of coins to the floor. "What will you do about it? Make me bow to your will?"

I lifted my chin with every last shred of my anger. "Come and do the session like you promised," I demanded firmly.

Darius stalked closer and the difference in our heights was made painfully clear as he towered over me and I was forced to look up at him.

"No," he breathed, his body coiled with tension that I could practically feel. "If you want me to train you, you'll have to make me. If you really are one of our kind then you're going to need to learn quickly that Fae take what they want and the only thing that matters to us is power. So if you want me to do something for you then you're going to have to force me."

I bit my tongue against the urge to start calling him names and remind him that he'd already agreed to this and replied in an icy tone. "How many Elements do you wield again, Darius?" I asked. "Two isn't it?"

I let the insinuation hang between us and I almost felt his hatred of me and what I was as it simmered inside him.

"Two are more than enough," he replied bluntly.

"Yeah... but having all four has got to be better." God, why the hell was I rising to the bait like this? I'd only wanted him to help me, I'd never had any intention of prodding him about my potential. Hell, I'd never even given my potential much thought but now it sounded like I was challenging him for the throne I'd claimed to have no interest in.

"I'm an apex predator. My kind aren't built to take orders from anyone. It's written in my DNA to rule over you. I could never bow no matter how powerful you might have the potential to be," he growled, clearly reading between the lines I'd never meant to draw.

"How can you know that? You don't even know what Order I am. Maybe I'm higher up the food chain than you think," I snarled. I had no idea what had prompted me to enter into this argument with him but now that I'd embarked upon it, I felt like there was no way for me to turn back.

Darius snorted a laugh as he moved to pass me in the doorway, pausing right in my personal space so that I was face to face with the rippling muscles of his bare chest. The scent coming off of him was enough to make me bite down on my lip. It was at once metallic and animal. A hint of smoke and cedar and something totally him.

"No one is higher up the food chain than me, *Roxy*," he purred, placing a hand either side of my head and pinning me in against the door.

I swallowed a lump in my throat as I tilted my head back to look up at him, my heart pounding with fear and exhilaration at his proximity. I pressed my palms to the door behind me, locking them in place in case they got any ideas about reaching for the beast before me. Because despite the fact that Darius Acrux was a complete and utter asshole who had made it his mission to make my life a living hell, he was still my exact brand of temptation.

This close to him I felt like an addict sitting before a lit pipe, just hoping the smoke didn't blow in my face before I caved entirely.

My gaze roamed over his features as the distance between us was reduced to millimetres. The heat between us was building, sparks of energy lighting my skin with a carnal need which I was sure only he could satisfy but I refused to acknowledge the fact.

"What Order are you?" I breathed, wondering why I'd never asked before. He always acted like a monster to me so I guessed I'd never needed proof of what his nature was. But as I stood before him I began to feel like coming here had been a terrible mistake. The look in his eyes said he might just devour me whole and I got the feeling that wasn't an empty promise.

"I'll show you mine if you'll show me yours," he replied mockingly and for a moment I could have sworn his eyes changed. They'd looked golden, the pupils shifting to reptilian slits before he blinked and the deep brown colour had returned. Perhaps I'd imagined it but I didn't think so.

"But I don't know my Order yet," I said. "Professor Orion thinks growing up in the mortal world suppressed our abilities."

Darius eyed me intently as though he were looking for a lie and I resisted the urge to try and shrink into the door he'd boxed me against.

He stepped back suddenly and unhooked his belt buckle before unbuttoning his jeans.

"What are you doing?" I gasped, my gaze locked on his movements as he dropped his pants, boxers and all and I was given an eye full of every single inch of him.

"When you stop eye-fucking me I'll show you what you're so desperate to know," he replied mockingly and I snapped my gaze back up to his face, throwing him a scowl.

"People don't tend to whip their junk out in the middle of a conversation," I quipped. "So if you didn't want me catching an eyeful of little Darius then you shouldn't have brought him into our discussion."

Darius released a breath of laughter and for half a second it was as though we didn't harbour eternal hatred for one another.

He leaned close to me again and I had to work hard on maintaining eye contact as his naked god-like body shifted so close that I could hardly breathe.

"If you come to my room uninvited again then it had better be because you're ready to bow to us or to beg me to bend you over that headboard and make you scream my name," he purred and the total confidence with which he said it made my traitorous libido kick into overdrive. I bit down on a reply, not wanting him to know the effect he had on my body as I pressed myself back against his door defensively. Thankfully the movement was minimal and I managed to maintain my disinterested scowl.

Darius turned away from me suddenly then took a running jump out of the open window beside us. I gasped in surprise, my heart leaping as I shot forward to look out at what had happened.

For no more than two seconds, Darius free fell from the ten floor drop before his body shifted with unexpected ease and a huge, golden dragon burst from the prison of his flesh as if it had been there all along.

My mouth fell open in shock as I stared at the glorious beast of legend as Darius gave a few flaps of his powerful wings and spiralled up towards the clouds. Each of his scales glimmered in the light of the setting sun like a million gemstones. The thin membrane of his wings let a soft orange glow through them as he banked hard, weaving across the landscape of the fire territory with more grace than should have been possible for such an enormous beast.

As if that display wasn't enough to make my heart pound and my desire for him grow ten-fold, he released a powerful roar which made the whole glass structure of Ignis House shudder. He followed that up with a blast of dragon fire so potent that it warmed the skin of my cheeks despite the huge distance between us.

My gaze stayed locked on him as he tore through the skies and I found myself desperate to join him in the clouds. I wondered if there was any chance that when my Order revealed itself, I would be granted the blessing of wings. Flying through the clouds seemed like its own beautiful kind of freedom and I knew that if I could experience it even once then I'd be able to die having lived a life fulfilled.

I stood watching Darius in his dragon form for way longer than was necessary but I couldn't help it. He was beautiful, magnificent, a king amongst beasts. He'd been right when he said that we'd find nothing to tame this hatred between us though. Mine and Darcy's very existence threatened his position as a monarch of this realm and I knew with one look at his shifted form that a creature such as him would never be tamed.

He was power and heat and war wrapped up in a single being. He'd fight to the death to maintain what was his. And while we remained at this Academy, we were a threat. But for the first time since I'd arrived here, watching him soar through the skies sparked something in me. It was like a primal ache to rise to the challenge he presented. I didn't want his throne or his kingdom but I did want something else from him. I wanted his respect. And with that knowledge I knew I'd never bow to him. So if he was determined to see me fall, he was going to have to try and make me break.

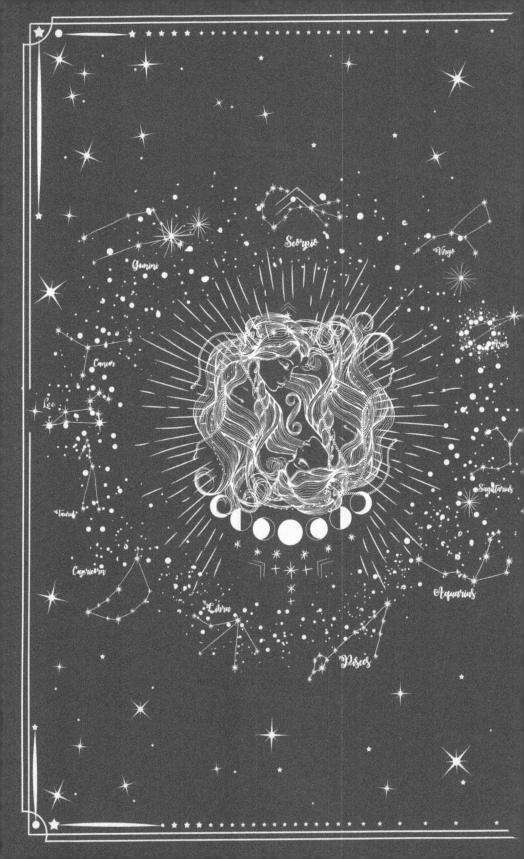

DARCY

CHAPTER EIGHTEEN

The Siren Order Enhancement class was held on the edge of the expansive lake in Water Territory. The sun was glimmering beyond the clouds, making a good effort at breaking through as we strode up the path to where around fifty students were gathering together for the class. Aqua House was far out at the centre of the lake, a group of beautiful domes, its sea green exterior sparkling in the morning light.

We hurried forward so we weren't the last ones to arrive and the Professor looked to us with a welcoming smile. "Good morning girls, I'm Professor Undine," she said, beckoning us closer. She was young with large blue eyes the colour of the ocean. Her hair was a rich crimson, braided down her spine and almost reaching her ass. She looked like a cross between Lara Croft and The Little Mermaid in her tank top and shorts. An outfit that it wasn't nearly warm enough for.

"Come on everyone, get in the circle," she called.

Everyone sat down in the grass and we dropped into a space between two guys, looking toward Undine at the heart of the group.

My gaze snagged on Max Rigel on the other side of the circle and my heart juddered. His arms were locked around his knees and his muscles were on show in the tight t-shirt he wore. Everything about him screamed Alpha male and I couldn't help but appreciate his masculine shape for half a second.

A slim blonde guy beside him muttered something in his ear and Max started grinning. He somehow looked even less approachable now he was smiling.

Undine took something from her pocket and I eyed the strange contraption with interest. A silver ball hung in a nest of wire and as she flicked a finger at it, the ball inside started spinning.

She tossed it at a girl across the circle who caught it out of the air.

"Happy," the girl announced, reading something off of the ball as it stopped spinning.

"Great," Undine said. "Who wants to start?"

Max groaned, seeming annoyed and I tried to work out what the hell was going on. "Can't we do fear again, miss?"

"We did fear last week," Undine said firmly. "And besides, you spend enough of your time terrorising the other students at Zodiac to get your fix, Mr Rigel. You don't need to get it here every week too."

"For fuck's sake," Max growled.

"*Language*, Mr Rigel. That's five points from Aqua," Undine shot at him. "You know how much I hate the Fs and the Ss."

"What about the Cs?" Max asked with a smirk.

Undine ignored him, glancing around the circle until her eyes landed on Tory and I. "Ah, this is a good opportunity to introduce you to our Order, girls. Come and stand up here with me."

We rose to our feet and my skin tingled uncomfortably as I felt everyone's eyes on us. We joined Undine and she gave us an encouraging smile.

"Think of a happy memory you've had this week," she instructed and I shared a look with Tory.

Happy? We hadn't had much time to be happy with everything that had gone on in the past few days.

"Er..." Tory frowned and I chewed my lip.

A couple of giggles sounded around us and a blush crept into my cheeks.

"You must have something that's made you happy in the last seven days? Or the last fourteen perhaps?" She raised her brows, seeming concerned as she glanced between us.

With slightly more leeway it was easier. Before Geraldine had been attacked, our night with Diego and Sofia had been a lot of fun. I tried to focus on only the good parts and nodded to Undine. "Got one."

Tory nodded as well with a grin.

"Okay." Undine pointed out ten people in the circle and they all rushed forward like dogs eager for a meal.

I shrank as five of them surrounded me and the other five ringed Tory.

"Take your coat off," a girl with dark ringlets urged and someone pulled it from my shoulders, tossing it on the grass.

"Hey!" I went to grab it but the five of them closed ranks.

"Hold that happy memory in your heads," Undine instructed.

Were we about to fly off to Neverland right now? Because I was pretty sure we needed fairy dust for that.

I tried to relax, knowing this was just the way of the Siren Order. And if I belonged to it, I had to try and fit in.

I conjured the happy memory again and the group around me pressed their hands to my bare arms. One even cupped my cheek.

The Sirens shifted in nearer, starting to smile. I realised one of them was the blonde boy who'd been sitting with Max and my stomach knotted.

"Tell us about your memory," a girl said and a wave of calm washed over my heart.

"I was out in town drinking with friends," I said, recalling how Sofia had consumed all four of Diego's shots before any of us had had a chance to grab one. A snort of laughter escaped me and the Sirens chuckled along with me.

"What else?" Max's friend asked, seeming less affected by my laughter. "I can sense something else in you, tell us about the rest of your evening." His eyes were hopeful as he brushed his fingers over my wrist. My tongue loosened under his influence and I felt myself drifting toward the later events that evening. "I saw Professor Orion."

One girl gasped then grinned keenly as she held onto my arm.

I frowned, but the blonde guy squeezed my flesh, a wave of their power calling me to keep going and my words kept flowing. "He was angry...he's so hot when he's angry."

Some of the group moaned and Undine suddenly clapped her hands. "Enough. We're not doing lust today."

Everyone released me and the reality of what I'd just said slammed into me. My cheeks burned as the Sirens headed away and I blew out a breath of annoyance at Max's friend.

I turned toward Tory but found she was still entranced by her group and I could almost see them feeding on whatever happy story she was telling.

Undine split the rest of the Sirens up into groups and they started recounting happy memories while their classmates drank in the power of their emotions. Max laid down in the grass, cupping his head with his hands, clearly not interested in participating.

The Professor moved to my side, giving me an apologetic smile. "You've got to keep your wits about you, Darcy. You can build shields and control which emotions Sirens can access." She rubbed my arm, leaning closer. "Orion is on your mind, huh?" She nudged me and I nodded as I recalled the way his dominating aura made me feel sometimes. Completely powerless and yet at the same time like I wanted to reach out and feel the graze of his stubble on my hands, run my fingers around the back of his neck and press my lips against his. He was intimidating as hell but there was also something about him that just...drew me in. And I'd *maybe* once or twice daydreamed about being spread across his desk under the full keenness of his rage.

Professor Undine sighed and I jerked away from her, realising what she'd done. "Hey," I snapped, furious.

Why is everyone after those emotions?!

And why am I even turned on by Lord Voldemort's hotter, younger cousin?

"Sorry," she said, but the smile pulling at her lips told me she didn't really mean it.

Leeches. All of them. In a way, I disliked this power more than the Vampires'. At least with them they only took magic, the Sirens could pull my darkest thoughts from my lips and feed on my feelings about them while draining my power.

Max suddenly pounced on Undine from behind, grabbing her shoulders. She squeaked in alarm and Max smiled keenly as he kept his hands on her to absorb her frightened reaction.

"We're not doing fear, Rigel," she snarled, throwing up a hand so a gust of air shoved him away from her. She stalked away, checking on the other students and Max hounded off after a couple of girls, looking like he wasn't done playing games.

I relaxed a little as I spotted Tory moving to join me, wondering if we could somehow ditch this class before any more of my thoughts on Orion were offered out like candy.

"I am *not* a Siren," she announced, seeming as pissed off as me as she arrived.

I nodded my agreement then noticed Max watching us as he stood with the blonde guy and some pretty girls. He stared at us for a few hard seconds then turned to his friends and started talking in a low voice.

"I don't like the look of that," Tory whispered as she scowled at them.

"Maybe Undine will just let us skip the rest of this?" I suggested hopefully. "We're obviously not part of this Order."

Tory nodded firmly. "I barely like hugging people let alone having heart to hearts."

Before we could broach the subject with Undine, she broke up the groups and gathered everyone to the lake's edge. She pulled off her shirt and I gazed at her in bafflement, leaning closer to Tory. "Does *every* Order have to get naked before they turn?"

She snorted a laugh. "Apparently."

She'd told me about Darius's dragon form and how he'd gotten butt naked in front of her before leaping out of a window. Everyone in Zodiac seemed to be body confident and ready to strip off at any given moment. But I just couldn't see myself doing it no matter what Order I was a part of.

As Undine tossed her shirt on the ground, my brows raised at the sight of her skin rippling and changing. Dark red scales glittered across her flesh, fanning out across her body, shimmering like oil in the hazy sunlight. They reached up to her chin and went no further so she appeared to be wrapped in a skin-tight suit made from a mermaid's tale. She ran toward the lake, diving in and disappearing under the waves with incredible grace.

"I'm not going in there," Tory announced and I nodded as we drew away from the shore and the deep water.

The rest of the students followed, their scales an array of colours from richest pinks, to pebble grey-blues and darkest green. I stared in wonder as nearly all of them jumped in and none returned to the surface.

My heart stalled as I found Max remaining on the shore with his friends, his shirt removed and his huge chest glimmering with deep navy scales. I was injected with an Aqua Man infused fantasy and caught myself before it got out of control.

Why were these Heirs all so devastatingly beautiful? At least one of them should have had skinny arms and a tuba for a nose. I could only imagine their parents were all gods from the heavens themselves.

Max grinned at us, stalking nearer until the weight of his power fell over us.

He took both of our hands, winding his fingers between ours. Calm rippled through my chest and guided my anxious thoughts away on swift wings.

"Hi," Tory whispered and Max smiled keenly at her.

"How're my favourite twins?" he asked, a conspiratorial note to his voice. His friends laughed, but none of them approached, respecting Max's boundaries as he held onto us for himself.

"Come sit with me," he said, his voice lilting and soft. He guided us toward the edge of the lake and we sat either side of him. His skin never parted from mine and I was vaguely aware that all the time he was touching me I was under his spell. But I couldn't seem to make myself pull away.

He wrapped an arm around each of our shoulders and the heavy fog over my mind thickened.

"What's your greatest fear, Tory?" he breathed in her ear and she gazed up at him, her eyes widening with the worst memory of her life. My throat constricted as I recalled that night a few years ago, the slicing terror of almost losing my sister.

Max sighed softly, his thumb caressing my shoulder as he kept his eyes on Tory.

I could see her fighting the draw he had over her and for a second I almost managed to tug away from him in a bid to help her. His influence pushed against my heart again, soothing me and I fell against him, resting my head on his shoulder. The scent of sea salt sailed over me and I listened quietly as Tory recounted that awful evening.

"My ex-boyfriend was driving me home late one night. We'd been fighting and he kept shouting at me. I told him to shut up and watch the road. He was driving like a maniac." Max rubbed her arm, pulling her closer. "We were heading back from a weekend in Wisconsin. The roads were so dark but he wouldn't slow down. He took a turning too fast and..." Her eyes glimmered with tears and I reached out to take her hand.

"We veered off a bridge and crashed into the river below. The car sank so fast and my ex...he got out. He left me. Just swam to the river bank. I couldn't get my seatbelt undone and I panicked. The air was running out and it was so, so dark." Tears ran down her cheeks and my heart strummed with sympathy. "I couldn't feel my fingers through the cold. And when the water went over my head I just thought that was it. I was going to die stuck in that shitty car while my even shittier boyfriend sat on the riverbank and didn't try to help me." She swallowed deeply and my own tears fell free as my heart squeezed tightly. "Luckily a farmer had seen us swerve off of the road. He swam out and cut the belt. He saved me. But since then I just can't go in deep water. It frightens the hell out of me." She shivered and Max soothed her, rubbing her arm.

He turned to me and I felt his power sinking deep into my bones, sucking out everything he wanted. "And you? What's your worst fear Darcy?" His voice was a deadly purr and my deepest fear rose in me the second he requested it.

"Every foster family we ever had got rid of us. We were barely in one home for more than a year. We caused trouble. Sometimes I regret some of the things I did so much. If I'd treated those families better, maybe they would have wanted me. That was almost bearable. I knew I was difficult to love but I didn't think I was entirely unlovable not until..." I fought against his power, my heart squeezing with the memory that had ended with my hair blue and my trust in humanity gone forever. It was mine and I didn't want to share it. I didn't even want to relive it in my own head.

"Go on," Max whispered, a hunger in his voice as his power wrapped around my tongue and pulled the words from my rebelling lips.

"This guy started pursuing me in school last year. I never really spent much time making friends with people but he was nice and it felt good to talk to someone who cared. We dated for around three months and I thought for one idiotic second I was actually falling for him." I shook my head at myself, sucking in a breath as I went on. "I lost my virginity to him at a party and afterwards he was so cold with me. He would barely look at me and I knew something was terribly wrong. The way the air changes just before a storm, that was how it felt. He'd gotten what he wanted and he just left me there after feeding me some bullshit excuse about how he wasn't ready for a relationship."

"Darcy," Tory whispered, as if trying to rouse herself from Max's power to stop me, but it was too late. He had this memory in his grasp and he was going to reel it in like a fish on a hook.

"He dumped me five *seconds* after he'd gotten what he wanted. I got out of there as fast as I could. And on my way home, I was crying and couldn't see properly. I tripped over on the sidewalk and bashed my right knee like the clumsy idiot I am. That night I sat in bed just staring at that bruise, wondering how a physical wound could look so bright and angry but emotional wounds stayed entirely invisible. I wanted my hurt branded on me, to remind me never to trust anyone again. So I dyed my hair the colour of that bruise. Black and blue. My own personal wound." My heart twisted and knotted as tears collected in my eyes. I turned away, a flow of shame running through my blood. I'd never voiced that part of the story to my sister, let alone Max who was feeding on every word of if. But my tongue kept moving, giving him everything he wanted. "My deepest fear is being cast aside, my heart crushed by trusting blindly again. So I'll never let anyone in again."

Silence descended and I could feel the tug of Max's power, draining me emotionally and magically. The tears had dried on my cheeks and the contact between us suddenly felt colder.

Max stood, leaving us on the ground as he stepped away. "Thanks for the meal Vegas. See ya." He dove into the lake and my thoughts slammed back into realignment. His friends laughed heartily as they jumped in after him with hollers of excitement.

Neither Tory or I looked at each other for a long time. We stared across the lake. And I decided Sirens were my least favourite Order of them all.

I was still feeling magically drained by the time Tory and I arrived at lunch in The Orb and I wondered how I was going to refuel the power the Sirens had taken. We'd barely acknowledged what Max had done to us and I felt sure she didn't want to talk about her fear as much I didn't want to talk about mine.

I spotted Diego and Sofia in a corner of the room and we headed towards them. I was quietly glad Geraldine wasn't here to lay out a table at the heart of the lounge for once, though I immediately felt guilty for it. The Nymph attack had apparently left her unable to heal as quickly as usual and her power was only just starting to restore.

The four Heirs were sitting on their usual couch and a hard wall built up in my chest as I surveyed them. Seth caught my eye and raised a hand to wave. I turned away, not trusting him one bit especially after one of his best friends had sucked my inner secrets out of me earlier. He'd probably heard all about what I'd told Max by now and the thought made me sick.

"Fuck them," Tory hissed as we headed over to join our friends.

We sat side by side and I relaxed a little, glad when Sofia took over the conversation and started telling us about her own Order class. Diego had spent his class with the Harpies and it sounded like he'd had more fun than we had.

"You didn't just ignore me did you, babe?" Seth dropped into the seat beside mine, wrapping his arm around my waist and sending a bolt of electricity through my heart.

"Go away," I said, scooting down the seat to try and escape him.

"What's up?" he asked as Diego and Sofia stared at him like the Loch Ness Monster had just joined our table.

"As if you don't know," Tory said dryly. "And can you stop pretending to like Darcy? No one's falling for it."

My heart stung at her words even though I knew she hadn't mean it the way I'd taken it. But after revealing my inner fear to Max, that old wound felt thoroughly picked open right then.

"I didn't mean that," she said quickly and Seth pulled me against his hip, leaning around me to glare at my sister.

"Well what did you mean, *Tor*?" he asked.

"Don't try that bullshit. We're twins, nothing gets between us," she snapped at him and I shoved him away again, shuffling back up to Tory's side in a show of unity.

Seth frowned, playing with something in his hand. He glanced around at the icy stares he was receiving from everyone at the table then stood up with a snort of irritation.

Before he left he leant over my shoulder, his mouth brushing my ear. "Read it when you're on your own." I felt him slip something into my pocket and he turned, marching back to his friends who were watching us with unconcealed scowls.

I shifted uncomfortably in my seat, still looking over my shoulder at Seth as he rejoined his friends.

Diego snapped his fingers by my ear. "Earth to Darcy, please tell me you're not interested in that perro?"

I didn't answer. Partly because I didn't know what perro meant, but also because I didn't know what the answer was. The note Seth had put in my pocket seemed to be burning a hole there, begging me to run away somewhere and read it.

"You can't!" Marguerite's voice suddenly filled the entire Orb and everyone fell silent.

I wheeled around, spotting her standing above Darius as he gazed up at her from his position on the couch, seeming annoyed that she was causing such a scene.

"It's over, move on," he said coolly, turning his cheek to try and dismiss her.

"Darius, baby, how can you throw away everything we have?" She clutched his hand and he prised her fingers off of him, attempting to continue ignoring her.

"Darius!" she shrieked, fire bursting to life in her palms.

The Heirs were suddenly on their feet and Darius practically snarled at Marguerite as he glared down at her, almost nose to nose. The flames in her hands extinguished and she backed up, muttering an apology and bowing her head. Several of her friends ran forward to group around her and I spotted Kylie amongst them. My tongue thickened as the tension in the room weighed down on me.

"This is about *them.*" Marguerite suddenly pointed at Tory and I all the way across the room and my heart rammed into my throat. "Ever since they arrived you've been acting different."

"Stop embarrassing yourself," Caleb shot at her, rolling his eyes. "You just can't deal with the fact that Darius got bored with you months ago. Move on, find someone else to screw. From what I've heard, it sounds like you need the practice."

Marguerite looked to Darius in horror. "But you love me."

Silence rang out and Darius glanced at his friends with a smirk. "Love you?" he laughed, turning back to her. "At what point in our once a week bed parties did you get that idea?"

She turned scarlet and her friends tried to pull her away, one of them petting her back.

Seth barked a laugh and Kylie shot him a death glare. "You're no better. I saw that video of you and Darcy fucking Vega at the bar last Friday."

Seth held his heart, faking a wound. "Sorry, babe, did I forget to ask your permission? You know I'm totally polyamorous right?"

She huffed at him, her hands balling into fists. "No Seth, you have *never* told me that."

"No?" he questioned airily, leaning his shoulder against Max's. "Well you can't go poly-shaming me now can you?"

She glared at him coldly. "You're a liar."

The four Heirs fell deathly still and my heart seemed to freeze with them. Max stepped forward, cracking his neck. "Wanna say that again, peaches?"

Kylie backed up, a glimmer of fear entering her gaze. "He's not polyamorous, Max, he's just cheating on me."

My brows raised and my stomach knotted. I had to give it to her. The girl was fighting her corner and she wasn't going to let Seth get away with anything.

Darius tried to walk around Marguerite and she grabbed his arm, holding on for dear life. "Please," she begged and dark clouds drew over his eyes.

"Let go," he said calmly, but nothing about him said calm.

She flinched back as if he'd been more abrupt and the other Heirs filed through the crowd of girls after him. They exited The Orb and the moment the door swung shut, mutters broke out throughout the whole lounge.

Marguerite wiped her eyes with the back of her sleeve and I realised I should stop staring a moment too late. She and Kylie locked sights on us like a missile and my heart jolted hard.

"Bitches incoming," Tory hissed as she tugged on my sleeve to get my attention.

My heart beat in time with their furious footfalls as they closed in on us. Sofia turned pale and Diego rested a hand on her arm, his jaw set as his eyes fell on the group of pissed off tigresses breathing down my neck.

Tory's fists were clenched and I could tell she was preparing to defend herself with her power. There was no sign of the A.S.S and most of the girls in Kylie and Marguerite's vengeance squad were sophomores or older. So that meant relying on our own poorly harnessed powers.

I turned, hoping to try and explain our way out of this before a fight erupted when the entire table flipped up into the air. I was thrown to the floor beside Tory and Sofia yelped as she and Diego were tossed aside too. The table shot up above us at speed and screams broke out as it burst into flames.

I threw up a hand to shield myself, panic flowing through me as glasses and plates cascaded from the fireball and smashed on the hard floor around us.

I rolled onto my knees in a bid to escape and Tory cast a rogue fireball from her hand. It flew too high, missing her target as it soared over the heads of our attackers and hit the far wall.

The table smashed back down to the floor behind us and I stumbled to my feet to escape the blast. I steadied myself and gazed back at the devastation, checking my friends were okay as my heart battered against my ribcage.

"What did he give you?" Kylie demanded, shooting forward and thrusting her hand into my blazer pocket.

I gasped as she clutched Seth's note between her fingers before unfolding it and staring at whatever it said for a painfully long second. With a choked sob, she threw it at me and ran away into the crowd.

"Get out of Zodiac, Vega sluts," Marguerite spat, her eyes spewing acid. She stormed away with her crew and my eyes fell to the note as it landed at my feet. Seth's words were written in a scrawling handwriting and what they said made my heart pound like crazy.

Be my date for the dance.

I heard the group of girls make it out of The Orb, slamming the door behind them. My heart shuddered and nausea gripped my stomach. Because I knew without a doubt, this was far from over.

TORY

CHAPTER NINETEEN

After spending a day dodging questions about the night I'd spent dancing with the Heirs, I was ready to admit that drunk Tory hadn't done me any favours yet again.

The following morning we spotted Marguerite and Kylie throwing glares at us the moment we arrived at The Orb as if their relationship issues came down to us instead of being a problem with the douchebags they'd selected for themselves. For the sake of avoiding their nonsense, we decided to grab breakfast to go which we ate on route to our lesson rather than deal with any more of their crap.

At the end of the day, I said a quick goodbye to Darcy as we left our Cardinal Magic class and headed in opposite directions along the vaulted corridors of Jupiter Hall. She was off with Diego and Sofia for a study session in Venus Library but I just wasn't in the headspace for more work. We had plans to meet in two hours for dinner at The Orb and in the meantime I had every intention of going for a nap. These early wake-up calls were wreaking havoc with my perfect sleep patterns and I just couldn't force myself into the habit of going to bed a minute before midnight. I'd always been a night owl and the crack of sunset was no time for me to be headed towards slumber. So I decided that I could catch up with a nap without having to try and alter my bedtime.

As I walked to the back exit of the building, a junior slammed his shoulder into me hard enough to knock my satchel from my shoulder and send all of my books flying.

I cursed him as I scrambled to retrieve them while the rest of the class swarmed around me and headed off down the stairs towards the exit. Thanks to some less than accidental kicking, I was forced to scurry about and grab a few scattered pages.

I knelt down as I tried to piece everything back together and refill my satchel and the sound of giggling reached me from the stairwell.

"Hurry up!" I recognised Marguerite's voice. "That jumped up little boyfriend thief is going to be here any second and we need to get every moment of this on camera," she hissed.

I stilled, listening for more as I got the feeling I knew exactly who she was waiting for.

"I didn't think you and Darius were officially dating?" another girl asked.

"He belongs with me," Marguerite growled. "Anyone with eyes can see that!"

"Careful with that Pegasus shit, Bianca!" Kylie snapped.

I straightened and half turned away from the stairwell, planning to go the long way around and avoid whatever glittery-shit filled hell they had planned for me but I stopped myself before I could scurry away.

I'd never been one to run from a fight before so why the hell should I run from a bunch of mean girls just because they'd claimed ownership over a man-whore and wanted to punish me for stumbling into his path?

I eyed the stairwell as I tried to come up with a solution. The stairs were narrow and spiralled tightly down to the lower floor and it sounded like the girls were fairly close by.

I still had very little chance of beating any of the older students head on with my magic but there was one thing I could easily do.

I lifted my hands with a smirk and summoned water, letting my power build and build before finally releasing it in a torrent that flew from me and flooded the entire stairwell.

The girls shrieked as they were drenched and I turned and ran the other way before they could come back for me.

Their footsteps were quick to follow from the stairs and I slipped into the closest door, grinning to myself as I listened for the sound of them passing. Their cries of anger and thundering footsteps passed right by outside and I had to bite my lip to stop myself from laughing. They hadn't seen me and that meant I had one less issue to deal with today at least.

"Hiding from someone?" an amused voice cooed behind me and my heart sank like a stone as I spun to survey the classroom I'd believed to be empty.

My gaze fell on Caleb as he smiled predatorily from the shadows where he was seated.

"Well damn, I've run straight from a pack of hyenas into the mouth of a crocodile," I muttered.

"Not a lion?" he teased and the fact that he hadn't even bothered to rise only confirmed the fact that I had no chance of escaping him.

"Oh no, they hunt together, you don't strike me as the type to need any help in cornering your prey."

"Sometimes it comes right to me without me having to do a thing," he agreed and I caught the trace of hunger in his dark eyes.

I took a steadying breath, pushing aside the urge to run. We both knew he had me and racing through the corridors filled with witnesses before inevitably ending up pinned against a wall and drained didn't really appeal to me. There was a quiet kind of dignity in just accepting my fate. One day I'd be strong enough to fight him off, but as much as it angered me, that day hadn't come yet.

"Shall we just get this over with then?" I asked, stepping towards him with purpose. If I was going to be used as a human juice carton I'd sooner do it on my own terms. I kept my stride even as I pulled my long hair over my right shoulder, baring my throat to him.

Caleb's gaze slid to my neck before trailing lower as he took in my curves, a different kind of hunger lighting his navy eyes.

Slowly, he pushed himself to his feet and I stopped a foot away from him, tipping my head to look up at him.

"You know, I can feel your power," he breathed, leaving the space between us empty and my heart began to beat a little faster. I wished he'd just get on with it but I didn't think begging him to get it over with was the best way to negate this torture so I just held my ground.

"Any idea on what I am then?" I asked, wondering if the different Orders of Fae tasted like flavours of pop. With a bit of luck, I wouldn't become his favourite.

"Sadly not. I can only feel the depth of your power, the strength of it. And you're *strong*. Once you learn to harness it, I have the feeling that I won't be able to take an ounce of it from you without permission." His lips twitched into a smile and I couldn't help but stare at them for a moment, wondering if I might like them a little more if only they didn't hide his fangs.

"Why the hell would I ever give you permission?" I asked, arching an eyebrow. Sure, I wasn't exactly fighting him off *now* but this wasn't permission; it was bitter acceptance. We both knew that I couldn't fight him off... *yet*. But if there was any chance in hell of me growing strong enough to manage it then I knew without a doubt that I would do just that.

Caleb reached out and brushed his cool fingers across the flickering pulse at the base of my throat. My skin skittered with nervous energy and a faint tingle of pleasure which I refused to acknowledge came along with it.

"You're an Heir too. If you make it past The Reckoning and complete your training here at Zodiac then the chances are that we will be in each other's lives for a very long time."

"I thought the whole point of your little boys club was to make sure my sister and I *didn't* make it through the Reckoning? Don't you want us gone?" I demanded.

Caleb shrugged one broad shoulder and I was struck with the sense that maybe he wasn't as desperate to get rid of us as I'd presumed. The four of them were such assholes but on an individual level, Caleb hadn't done much beyond hunting and biting me. The incident in the cave was a little different but even then he hadn't been overly nasty about it. He had a way about him that suggested all of it was some big game he was being forced to play but I never really got the same sense of malice from him as I did from the others. And now that I understood the way the Fae world worked, I knew that he'd do the same to anyone who challenged his position. So his behaviour wasn't necessarily as personal of an assault as it seemed.

"I'm interested to see how this whole thing will play out," he admitted. "Perhaps you'll fail and be gone by the end of the semester. Or perhaps you'll rise up and claim your birthright. Before your parents were killed our families were their councillors. We always would have held the power beneath you if things hadn't gotten so messy with The Savage King. So maybe you'll fail The Reckoning and be sent back to your boring, mortal lives or maybe the trials you're enduring now will only make you stronger in the end and you'll pass."

"So in other words, you're just going to keep going along with the other Heirs and their stupid stunts and whenever you're feeling peckish I'm still fair game," I snapped.

"Pretty much," Caleb chuckled.

I let out a huff of irritation. No knights in shining armour here. Not that

that was much of a surprise. Besides, I'd never needed one before so I wasn't going to look for one now. My sister and I had taken care of ourselves for a long time and as soon as we figured out how to harness everything we had from our Elements to our Orders, then these assholes would find out just who they'd been messing with.

"Can you just get this over with? I have a lot of studying to do." *Or napping to do but he doesn't need to know that.*

"Don't you want to hear my proposition, Tory?" Caleb asked, his voice caressing my name as he inched into my personal space.

"I can't imagine anything that you could offer me to make me a willing participant in your dinner schedule," I deadpanned.

"There may be one thing," he countered.

Before I could demand an answer, he caught my chin between his fingers and pressed his mouth to mine.

My heart stuttered in surprise as his lips captured mine, his tongue pressing into my mouth and sending a spike of desire flooding though my limbs. Of course I knew how attractive he was; you couldn't miss the cut of his chiselled features or the way his dirty blonde hair curled in that perfectly imperfect way.

I should have been pushing him back; he was one of *them*. But as I raised my hands to his chest with the full intention to shove him off, I found my fingers roaming over the hard plains of his muscles instead.

Caleb released a noise of satisfaction deep in the back of his throat as his hands moved to my waist and he walked me backwards until my thighs hit the hard line of a desk.

He lifted me easily, nudging my knees apart so that he could move between my legs and my heart thundered as the evidence of his desire pressed against me through the fabric of our clothes.

I slid my hands around his neck, drawing him closer as I devoured the taste of him and explored his hair with my fingertips.

Caleb's hand moved to my knee, his thumb skimming the top of my long socks before he began an ascent up my thigh.

My breathing hitched as his fingers moved beneath my skirt and I hooked my other leg around him, urging him on.

I didn't know if I hated him or not but I did know that my blood was heating and desire was unfurling in me like the wings of a bird. He was still going to bite me, steal some of my power for himself, but maybe this was the answer to my feelings on that. At least this once, I could take something from him too.

I could feel that cocky smile gracing his lips beneath mine and I drew his bottom lip between my teeth, biting down hard enough for him to pull back in surprise.

Caleb laughed as he surveyed me, his hand still beneath my skirt as he paused a millimetre from the edge of my underwear. I eyed him curiously. I didn't want him to stop but I wondered if this was just another of their twisted games.

"Why?" I asked breathily, needing to know that this wasn't some preplanned bullshit. "You can just take what you want from me. So why kiss me?"

"I can take your blood and power from you," he agreed darkly as his gaze slipped from my face to roam over my body. "But I desire more than that. And I'm a Taurus; when we set our minds on something it's not easy to turn us from it."

I scoffed lightly at that. I still found it hard to buy into every aspect of the star sign stuff. I guessed a little part of me just couldn't fully forget those silly suggestions in the daily newspapers that so many mortals clung to for reassurance. Though I probably should be believing all of it given my current surroundings.

I didn't know if I should trust him or not, I had notoriously terrible taste in men and I always, *always* picked the bad guy. But nothing could get my blood pumping like knowing I was playing with something I couldn't control and Caleb Altair was as unpredictable as the wind.

"You didn't seem so against the idea the other night," he urged as I failed to respond.

"That was drunk Tory," I countered. "She's notorious for making bad decisions so I wouldn't get too excited about anything you think she might have done with you. You shouldn't presume anything that happens when I'm wasted will have any bearing on sober Tory."

"And you think I'd be a bad decision?" Caleb asked with amusement.

My lips quirked. "I've been with enough bad decisions to recognise one when I see them."

"How many, exactly?" he asked, leaning in to run his lips along my neck, his stubble teasing my skin.

"Enough to let me know that it's a terrible idea." My breath caught as his mouth made it to the corner of mine. "Probably not enough to put me off entirely."

He chuckled darkly and the sound made my toes curl and my grip tighten on the edge of the table.

He held back for another moment, pinning me in those eyes the exact shade of the night's sky. There was a long pause as I tried to weigh up the pros and cons of this situation. It wasn't like he'd lured me here; this was just an accidental meeting and I couldn't deny the ache in my body to see this through. My heart was pounding, my skin alight beneath the pressure of his hand at the highest point of my leg and I really wanted him to move it just a few inches higher... Besides, making nice with one of the Heirs could hardly be a bad thing, given our predicament.

My gaze slid over his uniform and I bit my lip as I reached forward to unhook the top button of his crisp, white shirt.

Caleb's eyes hooded with a dark desire and he watched me as I worked my way down his buttons until I could push my hands inside his shirt and feel the hard lines of his muscles beneath my palms.

He shivered beneath my touch and pressed forward to kiss me again. This time I abandoned the last of my hesitation and gave myself to the moment. Being in this place hadn't exactly offered me much in the way of enjoyment so far and I was more than willing to take this pleasure from him.

He resumed his assent up my thigh, his thumb pressing down exactly where I wanted it and forcing me to release a gasp of pleasure against his lips.

Caleb began circling his thumb against me through the thin barrier of my underwear and I arched my back as my skin came alive beneath his touch.

His kisses grew more urgent as his other hand began to unhook my shirt buttons too and I continued to explore his body with my hands.

I could feel an ache building within me, demanding more from him as he continued to drive me towards the edge. His hand shifted and he pushed my underwear aside before driving a finger inside me.

I moaned encouragingly as the need in my body moved closer to unfolding and his other hand made it to my bra as he caressed my breast through it.

His mouth moved away from mine, carving a line of energy across my jaw and down my throat. I tensed as his lips touched against my hammering pulse but he didn't bite me, not yet, he moved lower and I tilted back to give him access to all of me.

Caleb pulled my bra down as his lips made it to my breast, his mouth claiming my nipple just as he drove another finger into me.

I moaned again, louder this time despite our surroundings, my eyes falling closed as I leaned back further and my muscles began to tense around him. He kept going, his grip on me tightening, his mouth demanding on my flesh as he felt me coming apart beneath him.

My breaths came in urgent pants as his fingers drove me on and I tipped over the edge with a cry of pleasure.

Caleb's mouth captured mine as he absorbed my ecstasy with a growl of his own desire and he guided me through the last throes of what he'd done to my body.

I melted against him as he kissed me sweetly, pulling his hand back with a twinge of regret.

He stepped back an inch, breaking our kiss and I blinked up at him in surprise.

"I have a student coming in a minute to learn the art of vampirism from an expert," he admitted reluctantly.

I chewed my lip as my gaze slipped over his open shirt, the perfection of his muscles which dipped into a v and disappeared beneath his waistband until I eyed the evidence of his arousal beneath his trousers.

"So that was purely for my benefit?" I asked in surprise as I slowly began to re-button my own shirt.

Caleb's jaw ticked with frustrated amusement. "Oh no, I got plenty from that too," he assured me with a look which made heart surge along my limbs.

He began to button his own shirt again and a pang of regret filled me as his body was concealed once more.

My legs still felt a little weak and I lingered on the desk as the silence spread between us. I wasn't sure what this meant; it was certainly no declaration of love but it felt like maybe we'd just come to a parlay. A middle ground where we didn't hate each other at least. And I was happy to admit I'd accept that kind of friendship from him any day.

His dark blue eyes slipped to my neck again and I sighed dramatically.

"You're still going to bite me, aren't you?" I asked, my fingers curling around the edge of the desk in anticipation.

"You could look at it as rewarding me for my efforts," he teased, clearly not even considering letting me off the hook.

"Well that makes me feel a little better about leaving you with blue balls," I replied with a smirk.

Caleb's eyes glimmered with promise. "Next time, I'll be sure to carve out a few hours to dedicate to you," he murmured. "And then neither of us will be left wanting."

My heart pounded excitedly at the prospect of that but I refused to let it show. "Next time?" I asked, raising an eyebrow.

Caleb regarded me for a few seconds before moving close to tuck a lock of my hair behind my ear. "Are you going to the dance on Friday?" he murmured and my pulse did a little trip over itself in surprise. Was he about to ask me to the dance? What we'd just done was fun but I was hardly about to start parading around the Academy with him, declaring myself as his somehow.

"Err, yeah," I said, waiting to see where he was going with this.

"Why don't you blow it off?" he asked and I blinked at him in surprise. Not asking me to the dance then, just trying to stop me from going and having any fun with my friends.

"What possible reason would I have to do that?" I asked, tilting my head just enough to make his hand fall from my face.

Caleb's lips twitched as he noticed the change in my tone and he ran the dislodged hand down my arm instead. "Because then I could sneak out and come to your room. We could have the whole House and an entire evening to ourselves," he said suggestively.

"That's pretty presumptuous of you, Earth boy."

"Earth boy?" he asked with a smirk and he held a hand out to me, a dark blue flower blossoming to life in his palm as he flexed his Elemental muscles.

"Perhaps I've gotten what I wanted from you now," I said, shifting forward to rise from the desk without taking the flower from him.

Caleb let the flower dissolve into nothing again as he stepped forward to stop me, a dark smile lighting his face. "I'm confident you'll come back for more," he assured me and the hitch in my pulse made me wonder if he was right. There was no way I'd be skipping the dance for his benefit though.

The door opened behind us and my heart leapt as I looked around and a Vampire who I'd seen in my Water Elemental class stepped into the room. His eyes widened as he spotted us in the compromising position but before I could do anything to cover for us, Caleb's fangs slid into my skin.

I flinched in surprise and fought back the urge to whimper in response to the pain as he fed on me. His hand fisted in my hair to hold me in place and I gritted my teeth as I rode it out.

After several long seconds had passed, he pulled back, his eyes meeting mine for a moment with a twinkle of amusement in them. My fist clenched with the desperate desire to punch him but I held back, knowing it was only likely to get me knocked on my ass.

"Lesson one for today, Teddy," Caleb said, turning his attention to the boy who'd interrupted us. "Always prey on the most powerful creature you can overpower. Tory here hasn't got a lock on her powers yet, so she's currently fair game. Although unluckily for you, I've already claimed her as my Source so keep your fangs off."

I pushed myself to my feet, pushing Caleb back a step as I retrieved my satchel from the ground beside us.

"Lesson two," I said coolly as I glared at Teddy who seemed inclined to try his luck with me despite Caleb's warning. "Don't underestimate the depths of vengeance. My sister and I have more power than the lot of you, and you'd be fools to think we won't remember what we went through while we were getting to grips with handling it."

I knocked my shoulder against Teddy's as I passed and he stumbled aside, clearly heeding my warning as I headed for the exit.

I pulled the door open but before it could close behind me, Caleb's voice followed me out.

"Until next time, Tory!" he promised. And as I adjusted my shirt self consciously, I found myself wondering if I was dreading that or looking forward to it.

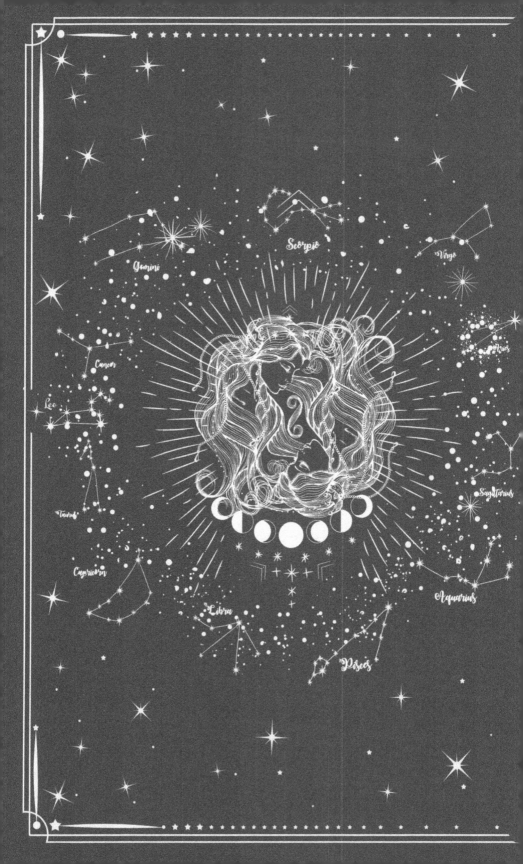

DARCY

CHAPTER TWENTY

The day of the dance arrived and Tory and I headed down to The Orb in our new outfits. Tory had ordered us dresses last minute and I was amused by the way she kept spending our inheritance like we already owned it. We still had to pass The Reckoning to even earn a place here at Zodiac. And if we wanted to see a dime more than our stipend, we had to graduate as well.

My dress was navy with lacy sleeves and fell down to my knees in a fan of silky material; Tory wore a plunging black maxi-dress which showed off her curves and a push-up bra that enhanced them even more. My hair was pulled up in a loose chignon bun while Tory's was curled and hung down her back.

The sky was an artist's palette of pastel tones, the clouds perfectly still as they sat in the endless pool of the heavens. Ahead, The Orb loomed, appearing a deep bronze under the hazy evening light. Students were arriving from every direction dressed in beautiful gowns and suits, an air of anticipation seeping through the atmosphere. I was caught up in it, too, enthralled by the buzz.

I spotted Sofia up ahead in a pale blue dress which danced around her calves. Her arm was linked through Diego's who wore a smart suit and I smiled at the sight of them chatting and laughing together.

Tory and I quickened our pace to catch up, but a hand caught my arm from behind and I was wheeled around into Seth's body. He brushed the tip of his nose against my temple and curled a finger around a loose lock at the nape of my neck, tugging gently to incite a deep shiver in me. "Hey, babe."

A deep, musky scent rolled from his neck and I fought away the inviting allure of it, pressing a hand to his firm bicep and stepping back. His hair was pulled up into a topknot which gave him a sort of preppy vibe. Especially paired with the fitted white shirt that was pulled taut over his muscular frame and dark pants hanging low on his hips. He looked good enough to eat and the grin on his face said he felt the same about me.

I cleared my throat. "Hi."

I felt Tory's eyes on me from behind but she didn't intervene and I vaguely wondered why.

"I had planned to walk you all the way from your room, but you weren't there." He cocked a brow as if that was a total mystery. "It's almost as if you weren't expecting me."

I rolled my eyes but a playful smile pulled at my mouth. The excitement on campus tonight was too addictive to ignore and I didn't see the harm in sharing a bit of banter with one of the Heirs for five seconds.

"I never accepted your offer," I said, then threw a glance over his shoulder, pretending to look for someone. "I thought that note must have been meant for your girlfriend and somehow ended up in my pocket instead."

He grinned darkly, stepping forward and I shot a look behind me, finding Tory had joined Sofia and Diego, the three of them waiting for me at the end of the path.

My stomach seemed to hover and I knew I should just end this conversation and walk away.

Seth shifted closer, his fingers winding around my wrist and sending a flare of heat into my veins. He leaned forward, moving his mouth to my ear. "I think she's got the message now. It's over."

"I thought you were polyamorous." I stepped back again, his closeness overly familiar as usual.

"I'm definitely the amorous part." He grinned widely and held his arm out for me to take.

I snorted a laugh. "No, Seth. I'm going with my sister."

"Ooh twincest," he said brightly.

I wrinkled my nose but couldn't fight a laugh. "You're twisted."

"*Real* twisted," he growled. "You wanna find out how much back in my room?"

"No thanks." I turned away from him and tried to pull off the cool stroll away, only I stumbled on my heels and muttered a curse as I joined my friends.

So smooth.

Tory raised an eyebrow and I gave her a *not now* expression that she surprisingly accepted without complaint.

Diego moved into the middle of our group and draped his arms around all three of us. For once, he wasn't wearing his hat and I was kinda surprised to find his dark curls fell down almost to his shoulders. "Can we pretend you're all my dates tonight? Make every guy in Zodiac think I'm er - cómo se dice? - the shit."

"Na you're good." Tory ducked out of his hold with a teasing grin.

"Hey!" he laughed and I slipped away too, giggling as he wrapped his arms around Sofia to hold onto her. She turned bright pink as he tucked her nearer and made no effort to leave.

"You're not going anywhere," he murmured and she smiled wider than I'd ever seen.

"Then you'd better make sure you don't drink so much and have to duck out early again," I teased.

"I can handle my drink!" Sofia protested, flushing red. "There was something wrong with those shots."

"Like the fact that you couldn't handle so many of them?" Tory asked with a laugh.

"No! Like they were too strong or there was something else in them or-"

"C'mon guys let's stop teasing her and just enjoy our night," Diego said, interrupting her mid-rant.

Tory and I exchanged a grin as we let the subject drop but Sofia continued to look a little annoyed about it.

As we closed in on The Orb, my Atlas pinged in my bag. I frowned, sliding it out and eyeing the notification on the screen.

Falling Star:
Our stars are finally in alignment.
It's time we meet.
I'm waiting in Venus Library.

I stopped walking abruptly, staring at the message in shock. Tory moved closer, noticing my reaction.

"What's up?"

In answer, I thrust my Atlas under her nose.

She read the message and her eyes rounded. Diego and Sofia grouped closer, a question in their eyes.

"Falling Star wants to meet," I told them and Sofia bobbed up and down in excitement.

"You have to tell us everything when you get back," she said.

I nodded, my heart hammering as I glanced over at Venus Library to the east of The Orb. The huge red brick walls rose up several floors, the deepening sunset casting them in blood-red light.

I made a move but Diego caught my hand. "Wait, is this a good idea? It might not be safe."

"It's fine," I promised. "Falling Star has helped us. Why would they hurt us?"

He seemed concerned, sharing a look with Sofia.

Tory rolled her eyes then started walking away. "It's happening Diego, get over it."

I gave him an apologetic shrug and hurried after my sister, my limbs fuelled with adrenaline as we quickened our pace toward the library.

"Do you think Diego had a point?" I asked when he was out of earshot.

Tory shook her head, her features set. "I wanna know who it is, don't you?"

"Of course," I agreed. "I just dunno if we should be bringing some backup..."

"Too late now," Tory shrugged as she opened the door to the library and jabbed me in the ribs to encourage me inside.

I gave up my protests, too curious to turn back anyway. I didn't want Falling Star to run off again if we hesitated too long. And it was time we found out who the hell had been messaging us.

What's the worst that can happen in a library anyway?

Tell that to the guy who was killed by Colonel Mustard with the candlestick.

The library curved around in a wide circle, the floor painted to resemble the night sky in tones of silver and deepest blue. Above us, an incredible globe hung from a silver chain, built in the image of Venus. A light glowed within it, changing from time to time and casting a hazy glow of green then blue, purple, red, pink.

At the back of the room was a high balcony above which were smaller silvery orbs hanging from the ceiling to light the place.

We crept through the first row of bookcases, the scent of old parchment tingling my senses. The library had plenty of shadowy corners to hide in and the thought sent goosebumps fluttering across my skin.

"Where are they?" I whispered, the place seeming to require silence.

"Here," a deep voice answered and a man stepped into the aisle in front of us.

My heart raced as I stared upon the face of Falling Star. He smoothed down his long grey moustache, taking a step forward out of the thick shadows.

Professor Astrum, our tarot teacher looked a little pale as he glanced between us. "Girls," he said softly. "I'm sorry for not revealing myself sooner." He smiled warmly and my thundering heart began to slow. "I was a good friend of your mother's," he said, pausing to let that sink in. "Merissa loved you both very dearly."

Tory folded her arms. "Is that why she dumped us in the mortal world to fend for ourselves?"

Astrum frowned deeply. "You don't understand, dear Roxanya."

"Tory," she corrected sharply. "Don't use that name. It isn't mine."

I pressed a hand to Tory's arm, giving her a pleading look. If we angered him now, he might not tell us anything. And I seriously wanted to hear what he had to say.

Tory gave me a nod that said she'd hold her tongue and I turned back to Astrum.

"Go on," I urged.

"Those times were dark. Your birth father, King Vega...The Savage King, he was the cruellest of rulers, barely a day went by without a public execution in the capital. Merissa was trying to protect you from him, from the way the world was too."

"What do you mean?" I asked, my heart pounding at the idea of being related to someone with such a terrible reputation.

"Nymph attacks rose every year and King Vega grew panicked, lashing out at his own people in response. He was deeply afraid of them. And in the end, that fear was valid. They murdered him, as you know, and the rest of his family."

My throat closed up as I thought of the two human twins who'd taken the fate that was meant for us. And that made me feel all kinds of uncomfortable things towards my birth mother.

How can we be related to people like that?

"And you think Darius's family is involved in that somehow?" Tory asked, her eyes narrowed in suspicion.

"There is much evidence to suggest it, yes. And the stars...they give me clues." He took a Tarot deck from inside his tan blazer, rubbing his fingers across them. "I consult with the heavens using these...they were your mother's. She was adept at reading the stars and we often consulted over them together. When she died...this pack arrived on my desk. She must have bound them to me." He sighed heavily, the pain of her loss clear in his eyes.

"What was she like?" I asked and felt Tory stiffening in my periphery.

Astrum gazed between us with a dark grief in his eyes. "Strong, beautiful, powerful. Her death still haunts me. For many years I tried to deduce from her cards what occurred before the night your parents were murdered. My instincts tell me the answers to my questions lies amongst them but they have only revealed some to me."

"So what have they told you?" Tory asked.

"They told me a dark conspirator was pulling the strings behind the murders. That the Nymphs were just pawns in a much bigger game," he said, his voice dripping with fear. His eyes flicked over our shoulders and I could sense he was getting jittery. "No Nymph would have gotten into the royal palace without help. And though they receive Fae power when they kill, rarely do they learn to harness it well enough to attack our kind with skill." He started thumbing through the cards in his hand, doing it so smoothly I imagined it was a habit he was accustomed to. "They were trained by Fae," he whispered and icy water seemed to spill through me. "And now that you have returned, I believe whoever controlled the Nymphs before is doing so again. I have long suspected Lord Acrux and now I think his son has taken up the torch too. With the help of Orion, a man whose family has deep roots in dark magic."

"Dark magic?" I breathed and Astrum nodded.

He looked over his shoulder, his thumb brushing through the Tarot deck at an increased speed. "The attacks are starting again and both Darius and Orion are linked to every scene. And each death is occurring frighteningly near to you both. If they are somehow controlling the Nymphs to try and-"

A creak sounded somewhere deep within the shelves and I stiffened.

Sweat beaded on Astrum's brow and his thumb suddenly halted on a card. He flipped it out of the deck, his eyes whipping across it back and forth. When he looked back at us, his face was as white as a sheet.

"Someone is listening to us," Astrum said so deathly quiet I almost didn't hear it.

My heart crashed against my ribcage and my breathing hitched as Astrum backed away.

He shook his head, seeming frantic as he continued to thumb through his deck. "Go now. I'll find you again another day. There is much more to be said." He darted into the shadows and Tory grabbed my arm, pulling me into a fast walk then a jog, then a run.

We fled through the library and out onto the path, my breathing ragged as we hurried away from the building.

I didn't relax until we were closing in on The Orb and the creeping feeling from the library finally started to wear off.

"What do you think?" I asked Tory as we stopped outside the huge golden dome. Laughter and music sailed from inside, the noise comforting after what had just occurred.

"I think he's one loose screw away from crazy, but he also has a point."

"But if Darius and Orion are after us, why do it this way?" I questioned. "They could have killed us a hundred times by now. Orion said himself students dying in accidents on campus is regular enough."

Tory shook her head, frowning as she tried to provide an answer. "Maybe they don't wanna risk getting caught, so they want a Nymph to do it instead?"

"Maybe," I said, thinking back to the night I'd confronted Orion. It might have been stupid, but I'd believed him when he'd told me he didn't want to hurt Tory and I. But what if I was just being naive? The guy wasn't exactly a moral martyr. He could be a pro liar and a seasoned killer. I didn't know him enough to judge.

I sighed, my insides in knots as I tried to figure out the answer. Because it felt like we were missing something vital.

"Come on," Tory sighed. "Let's enjoy the party at least. I'd rather not dwell on the fact that our father was some psycho king."

"And our mother swapped us for two random human kids who died in our place?" I added.

"And that," she agreed with a grim smile.

Someone shoved their way past us and I stumbled into Tory, spotting Marguerite heading up to The Orb, her arm linked with a gorilla-sized guy I recognised as a junior.

I straightened my dress, lifting my chin as I headed inside with Tory, irritation sparking through my gut. All thoughts of Marguerite were forgotten as I took in the incredible decorations laid out inside The Orb.

The lounge had been transformed into a ballroom that embodied the season of Fall. Golden leaves swept across the light wooden floor in an endless magical breeze. They dropped from a mass of beautiful vines which sprawled across the ceiling, turning green then orange, red, gold, finally falling to join those dancing on the floor. The process started all over again and I gazed up at the vines in fascination as we moved deeper into the throng of students.

I spotted Sofia chatting with a couple of girls with silvery hair and bright smiles. Something about the Pegasus Order held a calming kind of aura that made them stand out as what they were. The longer I spent at Zodiac, the easier it was becoming to recognise the differences in each one. But there were still so many I was yet to even learn about. And I was lost as to where we fit in.

I searched for Diego but before I located him, someone brushed my elbow as they stepped up behind me. My breathing hitched as the scent of cinnamon rolled under my nose.

"Evening," a deep voice murmured in my ear and I didn't have to look up to know who it was.

Orion moved past me and disappeared into the crowd before I could say a word in greeting. I was left with the lasting impression of his quarterback body fitted into a nice shirt and ebony slacks that clung to his ass and practically forced me to stare at it.

Great, now I'm eyeing up a potential serial killer.

If there was one final ass I had to stare at though...

Tory snatched a couple of shots from a waiter's tray and planted one in my hand with a devilish grin. I wasn't sure it was the best idea after what had happened last Friday. But then again, when had I ever said no to a free shot of tequila?

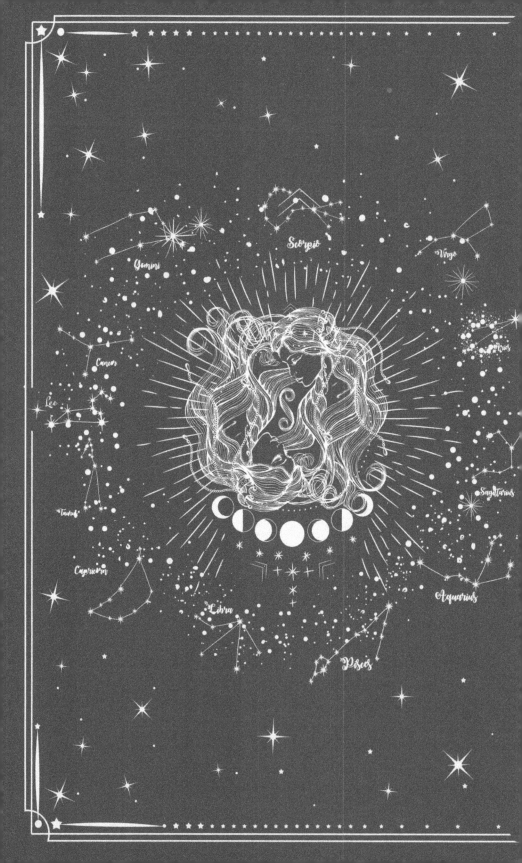

TORY

CHAPTER TWENTY-ONE

As the night wore on, I began to relax more and more. No one had come at Darcy or I with embarrassing forms of Coercion or jibing insults. I'd barely even caught sight of the Heirs at all. It was definitely looking like we were going to be able to enjoy our evening in peace. And with that thought in mind, I was in search of another drink.

An endless cascade of falling leaves in every colour of fall swept through a soft wind above my head, making the fire-based lighting flicker all around us. It was like something out of a movie, too impossibly beautiful to be real and yet there I stood, beneath it all.

The dance floor was full of couples who were locked together as a slow love song filled the room and I smirked as I spotted Diego and Sofia amongst them. She was looking up at him like he was the reason the sun appeared each morning but his attention was wavering a little. He alternated between looking back at her and glancing around the room. I just hoped it was because he was nervous and not because he was losing interest. She was in for some serious heartbreak if he didn't end up kissing her tonight.

Darcy had been convinced to join Seth for a dance too and though I wasn't exactly convinced that he held entirely good intentions it would have been pretty hypocritical for me to say anything after my accidental hook-up with Caleb. Not that I'd mentioned that particular judgement slip-up to anyone. I was sure Darcy would understand but my history of bad choices with the opposite gender made me want to hide my latest transgression. Typical Tory behaviour seemed to involve hot guys with questionable intentions or illegal activities more often than not so I was sure she wouldn't be surprised by me living up to that reputation but I'd still decided to keep it a secret for now.

I headed for the bar where drinks were being served in glasses made out of actual ice courtesy of the water Elementals. With all the excitement, I'd only managed one drink so far but it was time to catch up on myself if I was about to face the reality of going solo at a school dance. It had seemed like a great idea to turn down all of my well-mannered A.S.S suitors at the time but in reality it left me alone while my friends and Darcy coupled up.

I eyed Justin and the other A.S.S members across the dance floor as they chatted together and peeled off to dance. It wasn't too late to join them but I just wasn't sure I could take an evening of bowing and gushing voices calling me your majesty or Roxanya in the company of the ass club.

Nope. I wasn't above drinking on my own and right about now that seemed like a good option.

I reached the bar and ordered myself a double pink gin and tonic as I fiddled with a trailing curl of my hair.

"It's not too late," Caleb's rough voice came from beside me and I turned to find him leaning on the bar as if he'd been there all along. No doubt he'd used his Vampire speed to shoot into the position and I offered him half a smile as I eyed his pristine navy suit which exactly matched the colour of his eyes. He was stupidly attractive in sweatpants and a baggy T-shirt so the way he looked now was beyond words. Memories of his hands on my body, his mouth against mine came pouring in and a little flood of heat built in me.

"Not too late for what?" I asked, taking a sip of my drink which left the rim of the glass stained red from my lipstick.

"To sneak out of here and have some *real* fun," he replied, his fingertips brushing against my arm where I was leaning on the bar. The contact made a little flutter of energy run through me and I gave his offer a beat of consideration before shaking my head lightly.

"You'll have to work harder than that if you want me," I replied lightly.

He leaned a little closer, his mouth almost brushing against my ear. "I promise you, I'll work *really* hard."

Desire trickled along my limbs and I looked up at him from beneath my lashes.

"Tempting... but no." I shrugged.

I didn't want to be seen leaving with him. It was bad enough that Marguerite and her posse thought I was after Darius without me strutting out of here with another Heir on my arm. If anything was going to happen between Caleb and I again then it'd be on my terms and in secret. I'd had more than enough of everyone knowing my business and offering their opinions on it.

Caleb's lips pursed with disappointment and he opened his mouth to say something else just as Max and Darius appeared at the other end of the bar.

The Heirs didn't seem massively pleased to see me but then I wasn't thrilled to see them either.

Darius beckoned Caleb over and he straightened, pushing away from me a little.

"Off you run," I muttered and Caleb hesitated a moment, seeming torn between going to his friends and staying with me. But we both knew what he'd do and he smiled ruefully as he took a step away.

"I'm not switching allegiances, Tory," he said in a low voice, sounding resigned. "No matter how good you look in that dress. We still can't let you take our throne."

He walked away before I could respond and I watched him go with a flicker of disappointment which I quickly squashed. "I don't want your damn throne," I muttered but he couldn't hear me. None of them ever heard me when I said that.

They'd drawn a line in the sand and insisted that Darcy and I stay firmly on the other side of it no matter how little we wanted to engage in this fight. We didn't want their throne or their power or anything other than to find our place in this world that had been stolen from us for so many years. Why was that such a crime? Why did our very existence demand that we engage in this stupid war?

Darcy was now nowhere to be seen and Seth was conspicuously absent too. A prickle ran down my spine as I thought about what they might be doing. She was a big girl and perfectly within her rights to make her own bad decisions but something about the Wolf Shifter set me on edge. When he'd been holding me out over that ravine with Caleb, the look in his eye had made me think he really might have dropped me...

I finished my drink and placed my empty glass down on the bar as I turned away from it.

Darius caught my eye for a moment and a little spike of fear hit me at the coldness in his gaze. I resisted the urge to flip him off then thought better of it and raised my middle finger at him before turning my back on him to cement the insult. I wasn't afraid of Darius goddamn Acrux... or at least that was what I was going to keep telling myself until it became the truth.

I pushed through the crowd, keeping my eyes peeled for a sign of my sister while wondering where else she might be.

Before I got very far, a squeal of excitement caught my ear and I turned to find Geraldine hurrying my way. She was clad in a gauzy pink dress with balloon sleeves and enough ruffles to make her sound like she was wading through a pile of dead leaves at all times.

"Holy jammy dodgers on a diamond encrusted plate! Your maj-"

"Geraldine!" I interrupted her before she could dip her head to me. I was so pleased to see her up and about that I grabbed her into a hug which probably surprised me more than her.

"Oh my!" she breathed and I could tell that my embrace meant a lot to her. My heart softened a little despite myself. The A.S.S were annoying as hell but it wasn't really their fault that the Vega Heirs didn't want the throne.

"I'm so glad that you're alright," I said as I extracted myself from the layers of taffeta and grinned at her.

"Thank you. It took a while before I could get my magic to start replenishing itself again but I'm finally feeling like my old self."

More members of the A.S.S had noticed her return and were running over to greet her too. Bows, curtsies and formal greetings were getting tossed my way like missiles and I quickly extracted myself from the simpering group with the excuse of needing a bathroom break.

As I backed out of the crowd, I collided with a hard chest and turned to find Diego there with an amused smile on his face.

"Need a hand escaping the masses?" he teased and I laughed as I glanced back at the ass club who were all occupied with gushing over Geraldine's return.

"I think I made it out alone, thanks. Have you seen Darcy anywhere?" I asked.

"She was heading outside the last time I saw her," Diego replied with a faint frown. "Seth disappeared not long after. He's been hounding after her a lot recently. Do you think we should be worried...?"

"Don't be silly, I'm sure she's fine," I said, ignoring the little warning trickle that ran down my spine. "But I think I'm just gonna go and make sure."

"I can come with you," he said brightly, following me as I took a step away.

"Where's Sofia?" I asked, pausing again. I didn't want him leaving her for my sake. She'd been so excited about attending this dance with him and I wasn't going to let anything ruin it for her.

"She's grabbing a drink, I'm sure she won't mind if I just-"

"No." I waved him off as I stepped away. "Just look after your date. I'll be back soon."

Diego seemed inclined to argue further but I waved him off dismissively and headed for the exit. He liked to act all protective of us but if it came to an argument with Seth or any of the other Heirs I knew he'd just slink back into the shadows anyway. But that was alright; I didn't need anyone to fight my battles for me.

The cool air chilled my skin as I stepped outside and I paused for a moment, trying to figure out where to begin my search. I didn't want to interrupt Darcy if she was enjoying Seth's company but I just wanted to make sure she was okay.

Shimmering orbs of light marked a pathway to the left of the exit and I headed in that direction, eyeing the way the moonlight glimmered off of the silvery Lunar building ahead of me. This place really was beautiful.

My high heels clicked against the brick pathway and my breath rose in little puffs before me as I wrapped my arms around myself to ward off the chill.

I moved into the shadow of the curving Lunar building and stilled suddenly as I felt eyes on my back. Years of stealing bikes and skulking in the shadows had taught me to trust my instincts and I whirled around a moment before Darius reached me.

I gasped as I spotted him and he smirked like my fear amused him.

"Out for a walk?" he asked and I took a step back. He'd removed his jacket and stood before me in a pale blue shirt with the sleeves rolled back. His muscular chest pressed against the fabric in a way that drew my gaze but I refused to let myself appreciate it.

"Something like that," I muttered.

I glanced behind him but we were alone out here. His gaze trailed over me slowly and I shivered beneath his scrutiny as a beat of silence stretched a little too long.

"Did you want something?" I asked, holding my chin high.

"Last chance, Roxy. Take your sister and leave this Academy. Go back to your little mortal lives and leave Solaria in the hands of people who are worthy of the throne," he said darkly.

"I'm not going anywhere," I replied. "So you need to get over it."

"Is that your final decision?" he asked, taking a step towards me that made my heart leap with fright.

I held my ground despite the fact that my knees felt like they might buckle at any moment. "Yes," I snarled. He wasn't going to bully me out of here and I was done playing nice about it.

"Then I guess I'm going to have to change your mind," he said and it almost seemed like he was resigning himself to the fact.

I scowled at him as I made a move to turn away from him but his hand whipped out and he caught my arm, his strong fingers locking around me like a manacle.

"Let go of me," I demanded, trying to drag my arm out of his grip but he yanked me close instead of releasing me.

"No, I don't think I will," he growled. "You're going to learn a little lesson about respect. I won't have you turning your back on me again."

I struggled to free myself from him but he caught my other arm too.

"Don't fight me. And don't scream," he said, his voice thick with Coercion.

I threw all of my power into my mental shield but the force of his will tore through the wall I constructed like it was built of nothing but tissue paper and my eyes widened as I felt his commands take possession of my limbs.

Darius smiled at me but there was nothing warm in it. His jaw was set, determined and his grip on me unwavering.

He steered me towards the Lunar building and my traitorous legs went willingly beneath me.

My heartbeat thundered in my ears, and my limbs trembled with fear.

Darius Acrux had me in his clutches and I was completely at his mercy.

DARCY

CHAPTER TWENTY TWO

Seth had coaxed me into a few dances but I'd finally escaped, slipping outside The Orb to get some air. I was hot all over and had a knot in my stomach that kept warning me against Seth. I had to stop letting him draw me closer. I was starting to think maybe he wasn't so bad. And that was a dangerous position to put myself in.

He'll cut your heart out and eat it raw.

I circled the building away from the few students who were milling outside then pressed my back to the cool metal wall of The Orb and shut my eyes. I just needed a moment alone and some fresh air to knock sense back into me.

Goosebumps rose on my arms as the wind swept around me. I drank in the quiet and made a mental plan to go back inside and spend the rest of the evening with my friends. Something in Seth's wolf nature coaxed out a willingness in me I didn't like. When I was with him, I fell into the trap of his touches and stares like I was just another dog in his pack. One he could prompt and guide simply by being an Alpha.

A tingling feeling on my neck told me someone was approaching and I quickly opened my eyes. My heart squeezed with a mixture of emotions as I expected to find Seth, but Orion stood there instead.

"Oh," I breathed, a note of dread in my voice. The lamppost behind him meant he was cast in shadow and I was entirely encased within it too.

I glanced down the path, finding us completely alone.

Not good.

I pushed off of the wall, intending to try and make a fast escape but he stepped into my way.

"Professor," I warned, though I knew it was pointless. If he was here to bite me then I didn't have much choice but to let him. I couldn't imagine he was here for any other reason. He wasn't exactly going to kill me at the Academy formal...right?

His hand fell to my waist for the briefest of moments and his fingers pinched the material of my dress.

I sucked in a breath as goosebumps rushed across my skin which no longer had anything to do with the cold air. He extracted his hand and we shared this look that said we both knew he shouldn't have done it.

His breath rolled over me. One bourbon? Maybe two. The gleam in his beautifully dark eyes said he was letting loose tonight. But what did letting loose look like for him? It must have been so exhausting being as angry as he was all the time. And I wondered for a moment what caused such a deep, unworldly rage in him. But it definitely wasn't the time for those sorts of thoughts. If Orion was in a bad mood – which seemed to be a pretty much permanent fixture – then I needed to get away.

"Why do you keep flirting with the devil?" he asked and for a second I thought he meant him. "Seth Capella," he confirmed.

I folded my arms, tilting up my chin as I tried to front out his absolute rudeness despite my instincts telling me to run. "You're my Liaison, sir, not my life guru. If I want to date Seth, I will," I said coolly.

Did I want to date Seth? I mean, no. That was the right answer. But now Orion was trying to force me not to I was reconsidering my decision.

So you're going to date Seth to annoy Professor Orion? Real mature.

I internally berated myself. Of course I wasn't going to do that. Definitely not. No no no.

Orion glanced down the path then looked at his watch.

"Keeping you am I?" I asked in disbelief. It was like I was inconveniencing *him* even though he was the one blocking my path with his massive, hot body. The hot part was *so* not relevant, but also...

"Yes, now give me your wrist." He reached for it and I stepped back.

"Really? You're going to bite me tonight of all nights?" I hissed but he ignored me, throwing a look down the path again before moving forward to try and get his damn teeth in me.

Laughter bubbled in my throat as I suddenly realised why he was acting so oddly.

So this place does *draw lines. And Orion is sliding a toe across one. Which means I now have a weapon.*

I narrowed my eyes, my ammo locked and loaded.

He made his move, darting forward and pushing me back against the wall, baring his fangs.

My heart hammered as I forced my tongue to fight back before he got his meal. "Not strictly allowed this, is it sir?"

He paused, his hand locked around my arm as his gaze flickered from my neck to my face. "And where did you get that idea?"

"From the shifty way you're acting. Why did you follow me out here anyway? You could have bitten me inside."

He shrugged. "Seemed like easy prey."

I released a cold laugh and his hold on my arm eased a fraction. "I don't buy it."

"Why am I even tolerating this conversation?" he asked himself more than me.

I let him stew on that for a second, wondering if he'd come up with an answer because I certainly didn't have one. The closeness of his body and the heat seeping from his skin into mine was a sweet kind of pleasure I secretly wanted so much more of.

"Fine," he sighed wearily. "I shouldn't be here alone with you. It's not appropriate."

My brows rose. "We spend time alone in your office every Monday."

"That's different," he growled, seeming agitated as he threw a look at the path again.

I needed to work my angle to get out of this. He could bite me any second and I was kinda surprised he hadn't gotten it over with yet. "What would happen if I told Principal Nova about this?"

He gave me a dark stare. "Would you?"

His gruff tone sent a shiver through me and he shifted his hand on me as if he could sense my reaction.

"Try me," I whispered, quietly knowing I wasn't much of a snitch but maybe the threat was enough to hold him off.

His fingers slid up my arm and a carnivorous look entered his eyes.

I took a shaky breath as his hand slid to my neck. Something about his mouth against my throat right then seemed like a very bad idea. One that made my heart pump too fast and my thoughts fly away on the wind.

Orion leaned in and the mere flutter of his breath on my flesh felt like the most forbidden of kisses. I sucked in a heady lungful of air, tilting my chin up, a small but wilful part of me suddenly aching for his mouth on me.

This.

Is.

Insanity.

Someone cleared their throat and I jolted, spotting Seth at the far end of the path. He didn't approach, just stood there with an impatient expression.

"What's he doing?" I tried to push Orion back, not liking being seen in this compromising position.

"He's waiting for me to bite you," Orion said, pulling back an inch. "So he can have you back."

A shudder gripped my spine. "Well get on with it," I hissed. "Or are you going to continue playing with your food?"

His mouth twisted down at the corner and he leaned in, speaking into my ear. "Stay away from him. Go inside." Two seconds passed in which the heat of his breath made my belly squeeze deliciously and my heart hammer. I heard him swallow, sensed his lips a hair's breadth from my flesh, holding a lustful secret within that infinitesimal space.

In a flash of movement, he was gone and I was left reeling from the encounter, unable to believe he hadn't bitten me.

Seth jogged to my side, immediately winding his fingers between mine. "All good?" he asked brightly and I nodded, though I was anything but good. I was shaken to my core and not with fright for once.

Orion's words floated through my head and my forbidden desire gave way to a rush of anger. Who the hell was he to make demands like that? He wasn't my damn father. And that was more than clear by the way he'd just had his hands all over me.

Seth towed me along the path with a mischievous grin and dropped down on a bench under the orangey glow of a lamppost.

He pressed his face into my hair, pulling me flush against his thigh. "What's wrong, babe?" His mouth skated over my ear and my heart leapt at the touch.

"Nothing," I lied and he leaned back, tilting his head as his eyes trailed over my face.

"Liar," he teased. "Did Orion hurt you?"

"No," I said honestly.

A rustle sounded somewhere off in the bushes behind us and a tingle ran across my skin.

Seth brushed his fingers over my cheek, drawing me back to look at him. "If he bothers you, I can get my pack to make him back off. We don't normally take on professors but..." He smirked, leaning in closer, his fingers moving to cup my chin and tilt my mouth up. "You're worth it."

He leaned in and a hundred thoughts muddled in my brain at once.

I shouldn't be out here alone with an Heir. And I certainly shouldn't be thinking about kissing one.

But Orion had told me to stay away from Seth and that had riled me up something crazy. And as Seth's hand brush my knee, I felt myself giving in. Making a decision that I'd probably regret tomorrow, but right now felt like biting Orion back.

My pulse quickened as Seth's hand slid further up my leg, his thumb painting a delicate circle against my inner thigh. My thoughts scattered to the wind as my body responded to him, heat flooding into the base of my stomach.

I leaned in to meet his mouth.

His lips brushed mine, feather soft, then more demanding as his hands curled around my waist and dragged me against his firm body. I came apart as he drove his tongue into my mouth, the taste of beer and lust overwhelming my senses. He tugged me into his lap and my skirt rode up much too high.

I almost pulled away, but he released a low groan in his throat that had me undone and I tangled my fingers in his shirt as his mouth remained locked with mine.

Dog Boy was a ridiculously good kisser and I was starting to believe that maybe he really was sorry for the shit he'd done. That maybe he really did like me.

Probably shouldn't be kissing his face off right now though.

His hand roamed up to my neck and something cold brushed my skin. I flinched and his free arm suddenly locked around me. *Hard.*

"Seth," I yelped, breaking our kiss as his hold became painful.

He snatched hold of my bun then the world stopped turning as he sliced something sharp through it.

"No!" I gasped in absolute horror, shoving him back. But it was too late. He released me and I fell from his lap in a heap onto the path, grazing my knees.

A single lock of blue had come free from the bun he now held in his grip, fluttering down onto the ground before me. I snatched it up in desperation, my hands trembling and tears welling and welling and welling.

My hair, he took my hair.

But it wasn't just my hair. It was an age old wound and he'd cut it open deeper than before.

Don't trust anyone. That's what it stood for. And how fucking poetic that he'd tricked me, made me trust him then taken the one thing which had been meant to warn me against people like *him*.

A satisfied smirk pulled at his features. "Told you I'd get your hair," he said, his voice flat and cold and making my heart crawl into a shell to try and hide. "And since Max told me the little sob story behind it, I was even more determined to get my hands on it."

My lips trembled as tears ran over them, the taste of salt and betrayal running onto my tongue.

Giggles filled the air and Kylie burst out of the bushes alongside several more of her gang, her Atlas held in her hand. "I recorded the whole thing," she told Seth triumphantly.

Humiliation washed over me and I opened my palm in a flare of anger, willing magic into it but Seth rushed forward, closing my fist as he crouched before me.

"Nothing personal, Vega," he whispered. "It's the way of Fae. If you don't want things getting even worse for you, then take your sister and get out of our Academy." He winked, shot to his feet and slung his arm around Kylie, striding away while their laughter called back to me.

"Let's go to Lunar Leisure, I don't wanna miss the fun," Seth said and they started moving swiftly down the path, my blue locks still wrapped in his fist.

Silence fell and I reached up to clutch my head, too horrified to do anything but stay there on the ground a minute longer. My throat swelled with emotion as I found the choppy remains of my hair, shorter at the back than it was at the front – *and was that scalp I could feel??*

My hands started to shake as embarrassment caved in my chest. Tears poured down my cheeks as my heart turned to cinders.

How could I have been so stupid? How could I have thought for one second that bastard could be trusted? Why had I done this after everything I knew about the world?

Get up. Go back to Aer Tower.

But I couldn't make myself move. I just wanted to curl in on myself and hide away forever.

Panic rose in me as I continued to paw at my hair, knowing I had to get up. I had to disappear before anyone saw me like this.

Kylie had recorded the whole thing.

Oh God, please no. Soon, everyone in the school would have witnessed me kissing Seth then him slicing off my hair and taking it like some sick trophy. And me crying on the floor with grazed knees and the sky falling down on me.

A hand pressed to my shoulder and I jolted violently, wheeling around and throwing out a palm, desperate to defend myself. A huge crack tore across the path as earth magic left my body in a rush of energy and Professor Orion darted aside before it knocked him over.

My heart steadied despite the fact that my Cardinal Magic teacher wasn't exactly a guardian angel. But he wasn't Seth or his awful friends. I clutched my head, heat coursing across my cheeks as I tried to hide from him. There wasn't much more even Orion could do to me tonight that would break me any further. But he could laugh. And I waited for it to come.

He slowly knelt before me, his jaw set as his gaze swept over my hair. Shame burned a path through my body and I looked down at the ground, unable to bear being seen like this. "Have you come to say I told you so?" I bit at him, trying to cover my pain with rage. But no doubt he could see every one of the tears running down my face.

"Get up," he urged, taking my arm and pulling me to my feet.

"Why'd you come back?" I choked out, tugging my palm free and wrapping my hands around my head again.

"My spidey senses were tingling," he said, chuckling and I glanced up at him, my brow creasing.

"Was that a joke?" I asked in utter surprise, my voice raw.

His mouth hooked up at the corner and I couldn't believe he was actually smiling like *that*. I expected him to be laughing along with the rest of the school, not making jokes for my benefit.

"It was," he said. "A pretty good one I think." He tugged me nearer, his expression suddenly serious. "Now the blue is gone, how will I tell which twin is which?"

I tried to stop a surprised laugh escaping me but it broke free of my chest in the form of a hiccup. "You're right, however would you tell?" I sniffed, wiping at my damp eyes with my lacy sleeve. Mascara smeared across my hand and I inwardly cringed, knowing I must have looked like an extra in The Walking Dead right then.

Of all the people to make me feel better though, I would never have guessed it'd be him.

A scream cut through the air that made every nerve ending in my body sting.

Orion dropped his hand, suddenly alert and I started running before he could make any sort of decision.

Tory!

Fear scorched a hole in my heart.

The Heirs were on a war path tonight. And I had to try and stop them from hurting my sister.

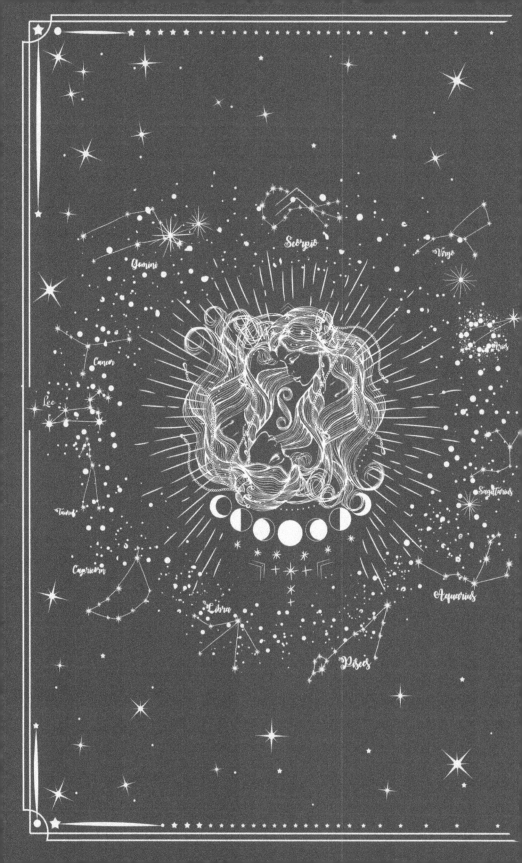

TORY

CHAPTER TWENTY THREE

Darius marched me straight into the Lunar building and swerved to the left once we were inside, heading for the gym.

"Where are you taking me?" I breathed, failing to keep the fear from my voice.

"We're going to see some friends," he said, not offering me any more than that.

We passed by the gym equipment and kept going to a part of the building I'd never visited before. I knew what we were heading for as soon as the warm air and scent of chlorine hit me and I frowned as Darius dragged me through a set of double doors and on through the changing rooms. He didn't slow his pace or lessen his grip on me and I was powerless to try and fight my way free of him while his Coercion still held me in its grip.

We made it out to the huge swimming pool and my lips parted as I spotted a crowd of people there. Marguerite and her friends shrieked excitedly as Darius dragged me towards them and my heart skittered as I hunted the sea of faces for someone who might help me.

A group of Seth's wolves started howling with excitement, jostling each other as they drank from bottles of beer and pushed each other close to the edge of the pool.

Darius steered me to the left and we skirted the long swimming pool, heading toward the deep end where a sign painted on the tiles announced that the water was six meters deep. A shiver raced through me at the thought of all that water, memories of being trapped in that car crash surfacing readily.

Three diving boards stood alongside the water and I had to tip my head back to look up at the tallest one. I'd seen divers using such things in the olympics on the TV but I'd never seen one in real life.

Darius kept hold of me, guiding me closer and closer to the diving boards where Max and Caleb stood waiting for us. Max's face was a picture of excitement and he was practically bouncing on the balls of his feet. Caleb's expression was set in a careful mask and he regarded me like I was someone he barely knew, let alone held any affection for.

I swallowed thickly. It was clear I wasn't going to be getting any help from him and I hadn't seen even one person here who seemed inclined to stop whatever Darius had planned.

Darius spun me to face the crowd of onlookers over the water and he slung an arm around me like we were friends.

"A lot of people have been talking about the return of the Vega Heirs like they're something special," he called, his voice bringing silence to the excitable onlookers. "But I am yet to see anything impressive about them. This one can't even fight off basic Coercion."

Darius tugged me against his chest but I stayed silent, unsure what my best move was here. My gaze kept travelling to the deep pool before me and the memories of rushing water were filling my ears. I'd been trapped in that car, waiting to die as it sank towards the riverbed and I fought against my jammed seatbelt.

My heart was pounding, my tongue heavy in my mouth but I couldn't let them see my fear. I was powerless here but the one thing I could control was my own reaction to whatever they had planned.

"To rise to the top, we fight against our fears and come out triumphant!" Max cried and the ever watchful crowd cheered in agreement. "So shouldn't one of the girls who claim to be our queens have to prove that she can do the same?"

I frowned at him. I'd never made any such claim and I knew Darcy hadn't either. Max stalked closer, holding my eye as he leaned in to speak just to me.

"Thanks for sharing your fears with me," he purred. "It made planning this so much easier."

Darius looked between me and his friend and I fought to keep my expression blank. My heart was thrumming in panic and a bead of sweat was running down my spine but I wouldn't give them my terror. I could see that they were set on this path and I wouldn't beg them to stop. I knew it wouldn't make any difference anyway.

Max leaned closer, brushing a finger down my arm and smirking knowingly as he absorbed some of my power laced with my fear.

"Come on then," Darius said, taking his arm from my shoulder and giving me a push so that I started walking again.

Caleb caught my eye as I passed him and he threw me a smile which was as mocking as it was cruel. A sliver of ice stabbed straight through my chest at that smile. It wasn't like I'd thought we were embarking on some epic romance but I had begun to believe that he wasn't all bad. That just maybe he wasn't determined to get rid of me and Darcy. And if I was being really honest I'd begun to think of him almost like a friend. The coldness in his gaze told me how wrong I'd been about that. He may not have been an active participant in this latest torture but he sure as shit wasn't going to be stopping it.

Darius walked me past the two lower diving boards and stopped me by the ladder that led up to the high board. A little sign informed me that it was a ten meter jump from the tip of that board to the water and my hands started to shake just a little.

"Come on then, Roxy," Darius growled, his breath warm against my neck as he leaned close. "Up you go."

"I can barely swim," I breathed, making sure he knew exactly what he was about to do to me. "I'll drown if I jump in there."

"Are you ready to bow to us then?" he asked. "And leave this school behind?"

I looked into his dark eyes, wondering if there was even a hint of humanity lurking in there. I didn't glare at him or scowl or throw my hatred into my gaze. I just looked and let him see the girl I was. Let him see who he was doing this to, while wondering if he was even capable of pity or remorse. I wasn't some long lost Heir come to steal his throne. I was just a girl trying to reclaim something that had been stolen from me and figure out my place in this screwed up world.

Darius's lips parted and something shifted in his eyes. For half a second I actually thought he was going to back off, let me walk away with my tail between my legs and be satisfied by knowing he'd won without forcing me to go through with this.

"*Start climbing! All the way to the top!*" Max demanded behind us, his Coercion wrapping me in its grasp with firm talons and forcing my limbs into action.

I turned from Darius, kicked my stilettos off and began my ascent up the ladder.

Up and up and up. My palms were slick on the metal rungs and my bare feet felt the chill of them sharply as I climbed ever higher.

The crowd of assholes below me started chanting and it took me a few moments to make out what they were shouting.

"*Jump! Jump! Jump!*" It wasn't an encouraging kind of chant though; it was eager, mocking, bloodthirsty.

My long black dress tangled around my legs as I climbed but I didn't slow as Max's Coercion urged me on.

When I finally reached the top, I pushed myself to my feet and stood on the long diving board which bounced slightly beneath my weight.

My legs were trembling and in my head I could hear the squeal of brakes, the screams which had torn from my throat as the car careered through the barrier and the swooping sensation in my stomach as the vehicle had dropped towards the river.

I was there again. Sinking, down, down, down and this time no helpful passerby was going to save me.

My ears were full of the terror of my memories but over the top of it I managed to hear another sound. Seth raised his voice in an excited howl as he raced into the room. His wolves howled in response to greet him and I balled my hands into fists to try and hold myself together.

"I was worried I was going to miss the show. I've just finished destroying the other one!" he called as he ran to join the other Heirs.

A hard stone dropped into the pit of my stomach at his words. Had he done something to Darcy? Had he hurt her? I wanted to scream at him and demand he tell me but the crowd of onlookers were chanting again and I could barely hear myself think let alone try and be heard from all the way up here.

Darius and Max moved towards the water's edge and raised their hands as they turned the smooth surface of the pool into a simmering vortex of movement.

I stared down at the deep water in horror. If I'd thought I had no chance of swimming in it before, now I was doubly sure that I was done for. Swimming lessons weren't exactly something that foster kids were offered regularly and aside from a few trips to the local pool, I'd never really learned how. I could get by, but I'd never attempt to hold my own in deep water, especially since the accident.

"Are you ready, little Vega?" Max called and the crowd of students started chanting louder, demanding the show they were promised as my knees locked into place.

I knew what was coming next. I threw every ounce of my power into my mental shield, hoping that I could fight off the Coercion the next time it came. It was meant to be harder to force someone to do something that could cause them harm and as I knew that this could kill me, I had to hope that they wouldn't be able to make me jump.

"*Jump!*" Max yelled and I felt his will smashing against my own.

I took a step forward but managed to fight off the desire to obey. I released a shuddering breath, wondering what would happen if I didn't jump.

Before I could get too excited about the idea, Seth raised his arms, grinning up at me as he called on his power.

I felt the wind building behind me as he directed it to throw me into the water. Panic gripped me and I made a run for it. I might not have wanted to go in at all but I knew that jumping in myself would be much better than getting tossed in by him.

My heart almost exploded as I leapt from the edge and the crowd screamed for my blood as raucous laughter rang out.

I plummeted towards the pool feet first as the water writhed beneath me. I didn't want to scream but I couldn't help it, the terror ripped it from my lungs as I plunged towards the water and my dress was whipped up around me.

I hit the water and shot beneath the surface as a torrent of bubbles raced from my lips. Down, down, down, the weight of my sodden dress dragging me to the bottom as it tangled around my legs.

I struggled against it, ripping the straps down and forcing it off of me as I tried to escape the confines of the material.

The water was cold, way too cold for an indoor pool and I knew I had the Heirs to thank for that.

I managed to force the dress off of me and shoved it away as I was left in my underwear. I twisted around and kicked for the surface with everything I had.

My lungs were burning, aching, demanding me to take a breath that would drown me.

My head breached the surface and I gulped down air as the water swirled around me.

I caught sight of the four Heirs standing on the edge of the pool, looking down at me with cold eyes as Darius and Max forced the liquid to bend to their command.

A huge spout of water rose up like a tower beside me and I tried to kick away from it even though I knew it was pointless.

With a flick of Darius's hand, the column bent and slammed down on top of me, submerging me again.

I was tossed beneath the churning water like a rag doll as I tried to figure out which way was up and the water pummelled me mercilessly.

My heart was trying to beat a path right out of my chest and I kicked for the surface again with a desperate need to escape.

As I swam, the water fell unnaturally still and the temperature seemed to plummet further, wrapping me in an icy embrace.

The light above me showed me which way to go and I started kicking again, wondering how many times I would have to endure this before they'd let me out.

I scrambled through the water, aiming for the surface as my panic and the freezing temperature slowed my progress and my lungs screamed their protest.

The light was just above me and yet it still looked impossibly far away. I kicked towards it again and my hands met with a solid surface instead of breaching it.

My eyes widened as I beat my fist against the slab of ice that had been constructed to keep me caught inside this nightmare.

I was drowning again. Back at the bottom of that river with the seatbelt cutting into me and no way to get free. Except this time I was free to swim but caught beneath the ice. The air I so desperately craved was mere inches away but it might as well have been miles.

I screamed as the panic swallowed me whole and the last of my air shot from my lips in a torrent of bubbles. I could feel my tears being swept away into the freezing water as if they were nothing and my heart was thumping a rhythm which could only lead to its own demise.

My magic warred beneath my flesh, desperate to save me and I drew on it, summoning fire to my hands.

The force of my power slammed through the ice and I managed the smallest gulp of air before Darius and Max strengthened the wall of ice to combat me.

I didn't know what to do. I had barely even begun to harness my powers and I had no idea how to shape my magic in a way that could help me. I was a blunt instrument hammering away at a wall of steel.

My magic flared again and this time a spiderweb of cracks shot out over the ice but it didn't break.

My limbs were trembling from the cold and the panic and I could feel the urge to take a breath swelling up inside of me.

I pounded my fists against the layer of ice as I kept kicking, sinking deeper and then bobbing up again. It was no use. Any moment now I was going to take a breath.

My heartbeat whooshed in my ears and each thump of my fist against the ice was weaker than the last. I was out of tears. I was out of time.

My lungs were burning and I fought as hard as I could against the inevitable but I'd already lost that fight.

Darkness prickled on the edges of my vision.

And I took a breath.

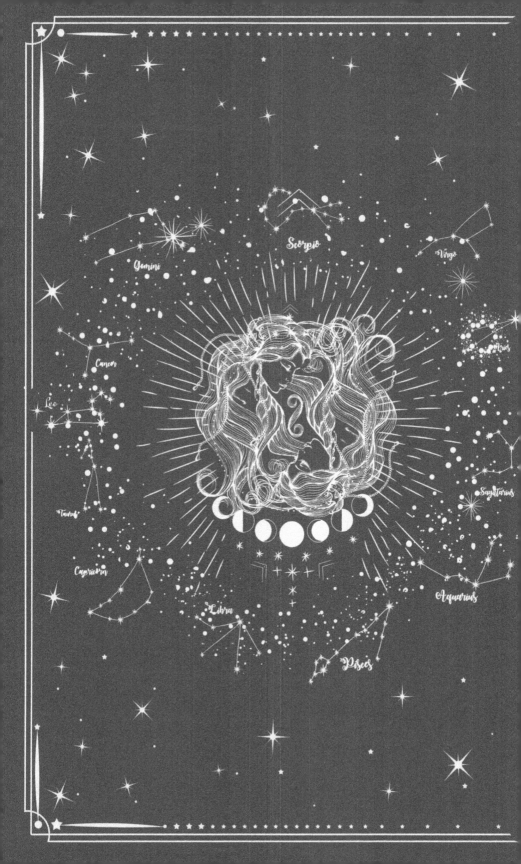

DARCY

CHAPTER TWENTY FOUR

Orion sped past me in a blur, using his Vampire speed to outrun me. My heart fractured as he darted into the Lunar Leisure building ahead and I poured every last ounce of energy I had into chasing him.

Mocking cheers and cruel laughter rang out from inside and I knew in the depths of my soul, my sister was in serious trouble. I burst through the door and turned down dark corridors before practically falling over my feet as I arrived at the swimming pool.

A crowd of students stood at the far end of the swimming pool which had been turned to ice. Orion dove from the edge of it, casting a torrent of water from his hands which melted the ice before he hit it. He disappeared under the surface and my throat constricted with confusion and terror.

A huge fissure ripped up the middle of the ice and Orion burst from under it, his arm locked around Tory. She looked unconscious – or was it more than that?

My world slowed and dread built in my chest.

No, she's not dead. She can't be dead.

My mind finally kicked into gear again and I ran to the edge of the pool, reaching for Tory as Orion brought her near. I caught her arm as he placed her down on the tiles at the edge and silence fell. The kind of silence that preceded a time of death announcement.

"Tory," I sobbed, gripping her freezing cold hand, every part of me trembling as I shook her.

Orion knelt beside her, dripping wet as he pressed a hand to her forehead. He shut his eyes and a deep red light glowed from beneath his palm.

I took a shuddering breath.

The room faded around me.

All that mattered was my sister and the magic flowing from Orion's body into hers.

Tory's eyes flew open and she coughed violently, throwing up water as Orion lurched aside just in time to miss it.

I fell onto her, hugging her close and Orion rose to his feet before I could thank him.

I spotted the Heirs walking along the edge of the pool, making a beeline for the exit.

Hatred tore at my insides as I glared at them, shaking from head to toe as I held onto my twin.

"IF A SINGLE PERSON IN THIS ROOM MOVES ANOTHER INCH, YOU WILL BE FACING IMMEDIATE EXPULSION!" Orion bellowed, the whole of the glass roof vibrating from his ferocious tone.

The Heirs stopped walking, falling silent. Darius scraped a hand down the back of his neck, looking riled for the first time ever. Seth was rubbing against all of them as if trying to soothe them and the sight of my hair poking out of his pocket made me want to scream.

"Face the fucking wall," Orion commanded in a tone that made my shoulders tense.

I watched through blurry eyes as the Heirs filed into line opposite Orion. I'd never seen him so angry and I wanted him to unleash every drop of his rage on them for what they'd done.

The rest of the crowd grouped closer together on the other side of the pool, seeming uneasy.

I brushed the damp strands of hair from Tory's face and she blinked up at me in a haze.

"Are you alright?" I choked out.

She nodded weakly and I fell forward to embrace her again, relief singing a song in my heart.

She shifted up to sit beside me and her deep green eyes dragged over my hair. Her upper lip peeled back as she hugged her knees to her chest and rested her head against my shoulder.

"I'm sorry, Darcy," she said in a raspy tone and I locked my arm around her, shaking my head in refusal of her apology.

"You have nothing to be sorry for," I whispered, my eyes falling on the four Heirs who I hated more viscerally than I'd ever hated anything in my life.

Orion stared at the back of their heads. They looked like they were lined up for a firing squad and I half wished they were.

The crowd of the Heirs' followers started muttering between themselves and some made a bold bid for the exit.

"No one is leaving this room until I hear what happened," Orion snarled at them and the straying students backed up into their ranks.

Orion prowled toward the Heirs, grasped Seth's hair in his fist and slammed his head against the wall with a loud crack. "Do you have anything to say about what happened to the Vega Twins tonight?" he snarled as Seth let out a hiss of pain between his teeth.

"No, sir," Seth said in a low voice and I ground my teeth as I shot daggers at him with my eyes.

Orion stepped toward Max beside him, pressing his face into the wall. "How about you. Rigel?"

"No, sir," Max muttered.

Orion moved to Caleb, leaning in to speak in his ear. "Have you been fucking with your Source, Caleb? You know that goes against the Vampire code and I might just be in the mood to get your fangs ripped out for it."

Caleb's broad shoulders tensed in anger. "I'm aware of the code, sir. I didn't do anything to her."

"Bullshit," Orion snapped as I stared at one of the monsters who'd tried to kill my sister.

Orion moved to Darius, resting a hand on his shoulder. Darius shrugged it off but Orion wrapped his arm tightly around him, pulling him close. "Are you going to lie to my face too, Darius?"

Darius shook free of him. "Can't lie to your face when I'm facing a wall, can I sir?" His tone was mocking and cold, his posture as rigid as if his spine was made of pure iron.

Orion whipped him around, releasing him in the same moment. He wasn't as rough with him as the others and I half wondered why. Darius was as bad as the rest of them and it made my blood chill to look at his expressionless face.

"One last chance," Orion said in a low voice just for him. "Explain."

Darius's eyes slid from his face to Tory, his jaw ticking before he looked back at the Professor. "We want them out. We're just trying to get them out - you know the pressure we're under. Max found out their fears and well...we brought them to life." He shrugged and my chest collapsed in on itself. Could they be any more cruel? We didn't even want their throne and they were still willing to try and break us so we'd leave.

Orion shook his head, his face painted with disappointment. "I thought *you* of all the Heirs were better than your parents."

Darius's face contorted as Orion turned his back on him, which I'd gathered was one of the biggest insults he could offer as a Fae.

"Everyone present in this room bar the Vega girls is now in detention with me for a full week. Capella, Altair, Rigel and Acrux, you will take two weeks and you're on a warning. One more stunt like this and I don't care if you're the sons of the stars themselves, you will be expelled from Zodiac."

"You know what, Orion? Go fuck yourself," Darius snarled, barging past him and marching straight out of the door.

Orion glared after him but didn't make a move to stop him.

"Detention?" Tory wheezed. "Is that it?"

Orion didn't answer and fury filled me. "How can you let them get away with this?" I demanded.

I noticed Marguerite and some of her vile friends pointing at my hair and giggling under their breath. My skin flushed hot and I turned back to Tory, wishing we could just disappear.

Orion crouched down before us and reached for Tory's hand. "You need more healing."

"Not here," she hissed, her eyes whipping to the onlooking crowd. "I just want to go."

He ignored her, pressing his hand to her shoulder and that strange red glow built beneath his palm once more.

I'd never felt so low, like the wind had ripped holes in the sails of my life and left them in tatters.

But I would fix them.

And I'd rise again.

Just not today.

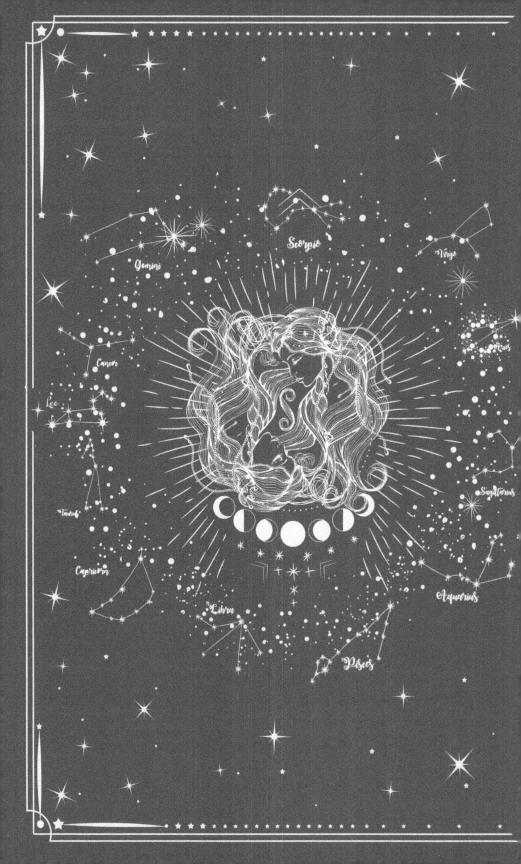

TORY

CHAPTER TWENTY FIVE

The burning in my lungs eased away as Orion's warm hands pressed against my skin. As I came back to myself, I started shivering, my teeth chattering as I curled my legs up to my chest.

Darcy was holding my hand, her olive eyes wide with concern as she looked at me and a lock of hair not even long enough to reach her chin fell towards me. I frowned at it, reaching out for the jagged ends of her hair and noticing the tear tracks which ran through her makeup.

"Draw on your fire magic," Orion muttered. "It'll help warm you up."

My gaze slid to him for a moment and I shifted away from him a little but he didn't release me.

"I'm just making sure all of the water is out of your lungs and healing any damage it did," he explained, his tone oddly flat.

"What happened to you?" I asked Darcy, my voice rasping through my raw throat. Drowning and screaming obviously went hand in hand.

Darcy's lips parted then closed again and her gaze flicked beyond me. I turned that way and found Seth, Caleb and Max still standing against the wall though they'd turned to look at us now that Orion's attention was off of them. Their faces were written with displeasure at the turn of events. The only one looking back at me was Caleb. His jaw was tight and his eyes full of secrets that I couldn't begin to fathom.

My heart leapt with another jolt of fear and I quickly looked away again as Orion released his hold on me. I took a deep breath and found it pain free at last. I knew I should have been thanking him but I couldn't quite bring myself to say the words. I dragged my knees closer to my body, aiming to cover myself as much as I could and hide my lacy underwear from view to the best of my ability.

I felt small, pathetic, laid bare for all of these assholes and stripped of every cocky, fiery part of me until all that was left was the girl who had never had any parents and always wondered what that kind of love would have felt like.

I was still shivering. Each time I reached for my fire, it slipped away from me again. I couldn't focus on it. It hadn't saved me when I'd needed it to. Being powerful hadn't helped me one bit. But it was the reason for this situation. It was why the Heirs had done this to me. If I didn't have my magic then they wouldn't have been interested in me at all.

"Caleb, take off your shirt and give it to Miss Vega," Orion snapped.

Caleb hesitated a moment before he started to unhook his buttons and I finally found my voice.

"I don't want anything from him," I said, my voice low, empty, but certain.

Caleb paused and Orion let out a low growl like this whole thing was a huge pain in the ass. Perhaps he'd like to be the one trapped underwater next time and see what he thought about accepting charity from the people responsible.

Orion shrugged out of his own jacket and handed it to me instead. Darcy guided my arms through the sleeves and I tugged my wet hair out of the collar as I got to my feet and buttoned it. The dark material swamped me, hanging to my thighs as I wrapped my arms around myself again.

I wanted to lift my chin, throw a scowl at the Heirs and their stupid followers but instead I knew I was doing a good impression of a kicked puppy.

I pursed my lips but failed to drag my gaze up from my toes all the same.

They'd wanted to break me. And maybe they had.

Orion looked at me and Darcy. "I'll walk you back to-"

A high-pitched scream filled with terror punctuated the air from somewhere outside the building and a shiver of fear raced through me.

"What now?" Orion growled as he turned and started jogging towards the exit.

Darcy snatched my arm and dragged me after him, clearly not wanting to get left behind with the Heirs and their fan club.

I forced my numb feet into motion, passing Caleb and the others without looking at them again.

Darcy yanked me into a run and I followed her lead as we caught up to Orion just before he reached the double doors which led out of the building.

There was more screaming now, people yelling for help and crying out.

Orion didn't slow, shoving the doors open and heading out into the night.

A huge crowd had gathered close to The Orb and beyond them, a flickering orange light reflected off of the shimmering gold wall of the building.

"Move aside!" Orion commanded and the crowd parted like a tide to admit him.

Darcy kept us right on his heels as we carved through the press of bodies. Everyone was twitchy, people were still crying out and the occasional scream cut the air apart.

"Who is it?" a boy muttered to my right.

"Do you think it was a Nymph?" a girl whispered fearfully.

We kept going until we reached the centre of the crowd and the heat of a fire brushed against my skin alongside a sickly smell that caught in my throat and made me gag.

"What the hell is that?" Darcy whispered in fear.

We fell still at the front of the crowd but Orion moved forward with a curse.

The fire blazed brightly right before us and my heart pounded a warning I didn't understand.

"I've only ever seen Dragon Fire burn like that," Diego's voice came from my left and I turned to find him beside me in the crowd of bodies.

His gaze was set on the blaze before us, his lips parted in shock and he didn't seem to have noticed the state of my sister and I. Before I could ask him what was going on, Orion raised his arms and directed a torrent of water to douse the flames.

Several of the surrounding students summoned orbs of silvery light to hang above us as we were plunged into darkness and I inched forward as a dark shape was revealed on the ground before Orion.

My bare feet pressed down on the cold path and a warning shiver raced along my spine but I didn't stop. Something drew me closer. I needed to know what that shape was.

Darcy stayed beside me as we moved into the ring of empty space left by the crowd and sidestepped Orion to get a better look.

"Holy shit," I breathed and Darcy clapped a hand to her mouth.

A body was curled on the ground before us, their flesh burned to a blackened crisp and their limbs coiled up in a foetal position.

Orion straightened and started yelling at the students to disburse, commanding any witnesses to come forward and directing someone to fetch Principal Nova.

I stood transfixed by the gruesome sight, my limbs locked into place and my eyes wide.

"We should get out of here," Darcy breathed but my feet were rooted to the spot as though I had some reason to stay.

"Wait," I breathed, not really knowing why as I took a hesitant step forward.

The ground ringing the body was blackened with soot and wet from Orion's magic. My bare foot pressed down in the muck and I shuddered.

I could feel a strange kind of tug on my magic right in the centre of my chest and as I focused on it, a faint tingling came to my fingertips.

"Do you feel that?" I asked, my voice low.

Darcy nodded warily and that was all the confirmation I needed.

I gave in to the pull of my magic and let it slip into my fingers as I set it loose.

The corpse before us twitched, its arm shifting as its charred fingers fell open. I almost screamed, staggering back and bumping into Darcy as horror gripped me. But before the sound could make it from my lips, something flew from the corpse's fist and shot straight towards us.

The dark card slapped against my chest and I gripped it automatically, glancing down in surprise. It was smooth and firm in my grip, miraculously undamaged by the flames which had destroyed its owner's body.

Students still lingered despite Orion's attempts to disperse them and more than one camera flashed.

"IN FIVE SECONDS I'M DOUSING ANYONE STILL HERE WITH ENOUGH WATER TO WASH YOU RIGHT OUT OF THE GROUNDS!" he bellowed and the lingering students hurried to comply, a few releasing squeals of fright.

"What are you two still doing here?" Orion barked and I spun towards the sound of his voice, instinctively shifting the card into the pocket of the large jacket I wore.

"We were just..." Darcy began, trailing off as she failed to come up with an appropriate excuse.

Orion's hard gaze was punctuated by his ticking jaw.

427

"Get the hell out of here!" he snapped, all echoes of his compassion towards us banished.

Darcy flinched as if he'd hit her and we stumbled away from him, scrambling back along the cold path.

We followed the dispersing crowd until we'd rounded a corner and I stopped to pull the card from my pocket.

Darcy gasped as her eyes fell on the picture of a cloaked skeleton riding a horse, its empty eyes were staring up at us in warning. At the bottom of the card was a single word: *Death.*

Darcy reached forward to take it and as her fingers brushed the card, the warmth emanating from it flared to a burn. I almost dropped it in surprise but a set of pale eyes seemed to blink at me on the edges of my consciousness and for a second it was as though Professor Astrum was standing before us. The image was gone as soon as it had come and I frowned at Darcy in confusion as I flipped the card over.

On the back of it were words written in a swirling silver script and as I read them, my heart plummeted into the pit of my stomach.

I made a mistake and now my time is up.
The Shadow has discovered me and there is no hope for me to escape their wrath.
The answers you seek are hidden between Leo and Libra.
Don't trust the flames.
Claim your throne.
- Falling Star

Fear took hold of me in taloned hands and it squeezed until I couldn't breathe. Professor Astrum had been murdered. The only person who'd tried to help us in this screwed up Academy was gone. He'd been so afraid, as if he'd known something terrible was going to happen. And now it was too late to do anything about it.

We were alone against the Heirs.

And I was beginning to think we were destined to fall at their mercy.

ALSO BY
CAROLINE PECKHAM
&
SUSANNE VALENTI

Brutal Boys of Everlake Prep
(Complete Reverse Harem Bully Romance Contemporary Series)
Kings of Quarentine
Kings of Lockdown
Kings of Anarchy
Queen of Quarentine

Dead Men Walking
(Reverse Harem Dark Romance Contemporary Series)
The Death Club
Society of Psychos
**

The Harlequin Crew
(Reverse Harem Mafia Romance Contemporary Series)
Sinners Playground
Dead Man's Isle
Carnival Hill
Paradise Lagoon

Harlequinn Crew Novellas
Devil's Pass

**

Dark Empire

(Dark Mafia Contemporary Standalones)

Beautiful Carnage

Beautiful Savage

**

The Ruthless Boys of the Zodiac

(Reverse Harem Paranormal Romance Series - Set in the world of Solaria)

Dark Fae

Savage Fae

Vicious Fae

Broken Fae

Warrior Fae

Zodiac Academy

(M/F Bully Romance Series- Set in the world of Solaria, five years after Dark Fae)

The Awakening

Ruthless Fae

The Reckoning

Shadow Princess

Cursed Fates

Fated Thrones

Heartless Sky

The Awakening - As told by the Boys

Zodiac Academy Novellas

Origins of an Academy Bully

The Big A.S.S. Party

Darkmore Penitentiary

(Reverse Harem Paranormal Romance Series - Set in the world of Solaria,
ten years after Dark Fae)

Caged Wolf

Alpha Wolf

Feral Wolf

**

The Age of Vampires

(Complete M/F Paranormal Romance/Dystopian Series)

Eternal Reign

Eternal Shade

Eternal Curse

Eternal Vow

Eternal Night

Eternal Love

Forbidden Fairytales

(Complete M/F Fantasy Series)

Kingtom of Thieves

Kingdom of Wishes

Kingsom of Shadows

**

Cage of Lies

(M/F Dystopian Series)

Rebel Rising

**

Tainted Earth

(M/F Dystopian Series)

Afflicted

Altered

Adapted

Advanced

**

The Vampire Games

(Complete M/F Paranormal Romance Trilogy)

V Games

V Games: Fresh From The Grave

V Games: Dead Before Dawn

The Vampire Games: Season Two

(Complete M/F Paranormal Romance Trilogy)

Wolf Games

Wolf Games: Island of Shade

Wolf Games: Severed Fates

The Vampire Games: Season Three

Hunter Trials

The Vampire Games Novellas

A Game of Vampires

**

The Rise of Issac

(Complete YA Fantasy Series)

Creeping Shadow

Bleeding Snow

Turning Tide

Weeping Sky

Failing Light